Praise for Shirley Dickson

OUR LAST GOODBYE

"Readers who enjoy the books of Sarah Sundin, Pam Jenoff, and other gentle historical fiction authors are sure to delight in Dickson's tale." —*Booklist*

"Against the backdrop of World War II, this complex romance is the perfect example of how the right person will accept another's flaws unconditionally." —*Library Journal*

"Historical fiction fans will quickly become immersed in May's heartwarming story." —*Publishers Weekly*

The Lost Children

ALSO BY SHIRLEY DICKSON

The Orphan Sisters
Our Last Goodbye

SHIRLEY DICKSON

The Lost
Children

FOREVER

New York   Boston

Cover design by Debbie Clement. Cover photographs © Lee Avison/Arcangel, Shutterstock. Cover copyright © 2022 by Hachette Book Group, Inc.

Forever
Hachette Book Group
1290 Avenue of the Americas, New York, NY 10104
read-forever.com
twitter.com/readforeverpub

Originally published in 2020 by Bookouture, an imprint of StoryFire Ltd.

First Forever Edition: July 2022

Forever is an imprint of Grand Central Publishing.
The Forever name and logo are trademarks of Hachette Book Group, Inc.

The publisher is not responsible for websites (or their content)
that are not owned by the publisher.

The Hachette Speakers Bureau provides a wide range of authors for speaking events. To find out more, go to www.hachettespeakersbureau.com or call (866) 376-6591.

LCCN: 2021952457

ISBN 9781538708439 (trade paperback)

Printed in the United States of America

LSC-C

Printing 1, 2022

To my lovely grandchildren,
Gemma, Tom, Will, and Laura—who is an inspiration! xxxx

The Lost Children

PROLOGUE
South Shields, North East England

January 1935

Martha Moffatt made her way along cobbled Frederick Street, the dim glow from the streetlamps lighting her way. Her breath steam-like in the frigid air, she pulled up the fur-trimmed collar of her coat as she turned the corner into Hake Street and entered the garage forecourt.

"Happy New Year, lass." The tall, lanky figure of Alan Pearson, one of the mechanics, loomed out from behind a petrol pump. He stamped his feet and blew into his hands.

"Alan...what a fright you gave me."

"Sorry, lass. But am I glad to see yi'. I'm frozen stiff standing in the cold. Hurry and open up." As he made for the office door, he called over his shoulder, "Are yi' feeling better now?"

Martha followed him, her high heels tapping on the concrete. "Yes thanks."

"I hear it was the flu. Nasty that. There's lots of it about. Did it spoil Christmas?"

"A bit. I kept feeling sick."

She still did. Bile rose in Martha's throat and she swallowed hard. If only she dared ask someone if feeling sick occasionally at four months was natural...But there was no one she could trust. Intrusive and worrying thoughts invaded her mind and a rush of panic seized Martha. Her hand shaking, she fumbled in her bag for the key. She told herself she couldn't go on like this. Her mind was made up; when she next saw the father, it was time to tell him that she was expecting his bairn.

She opened the office door and led the way into the office-cum-spare-parts shop. Switching on the light, she hurried behind the counter and turned on the two-bar electric fire.

"Have you heard the latest?" Alan took the large key for the workshop from its hook. He turned and his deeply lined, good-natured face broke into a grin. "Fenwick and Son are going to open a second garage."

Martha wasn't surprised. "It makes a lot of sense. The haulage side of the business is profitable. And it's well-known the boss is a man with ambition."

Four years ago, after she left school, Martha had done a stint at college learning secretarial skills, presentation and decorum. Seeing an advertisement for a secretary and cashier at Fenwick's garage in Laygate, Martha had applied for the job. In the interview, Mr. Fenwick, the owner of the garage—a tall and rather handsome older man wearing a smart double-breasted suit, crisp white shirt and flamboyant red and gold tie—had given her a charming smile and asked if she could start straight away.

She worked in the office with Mr. Fenwick's son, who also carried on the family name of Edward. As they chatted on their tea breaks, Martha grew to enjoy his company and they'd quickly become close. Edward—he insisted she call him by his Christian name when they were alone—was two years older than her, and she'd found out he was an only child and had no mam.

"I was five when Mum died of the Spanish flu," Edward had told her, his intelligent and gleaming brown eyes clouded with sorrow.

"Oh, I'm sorry," Martha had said, full of sympathy for him.

Edward had shrugged. "I can barely remember her."

"Who brought you up?"

"Mum's parents wanted to, but Dad was having none of it."

"Gracious, did he bring you up on his own?"

"Apart from the holidays, which I spent with my paternal grandparents, yes."

Martha's admiration for Mr. Fenwick had grown.

Her reverie was interrupted by Alan letting out a relieved sigh.

"It's champion news about the garage, isn't it? I mean, in this climate nobody's job's safe. The news last night said industrial conditions are better than any other time since the slump in thirty-one." He pulled a skeptical face. "I dunno where they get their figures from but it's certainly not this part of the country. Folk in this neck of the woods are scared to death of the dole and that bloody Means Test." He gave a shake of his head. "Sorry for the language, lass, but it makes me blood boil. Me neighbors next door were denied dole money because they've got two spare dining chairs and a piano they can sell. It's criminal. You've got to be nigh on poverty stricken before—"

At that moment the door opened and Edward Fenwick junior entered, accompanied by a cold blast of air. He gave Martha a shy smile, then turned to Alan. "Are you sounding off again?" His tone was convivial.

Martha could never get over the physical likeness between father and son. Both were tall with broad shoulders, a rather pleasing muscled physique and sandy-colored hair. The difference between them was the color of their eyes. Edward senior's were a piercing blue, while his son's were chocolate brown. In personality they were dissimilar too. Mr. Fenwick was commanding, whereas Edward had a more amenable manner—though he seemed tense whenever his father was around, as though he felt under pressure to please his dad.

"Look sharp," Edward told the mechanic, "the lad's outside waiting for the workshop to be opened."

The lad was young Terry, employed as an apprentice.

As Alan made for the door, Martha moved to the cracked mirror on the office wall and placed her cloche hat on the shop counter. Smoothing her blonde waves into place around her face, in the mirror she saw Edward's eyes lingering on her.

She met his gaze, and he looked away.

Martha checked her reflection, making sure her lipstick didn't need replenishing. Smiling, she inwardly thanked the elderly lady she'd sat next to on the tram all those years ago who'd given her such sound advice.

"I won't set a foot outside without first putting my face on. A bit of lippy, some attitude and drop the Geordie accent"—she'd winked knowingly—"and you can fit in anywhere."

Martha had never forgotten the woman's words and did as she'd advised, putting her makeup on before venturing out and being careful to speak properly. She had the same light blonde hair as her screen idol, Carole Lombard (although she did wonder if Carole's was dyed), and tweezed her eyebrows into the same elongated line, rimmed her eyes with black pencil and painted her cupid bow lips with bright red lipstick, much to Mam's disgust.

"You look like a trollop with all that muck on your face," Mam told her, her arms folded. "I don't know, these days folk haven't a ha'penny to their name and go around looking as though they're made of money."

"Mam, I pay my board and lodgings and I'm careful with the rest. If I treat myself at times, it's because if I look good it makes me feel good."

"Mark my words, my girl, one day you'll get your comeuppance."

That day had arrived, Martha thought, as she turned around from the mirror and faced Edward.

It had only happened once in the upstairs flat when she'd had her first taste of champagne—that is, first glass or two of champagne—and she'd felt rosy and giggly. Only now she was paying for her transgression. He'd given her a string of pearls and professed his love for her, as she had to him.

Everything would turn out right, when she told him, she reassured herself. Wouldn't it?

Alan slammed the door behind him, and Martha jumped, her mind returning to the present.

"D'you know who's going to run this new garage?" she asked Edward.

"You know Dad never tells me anything." His lips pressed together in a mutinous fashion.

Martha knew from experience to drop the subject, as he was touchy when it came to his father. Edward wanted to strike out on his own and was biding his time until he would tell his dad— so he said.

Just then, the door opened and the man himself, Edward Fenwick senior, walked into the office, a blast of cold air from outside making the naked bulb that hung from the ceiling swing back and forth. Martha shivered. Mr. Fenwick was a dashing man and she had to admit that whenever he entered the room, she was rather awestruck by him.

"Morning." He removed his leather gloves and undid the belt of his double-breasted topcoat, shrugging it off to reveal a tailored suit. Hanging his coat on a hanger behind the door, he strode over to the electric fire and, reaching behind his back, clasped his hands together.

"It's gone half past eight." He glowered at his son.

"I was just about to open the showroom." Unease emanated from Edward. Martha, frustrated, wondered if he'd ever find the courage to stand up to his dad.

The boss turned to Martha and raised a disapproving eyebrow.

She took the hint. "I was just about to start on invoices." Knowing the boss's black mood was not one to be toyed with, she made for the typewriter at her desk.

But not before removing her coat. Hanging it on a vacant peg, she turned to see both men staring at her, their eyes nearly popping from their sockets.

She looked down at her abdomen and saw, where her white blouse had risen from the waist of her slim pencil skirt, the small mound.

"Are you expecting?" Mr. Fenwick's voice thundered.

Martha felt a flush creep across her cheeks. She hadn't planned on it being revealed like this. She pulled back her shoulders. Maybe fate had intervened and it was for the best. "Yes, I am."

His eyes went scarily dark and the atmosphere in the room turned ominous. "We can't have customers seeing a pregnant woman on the premises."

Edward looked stricken. "Dad, what are you saying? You can't—"

"Edward, keep out of this." Mr. Fenwick moved toward Martha and took her coat from the peg. He handed it to her. "Go home. You're sacked."

Martha's knees felt as if they were about to buckle. "You can't do this, I—"

"Silence. I can dismiss you and I will and there'll be no argument." His expression was menacing as he towered over her.

Shocked, Martha looked at Edward for support, but his face turned gray. He avoided her eyes and stared at the ground. What was the use? She should have known he would never cross his father.

Without another word, Martha left the premises to an unknown and frightening future.

CHAPTER ONE

When Mam first saw the evidence of Martha's pregnancy, her scrawny body bristled with outrage. "Don't you dare tell me you're expecting."

Martha's went mouth dry, and she could hardly speak. She swallowed hard. "I am."

They stood staring at each other in the kitchen cum living room of their two-bedroomed flat. Mam's lips a thin line of disapproval, she lashed out, "I hope whoever he is, he's prepared to have a shotgun wedding. Because I certainly won't be shamed or willing to take on his child. Who is he?"

Nothing would induce Martha to disclose the identity of the father; she was too ashamed to admit what a fool she'd been to expect someone like Edward Fenwick to stand by her. And yet, although on one level she'd lost all respect for him—Edward had betrayed her trust and treated her badly—deep in her heart, Martha couldn't help but still love him. She swore she'd never trust another man again.

The future looked bleak, for who'd employ her now that she was an unmarried mother? And if she couldn't support the bairn she carried, what was the alternative? The thought of poverty and the workhouse terrified her.

Even if Mam did offer to help, there was no way she could earn enough to feed and house the three of them.

Mam had worked as a cleaning lady ever since Dad had been killed when a roof collapsed in the mine in the winter of 1925.

Mam was held in high regard and she worked in some of the big houses in town.

"Silly bugger," Mam had said at the time of her husband's death, her face white with shock. "Your da survived the Great War without a scratch, then came home and got himself killed." She never cried or spoke Dad's name from that moment on.

Money was tight but Mam managed to keep a roof over their heads, renting a downstairs flat in Havelock Street with her earnings from working long hours. She had big hopes for her daughter and she had encouraged Martha to acquire the qualifications needed to work in an office.

"I'll not have you working as a skivvy like me. They'll treat you right in an office job and I hear the pay is grand."

The one pound seven shillings a week Martha earned helped with the rent and household bills. Mam had been overjoyed when she got the job because it meant she could lighten her workload by a few hours, as the arthritis in her hands was playing up something rotten. Each week Martha proudly handed over her board and lodgings to Mam and the rest she spent on personal items such as clothes, makeup and her favorite pastime of going to the flicks.

"You should save your money for a rainy day," Mam scolded. "Just look around you in the streets; in these desperate times you never know when your luck will run out."

Mam had led a hard life, and as a result she was cagey about the future. Her biggest fear was she'd be thrown out of her home and end up a pauper on the streets.

Until now, Martha had never had reason to worry. But that was before the bombshell of her pregnancy and her dismissal. Now, Martha's mind was in turmoil; she couldn't believe that Edward had been using her. She didn't know what to do or who to turn to. With no way to prove who the father was, it would be her word against his and pride wouldn't allow her to beg.

Mam had been right all along; caution paid, but Martha had learned too late.

It was Bessie Todd, Mam's oldest friend, who eventually solved Martha's problem.

Early one morning, when Martha was cleaning the windows of the downstairs flat—this was her penance, to help Mam around the house as much as she could—Bessie appeared at the front step.

"I'm calling in to see your mam."

"Go in. Mam said she was expecting you."

Bessie gave a friendly smile. "If ever yi' fancy a cup of tea, hinny, and a chat, you're welcome to call in at my place because I'm starved of female company. The lads are away at the pit and when there's no work at the shipyards me old man is mostly at the allotments, heavens be praised, because he drives me mad moping about the house."

Why not? Martha thought. She had nothing better to do than housework or stare at the four walls while she listened to the wireless. Now, in her seventh month, she didn't venture far from home; with no money to spend and folk spurning her, what was the point? Besides, her feet were swollen like puddings and her back ached.

"That would be lovely, thank you. It would be pleasant to have a change of scenery," she admitted.

On a chilly April day, Martha caught the trolleybus and made her way to Bessie's upstairs flat.

Bessie, wearing a turban-style headscarf covering her light brown hair, and an apron over a faded floral summer frock, appeared delighted when she opened the front door.

"Martha, how lovely to see you. Come in, hinny."

Bessie led the way upstairs into the kitchen–living room where there was a mouthwatering smell of something delicious baking in the range oven. With its brightly burning red coals and evidence of family clutter, the room was welcoming.

"Make yourself at home and I'll make us a cuppa." Bessie nodded to a horsehair couch that had seen better days and she disappeared into the scullery.

"So, what's goin' to happen," she asked, when she returned and handed Martha a cup of tea, "about this bairn you're carrying?"

Martha, taken aback, was at a loss what to say and took a sip of tea while she thought.

"I've asked your ma but she stays tight-lipped." Bessie shook her head. "A problem doesn't go away just because you ignore it." She let out a heartfelt sigh. "Don't I know it with my lot."

Martha blurted, "I don't know what to do, Bessie. Mam looks furious most of the time and hardly speaks. I'm sure she hates me now for what I've done." She stared down at the large mound of her abdomen. "The worst thing is, I don't want it, but I know it won't go away."

Tears blurred Martha's eyes and her nose ran. She wiped her face with the back of her hand. She loathed herself for giving in to sniveling. Bessie fumbled in her apron pocket and handed Martha a clean handkerchief.

"As you know, me and your ma have been friends for a lot of years. She can be hard as nails sometimes, but that's what's seen her through the bad times. Inside, the woman has a heart of gold. She's only ever wanted a better life for you and this business of you expecting has floored her. Something else I know is, you mean the world to her, lass, even though the woman will never show it."

A lump squeezed in Martha's throat and her eyes went watery again. That was the trouble these days, she got upset and weepy about the slightest thing. What a selfish cow she'd been, taking Mam for granted over all the years. She'd worked her fingers to the bone to give Martha a good start in life and this was how she'd repaid her, by becoming the scandal of the street. Mam didn't deserve this.

"I'm a disgrace," she wailed. "I'd do anything to put things right."

Bessie shook her head. "It makes me blood boil how it's always the lass that gets crucified and the lad walks away scot free. I've got two laddies and, by God, I'll teach them better. If one of them dares to treat a lass the same way, he'll have me to answer to." Her eyes flashed in anger.

If Bessie's lads knew what was good for them, they'd think twice before crossing their mam, Martha thought as she blew her nose.

"It's hopeless. I've ruined everything."

Bessie folded her arms, looking businesslike. "I've had a talk with your ma and there is a way out."

Martha wiped her eyes. "You've talked with Mam?"

"Yes, because I knew she'd never broach the subject. You see, your mam's just as scared as you about the future. I know I would be. She can't discuss the problem because likely the worry will spill over into a fury she knows she'll take out on you."

"She does. If I say a word, she bites my head off."

In the silence that followed while they sipped their tea, Martha found herself thinking that she hoped she'd turn out as wise as Bessie when she was older. Though she doubted it, the mess she'd made of her life so far.

"You said you've thought of a way out?"

Bessie, putting the cup and saucer on the floor, sat up and looked at Martha.

"I'm lucky, hinny, I've had two bairns, three if I count the one who came before her time." Her face sagged in sorrow. "There's couples out there that can't have any, and they're desperate for a family, so they're looking to adopt."

"Adopt?" Martha reeled.

Bessie's candid eyes met Martha's. "Aye, lass. And there are places that organize such things."

"You've spoken about this with Mam?" Martha was incredulous. It was unbelievable Mam hadn't mentioned something as important as this.

Bessie screwed up her face as though she felt awkward. "I did and she said it had gone through her mind as well."

A wave of disappointment at Mam washed over Martha. "Why didn't she say?"

"I think she would have done, pet, eventually." Bessie's tone was conciliatory. "She's probably biding her time, like you do when something's difficult and you've to be in the right frame of mind before you speak out."

Martha sagged. The enormity of what Bessie was saying was difficult to take in. Could she really walk away from her child? She tried to think of the subject dispassionately. Her baby would have a good home and it would make life so much easier.

"Think on it this way, you'll be doing some poor souls a great service and the bairn will never want for anything. And, you can get on with your life and everyone will gain." Bessie smiled reassuringly.

She made it sound so easy.

Martha held out her hands, palms upward. "Is Mam happy with this?"

Bessie nodded. "She sees adoption as a solution."

Martha reasoned she wouldn't be doing it just for herself. Mam would benefit as well. She wouldn't have the worry, the weight on her shoulders of providing for the small family, the shame of others around knowing her daughter would never likely marry. And the bairn wouldn't live a life of shame branded a bastard.

As she felt the life inside her move again, a sense of wonder overcame Martha and she experienced a niggle of self-doubt. Was she being selfish putting her future above the bairn she carried? Would she regret her decision forever? Then, thinking of the benefits Bessie described, and of her mother and the bairn, Martha hardened her heart and brushed the intrusive thoughts away.

She made up her mind; for everyone's sake she would stay strong and let go when the time came.

CHAPTER TWO

Two weeks before the baby was due, Martha, accompanied by Mam, traveled to the Mothers' Hospital in Newcastle. Bessie had kindly made the arrangements for the birth and adoption as Martha, in some kind of mental stupor about the whole thing, hadn't felt capable.

Matron, wearing a beige uniform, answered the door and led them to her office on the ground floor. Sitting behind her large mahogany desk, she booked Martha in, then told them, "The houses are used as administrative offices and nurses' quarters, there's also a dining room and kitchen." She spoke with the crisp voice of authority. "The wards, including the labor and delivery room, are housed behind in the large gardens. Follow me and I'll take you to your ward."

Mam, avoiding Martha's eyes, declined the offer with a shake of the head, and got up to leave. "I'd best be off."

Fear gripped Martha. "Will you visit?"

Her hand on the doorknob, Mam didn't turn. "I'll try, on me day off."

Then she was gone.

As Matron took Martha to the six-bed ward which she would share with five other pregnant girls, a feeling of being forsaken overpowered Martha.

"Welcome to the house of shame," a brunette occupying the next bed told her when Matron was out of earshot. "I'm Mavis."

Martha gave a brief smile. She was still getting her bearings and couldn't believe her life had come to this. But she'd rather be here than at home where recrimination festered in the atmosphere.

Life at the Mothers' Hospital was made more bearable by the camaraderie Martha struck up with the other girls in the ward, who were in the same pickle as her.

"Dad banished me from the house when he found out I was expecting," Betty, in the first bed on the ward, told the others. It was after lights out and they were all in bed staring at the ceiling in the darkness. "He said I had to get rid of it or I wouldn't be allowed back home. I was sent away to live with an old aunt till it was time to come here."

Mavis's voice piped up. "Mine said if I'd kept me legs closed, I wouldn't be in this jam."

"Does the father of the bairn know you're pregnant?" Martha couldn't help but ask.

There was a long pause and then Mavis gave a sigh. "I met Mike at a dance hall. He was dreamy and I couldn't help but fall for him. I was stupid and naive enough to think he loved me but all he wanted was a bit of hanky-panky. He scarpered when I told him."

None of the others spoke. Martha guessed that Mavis's experience mirrored theirs, as it did hers, reminding them of their own ignorance and gullibility.

She changed the subject. "Why do we have to stay three weeks after the birth?"

"It's so we're given the chance to bond with our bairns and maybe decide to keep them." Betty's voice was wistful. "I've heard there're places where the baby's taken off you straight after the birth." Her voice quivered. "I wanted to keep mine but Dad would never allow it." She gave a sob. "It's probably for the best as

I don't want mine to have the same upbringing as me. I want the best for my baby."

Martha was surprised how the others thought of their babies as a person. In her mind she had an *it* growing inside her—because she found it safer that way. But most of the time she tried not to think of *it* at all.

That night Martha was kept awake by Betty crying in bed. The lass was due any day now, but you wouldn't think it to look at her as she was tall and slim and her mound was well hidden beneath the loose maternity top she wore. Martha's abdomen was enormous and she couldn't see her feet. She worried about how it would get out as surely it was bigger than the opening down there. She was ignorant about such topics as birth as it was something you didn't talk about, especially with your mam—that would be excruciatingly embarrassing.

Next morning, after breakfast, a nurse with a stern expression walked over to Martha's bed and pulled the curtains around them. She put her notes on the bedside table. "Hello, Martha." She gave a brief smile. "Just an initial examination to check you and baby are doing fine. I expect you know the routine."

Martha didn't. Neither could she admit she'd never been to see the doctor, an old gentleman she'd known since she was a child, as she was too ashamed. She couldn't bear to see the judgmental expression on his face. Besides, there'd been no need as she'd been fit all throughout her pregnancy and it had grown to this huge size without any problems.

She felt nervous, and she didn't know what to expect.

The nurse asked her questions about her pregnancy and took Martha's blood pressure, all the while writing things down in the notes.

"Pull up your maternity top," the nurse instructed.

Lying there, the enormous mound of her stomach exposed, Martha felt self-conscious.

The nurse brought out what looked like an ear trumpet and placed it on Martha's belly. She bent over and listened. Martha guessed she must be trying to hear the baby's heartbeat. Moving the trumpet to different areas of Martha's belly, the nurse frowned as she concentrated.

A moment of worry seized Martha. "Is... is it all right?"

The nurse stood and her smile was back. "Two strong and healthy heartbeats."

"Pardon me?"

"The twins are doing fine."

"Twins...?" A rush of panic coursed through Martha. "There must be some mistake..."

The nurse studied her, her eyes pitying. "Did you not know you're expecting twins?"

The thought had never entered Martha's mind. She felt weak with shock.

She was carrying two babies. The enormity of it sank in. Did she really have the strength to place two bundles in another woman's arms? Angry at herself for getting into this pickle, tears of remorse stung Martha's eyes. What if, she thought, having twins lessened her chances of having them adopted.

A feeling of dread overcame her as she realized she would have to tell Mam.

Mam came to visit the next week. She looked furtively about and spoke in a low voice. "I don't want you looking like something the cat brought in." She opened the brown paper parcel she carried and handed a cotton nightdress with buttons down the front to Martha. "It's not new but I haven't the money to splash on something you'll only be wearing for a couple of weeks."

"Thank you." Martha shook out the folds and looked at the tent-like nightdress. She had to stifle a nervous giggle with a cough.

They sat in silence after that, Mam looking as if she wished she were someplace else, while Martha tried to find the courage to tell Mam the catastrophic news that she'd received last week.

"Bessie says hello. She hopes you're—"

"I've got some news..." Still reeling herself, Martha dreaded telling Mam. She felt lightheaded and faint. Best to get the deed over with. "I'm expecting twins."

Mam looked at her, eyes wide with shock. "Two?" she exploded.

Martha braced herself for the usual rant: how she was an ungrateful wretch and how Mam had worked hard to give her daughter a better life—which was true, Martha knew—and this was her repayment.

But Mam, her face now stony, stood up to leave, her lips pressed in a severe line, as though the news was too much even to comment on.

The fight went out of Martha as she watched her mam leave the room; she wasn't even worth shouting at.

When Betty's baby was delivered, she was insistent that the motions for adoption were started immediately after the birth. The night before the baby was taken away, she cried and cried all night through. The next morning the damp patches on the front of her nightdress looked as though her breasts were crying too.

The last time Martha saw her, the whites of her eyes pink, her face pale, Betty was inconsolable as her mam led her, shoulders drooping in despair, through the hospital front door.

That wouldn't happen to her, Martha told herself. She felt no attachment to *them* whatsoever. She was doing the best for all concerned. She'd walk away and carry on with the life she'd been leading before she ever set eyes on Edward Fenwick, all those long months ago.

Martha's waters broke in the middle of the night. She thought she'd wet the bed and lay there shivering, unsure what to do.

She whispered in the dark, "Are you awake, Mavis?"

"Yes," came the reply. "What's up?"

Martha explained her predicament. All she could think of was that the nightdress Mam had brought was wet through.

She heard a rustling and then Mavis stood by her bed. "I think we should tell somebody." She took Martha by the hand to help her out of bed and gently led her down to the labor ward.

Martha spent much of the next six hours in the labor room on her own, battling with the all-consuming pains she thought would never end. She was scared, and lonely in a way she'd never experienced before. In a haze of pain, she wished Mam was at her side. Mam was her security, Martha realized with surprise.

As another tightening pain rose in her back and battled its way into her belly, exploding with a force that made her want to cry out, Martha resisted and dug her long, sharp fingernails deep into her palms instead.

"Now comes the hard labor part," the nurse said, after she finally bustled in and examined Martha. "This is close to the end. You're ready to push. Not long now before your first baby is born."

After a time of mighty pushes when Martha thought she'd surely burst a blood vessel, the nurse told her, "Gently does it."

She gave another push, and then Martha heard a baby cry.

"It's a boy," the nurse proclaimed, wrapping the baby in a white towel and handing the bundle over to Martha.

Martha looked down at its rather squashed red face. Blue eyes stared up at her and, as she unwrapped its sturdy, naked body, an unexpected feeling of all-consuming love for her little boy took Martha's breath away.

"Hello. You've got such a serious face. You look like a Jacob," she said.

Another nurse entered the room and took the baby away. "Sorry, but you've more work to do yet."

At the thought of going through all that pain and hard work again, Martha sagged back against the pillows and, depleted of energy, she panicked. She felt something akin to a prisoner unable to escape punishment.

For a moment she rested, but then the compulsive need to push started over again, overwhelming her until she felt out of control. She prayed she had the strength to bring another baby into the world.

Exhausted, she shrieked, "I can't do this any more!"

The nurse told her, "Martha, listen, your second baby is in a good position, and should be born soon. Well done. You should be proud, you've worked hard and done a great job."

Her words gave Martha the encouragement she needed to keep going.

"Martha, don't push, we're nearly there."

She took deep breaths and it took all her willpower to over-come the desire to push. She couldn't endure any more pain and her tired body screamed for the punishment to stop but when the nurse said, "I can see the baby's head," Martha gave one final push and then she heard the wonderful words, "Martha, you have a beautiful daughter."

Collapsing back on the bed, instead of being drained, Martha felt an exultation she'd never experienced before. Through her elation she became aware of muttering between the nurses at the bottom of the bed.

Martha, hauling herself up, balanced on her elbows. "I want to see her... my baby. Is something wrong?"

The nurses ignored her and one of them carried the baby over to the far side of the room. Martha couldn't see what they were doing, but she could hear whispering, before an edgy, threatening silence filled the room—a silence she could barely endure.

Then, gloriously, the baby cried.

"Let me see my baby."

The nurse handed the bundle over, and Martha examined every inch of the tiny wisp of humanity that was her daughter.

"What a fright you gave me. You're not as robust as your big brother but you're a Moffatt and I know you've got what it takes inside. What shall we call you, then, eh?"

The day after the twins were born, Martha battled with both feeding and her emotions. As she fed each baby and looked into their searching, worldly-wise eyes, the need to watch her babies grow, and the overwhelming desire to protect them from all the evils of the world, enveloped Martha.

The idea of adoption, especially when Matron told her that the twins could be separated, was too much for her to bear. But the voice of reason nagged. Being on her own and with no money, keeping the twins was just not possible. Besides, she was being selfish, and like Betty, she needed to think about what was best for the two babies.

She could sympathize with Betty now, though, as she knew the extent of what the lass had gone through. Martha hadn't slept as all she wanted was to steal into the nursery and hold her two precious babies in her arms. But, still in pain down below and too weak and wobbly, she wouldn't make the nursery even if she were allowed. It was only a few hours since the twins were born and yet already they'd become an integral part of her. How could she part from them? Martha, tasting salt tears on her lips, realized she'd miss out on seeing them grow, seeing the people they'd become. Could she bear such heartache?

On the second day after the twins' birth, Mam appeared on the ward. As she walked purposefully toward her bed, Martha tried to discern her expression. The visit was unexpected, and she wasn't mentally prepared. She sat up in bed and hoped she didn't look as vulnerable as she felt.

"I've had a look at the bairns in the nursery." Mam's animated expression surprised Martha. "The laddie looks the spitting image of your da." She put the paper bag she was carrying on the bed and rifled in it, pulling out two white knitted matinee coats. "I've had time on me hands after work with no one in the house and I've made these. We don't want folk to think nobody cares. Besides, they're listed on the adoption sheet as things we're supposed to provide."

"Mam, about the adoption, I'm—"

"I want to talk about that." Mam pursed her lips and Martha knew there was no use arguing, she had to hear her through first. "I know you're keen to have the twins adopted and I thought the same thing, but I've had second thoughts. Families should stick together. These bairns are our flesh and blood and you don't give family away no matter how hard the going is." She took in a huge lungful of air and gave Martha a warning stare that suggested she disagree with her mother at her peril. "You're not giving them away and that's final."

Too flabbergasted to know what to say, Martha simply stared in amazement at her mother.

"I've a bit of money put by for a rainy day and that'll see us through for a time, till you can find work and become the wage earner in the family." A smug look crossed her face. "See, wasn't

I right getting you to work hard and get those qualifications to secure a good job with decent pay? It will now come in handy."

Trust Mam to want to rub it in, but there was no denying she was right.

"Mind you, we'll have to move and find a cheaper place to rent. But that wouldn't be a bad thing as our nosy neighbors would have a field day with their wagging tongues. No, we'll start afresh." Her head inched closer to Martha's. "From now on we'll tell anyone who asks, the father died."

Martha found her tongue. "What will we tell the twins?"

"The same. I've always thought a lie didn't do anyone any good but in this case it's for good reason."

"But who'll look after them?"

"Me, of course. I'm not that past it that I can't see to a couple of bairns. I'll grant you it won't be easy, but it'll be better than being on me knees for most of the day scrubbing other folks' floors." For a moment Mam looked unsure. "So, what d'you think?"

As she thought of her two kiddies lying in the nursery, defenseless and needing a mother's love, Martha's throat tightened. "Mam, I think you're wonderful. When I saw the twins after they were born I...oh, I can't describe how I felt...emotions I've never experienced before. The idea that I'd have to give them to someone else to bring up..."

The tears came then, unbidden, rolling down her cheeks and dripping off her chin.

Mam folded the matinee coats and put them in the locker beside Martha's bed. Settling back in her chair, she took a deep breath. "I know, it was the same with me when I first clapped eyes on you." Her face softened at the memory and she stared into the distance. Martha watched her, knowing her mam was reliving a time gone by when she was a young woman with a child, before tragedy struck.

After a few minutes, Mam's eyes focused and she stared around as if surprised to find herself here on the ward. She smiled and hesitated before she said, "After your da died, I couldn't feel anything...I didn't know how to..."

The words, too difficult to utter, were left unsaid.

But it was enough. Martha knew she was loved and valued, even if Mam couldn't express it. Things would be different with the twins, Martha vowed; she wouldn't shy away from demonstrating her love with words of endearment and hugs.

Mam sat up and pulled back her shoulders, becoming her practical self again. "I expect, like me, you'll have to bring the bairns up on your own. It would take a brave man to be saddled with kids that weren't his, especially twins."

Martha gave a disbelieving shake of the head. Mam would never change but, on reflection, Martha realized she didn't want her to.

Mam's expression became thoughtful and Martha didn't know what to expect next—was this something new, something softer in her, or was she simply contriving to get her own way about one thing or another?

"I'm thinking, if I'm to look after these bairns, I think it's only right and fair I should have a say what they're called. How about Sid after your da for the laddie and Molly for a girl, as it's your grandma's name."

Molly—Martha liked the sound of it and somehow it suited her daughter—but no way would she call her son Sid. Martha's heart was set on Jacob.

But for now, experiencing a sense of well-being for the first time since she'd found out she was pregnant, Martha was disinclined to disagree with her mother as she didn't want to spoil the harmonious atmosphere. The argument about names would keep for another day.

CHAPTER THREE
May 1943

"Thank heavens I made it in time," Martha told Vera Gillespie breathlessly as she caught up with her on the road that led from the hostel to the ordnance factory gates. "This overtime is killing me. I can't get up in the morning."

It was a bright and sunny morning without a cloud in the powder blue sky, and it felt good to be alive. Martha wished she was at home to take Molly and Jacob for a walk around Readhead Park. This used to be a favorite pastime when they could all be together and something the twins loved, especially when they stopped at the park and Martha pushed them to and fro on the swings.

Vera yawned, covering her mouth with a hand. "Lazy sod. You're not a special case, it's the same for all of us." She gave a heavy sigh. It never ceased to amaze Martha how Vera could swear with such ease. Mam would have knocked the living daylights out of her if she'd used such language. "I tried to wake you, but you were like the sleeping dead. Then I figured it was time you learned the hard way if you were late for work." She liked Vera, and they'd become firm friends since day one, even though the lass acted like an authoritative parent at times. Vera had this ability to see the funny side of things and where they worked, with its constant danger, you needed a sense of humor.

Martha shrugged with a nonchalance she didn't feel. If

factory workers were even five minutes late, their pay would be docked for fifteen. Every penny of her salary was precious as she sent most of it home to Mam.

The two women walked among the throng of workers toward the factory where beyond the entrance gates lay a sprawl of low camouflaged buildings. Here was where the Munitionettes filled bombs and shells, the hard graft they did to help the boys in the forces—their loved ones, fathers, brothers, husbands—to win the war.

Vera yawned again. "At least it's reasonably light, though there's nothing to see except bleak countryside." Raising her eyebrows, she pulled an ironic face. "When I was called up, I'd visions of excitement in the WAAF or the WRNS, not this bloody life in the middle of nowhere where I could be blown to smithereens."

"What if you'd been sent abroad?"

Vera gave a dimpled smile. "That was the whole idea: to see a different part of the world *and* to meet some gorgeous bloke in uniform who'd fall instantly in love with me. And, of course, he'd be an officer and gentleman." She sagged. "But the directive at the labor exchange put the dampener on that. So here I am posted in deepest County Durham working in munitions."

"Where you were thrilled to meet up with me." Martha gave a cheeky grin.

The pair of them walked through the gates, showing their passes to the security men. Vera handed over cigarettes and matches, while Martha took off the tiny silver cross that hung around her neck on a chain. The necklace was Mam's, but she'd given it to Martha when she'd left home three years ago to work at the factory.

Security at the factory was strict and all personal items—such as jewelry, coins, hairpins or anything metallic—were classed as contraband and had to be handed in, as if they caused even the tiniest spark, it could trigger an explosion.

As they made their way to the shifting house, Vera said, "I'll admit I've become rather fond of northerners. You're a friendly bunch, in the main. Thing is, though, I'm pleased it's you I'm sharing a room with as I can't understand a bleeding word that some of the other women are saying, in their broad Geordie."

"Don't worry. We'll educate you yet."

Vera rolled her eyes. "The main thing that helped settle me in was the living standards are so much better than I imagined and being comfortable is a prime requirement of mine."

"So, you thought northerners were heathens?" Martha raised her eyebrows, her expression comical.

They both laughed.

Living in the purpose-built hostel as Martha did—with hot and cold running water, inside lavatories, and wholesome meals in the canteen—the first-rate living standards caused her to have pangs of guilt. The flat where the twins lived with Mam had no such luxuries. With drafty sash windows, a lav in the backyard, and only cold water, the downstairs flat was by no means ideal, especially as Molly was a sickly bairn. Then there was the shame of Mam bringing up the twins. What with rationing and keeping the twins clean, fed and healthy, Martha continuously worried that it was all too much for Mam.

She often wondered if she'd done the right thing denying Jacob and Molly the chance of being adopted by a better-off family—but in her heart Martha knew she'd never have been happy if she'd given up her bairns. And she knew Mam felt the same way, as she adored her grandchildren.

*

The first years of the twins' life had been a struggle. The family lived on Martha's pitiful wage as a cleaning lady by day and she worked in a public house at night. The move to a cheaper flat in what was classed as an undesirable area at the bottom end of Perth Street did help their finances, and Martha found the folk in the neighborhood the salt of the earth and always on hand to help out.

Mam had given Martha her wedding ring to wear, saying, "Nobody needs to be any the wiser about your marital status."

But the folk in Perth Street couldn't care less whether Martha was married or not because everyone had their own troubles to contend with.

Martha, determined to improve the family's living conditions, had set out to find employment as a typist where the wages would be better, but jobs like that were like gold dust.

Her favorite part of the day had been before she set off for her shift in the pub each night, when she'd bathe her two adorable kiddies in the large china sink in the scullery. Then, after reading them a bedtime story, she would watch as, drowsily, they snuggled beneath the blanket and fell into oblivious slumber.

Working behind the bar, Martha had had no trouble because wearing Mam's wedding ring meant there was only friendly flirtation and banter between her and the regular customers. And anyway, that part of Martha's life was over because, curse him, her heart still belonged to Edward Fenwick.

In September of 1939, Martha had been shocked when war was declared, as, like many others, she'd believed Neville Chamberlain in his speech the previous year when he'd spoken of returning from Munich with "peace for our time."

The war became real for Martha when children from big cities and towns began to be evacuated to places out in the countryside for their safety.

She told Mam, "Folk are saying because of the shipbuilding industry on the Tyne, the town will be a prime target for bombing raids by aircraft. I don't know what to do for the best. Maybe we should send the twins to the countryside to keep them out of harm's way?" She'd shaken her head with worry.

Mam had looked horrified. "What! And have them live with

people we've never met? I should think not. What about Molly with her infirmity? I doubt strangers will be willing to take her. And Jacob won't go anywhere without her. Leave them be, is what I say."

Mam didn't add that she would be lost without the twins, but she had a point when it came to Molly. Folk who didn't know her, and couldn't see that she was a normal little girl and as bright as a button, judged her by her disability.

Martha had opted to take Mam's advice and keep the twins at home. At first it seemed she'd done the right thing as, for months at the start of the war, no bombs dropped and folk talked about the phony war.

Martha wanted to enlist but there was no way she could leave the twins with Mam when they were so young and such a handful. But when the twins were five and had started school, Molly had suffered another bad chest infection. Martha blamed the black mold that grew on the bedroom walls, and decided to join up, even if it would mean having to leave home for a while. She needed to earn more money to afford better living conditions for her children.

It was seeing a poster on a billboard one day that spurred her on. The poster—featuring a female worker in a factory, with a soldier behind holding a shell—read, *On her their lives depend... Women munition workers... Enrol at once.*

So, the very next day, Martha visited the labor exchange in Wawn Street to enlist and subsequently was posted to an ordnance factory built for the purpose in an unpopulated area of County Durham. It was too far away to travel home each night, so Martha opted to board in the factory's hostel. The lure of working in such dangerous conditions away from home was the four pound pay packet that could rise to a heady eight pounds if she worked overtime. Although she missed the twins terribly, Martha convinced herself that it was for the greater good of the family.

*

Now, as she followed Vera into the changing rooms, Martha took off her outdoor clothes and hung them in her locker. A wave of fatigue overcame her. She was dreading the long shift ahead. She changed into a white cotton jacket and trousers, turban-style headscarf and rubber boots, and picked up the obligatory gloves and mask that protected against poisonous fumes.

Punching their cards in the timing house, Martha mentally prepared to begin the six o'clock shift.

"Another day, another dollar." Vera waggled her head comically. "I know. I've been watching too many Yank films but I do love them—when I can stay awake, that is. The last movie I saw was *Casablanca* with dreamy Humphrey Bogart." They took their places on the line with the other women, and Vera raised an eyebrow at Martha before adding, "Oh, for time off and a night at the flicks."

Before Martha could answer, Rita, the supervisor, barked, "No chattering. Time to concentrate."

Everyone knew the beefy and no-nonsense Rita meant business. At the drop of a hat, you could find yourself suspended for the slightest misdemeanor. But, considering what was at stake when you worked with explosives, Martha knew that Rita was only doing her job.

Their voices subsided and all that could be heard was the sound of Joe Loss and his band blaring from loudspeakers.

The war was in its fourth year now, and folk were war weary. But the pressure to keep up production quotas at the factory meant that women were expected to work a grueling twelve-hour shift and leave of absence was canceled except on grounds of compassion. Martha was exhausted and missing her family—for it had been two whole months since she was last granted leave to visit Mam and the twins. And with the growing fear of the personal danger she faced each day, Martha suffered terrible nightmares and was afraid to close her eyes at night.

Her fear was not death itself, because that would be quick; her anxiety took the form of imagining some disabling injury which would mean she'd be a burden to her family for the rest of her life. Martha never spoke of such fears—even to Vera, to ask if she too endured vivid nightmares—because explosives and a worker's nerves could be a lethal mix. Those who suffered were considered a danger at the factory and moved to another sector, or simply dismissed. Martha needed her bulky pay packet for the sake of her family's future, and so she had to keep her troubles to herself.

Martha eyed the safety notices placed at strategic intervals around the factory walls, and the never-ending rules. A heavy sigh escaped her. The danger of continuously filling bombs with toxic chemicals was getting her down, and Martha knew she needed a break before her nerves got the better of her. At the thought of the twins, the need to see them overwhelmed her.

The clattering conveyor belt began and as the empty bomb cases rolled down the line, Martha decided that in her half hour's tea break she'd visit the office and ask the factory manager's permission for compassionate leave to visit home.

Mr. Broadbent, a man with an irritating nasal voice, had a hint of civility behind his mask of officialdom, and she knew he had a heart. Surely, if Martha explained how long it was since she'd last seen her kiddies, he'd relent and bend the rules.

CHAPTER FOUR

Martha sat on the Newcastle-bound train, her forehead pressed against the window watching the world go by—frisky lambs in vibrant green fields, cows idly munching grass, an expanse of trees in the distance. She was disappointed when the landscape changed and built-up areas came into sight.

It was still early morning, and the day promised to reach a reasonably high temperature. Dressed in an emerald green frock with buttons down the front and a white cardigan, her face made up, Martha felt feminine for the first time in an age.

The train, billowing steam, roared into Newcastle station and Martha hauled her ancient brown leather suitcase down from the overhead luggage rack. When the train stopped, she alighted from the compartment and, assuring a waiting porter she could manage her luggage, she made her way to platform three. Here, as she waited for the South Shields–bound train, excitement fizzed within her. Impatient to see the twins, Martha found it difficult to sit in the waiting room and marched back and forth on the platform.

Her thoughts turned to yesterday and the uncompromising expression on Mr. Broadbent's face when she'd made her request.

"Out of the question." Sitting behind his inlaid office desk, the manager had avoided making eye contact.

"I haven't seen the bairns for months; they'll have forgotten what I look like," Martha had implored.

"I won't make exceptions."

A sense of urgency made Martha daring. "Please. The twins will be pining for me."

"As I say, there will be—"

"Do you have bairns of your own?" Martha had butted in before the manager had the chance to utter a firm no.

He had been stony-faced and Martha feared she might have overstepped the mark.

She spoke out of desperation. "Only, if it was you, wouldn't you beg and plead, not for yourself but for the sake of your kiddies? They need to see me occasionally. I promise when I return, I'll be a model worker."

In reply, Mr. Broadbent looked at his watch and told her, "Your tea break's over. I suggest you get back to work." The finality in his tone disheartened Martha.

After a morning's tedious work, followed by a meal in the canteen of soup and a portion of minced beef pie and chips, despite a sing-song with the lasses as they sat around a large round table, Martha had made her way back to work feeling glum.

But Rita had collared her as Martha resumed her place in the line. "Moffatt, the boss has sent word that you're to have leave of absence for two days starting tomorrow. You've to be back at work sharp on the twenty-sixth to start the afternoon shift. Is that clear?"

Boarding the South Shields train, Martha found a compartment with only one other occupant, a bloke with a balding head and spectacles, reading a newspaper. She sat down opposite him in the window seat, and he looked up and gave a brief nod.

Listening to clickety-click of the wheels as they ran over the track, Martha removed her white gloves and glimpsed Mam's wedding ring. Everyone on her shift assumed, because of it, that she was married. Like most married women at the factory, she stuck tape over the ring while she worked, fearing it might get lost if she took it off.

People—including Vera—knew she had bairns, but not the fact they were fatherless. Martha knew that Vera was the last person to be judgmental, but she needed to protect herself. She didn't want to see a hint of scandal in anyone's eyes. For, truthfully, Martha considered herself a disgrace and, like a ship pulling at its anchor, the shame of her wrongdoing dragged her down.

This feeling had started one day when Molly was saying good night in bed, looking at her with trusting, innocent eyes. Martha had felt a wave of guilt; she hadn't considered anyone but herself when she fell in love with Edward Fenwick and gave in to her passion that one time. It was her fault that those gorgeous kiddies bore the stigma of her actions.

When Jacob, with his forthright manner, had asked why he didn't have a dad like everyone else at school, it was Mam who'd answered, "Your daddy died, pet." She gave Martha a meaningful look that said she was handling this and it was for the best.

Instead of correcting her mother, Martha, frozen like a statue, had kept silent.

"How did my daddy die?"

Mam looked momentarily at a loss. "He died at work," she improvised, then enlightenment dawned on her face. "He worked down the mine and one of the roofs fell down on him." She at least had the decency to look guilty when Martha caught her eye afterward.

"Do you have a better solution?" Mam had hissed later when Martha confronted her after the bairns were in bed.

Martha admitted that she hadn't. She knew Mam had done it for the right reasons, though it still stung that those two little innocents had been lied to. But it was better for now, she reflected, than them knowing the truth and being brokenhearted. Martha vowed that no matter how difficult it was, she'd tell the twins the true story of their birth in the future when they were old enough. She owed them that.

The compartment was humid and Martha felt her eyes drooping. She saw the twins in her mind's eye. They were almost eight now, and they weren't identical; she'd learned that boy and girl twins never were except in extremely rare cases. Jacob was square and stocky with brown opaque eyes. She could never fathom what he was thinking. Molly was smaller, with long, shiny sand-colored hair past her shoulders, match-like limbs and enormous brown eyes. Though they were so different, you could tell by their similar features they were brother and sister.

With these thoughts flitting through her drowsy mind, Martha yawned. There hadn't been time to tell Mam she was coming home and the twins would be at school when she arrived. Imagining their excited faces when they saw her, Martha's eyelids closed and she fell asleep.

The next thing she knew, she awakened with a start as a young soldier in khaki uniform entered the compartment and sat opposite her. Embarrassed that she'd nodded off, probably with her mouth wide open, Martha sat up straight. The skirt of her frock had risen above her knees and she smoothed the hem down.

The soldier, who had fair hair and a kind face, gave a friendly smile. Martha nodded in return. As the train pulled out of what looked like Jarrow station, she looked out of the window toward the empty platform.

"A right carry-on last night. Jerry was out in force." The soldier spoke to the man next to him. "You from Newcastle?"

The older man laid the newspaper down on his lap and took off his spectacles. "I am, son."

"Jerry do any damage?"

"Aye. He kept me awake for half the night." The gentleman

rubbed his eyes. "I heard a blast and it was an AA shell, apparently, fell through the roof of the local printers. It exploded on the top floor where the machinery was. So, no real harm done or loss of life. Thank the Lord." He turned to the younger man. "You?"

"Nah! The raiders just roared over. I reckon the coast took the brunt of it. It's likely Jerry was after the shipyards. Rotten buggers." He looked over to Martha, looking sheepish. "Sorry, miss."

"The shipyards..." she repeated.

"Aye, miss, it was a full-scale raid."

Martha's mouth went dry and she had to swallow before she spoke. "Full-scale, you say," she repeated stupidly.

"You got relatives in the town?"

Martha, not trusting herself to speak, nodded. As if understanding her situation, the two men lapsed into silence.

Martha gazed out of the window, the anxious thoughts zipping through her mind causing her stomach to clench. She told herself, *Mam and the twins don't live by the coast but in a residential area which isn't likely to be a target by raiders.*

But until she saw them with her own eyes, the thought would bring Martha no comfort.

The train slowed and Martha leapt from her seat. As she reached for her suitcase, the soldier stood up and, beating her to it, handed her the luggage. His eyes lingered on her.

"Thank you." She felt herself blush.

As the train crossed the bridge over King Street, Martha took in the scene. Folk below bustled about in the main street, while way above in a blue expanse of sky, a dazzling sun shone. For all the beauty and tranquility, the icy shiver down Martha's spine caused her to shudder.

Martha was first to open the train door and step onto the platform. Hurrying down the hill she waited at the bottom of

Fowler Street at one of the bus stops. An elderly woman who wore a headscarf over her white hair, noticing her as she passed, said, "It's no use waiting there, pet. The trolleybuses aren't running because of the raid. Terrible wasn't it?"

"I don't know, I've just arrived in town."

The woman's shook her head. "I live behind the Town Hall and I thought the planes going over would never stop. I've never been so scared in all my life."

"D'you know which district?"

"My next-door neighbor is a fireguard and he reckons the Westoe area took a hammering."

Martha felt herself sway slightly. "What about the bottom end of Perth Street? I've got family living there."

"He didn't say. He only spoke of the shops and houses that were seriously damaged and that included the Dean Road Warden's Post."

Unable to stand still another minute, Martha began to move away. "I have to go."

"Good luck, pet," the woman called. "I hope to God your family's safe."

Martha raced all the way up Fowler Street, passing the sweep of steps of the Town Hall, and made toward Westoe Bridges. Out of breath, her legs turned to jelly, Martha crossed the road between two anti-invasion blockades. She stopped on the other side of the street and, catching her breath, she sniffed the air. Instead of the usual sickly stink emanating from the brewery, the air smelled acrid.

Trying to keep the hysteria rising inside at bay, she hurried on. Two Women's Voluntary Service vans stood in the road two blocks up, while farther up the hill workmen, wearing brown overalls and flat caps and carrying shovels, were digging rubble piled high in the road. Ladders leaned against houses whose windowpanes were blown out and roofs, their slates missing, had gaping holes in them. But worse by far were the ominous gaps between the houses.

Mam. The twins.

Adrenaline rushing through her, Martha hurried along the road. She turned into Perth Street. The scene that met her eyes was one of devastation.

"I can't, pet. I can't let anybody pass." A wiry-looking workman blocking her way nodded at the notice in the middle of the road.

Road closed. Unexploded bomb. A.R.P.

"The Warden will have me guts for garters if I make exceptions."

"I want to see me house, to see if me family's all right. Please let me through."

She could see from here that the side wall of the corner house on the second block in the street had collapsed. The floor of the upstairs had caved in and downstairs there were just piles of rubble and the timbers of the roof hanging down.

In her distress, Martha was aware she'd lapsed into Geordie dialect but what did it matter if she didn't talk properly? What did anything matter except that her family was safe.

The workman, his arms folded, wasn't going to budge.

Please God, she thought, then she saw a movement out of the corner of her eye. She looked over to a downstairs flat doorway where a woman of indeterminate age stood with a toddler in her arms. The woman, lank hair straggling to her shoulders, wore a frock that looked no better than a rag beneath her faded pinafore.

As one mother to another, she gave Martha a knowing look, then with a nod, she indicated with a movement of her eyes up the street. Martha, needing no further encouragement, dropped the suitcase she was carrying and, like a bullet out of a gun, shot past the workman.

"Miss, come back. D'you want to get yourself blown up?"

Martha didn't care. What was the point of living if she didn't have Mam and the twins?

Halfway up the second block, Martha climbed over the rubble in the road that was once a house. Her gaze traveled up the street to where her own house had once stood.

The front façade of the building was missing and Martha could see through to the back wall. With no roof, the sun beamed light into dark corners. Nothing was left inside except bricks and mortar piled high on the ground.

She dropped to her knees and screamed.

"Mrs. Moffatt, here…" The voice penetrated Martha's numb mind and she looked up the street. A small crowd of people were huddled behind another notice board and an old woman among them called out, "Mrs. Moffatt, there's an unexploded bomb. Take care how you go."

Martha recognized old Mrs. Mallows.

"The bairns…Mam…What happened to them?" She ran forward up the street, oblivious of danger until she reached the crowd.

"Lassie, d'you want to get yourself killed and have your bairns motherless?" Mrs. Mallows tutted and shook her head.

"The twins, they're alive?"

The woman patted her arm. "They are, hinny." Relief flooded through Martha. "The Lord be praised. They were found under the stairs. Folks clawed with their hands to get them out. That was before anybody knew about the danger of the bomb." She exhaled a great sigh. "Prepare yourself for a shock. I'm sorry to say your ma didn't make it. She'd thrown a heavy bedspread over the bairns and covered their little bodies with her own." Her eyes swam with tears. "She was a brave woman. She lived for those kiddies, and poor soul, died for them too."

It seemed to Martha that old Mrs. Mallows' voice came

through a long tunnel. And though she heard the words the old woman spoke she had difficulty taking them in.

"Mam's dead?"

"She is, pet, and if it's any consolation it would've been quick."

"Where are the twins?"

"The ambulance took them to the infirmary. Lass, hold on. You need time to take it all in."

But Martha was running pell-mell up the street, passing bombed buildings, the wrecked Regent Cinema, heading for the Ingham Infirmary.

CHAPTER FIVE

Jacob strained to hear what was being said on the other side of the curtain around his bed.

"Understandably they're both in shock." A lady's voice spoke.

The curtain was then drawn back and a nurse in a navy uniform and starched white cap stood there with someone at her side.

"Mam!"

Though she was wearing red lipstick and rouge on her cheeks from the little round pot that she kept in the dressing table drawer and that the twins weren't allowed to touch, Mam's face was the color of milk and her eyes glistened.

Jacob fought back the pesky tears threatening to fall. Old Mrs. Mallows had told him when he'd fallen off his bike and grazed his knee, "Big boys don't cry."

Mam, her arms outstretched, rushed over to the bed and enveloped him in her arms, hugging him tight. "Thank God, Jacob," she whispered in his ear in a shaky voice.

The warmth of her skin through her cardigan and familiar smell of the perfume she wore, like summer flowers, caused an ache to squeeze in Jacob's chest.

"Granny took me and Molly under the stairs and she—" he started to say, then his mind went blank. The noise of droning planes filled his head, and a shrieking, whistling sound that made him scared. Struggling free from Mam's arms, he put his hands over his ears.

"Jacob, love, it's all right, Mam's here."

A big lump in Jacob's throat tested his resolve not to cry but he refused to give in. His body ached, as if someone had been hitting him in a fight. If he moved, he discovered, a sharp pain stabbed him in his side, making him gasp and cry out.

Mammy cradled his head against her chest. "You'll hurt for a while," she told him in a crooning, soft voice as though she was talking to herself. "You have no bones broken—only a sore rib and lots of bruising and a black eye." She stroked his hair back from his forehead. "You can tell me what happened but if you don't want to that's fine."

It all came back now, and though the night's events played in his head, Jacob couldn't tell Mam. Him lying in the bed with Molly next to him, being woken by the noise outside that, at first, he'd thought was Silky, the upstairs neighbor's cat, yowling on the backyard wall to be let in. The bedroom door bursting open and Granny's voice saying in the dark, "Quickly, you two, it's the siren. Put your dressing gowns on and get yourselves under the stairs."

The light clicked on, but Granny had disappeared. Molly, sitting up in the bed, had rubbed her eyes.

"Hurry, Molly, you heard what Granny said," Jacob told her because he was used to looking after her.

"Where's Floppy rabbit?" She looked around the bed then dived beneath the bedcovers. "Found him," she called, reappearing.

Jacob was relieved because his sister wouldn't go anywhere without Floppy and sometimes Jacob felt jealous of the rabbit.

With a sense of urgency, Jacob had hopped out of bed and, helping Molly from her side of the bed, he took her hand and guided her as she walked up on tiptoe, in that lopsided way of hers, through to the passageway.

It was then Jacob heard the drone of airplanes and guns blazing from the ground. As the raiders came closer, and the sound of terrific explosions started, Jacob led his sister to the safety of the under-the-stairs cupboard.

The confined space smelled of damp and sweaty shoes, and paper was peeling off the walls. He helped Molly to sit down, then sat beside her on the floor beneath the shelf that was filled with bits and bobs—umbrellas, boxes of books, musty smelling pillows and a cricket bat.

Granny appeared carrying a torch, a flask, and the big bedspread from her bed. She closed the door behind her.

"Here, put this over you to keep warm," she yelled as planes roared above the rooftops.

In the semi-darkness, Jacob felt Granny's presence shielding the doorway. The sense of being suffocated overcame him, making his mouth dry and his heart beat faster. In times like this when he was afraid, Jacob thought of Biggles. In his latest book, *Biggles Sweeps the Desert*, his hero and his squadron took on a dangerous mission. Jacob could get through by sitting here in the dark, and pretending he was his hero on a perilous mission.

Planes roared overhead, then there was a deafening whistling noise that hurt Jacob's ears, followed by a huge explosion, and plaster fell on the top of his head.

Another whistling noise, and a dull thud that seemed to reverberate beneath where Jacob sat, a piercing scream from beside him, then something heavy landed on top of him. For a moment everything seemed to stand still, then there was blackness.

When Jacob opened his eyes, he had been surprised to find himself lying on the pavement on what appeared to be a wooden door. He looked around, searching wildly for Molly.

She was lying next to him, also on a door. "My eye hurts and my arm," she told him.

Though his body hurt, Jacob tried to sit up to look at his sister's face, but he fell back, his arms too weak to hold him up.

As the day got light, he could see from where he lay that one of Molly's eyes was swollen. An ambulance pulled up in the road and two men came over and heaved the door Molly lay on from the ground, carting her away.

"Where are you taking Molly?" he cried.

"It's all right, sonny," one of men called over his shoulder, "we're taking her to the hospital where she'll be looked after. We'll be back for you."

Then they were gone.

Jacob looked all around for Granny. He couldn't believe it when he saw her stretched out on the green-painted front door from their flat beside the mountainous pile of rubble that must have once been their home. He shuddered with fright as he saw Granny's eyes were closed and her face was the color of chalk but the usual riddle of lines on her skin had somehow smoothed.

Jacob wished Granny would open her eyes and speak—something was wrong with Granny and he was scared that she'd never wake up again.

One of the ambulance men had appeared and Jacob had watched as the man covered her body with a blanket; a tremor of shock ran through Jacob. He couldn't quite take in what was happening.

Now, Jacob struggled to sit up in the hospital bed. "Granny, she's—" he began.

Mam shushed him. "She's gone to sleep and she's"—Mam's chin trembled—"happy to be in heaven with Grandad."

Jacob knew Mam was only trying to make him feel better. He wanted to stay brave like Biggles but tears leaked from his eyes and big sobs hurt his chest.

Mam, holding him, told him with a croaky voice, "There, there, son, let it all out, it'll make you feel better."

*

Two days after the bombing, and with no place to call home, Martha and the twins found themselves living in a rest center at the local church hall, where the family slept on raised canvas stretchers until they could be rehoused.

That morning, leaving the twins with a WVS lady at the rest center, Martha made her way to the red telephone box in Imeary Street to phone Mr. Broadbent. She explained about the bombing and her plight.

"So," she finished, "I won't be coming back to work."

"D'you mean for good?"

"I've no one to look after the twins."

Mr. Broadbent, though sympathetic, did not sound delighted with this news, from the clipped way he spoke. "Production's at a premium. Your place will be waiting if you do return." The line went dead.

But Martha had more pressing things to worry about. Leaving the telephone box, she headed for Mr. Newman's funeral parlor in Whale Street, to see about organizing Mam's funeral.

As they sat in the parlor, Martha felt oddly that this wasn't real, that Mam couldn't really be dead. She didn't want to stop and think because if she did she knew she couldn't handle the grief. She took deep breaths. Best to keep going, and focus her mind on matters in hand.

Mr. Newman, looking sober in a black suit, told her, "You'll still be numb with shock. Unless there's anything specific, you can leave the particulars of the dearly departed's funeral to me. I'll keep costs as low as I possibly can."

It all seemed to be carried out in a perfunctory manner and Martha was glad because she couldn't handle words of comfort or sympathy.

Martha, knowing his good reputation in these parts, told Mr. Newman, businesslike, that she wanted the simplest funeral, for although Mam believed, she didn't go to church.

It was when she left the funeral parlor and closed the door behind her that the words played, as if in capital letters, in her mind. *Mam was dead.*

As she struggled to find the next breath, tears spilled from her eyes and rolled down her cheeks.

It was at Mam's funeral that Martha saw Bessie Todd. Martha reflected how good it was to see Mam's friend and that Bessie hadn't changed over the years.

A few people had turned up to pay their respects: neighbors from Perth Street, folk Mam had worked with in the big houses and Bessie—who was the only other person, apart from the vicar and Mr. Newman, who joined Martha at the graveside.

"Lass, I'm sorry for your loss," Bessie said when the others had left and Martha had refused a lift from Mr. Newman.

Walking up the path, Martha looked back at the grave heaped with flowers. Two gravediggers, spades in their hands, were filling up the hole, where Mam would spend eternity, under brown sodden earth.

The two women walked together past tall Victorian gravestones toward the cemetery entrance gates.

Bessie turned to Martha. "I was horrified when I saw the notification in the paper. I couldn't believe my eyes. Your mam, dead. I only saw her last week when I called in. Bloody Jerries..." She sniffed back the tears. "She was taken before her time."

They chatted as they walked, Martha feeling relieved to have someone to talk to about Mam. She still couldn't get used to the idea she was really gone. It was as they passed the park, when they were about to go their separate ways, that Bessie inquired about the twins.

Martha heaved a great sigh. "They're very subdued; it's a lot for them to take in."

"You too, hinny," Bessie sympathized.

"I agonized over whether or not the twins should come to the funeral but decided against. It's too much for them just now. I'll bring them later to put flowers on Mam's grave."

"I think that's best. Who's looking after them?"

"A kind WVS lady at the rest home where we're staying."

Bessie's brow wrinkled in puzzlement. "What happened to the flat?"

"It didn't survive the raid."

"You mean they weren't in the shelter when the bomb dropped?"

"Mam preferred to be under the stairs. She liked the upstairs neighbors, but she said the husband took over in the shelter." Martha gave a weak smile. "And you know how Mam liked doing things her own way."

Bessie's eyes grew large in alarm. "So, you've got no roof over your heads?"

Martha, too emotional to speak, nodded.

"Well, you have now. Go and collect them bairns and come home with me."

CHAPTER SIX

June 1943

The Monday after the funeral, Martha was sitting in Bessie's kitchen cum living room, the kettle whistling on the hob. She gazed into the fire, as if the answer to her problem of what to do in the future would magically materialize in the embers.

She mourned Mam's loss every single day, not only because she loved her dearly, but because her looking after the twins meant Martha could go out to work and earn a living. Though she adored her kids, Martha liked the independence of a working life rather than being a drudge at home all day.

But now she had no money and no means to earn any, she didn't know how she was going to manage to raise the twins, and she could forget moving out of the area. Her little family was doomed to live a poverty-stricken existence and unless she could work, there was no way out.

Mam's death preyed on Martha's mind, and the idea that the twins were in danger from raids haunted her. She couldn't leave them, not with the uncertainty that she might never see them again. If anything should happen to her bairns, Martha's life wouldn't be worth living.

"I've been thinking, about you and the twins staying here..." Bessie said, as she bustled into the kitchen and took the whistling kettle off the hob.

Martha tried not to panic; she knew she and the twins needed to move out, but she didn't know what she'd do if Bessie couldn't keep them there at least until she'd come up with a plan.

Bessie turned toward her, her face creased in concern. "That attic bedroom where you're all sleeping is cold and cramped and no place for a disabled bairn to be sleeping, especially on a makeshift bed on the floor."

Martha stiffened as she always did when anyone spoke of Molly's frailty, because that's how she thought of the weakness her daughter had down one side of her body. Folk could be infuriating the way they sometimes treated Molly as if, just because she was physically frail, there was something wrong with her brain.

Sometimes she could be too prickly and protective, as she knew she was being now with Bessie.

Bessie went on, "Molly needs rest to help that eye to heal. I'm thinking it's for the best if my two lads swap bedrooms and you can all sleep in a comfy double bed." She smiled. "My Fred teaches the lads to be chivalrous."

Overcome with relief, and shame at having been sensitive about Bessie's remark when she only had Molly's well-being at heart, Martha's cheeks burned.

But with her loss, nowhere to call home and no idea what to do next, she felt...unhinged, was the only way she could describe the mixed emotions inside.

Bessie, pouring the boiling water into the teapot set on the table, nodded as if she knew the turmoil Martha was going through. "Your mam was as proud as punch of all you achieved what with your typing skills and then working for such a big wage at the munitions factory."

"She wasn't proud of everything I did."

Bessie stopped what she was doing and her careworn face looked irritated.

"If you're alluding to the twins, then you should be ashamed. Your mam may have been shocked at first, and who wouldn't be, but the woman thought the sun shone out of those two kiddies' backsides. She was proud of you, especially the way you got on with life and took no heed of what people said behind their hand." She nodded. "Her very words to me before you left the old place for Perth Street were, 'I never thought I'd see the day when Martha would get her hands dirty. And she's doing it for those bairns. I'm proud of the way she's acting. She's a proper mam, the way her bairns always come first.'"

"Mam said that?"

Bessie folded her arms beneath her bosom. "I don't make things up just to make folk feel better."

Isn't that the truth. Martha smiled but felt teary all the same.

Bessie poured their tea and then rubbed the small of her back. Thin as a rake, she looked as though a puff of wind would blow her over. The woman had enough to deal with without having extra folk cluttering her home.

She looked squarely at Martha. "I'm just going to say this straight out and I want you to think before answering. Why don't you all stay here for as long as you need to? This war can't go on forever."

Martha couldn't believe Bessie's generosity. She felt her throat tighten in immense gratitude. But there was no way she could accept—she couldn't continue to be a burden on Bessie—though she didn't have the resources to find a place of her own.

Her thoughts turned to Edward Fenwick. The last time she had seen him was last year in a wedding photograph in the *Gazette*. The picture had shown Edward junior standing outside the church with his new bride, Edward senior beside him and her parents beside her. The bride was surprisingly plain; she wore spectacles and a cloche hat and was the same height as Edward. But she had a pleasant smile and intelligent eyes. Beneath the photograph was the wording, *Local teacher walks on gold when she marries at St. Michael's church.*

No way would the family want any association with Martha or the bairns, even if she could convince them the twins had Fenwick blood flowing through their veins. No, she was on her own, and some might say it served her right.

"Bessie, I couldn't possibly accept—and no arguing. You've got enough on your plate. But thank you so much for the offer."

Bessie rolled her eyes. "I knew you'd say that. And how are you going to manage?"

Martha gave a sigh of resignation. "I expect I'll get rehoused and manage as best I can like all mams do. I've got a bit of money put by."

This was a lie and only said to keep Bessie happy. The reality was, the last of Martha's money had gone on Mam's funeral bill.

"If you're anything like your ma, once you've made your mind up, nothing will change it." A look of sadness crossed Bessie's face as she remembered her friend.

That night as Martha lay in the double bed in the boys' bedroom—strewn with Jacob's toys, cars and soldiers in the middle of what looked like a raging battle—she mulled over her options. It was one thing to say she'd make it on her own, Martha realized, but quite another to make her decision a reality. She couldn't apply for benefits like the widow's pension as it would be discovered she was an unwed mother. Martha's greatest fear was that the twins would be taken away. Or worse, they'd all be classed as paupers and sent to the workhouse where they'd be separated. Martha knew that women in her position had no say in the matter.

Molly, beside her in the bed, stirred, and automatically she reached for her rabbit which Mam had knitted for her when she was a baby. A wave of maternal love overcame Martha.

None of their belongings had been recovered from the flat and the only clothes the twins had were the pajamas they'd stood in, or rather, lain beneath the rubble in. The lady from the WVS at the rest home had kitted them out and Bessie's lads had provided Jacob with toys from their childhood.

When the twins were discharged from the hospital, Molly, quiet and withdrawn, had refused any toys offered at the rest center. Floppy rabbit, which the workmen had found beside her in the rubble, was the only toy she wanted, and nothing would induce her to let go of him.

Martha was concerned the twins, especially Molly, would have nightmares from being buried alive in the rubble. She snuggled beside Molly's warm, slim body beneath the sheet to provide some comfort. Jacob's even breath could be heard the other side of his sister.

Both twins were slowly recovering from their ordeal and, after the loss of their granny, they needed their mam to be constant. Martha worried about the future; she didn't know what to do and feared, yet again, that she'd let her children down.

CHAPTER SEVEN

July 1943

"How about you get a job while you're still living here?" Bessie looked up from shuffling the playing cards. "Then when you do get a place of your own, I could collect the twins from school and bring them here until you're finished for the day. And I could have them in the holidays."

With a broad smile, she dealt a hand of cards on the green felt card table.

The twins sound asleep in bed, Bessie had suggested a game of gin rummy.

As she collected her hand of cards, Martha smiled and mulled the idea over. It was such a kind offer, but Bessie had always said how glad she was her lads were grown because bringing up kids was hard and that was why you had them when you were young.

"Hawway...concentrate." Bessie interrupted her thoughts. "You're miles away."

"I'm thinking over what you've said. It sounds great but the twins would be under your feet after school, and all day in the holidays. And in wintertime with the bad weather, Molly's often off school for weeks at a time."

"Aw, lass, she'd be no bother. We all love having her here. Jacob too, of course." Bessie laid her playing cards down on the table. "I missed coming to call on your mam when the family moved to Perth Street." She grinned. "Me and your mam had some rare conversations, some that would make your hair curl." She let out a sigh. "Then when you moved, we lost touch, more's the pity."

"Mam was kept busy with the twins. I felt guilty but we couldn't have managed otherwise. Looking after them was a full-time job, especially when she had Molly's exercises to do morning and night."

There followed a contemplative silence, and then Bessie asked, "Did you always know about Molly? It must've come as a shock."

"I didn't at first. It was when she was a few months old and I tickled the sole of her left foot and she didn't react I thought it odd, especially when she squirmed and giggled if I did the same with the other one..." Martha studied her hand of cards, then laid them down. "From then on I used to compare the twins and watch for differences."

Bertha gave a puzzled frown. "What kind?"

"Molly didn't roll over like Jacob, or get up on her knees to crawl. But what really concerned me, was when she didn't reach for shiny objects with her left hand, or attempt to grasp the bottle or spoon when she was feeding."

Bessie nodded. She contemplated Martha. "I think this conversation calls for a tipple." She stood up and went into the tiny scullery, coming back with two stemmed glasses filled with a rich brown liquid. She grinned cheekily. "Me secret stash of sherry for such an occasion as this." She handed Martha a glass.

Martha only drank sherry at Christmas, but with the twins tucked up in bed, she thought, *why not?* She couldn't remember the last time she had relaxed.

Settled back in her chair, Bessie asked, "Did you do anything about Molly at the time?"

"Not then, I'm ashamed to say. I kidded myself Molly was a late developer."

"I'm surprised your mam didn't notice anything."

"She did. Molly was about fourteen months and had just started to sit up while Jacob was toddling everywhere. Mam noticed she didn't use her left hand and was making no attempt to walk." Martha had felt guilty, she recalled, as if it was retribution for her past sin. "It was Mam who brought me to my senses. She insisted we take her to see Doctor Bryant."

Bessie beamed. "I like him. He's a proper hands-on doctor. What did he have to say?"

"Enough to scare the wits out of me." Martha sighed, as she put the glass on the table. "He confessed he hadn't been taught this condition in medical school, but he'd come across two cases before."

"What condition?"

"He suspected it was cerebral palsy." Martha hated saying the name of the condition out loud.

Bessie gawped. "What the heck's that? I've never heard of it."

"Neither had I. All I wanted to know was if it was curable. I told the doctor not to hold back." Martha paused at the memory. "He explained that he'd been informed some children are never able to sit up, use their hands or walk."

As she relived the shock of the time, her eyes welled with tears, which she quickly brushed away. She'd long ago decided there'd be no wallowing in self-pity.

Bessie laid a hand over Martha's on the table. "Aw, pet. You've had a raw time. It's a good job you're made of stern stuff."

Bessie didn't know the half of it. Martha had gone to pieces at the time, and when Doctor Bryant eventually made an appointment for Molly to be seen by a city specialist, the situation had gone from bad to worse.

Mr. Kennedy—an irritating, obnoxious man, who spoke with his eyes closed—had an imposing presence, reminding Martha of Edward Fenwick senior.

She told Bessie, "We saw a specialist at the time, but he was no help. He said nothing could be done for 'the child'—as he called

Molly. His very words were, 'Take the child to Trevally's home for crippled children.'"

"Gawd! Has the man no compassion?" Bessie shook her head in disbelief.

Martha felt in need of another sip of sherry, but she continued, "I was outraged, Bessie. I informed him there was no way I'd put Molly in an institution."

Bessie's lips pursed. "Was your mam there? Surely she had a say in all of this?"

A lump grew in Martha's throat as she thought of Mam's saddened expression.

"She told me to take no notice of what the numbskull specialist said."

Bessie gave her a knowing look. "That sounds like your ma."

"She said"—Martha's chin wobbled—"'You, Martha Moffatt, will have none of that. You'll bring Molly up to be the best she can be and to find her own place in the world.'" Her voice cracked, and she swallowed hard. "I swear, Bessie, as I looked down at Molly, gurgling and looking gorgeous in my arms, I vowed that's exactly what I would do. I swore I'd make no distinction between the twins and let Molly have as normal a childhood as possible."

"That's what you've achieved, pet, and you've made a good job of it." Admiration shone in Bessie's eyes. Then her expression grew thoughtful. "But when did she get her caliper?"

"Molly was late walking and when she did it was with difficulty." Martha visualized her small daughter in those days. Unaware of her difficulties, she was happy just to be upright like her brother. "Her left leg was weak, and the hamstring had tightened so she ended up walking on tiptoe. A few years later I saw a notice in the *Gazette* stating that a cerebral palsy specialist from London would be at the local clinic for the following few weeks. I took Molly to see him."

"That was brave, lass—after the experience you'd had with the last one."

Martha shrugged. "I figured I'd nothing to lose."

"So, what was he like?"

"Mr. Williams was quite old, with snowy white hair, sharp eyes and the warmest smile. What I liked best about him was his attitude toward Molly." Martha gave a fond smile at the memory. "She had his full attention and he called her, 'my little cutie.'"

Bessie gave an approving nod. "Ahh! The man had a heart."

"He told me, 'This little charmer is bright and mentally alert and don't let anyone tell you anything different.'"

"That must've been music to your ears."

Martha, exhaling, smiled and nodded agreement. She remembered asking if she could have caused Molly's disability somehow. His frank eyes had met hers. "There are many theories, Mrs. Moffatt, but I suggest you don't concern yourself with a matter that is most unlikely and concentrate on what can be done to help Molly with the activities of daily living." His smile was sympathetic. "You're not alone. A lot of women ask the same question."

She told Bessie, "Mr. Williams explained Molly's handicaps could be improved with stretches and exercises. Over the next few weeks, he showed me how to do the exercises for Molly's leg and fingers."

"And you've done them religiously ever since." Bessie's tone was warm.

"I had to, Bessie. Mr. Williams told me that the stretches mightn't be enough, and if they weren't, he recommended that when Molly was older, she wear a caliper to help stretch the tight hamstring and heel cord." Martha involuntarily shuddered. "Otherwise, she could end up with deformities." Martha remembered the shockwave that had gone through her and the vow she'd made that she wouldn't allow such a thing to happen.

"Then he went on to tell me that though I'd have a fight on my hands, he strongly advised that Molly should attend normal school."

Bessie's brow corrugated. "But you didn't have any trouble, did you?"

"No. But only because I prepared for the day. I made sure the twins could read before starting school." Martha saw in her mind's eye the two adorable little faces concentrating as they spelled out the word she pointed to. "Simple books, but I reckoned if I could prove Molly was bright, I'd have less trouble getting her into school with Jacob."

"And you succeeded."

"I can't take the glory, Bessie. It was Molly's determination that won through." Her voice cracked at the thought of her daughter's struggle. "Her leg was weak and she couldn't lift it enough even to go up a low step, and her cumbersome walk meant she couldn't go very far. That was besides having a disabled hand."

"God love her." Tears sparkled in Bessie's eyes. "She just gets on with it, doesn't she, and never gives in?"

They sat for a while in thoughtful silence.

Bessie wiped her eyes with her fingertips. "So, how did the bairn manage getting to school and back?"

Martha raised her eyebrows. "Would you believe, at first, by a sturdy Tansad pushchair I bought secondhand. Then when her leg was stronger, she wore a caliper to school. As far as her hand is concerned, Molly solves the problem by improvising with her good hand."

Bessie raised her glass. "Despite what you say, lass, you're a marvel."

Martha held up her hands, refuting the fact. "No, Bessie. I did what any mam would do. The thing is, the twins are inseparable and Molly would be like a flower denied water if she didn't have Jacob by her side."

Placing her glass on the table, Bessie picked up the playing cards. "So, what d'you think?"

"You'll win because you always do and—"

"Not about the cards! About me looking after the twins while you go out to work."

"You're very kind, Bessie, but like I said you've got enough on your plate as it is."

"As long as you know the offer's always there."

Later, when Martha was in the bedroom changing into her nightdress, she agonized over how she was going to solve the problem of bringing up the twins on her own with no finances. What terrified her most, she thought as she slipped between the cold sheets, was if there was another air raid and she lost her children.

The unthinkable had happened to Mam.

As though the gods were listening in, a sound broke into Martha's consciousness and she sat up with a start. Hearing the air raid sirens wail, fear gripped her heart.

Molly, beside her, awoke and let out a pitiful scream.

They got out of bed and headed down to the chilly and dank washhouse-cum-shelter, where Bessie, Martha and the twins huddled beneath blankets and leaned against cushions. Fred was working at the docks as it was high tide—the only time ships could float into the docks. Bessie's two lads were doing the night shift at the coal mine. Bessie admitted she'd forgotten to replenish the oil for the hurricane lamp and so light came from a flickering candle that cast shadows on the far wall.

Planes flew so low they seemed to skim the rooftops and loud bangs came from guns on the ground. Then, there was an almighty explosion in the distance. The shelter walls appeared to sway but mercifully didn't come crashing down. As raiders shrieked overhead, then sped into the distance, Molly put her small hand in Martha's.

"Will we die like Granny?" she asked in the smallest of voices that Martha could only just hear over the retreating drone of planes.

"No. I won't let that happen." Martha, looking at Jacob's round and terrified eyes and Molly's ashen face, was now convinced she knew what to do.

In the eerie candlelight, Bessie looked at her questioningly as if she knew something was afoot.

All quiet now in the air, and with no sound of further attack, Martha looked Bessie square in the eye. "I've come to a decision. I know it's late in the day but I'm going to see about having the twins evacuated to the country where they'll be safe. I couldn't bear it if anything happened to them."

Bessie looked thoughtful. "I never regretted sending our Jimmy, me youngest, who was only thirteen at the beginning of the war. It was the time of Operation Pied Piper and kiddies were being sent away to the countryside in droves."

Martha nodded. "Mam wouldn't hear tell of the twins being sent to strangers, so we decided they would stay home with her. I would do it differently now though. A war only lasts for a time but if you cop it, it's forever."

"I missed our Jimmy something rotten. When it was the phony war and nothing happened, I nearly cracked and sent for him to come home."

"Why didn't you?"

"I saw a poster on a billboard. A mother sitting in the countryside looking thoughtful, her children playing at her feet on the grass. Hitler was behind her saying, *Take them back!*, and the writing underneath on the poster read, *Don't do it, Mother. Leave the children where they are.*" Bessie shrugged. "The poster did its work. I left Jimmy where he was and I've never regretted it." She turned toward Martha and her expression was sympathetic. "I do know what you're going through. A mam does anything to protect her bairns."

They waited in silence until the all-clear sounded. Martha looked at her watch. Just after half three—another sleepless night. Then she felt guilty; others mightn't be lucky enough to see another day.

The twins, sitting subdued, had been listening in to the conversation and Martha felt bad that they'd found out about her deciding to evacuate them in this way. With a pang of regret, she thought of Mam and a sense of relief at being alive overpowered her. She squeezed the twins tightly as they sat huddled together.

Bessie stood up and started to fold her blanket. "What about you? Will you go with the bairns? I'll be sad to see you leave but there's nothing to keep you here."

"I'll go back to work at the factory. I'm determined to save so that I'll have the cash to rent somewhere decent for us all when the war finishes."

The problem is, a voice in her head said, *will a home be found for Molly, an evacuee with physical difficulties?*

CHAPTER EIGHT

October 1943

Jacob, holding a suitcase, trotted along on one side of Mam, while Molly held her hand on the other side.

Molly still limped as she walked, Jacob thought, trying to distract his mind from what was happening, though the good thing was her leg was strong enough now for her to lift it to walk up steps. But she still got called names and was pestered at school, Jacob knew. If Jacob had his way, he'd bash the culprits who mistreated his sister, but Molly had pleaded for him not to interfere because she was afraid that it would only make matters worse.

"Besides," she'd told him with that intense look on her face, "I can stick up for myself."

Which she never did. Molly's way of dealing with bullies was to ask them, with a hurt look that made a pain squeeze in his heart, "Why don't you like me? If you wore a caliper it wouldn't stop me from being your friend."

Molly was like that; she just came out with whatever she wanted to say. Granny used to call the way she talked "black and white straightforward"—whatever that meant.

He was sad when he thought of Granny. He missed her and didn't like the idea of her being buried underground. Wriggly worms weren't so bad, but he wouldn't like to be stuck in a wooden coffin and wondered how she got out when it was time to go to heaven.

As he walked toward the railway station entrance, Jacob

scratched his neck where the collar of his shirt itched. The shirt, like the short trousers he wore, was a hand-me-down from the clothes depot where Mam had taken the twins to be fitted out after the bombings when they stayed at the church hall.

The three of them had stood in a long queue and when it was their turn, the harassed-looking lady who wore the green uniform of the WVS had told Mam in a voice that meant business, "Be sharp. I haven't got all day. What are their sizes?" She'd handed Jacob a pile of clothes and a pair of shoes that had creases where someone else's feet had been. Jacob had sniffed the clothes and they smelled of someone else too.

Then the other day, Mam had taken them back to the clothes depot. It was an older WVS lady, who had gray hair, that served them this time.

"I don't suppose you've any slippers or sandshoes, and a winter coat each," Mam had asked politely, "because the kiddies are being evacuated and that's one of the requirements on the form." Mam took a piece of paper from her handbag and, as she glanced at it, Jacob noticed her hand trembled. "I think that's everything."

He was alarmed. Ever since that night of the raid when he'd heard Mam and Bessie talk about evacuation, he'd been scared. Then when nothing happened, he was pleased because he thought Mam had forgotten all about sending them away—because Jacob knew that's what evacuation meant.

The lady's eyes crinkled as she smiled kindly at Mam. "You're doing the right thing, dear. We've had a few in that's doing the same after the last raid in July."

Mam checked behind to see if anyone was listening in. She told the lady, "I've kept putting it off but I've finally taken the plunge." She took a deep breath. "I'd never forgive myself if . . . you know."

The lady nodded. "You won't regret it, my dear. And before you know it, they'll be back home again safe and sound."

A man and lady came to stand behind Mam.

"Now let's see about finding you those sandshoes," the WVS lady told the twins.

For the rest of that day Jacob felt jittery inside and it was at bedtime that night that Mam mentioned the word evacuation. She explained that the twins would be far away and live with a stranger, who would be in charge. They'd start a new school, have different friends and live out in the countryside where they'd never been before and which they knew nothing about, except there were animals and tractors in the fields. Jacob had been upset and couldn't get to sleep that night but he never let on to Mam because he knew she had enough worries.

The one good thing that appealed was that living in the country, hopefully, there'd be fewer planes flying overhead. Since the bombings when Granny was killed, Jacob, as he lay at night in the dark in bed, would go stiff with fear if he heard the droning of planes. He never told anyone because they'd think he was a sissy.

The same harassed-looking WVS lady who'd been behind the counter at the clothes depot the first time stood at the station with a wide-eyed little girl and a woman who looked like her mammy. The WVS woman, wearing a green blouse and skirt that had creases across the front where she'd been sitting, and a brimmed hat with an interesting-looking badge on it, looked up when the three of them approached.

"I'm Mrs. Walters," she told them. "I'll be traveling with you. I see you have the required gas mask in its case."

Jacob thought the lady wasn't mannerly as she didn't even say "Good morning" to Mam.

"Yes, all ready and correct," Mam replied in a pretend light-hearted voice she used when really, she was feeling sad.

"The twins have underclothes, night clothes, day clothes and plimsolls—newly bought." She raised her eyebrows at the WVS lady and continued, "Spare socks, toothbrush, comb, towel, soap, face cloth, handkerchiefs, a wooly jumper and coat."

Jacob felt the need to add, *so there*, but knew Mam wouldn't approve as she liked him to be polite.

"Can we not go inside the station?" Mam asked. "Because this northeasterly wind is perishing."

"I'm afraid not. A parent who can't face saying goodbye in the actual station has requested she meet us outside."

"I understand." Mam's voice went wobbly.

All this time Molly was clinging onto Mam's hand, her fingers white as if she'd never let go. She was nervous of meeting new people, Jacob knew, as she didn't like them staring at her wasted leg or drooped shoulder, with the limp arm that hung at her side.

At such times, Mam, noticing, would say in a sing-song voice, "Molly Molly Moo. We love you. Don't we, Jacob?"

He'd reply, "Yes, we do." He wanted them to say it now, but this wasn't the right time.

The woman with the girl gave the twins a kindly smile. "I don't know about you, but this is the first time Monica and me have been away from home." She turned to Mam. "The raid the other night was the last straw. Me house is unlivable. I've had enough. I'd never forgive myself if something happened to the bairn but I didn't want to be separated from her and so we're off to me sister's in Allendale. I plan to stay till the war's over. Me hubby's stationed abroad so there's nothing to keep us here."

"Same. Only I'm staying." Mam hesitated as if wondering if she should go on or not. "I intend to work. I plan to save up to set me up for when the war finishes."

"That seems sensible."

Another woman hurried toward them, wearing a black-and-white check coat with the collar up. A boy, who looked younger than Jacob, walked at her side, a suitcase and gas mask in his hands.

He wore a brown label with his name and address pinned to his coat, the same as all the children.

"All present and correct." The WVS lady looked directly at

the lady wearing the black-and-white coat. "We're ready to go into the station now."

The lady dropped on one knee by the little boy. "Be a good boy, Andrew. Mammy and Daddy will come and see you whenever we can. Remember to clean your teeth." Her chin quivering, she turned and she walked away. Tears rolled down Andrew's cheeks.

Jacob sniffed. Big boys didn't cry.

At any other time, at the thought of a train ride, Jacob would be beside himself with excitement, but this was different. He didn't know where he was going and the fact he'd be living with strangers made him jumpy and nervous inside.

Mam took his and Molly's hands and walked them, at a slow pace to allow for Molly, to the platform where an amazing train, bright green with a black funnel billowing steam, waited.

Mam knelt beside the twins, her face level with theirs. "I promise I'll come and visit the minute I can, meantime I'll write." She gave each of them a red lipstick smile. "I know you'll stay brave. And I want you to remember, this is for the best. The war will be over soon and we'll be together again." She spoke in a bright voice. "I love you both, dearly."

"Love you," they replied. Jacob knew his voice was shaky.

"Molly, if you need anything at all, don't be afraid to ask a grown-up for help. And remember to put your caliper on every day. I know it hurts sometimes and I'm sorry, but you want to wear pretty shoes, don't you, when you grow up?" Mam gave her best pretend smile.

"Yes." Molly made a peculiar sound, as if she had hiccups.

Mam gave her a kiss on the cheek that left a red lipstick mark. "Now, go find Mrs. Walters."

Molly hesitated. "Don't want to. I want to stay here with you and Jacob."

Jacob saw Mam bite the inside of her lip like she did when she seemed unsure of what to do.

"You're a big girl now. You have to learn to do things on your own. If it's something you don't want to do, then you have to be a sport and grin and bear it." She paused and gave a weak smile. "Imagine when you're bigger and have a boyfriend and the pair of you can't go anywhere because me and Jacob are tagging along."

The twins laughed at the silliness and when Mam joined in, Jacob's tummy relaxed for a bit.

Molly, walking with a lopsided gait, moved off.

That's how Mam made Molly do things if she went shy or was afraid; she made a joke and it worked by helping his sister feel better. Mam was clever like that.

"Jacob." Mam's voice sounded serious, and he noticed the whites of her eyes had turned pink. "Look after your sister. Whatever you do, don't get separated. And no complaining."

A sinking feeling came into his tummy. Now he had something else to worry about. He had never dreamt Molly and he would be separated. Rather than worry Mam with lots of questions because she looked harassed, he answered, "I promise, I will."

"Something else." Mam opened the clasp of her black handbag and pulled out a small envelope. "I want you to put this in your pocket and keep it somewhere safe when you get to the new place."

"What's in the letter?"

"Listen carefully. You're never to open it unless you or your sister are in . . . real trouble, promise me."

"In danger like Biggles' adventures in the book?"

"Not quite the same. I mean when something very bad happens to make you upset and you've nowhere to turn."

"I could tell you."

"I mightn't be on hand for some reason. Find a grown-up, Jacob, whom you trust and give the letter to them. D'you understand?"

Jacob felt alarmed because he didn't. "What kind of trouble?"

Mam looked over to where Mrs. Walters was beckoning to them. She kissed him on the cheek, then stood up. "You're a sensible boy, Jacob, you'll know when real trouble happens. Now it's time to go. Promise you'll write as soon as you can."

"I promise, Mam."

She folded the letter and put it in his trouser pocket. Then, she opened her mouth as if she wanted to say more, but no words came out. Instead, she hugged him so tight that it took his breath away.

As the train moved away from the platform with heavy *chuff-chuff* noises, the twins stood at the carriage window, waving to Mam, who was looking as lost and sad as Jacob felt.

Running along the platform, Mam blew a kiss and waved vigorously. *Don't forget to write*, she mouthed.

Then the train, gathering speed, whistle blowing, clouds of steam billowing in the atmosphere, chuff-chuffed out of the station, leaving Mam behind, and a frightened and yet excited feeling overcame Jacob.

"Come, children, sit down. I've kept seats for you." Mrs. Walters' voice held a gentle note and her being kind made him feel weepy.

Jacob, thinking of his hero Biggles, who courageously faced any situation, squared his shoulders. He'd Molly to take care of, and she'd be missing Mam already, just like him.

"Molly, you can sit by the window," he told her.

She gave him one of those sweet smiles that said thank you with her eyes.

Watching the world whizz by outside the window—houses with long gardens, some with washing on the line blowing in the breeze, and bombed out buildings—Jacob had a sense of things being unreal. He did something he'd never done before:, he put his arm around his sister's shoulder. Not to comfort her, but more to reassure himself that she was actually sitting beside him. Turning her head from looking out of the window, Molly looked at him and her heart-shaped face held a sorrowful expression. Then she did something she'd never done before and laid her head on his shoulder.

"I don't want to leave home and live with some stranger," she whispered.

Neither did Jacob but he knew if he didn't keep strong like Biggles, the pair of them would end up in tears right here in the carriage where everyone could see and that would be embarrassing.

Mam had showed them on a map where they'd be going and had told them, "It's a little village called Leadburn, way in the country where you'll be safe from the bombing."

What would Mam do now? Jacob wondered and searched his mind for a joke; then he caught his eye on the label with Molly's name and address written on it, pinned to her cardigan, just like the one Granny had once knitted. The thought made his eyes moisten and he blinked rapidly.

"We look like two parcels being delivered, don't we, Molly?"

Molly sat up and, her long eyelashes moist, she wiped them with a hand. She looked at Jacob's label and for a time he thought the joke hadn't worked. Then, her face lit up and she started to giggle. Proud of himself for making her laugh, Jacob joined in. Neither of them could stop and—much to Mrs. Walters' disapproval, as she pulled an irritated face—they kept laughing until their sides ached and tears ran from their eyes.

Whether they were happy or sad tears, Jacob wasn't sure.

The journey involved traveling on another train to a place called Hexham, but this train ride was different. Jacob, gazing past Molly out of the window, was amazed at the open space outside; he could see countryside for miles into the distance where the sky seemingly met the hilltops, but it was a bit scary as there were no shops or houses. In the fields, there were cows and sheep; Jacob only knew them because he'd seen them in a book. Molly, looking out of the window too, kept saying, "Look at that, Jacob," pointing to a scene they'd never encountered before, like now when they saw a river rushing past not so very far from the railway track.

At home in South Shields, there were rows and rows of streets filled with terraced houses with tall chimneypots puffing out grimy smoke that dirtied Mam's newly washed clothes hanging on the line in the back lane. As his thoughts turned to home, a longing to be back overcame Jacob. He wanted to be there, to see the people he knew, the places he was used to, but most of all to have the security of being with Mam.

At Hexham they made their way to the bus station, where the lady with the girl called Monica left them to catch a bus to Allendale where her aunty lived. Feeling a stab of envy, Jacob wished someone he knew was waiting for him at the end of his journey.

"Best of luck," the lady called as she headed off to a different bus stand.

The little boy, Andrew, was all alone and his shoulders drooped. Jacob felt sorry for him and took the little lad's hand.

"Are you coming to Leadburn?" Jacob asked.

The boy looked up, his face blotchy red. "I dunno, but if you are, I hope I am as well."

Mrs. Walters ushered the three of them onto the bus and the conductress tinged the bell.

This part of the journey included traveling along twisty, narrow roads that made them all hang onto the seats in front, but at least it didn't take long.

Molly was looking with wide eyes at the tall trees lining the road and obscuring the view outside the window. "It's like the story Mam read to us when we were small where the children were taken away into dark woods—"

"To the gingerbread house…" Andrew, sitting just in front of them beside Mrs. Walters, turned around, his eyes round with fear.

"It's only a story." Jacob made big eyes at Molly.

"Made up to frighten little boys," she agreed. But still, Molly looked a bit shaken.

A bell tinged and the bus slowed then stopped at the side of the road where nothing was to be seen but fields, trees and a bus shelter with a wooden seat. Two older girls at the front stood up from their seats and alighted from the bus.

As she looked out of the window, Molly's eyes followed the girls as they crossed the road. "What kind of uniform are they wearing?"

Mrs. Walters turned in her seat. "They're Land Army girls, you'll see lots of them around here. There's a hostel, I'm told."

The bus started up again and after a while, turned right and trundled along a smaller road lined with houses with long front gardens. It then came to a halt outside a house with a red post box built into a stone wall.

"Who's for Leadburn?" the conductress called.

Jacob alighted from the bus and sniffed the air. It smelled differently here, not sooty but clean with a kind of sweet smell he couldn't fully describe. He turned and, taking Molly's small suitcase, helped her from the platform. Andrew came next, followed by Mrs. Walters.

The bus moved away and they were left looking at a scene that made Jacob gasp.

"It's like looking at a picture story book," Molly said in wonder.

Jacob gazed over a large grassy verge and fast running stream, to a gnarled tree on the other side. "I've always wanted to climb a tree."

Molly smiled. "Look. Doesn't that tall church steeple behind that house look as if it's poking out from the roof?"

"The army's here," Andrew chipped in and pointed to an area of grass farther up the village where a big tent had been erected and soldiers in uniform milled around.

"It's a NAAFI tent." Jacob showed off his knowledge of the forces. He knew a lot about vehicles and everything about airplanes after reading the Biggles comics.

"Hurry along, children. I have to make the return journey home and it'll be suppertime before I get back," Mrs. Walters grumbled.

The word home reminded Jacob of their predicament and his tummy seemed to nosedive like an airplane. A feeling of abandonment overwhelming him, he took Molly's stiff-fingered hand in his because he knew she felt the same way too.

Mrs. Walters led the way, carrying Andrew's suitcase while he trailed behind.

"Andrew, pull your socks up, you," she told him. "You want to look smart for when your new family come to collect you."

Poor Andrew's thin face went white and Jacob could tell that all he wanted was to return home to his mam, as Jacob did.

Jacob's tummy rumbled. It was afternoon and all he'd eaten was two chicken paste sandwiches that Mrs. Walters had handed out in greaseproof paper after they'd boarded the train for Hexham.

They crossed over a little white bridge, water swirling below, then passed the red telephone box and the store where you could see inside rows of shelves with hardly anything on them.

Mrs. Walters stopped at the door of a low roofed building. "Here we are."

"Where are we?" Jacob asked.

"The village hall"—Mrs. Walters opened the creaky, wooden door—"where you'll be billeted to a family." She walked in the building. "Hello, is anyone here?"

Jacob waited for Molly, who lagged behind with Andrew, to

enter together. The room was long and low and had a stage at one end, while a trestle table with high-backed wooden chairs surrounding it stood in the middle.

An elderly lady came out of a far door, drying her hands on a wraparound apron. She was plump with twists of white curls surrounding a smiley, pink-cheeked face that surprisingly didn't have any deep lines like Granny's did.

With a shock, Jacob remembered Granny wasn't here any more and a tightness came into his chest, with the feeling he couldn't breathe properly.

"Are you all right, son?" The lady moved toward him, her body stooped. "What's your name?"

"Jacob, and this is my sister, Molly."

The lady's smile was kind. "How d'you do."

"The boy's fine. Tired, that's all." The WVS lady became her bossy self. She held out her hand. "I'm Mrs. Walters. I was expecting the billeting officer."

The smiley lady shook hands. "Mrs. Leadbeater's sorry but she can't make it. She's asked me to stand in for her." She looked at the three children as if she talked to them too. "Mrs. Leadbeater's a busy woman and works far too hard, running the post office and doing the mail for the comforts fund for our boys fighting for their coun—"

Mrs. Walters gave a rude and impatient tut. "When will the host families be here?"

"I'm sorry you're stuck with me." The lady didn't look sorry at all but kept on smiling. "I'm Brigit Merryfield, by the way." She twinkled a smile at the three children. "Your host families will arrive soon. They were told two o'clock." She looked up at the large round clock that hung on the opposite wall. "You've a quarter of an hour to wait. How about a nice cup of tea? There are shortbread biscuits in the tin." She winked at Andrew, then prattled, "There was a whist drive here last night and so I baked for that. One of Mrs. Leadbeater's fund-raising events. I'm here to tidy up. It's a small thing but I like to do me bit."

For the next quarter of an hour, sitting around the table, sipping tea and munching biscuits, they listened to the nice lady talking nonstop, telling them about the village.

"Mr. Dodds drives his bread van from the next village and most folk agree it's high time we had our own bakery. Then again, with time on my hands I make my own. Mr. Nichol from the local farm arrives every morning driving his horse and cart, delivering milk around the doors and the school. We have lots of goings on here in the hall, all arranged by Mrs. Leadbeater: collections for rags, cardboard, bottles—"

At that moment the village door swung open. Mrs. Merryfield, looking expectantly to see who came in, stopped mid-sentence.

A lady who held the hand a little girl of about four came into the hall. She looked quite young, Jacob decided, and wore a gray, wide-shouldered suit, black gloves and shoes to match—Mam would approve of the lady's smart appearance, he thought.

"Mary." Mrs. Merryfield stood and walked over to the young lady. "How lovely to see you. I hear you're after an evacuee."

"Mrs. Leadbeater said they were short of billets so I volunteered. I wouldn't want my Susan"—she nodded down to her daughter—"to be stuck in the bombings. It's my way of doing my bit. Besides, with Eric being away, Susan and I could do with the company."

Mrs. Merryfield turned and told the children, "Eric's in the Royal Navy and it's an age since we last saw him in the village."

"Uh hum!" Mrs. Walters, giving an exasperated shake of the head, stood and moved over to the lady.

"Which evacuee will you choose? Stand up, children, please." She addressed the lady again. "That's Molly and Jacob, they're twins. The little boy is Andrew."

"Oh! I don't know." The lady looked as uncomfortable as

Jacob felt. "Point to the kiddie you'd like to come home to live with us," she told Susan.

Susan looked them up and down as if they were lollipops in a jar and she'd to choose a color. "That one." She pointed to little Andrew.

"Good choice," her mam told her, "he's more your age and you can play with him."

Mrs. Walters went over and fished some papers out of her briefcase and the two women with the two children sat talking for a time.

Then the door opened and another lady, older this time, came in. She wore a black coat that reached practically to her ankles and wellington boots and had a no-nonsense expression on her thin face.

She eyed the twins up and down. "Is this all that's left?"

Mrs. Merryfield, the smile gone, answered, "Most kiddies have been evacuated before this late stage of the war, Nora. But this bunch are as lovely as ever."

Nora sniffed in answer. She looked Jacob up and down again. "I don't want no boy. I need help around the house."

Jacob's first reaction was relief but, as the lady approached Molly, he felt panicky. "We're twins," he gabbled, "Mam says we're not to be parted."

The lady turned toward him. "Your mam isn't here, though, is she?"

It was all too much for Molly, Jacob knew, as she inched toward Mrs. Merryfield. She looked up at the old lady. "Please, Mrs., I want to stay with Jacob."

"Don't you worry, my love. You and your brother can come home and stay with me."

"You can have them." Nora looked down at Molly's caliper and, turning on her heel, she made for the door. "No amount of government money would induce me to take on a cripple. What use will she be?"

CHAPTER NINE

"Are you sure you can manage?" Mrs. Walters looked uncertain as she made for the door.

Mrs. Merryfield winked at the twins. "I'm not in me dotage, yet."

Mrs. Walters, her hand on the doorknob, rubbed her chin. "How about you arrange with the billeting officer that you look after the twins until another billet is available?"

"There are none. Even though some of the evacuees have returned home, the village is stowed out with soldiers. And I don't want *her*"—she nodded to the door—"deciding she does want government money offered to host families, after all."

A look of relief spread over the WVS lady's face. "Then I'll be off."

As the village door closed, Jacob, rooted to the spot, was dismayed to see Mrs. Walters go, not because he liked her particularly, but she was the last link to home—and Mam.

Mrs. Merryfield removed her apron. "Come on, you two, I want you to meet Smoky the cat. She'll love you."

Mrs. Merryfield lived at the other side of the village. Crossing the stream by another bridge farther down the village this time, Jacob couldn't see over the high stone sides that were covered with green moss.

The twins followed Mrs. Merryfield along the road for a time, then, turning left, she started up an earthen path where tall, skinny trees grew on either side. Mrs. Merryfield, being older, didn't walk very fast; or else, Jacob thought, she was allowing for Molly to keep up.

Jacob rather liked Mrs. Merryfield, he decided, because she didn't feel like a stranger.

He knew his sister was upset about being called a cripple; it had happened before in the play yard at school at home. Afterward, Molly had told Mam (who was home at the time) that she didn't want to attend school any more. Mam must have suspected that Molly was being taunted because she'd said, "Molly Moffatt, you will go back to school, you've got nothing to be ashamed of. And if other kids call you names it says more about them, what kind of person they are." She appeared good and mad. "What person in their right mind would want them for a friend? And I won't have you"—she turned to Jacob, who sat innocently eating a slice of dripping and bread—"taking it upon yourself to fight other people's battles for them. In fact, I don't want fighting at all. Is that clear, Jacob?"

Jacob had tried to look as though he didn't know what Mam was talking about, but it hadn't worked because his discolored eye gave him away. All he knew was the fight had been worth it because the culprit had promised he'd never call Molly names again.

Now, they walked up the earthen track, birds tweeting in the trees up above, and the path opened up to reveal a pretty stone cottage. It had a small front garden with a wooden bench against the house wall. Pretty, feathery pink flowers that gave off a heavy scent climbed up a wooden frame surrounding the yellow front door with its gleaming brass knocker and handle.

Mrs. Merryfield opened the gate and crunched up the side path. The twins, following her, came across an area of sweet-smelling newly cut grass—what Jacob had smelled, he realized, when he first arrived and got off the bus—behind which were rows of greenery that resembled the allotments at home.

"This is home, dears. You can roam anywhere except the herb garden." She pointed to what Jacob had thought was the allotment.

Just then a black cat appeared. "Hello, Smoky." The cat, whose long upright tail was swaying left to right, brushed against Mrs. Merryfield's leg.

"I'm pleased to see you too." She turned to Molly: "D'you like cats?"

"I like Smoky."

"Then stroke her. She especially likes her ears being tickled."

Jacob knew Molly was unsure. The only time they saw a cat at home was if one strolled on the top of the backyard wall, and then Granny would clap her hands and shoo the cat away.

Mrs. Merryfield picked Smoky up and placed her in his sister's arms. Molly began to stroke the sleek fur and a rattling noise came from the cat's throat.

"You've made Smoky happy. She's purring."

Eyes shining, Molly cuddled the cat into her chest, rubbing her cheek against the soft fur. She smiled. Mrs. Merryfield, looking on, appeared satisfied, as if she knew this was what Molly needed to help forget her shyness.

Inside Mrs. Merryfield's cottage—with its dark cozy interior, low kitchen ceiling, and comfortable-looking saggy chairs with bright colored crocheted cushions just like Granny's, and lots of interesting ornaments on all the window ledges and furniture surfaces—the peculiar thing was that Jacob felt right at home.

The sun shone through a window and light fell on a piece of colored glass on a wall shelf, making colored sunbeams dance on the walls.

"It's one of my crystals," Mrs. Merryfield told the twins. "The house is welcoming you." Taking a square of material off the mantelpiece to protect her hand, she took the kettle off the hob. "How about tea and a homemade scone and then I'll take you upstairs to see your bedroom. It'll be lovely having someone here to bake for, won't it, Smoky?"

"Thank you, Mrs. Merryfield." Molly surprised Jacob by speaking up, as she usually left talking to people they'd just met to him.

"You're welcome, dear, but my name's Brigit." A thoughtful look crossed her face. "I expect you'll feel strange calling an old lady by her first name. How about calling me Aunty Brigit? Or is that too familiar?"

The twins passed a look.

"We'd like that," Jacob confirmed.

That first night, Jacob felt a bit awkward living with Aunty Brigit, and after he cleaned his teeth and hopped into the double bed beside his sister, he could tell, by the way Molly sat stiffly next to him, that she felt the same way.

He saw her caliper leaning against the wooden locker by the bed. "You've manged to undo the strap yourself?"

He was surprised as it was Mam who usually unfastened the buckle on the strap.

"I managed with my right hand." Molly looked uncertain. "Mam told me to ask the people I live with if they'd help do my exercises and stretches. She said it was important and that I should tell them what to do."

"She never said anything to me." Jacob felt left out.

"Mam said it was time I learned to do things for myself. And that though Granny was kind it meant she sometimes spoilt me. I want to do as Mam says 'cos she's right, but Jacob, I don't like asking people..."

"I'll do it."

"You'll be spoiling me then."

"I want to help."

Molly clutched Floppy rabbit to her chest.

Jacob didn't know what to say to help. "You'll feel better in the morning."

That was Mam's cure-all for any of their worries at night.

"I've got to be brave sometime. I like Aunty Brigit, she's kind. Besides I don't want to end up with them formities like Mam said I would if I keep walking on my toe."

Jacob was sure his sister hadn't said the word correctly.

"Jacob."

"Yes."

"I'm scared to start a new school."

Although Jacob loved Molly, she frustrated him sometimes. He didn't want to be worrying about her when he was trying to stay brave himself. He let out a sigh. Though he knew he was being unfair, because he didn't have a disability and the fear of a classroom of children gawping at him.

"Don't worry, Molly Moo, I'll be there too."

At that moment, Aunty Brigit came into the room. "Would you like me to read you a story or can you do it yourselves? I've forgotten when my daughter, Tabitha, started, it's so long ago."

The twins politely refused because Mam was the one to do that—even though the twins could read for themselves. Mam said it was their special time together.

"I'll leave a torch in case either of you need to get up in the night." Aunty Brigit placed the torch on the locker beside the bed, then turned back toward them. "Molly dear, I have a special rub I've made up that might do your leg good. I could give you a massage with it, if you like."

Jacob wondered if Aunty Brigit had been listening at the door, but he was sure he'd heard her coming up the stairs just before she came in.

"Mam says I should still do my leg exercises every day or I'll get formities."

Jacob was surprised Molly had spoken up for herself.

"Deformities, dear. How about I help you with the exercises?"

"And stretches," Molly prompted. "I could show you what Mam does."

"What a good idea." Aunty Brigit switched off the light. "Night, night, I'll see you in the morning."

As Jacob lay staring in the dark, an ache of longing overwhelmed him.

Molly's voice came through the darkness. "Jacob, I'm glad we're sleeping in the same bed together like at home."

Though they had to use a bucket at home at night as the lavatory was down the yard, and the bedroom had black moldy spots on the walls that resembled dead flies, Jacob knew his sister felt the same as he did and would rather be back there. With a pang of longing, he realized they didn't have a home any more.

"Cheer up," he told her. "Things will look different in the morning." Another of Mam's sayings.

It was then Jacob remembered Mam's letter still in his trouser pocket, and her telling him if they were in trouble to give it to someone he trusted. Jacob wondered where he could hide the letter. He felt bad keeping it a secret from Molly, then he recalled she and Mam kept things from him too. He tried to think what his hero would do. Hide the letter beneath something, a voice in his head said, where no one would think to look.

But where? his tired mind asked. Beneath the floorboards? The shelf of a wardrobe? This was Jacob's last thought before falling asleep.

When the twins awoke the next morning, they dressed and, after Jacob had fastened the strap on Molly's caliper, he said, "Mam usually helps you with stairs. Will you manage?"

"I have to try, Jacob. You won't always be here."

Jacob stood at the top of the narrow staircase, watching Molly as she maneuvered herself to sit on the top step and bum shuffle each step at a time to the bottom. Then, with her right hand on the banister rail, she hauled herself up.

She grinned up at him proudly. "I've only got to find out how to get up now."

"I'll be there in a minute," Jacob called as he made his way back to the bedroom.

Rolling back the corner of the carpet, he was disappointed to find that there were no loose floorboards like at home. And no wardrobe, only a tallboy chest of drawers. Opening one of the drawers, he moved what looked like folded curtains in it to one side and saw flowered wallpaper lining the bottom of the drawer. Taking the letter from his pocket, Jacob placed it under the wallpaper and, moving the curtains back in place, he shut the drawer. His mission accomplished, imagining what Biggles would do, Jacob looked around the room to see if he'd left any evidence. Satisfied everything was in its place, he left the room and went down to breakfast.

"It's school today," Aunty Brigit told the twins as they all sat around the breakfast table, "but with all the upheaval yesterday I think you two could do with a day of rest." The twins agreed with a vigorous nod. "Before you do anything, though, I suggest you write to your parents. They'll be worried about you."

As Aunty spoke, Jacob watched Molly struggle to put jam on her bread with a knife. The problem was her stiff fingers. If she moved one, the others automatically followed.

"We've only got Mam," Molly said, holding the bread down with her left hand, and spreading the jam with her right. "Our daddy died when the mine roof fell on top of him."

"Dearie me, that's so sad." Tears came to Aunty Brigit's eyes. "What a mam you must have to bring you up on her own."

"Granny helped but then she died in the bombing."

"Oh my!" Aunty Brigit clapped her hands on her cheeks. "What you two have been through. We'll have to make it up to them, won't we, Smoky?"

The cat, curled in front the fire, looked up as if she knew she was being spoken to and let out a loud meow.

After a breakfast of Weetabix, a slice of bread and homemade raspberry jam, the twins sat at the table writing a letter to Mam, while Aunty washed the dishes at the big sink.

When Jacob had finished the letter in his big loopy handwriting, he slid the sheet of paper over the table for Molly's inspection.

Aunty Brigit turned from the sink. "Did you tell your mam you're safely here? And that you're missing her, but you're being brave and getting on with things? Because that's what mams like to hear."

That's exactly what Jacob and Molly had written because they didn't want to tell Mam the truth: that, although traveling to see somewhere new felt like an adventure at first, they now wanted to come home.

"I've told Mam about Smoky," Molly said to Aunty as Jacob licked the edge of the envelope to seal it down.

Smoky, strolling over, jumped on Molly's lap and nestled down.

"I reckon Smoky's adopted you." Though it was her cat, Aunty Brigit didn't seem to mind. "Right, off you two go to the post office and get that letter in the post. Your mam will be anxious till she receives it."

"Go by ourselves?" Molly looked shocked. They were never allowed to cross main roads on their own. Granny said they had to be at least ten.

"The postie's only a few yards along the road from here, and the post box is in the wall of a house. You can't get lost and the roads are quiet here. You'll pass the school on the way; why don't you take a look?" Aunty Brigit dried her hands on the tea towel.

"I'm just popping out to get the rations in, so don't worry if I'm not here when you get back. I won't be long. I'll leave the door on the latch." Continuing to dry the dishes, she began to hum, *run rabbit, run, run, run.*

After they'd stuck a stamp on the envelope, given to them by Mrs. Walters for this very purpose, the twins left the cottage by the back door and, crunching over the gravel at the side of the cottage, made their way down the earthen path and along the road.

They walked along the narrow footpath past the lovely big stone houses that had space around them, set back from the road by huge gardens and their own front paths. It wasn't like home where your front door opened out to the pavement.

"Isn't the village nice," Molly remarked, stopping for a moment to look around. "But I'd still rather be in me hometown."

Jacob frowned; if Mam had been here, she'd have told Molly, "It's *my* hometown." Mam liked them to talk properly.

Thinking of Mam made Jacob's eyes sting with tears.

Voices came from behind them and Jacob turned. A few yards back, a group of school children walked along the path, talking and laughing.

One of them, a boy, bigger than the rest with a mop of curly fair hair that Mam would never allow a boy of hers to have, said something and the others all stared curiously at Molly.

Molly's cheeks flushed pink, her upper body hunched and she attempted to hurry away, which made her lopsided walk more noticeable.

The boy with the fair hair started to laugh and began to imitate Molly's walk.

The fury that rose in Jacob was instant and, with a pounding in his ears, he clenched his fists. He didn't care about the consequences, he just wanted to punch the living daylights out of the cruel lad. Then, a girl with red hair caught the boy by the arm and as her face scrunched, she said something to him—it appeared as though she told him off.

The boy shrugged and moved on, but not before he glared with dislike at Jacob—and Jacob knew he'd made an enemy on the first day.

How Jacob wanted to run up to the boy and punch him in the face, but what stopped him wasn't Mam's warning, but Molly. He didn't want to embarrass her any further.

The pounding in his ears gone, but his body still tensed for a fight, he hurried and caught up with his retreating sister.

"Look, there's the post box in the wall," Molly said, as if nothing had happened.

Jacob heard the group of children not far behind.

"Let's go inside the post office and look around." And avoid the bully, Jacob thought, because he didn't want Molly to suffer any more harassment.

The bell tinged.

The post office smelled of paper, cardboard and, curiously, glue. The lady behind the counter was busy writing something down but she looked up as the twins walked in.

"Hello, I've not seen you two before."

The lady had blonde hair, a milk-colored face and friendly smile and she wore a post office uniform.

"We came yesterday…" Unusually, Jacob felt tongue-tied; everything here was new and daunting.

"Ah! You're two of the evacuees. The twins."

"How d'you know?" Molly blurted.

"Because you resemble each other, and because I'm Doris Leadbeater, otherwise known as the billeting officer. Sorry I wasn't there to welcome you and see you settled with your host families." She smiled. "I hear Brigit Merryfield has taken you in."

They both nodded.

Molly ventured, "Aunty Brigit's got a cat that I'm allowed to stroke."

Jacob wasn't surprised that his sister found it easy to talk to Mrs. Leadbeater. The lady had a friendly face and appeared really interested when you spoke. Somehow, he felt like he'd always known her.

"Aunty! That will please Brigit. She misses her daughter sorely."

"Why, where is she?" Molly wanted to know.

"Tabitha married and moved to Yorkshire. She wanted her mam to go and live with them but typically Brigit didn't want to go because she felt she'd be in the way."

Jacob was used to people being friendly and gossipy and talking to strangers, because that was what it was like at home, but here, everyone in the village seemed to know each other and all their business.

"The reason I've never billeted evacuees to Brigit before," Mrs. Leadbeater sighed, "despite her nagging me, is because at her age she'll probably find it hard to cope. Though, she'd never admit it. So, you two had better pull your weight." She gave them a no-nonsense stare, then looked at Molly's caliper. "And help as much as you're able."

Mrs. Leadbeater reminded Jacob of Mam, who always spoke her mind. Jacob liked that in grown-ups, because then he knew what to expect.

"We will," they chanted together.

"Now then"—Mrs. Leadbeater's friendly smile returned—"what was it you wanted?"

"For this to go into the post bag, please." Jacob handed the letter to Mam over the counter.

Later, as they made their way back to the cottage, Jacob decided he'd help Aunty Brigit as much as he could. Because if he and Molly did prove to be too much work for Aunty Brigit, they might be sent to live with the Nora lady.

CHAPTER TEN

"Tuck in," Aunty Brigit told the twins as she bent down to the floor and filled Smoky's saucer with milk. "You'll need sustenance for all that learning."

As he ate his dippy egg, Jacob marveled at such luxury because at home, with rationing on, eggs were scarce and sometimes the twins were lucky to get one a week.

Aunty Brigit came out with some queer sayings and she used words that sometimes he didn't understand. He knew her meaning today though, as the twins were about to start school.

She told them, "Ignore the children who don't mix, and be happy with the ones who do. They'll prove to be your friends and you'll get by without the others."

The whites of Molly's eyes went big. He knew it was the ones who didn't mix she was afraid of—and the things they might call her.

Breakfast over, Jacob, ready with a battered leather satchel slung over his shoulder and Molly with a book bag that Aunty Brigit had found in the cluttered under-the-stairs cupboard, wrapped up in their warm coats, hovered at the door ready to leave.

Aunty Brigit didn't attempt to put her outdoor coat on.

"You don't need me to take you to school," she told them as she hauled up the brass scuttle from the hearth and slung coal on the range fire. "It's best you go on your own and show how brave you are. Ask for Miss Templeton, the headmistress; we go back years. She taught my Tabitha when she started as a teacher. She's a stickler for rules but fair with it. She'll keep you right."

His insides quaking, Jacob didn't feel brave. But he thought of Biggles and stood tall. What was a first day at school compared to the dangers Biggles met?

"Come on, Molly. Don't be a sissy. I'll look after you."

"Is it frosty outside?"

Jacob told Aunty, "Molly can't walk out in slippy weather and Mam lets her stay off school."

"Molly, dear, whenever the weather's bad you can stay at home with Smoky and me." Aunty looked out of the kitchen window. "Today's drab and you'll be fine." She gave Molly a sympathetic smile. "Doing something new is always frightening but it's only till dinner time and then you'll be back here where Smoky and I will be waiting."

Molly looked pleased at the idea she wouldn't be staying for school dinners.

The weather was dreary, the sky hanging over the rooftops like a gray blanket. As the twins walked along the street, the air was damp and their breath turned into smoke-like puffs.

The school was halfway along the road, just before the post office. A two-story stone building, with a long corridor, peaked roof and with long narrow windows, the school seemed to Jacob like a church. A low-walled forecourt garden separated the entrance steps from the front street.

Molly struggled climbing the four steps, and when the twins passed through the doorway, they found themselves in a small, dim hallway.

"No assembly in the yard this morning, it's too damp," an older lady, who wore a navy suit, white blouse and had slate gray wavy hair, told everyone. "Coats in the cloakroom and go straight into the main room for school assembly."

Jacob went up to her. "We're new here, miss."

"You must be the twins." She flashed a distracted smile of greeting. "I'm your headmistress, Miss Templeton. Hang your coats up and follow the rest. You can't get lost."

Jacob thought there was nothing else for it, so that's what they did.

Compared to their school at home, there weren't many children, but with everyone talking and laughing in groups, the fact the twins didn't know anyone and couldn't join in was overwhelming.

Someone was waving at the twins and Jacob realized it was the red-headed girl they'd seen yesterday.

She came over and, as Molly shrank beside him, the instinct to protect her overcame Jacob.

"Hello. I'm Denise Curtis. I live in the village. What's your names?"

"Jacob and—"

"I'm Molly." Jacob was both surprised and pleased his sister had answered.

"Where d'you live?"

"South Shields, but we're staying with Mrs. Merryfield."

Denise smiled. "People say she's a bit dotty but my nana, who runs the village store, says there's no harm in her and she's got a heart of gold."

Jacob liked Denise's nana.

"Quiet everyone, please." The room hushed and Jacob saw Miss Templeton standing on the platform at the front.

Denise whispered to Molly, "You can come and play at my house sometime if you want."

Molly gave a shy smile and nodded. Jacob was glad his sister had made a friend.

Prayers were said and then they all stood up and sang "O God, Our Help in Ages Past."

Then, Miss Templeton's eyes circled the room. "Two notices

only this morning. All milk bottles are to be either handed to milk monitors or put back in the crate. Don't leave them lying around where they can get broken. Is that understood?"

"Yes, Miss Templeton," the company of children chorused.

"Next, we have two evacuees joining us. Molly and Jacob Moffatt." She looked directly at the twins. Everyone turned their heads to see who they were. Discomforted by being on show, Jacob felt he now knew what it was like to be a goldfish in a bowl.

"Remember your manners and help them settle in. Leadburn School is noted for both hard work and a warm welcome to new classmates." She peered over her spectacles at them all. "And where you can, lend a helping hand."

"Yes, Miss Templeton."

The twins stared at one another. It would be just like Aunty Brigit's kind self to have told the headmistress about Molly's weakness.

It was then Jacob noticed the boy with fair curly hair, a head bigger than most of the others. He smirked at Jacob. The boy, obviously, wasn't about to heed the warning.

*

Molly was surprised that there was only one classroom and it had all age groups in it. Miss Crow, their teacher, was a skinny lady who strangely had two differently colored eyes—one green and one brown—and an expression that looked as though she was dissatisfied all the time.

The twins sat at a two-seated wooden desk that had cast iron legs. For the first part of the morning, the class stood and chanted the five times table, which was an easy one. Sums came next when Miss Crow wrote figures on the blackboard with chalk. Molly was aware the other children kept staring at them. Denise, who sat at the desk over the aisle from her, smiled, though, which made her feel better.

Molly, determined to be bold, smiled back.

At playtime in the school yard, Molly looked out of the rusty-colored railings to a field where wooly sheep grazed. She limped through the groups of children over the yard that had a netball court painted in white on it and waited for Jacob to emerge from the building that housed the row of outdoor lavatories.

She tensed as the boy with the fair hair who'd imitated how she walked yesterday moved toward her. Surrounded by a gang of children, he sneered, "Hey! Matchstick leg, I'm not lending you a hand. I need both of mine."

The others laughed as if what he'd said was the funniest joke, but their eyes were wary.

The lad's lip curled. "Mam says what you've got might be catchin' and you shouldn't be let out. Go home, matchstick leg, we don't want you here, do we?"

Some of the children looked uncomfortable but they all kept staring at Molly as if to see her reaction.

Being stared at was the worst but Molly found herself blurting, "Why are you being so mean to me?"

"Roger, don't be horrible." Denise seemed to appear from nowhere. She came to stand by Molly. "She can't help it if her leg's disabled. Besides, they wouldn't let her come to school if it was something infectious."

This was worse, as now even more children had gathered around to stare. Molly was frozen to the spot.

Someone pushed their way through the gawping children.

Jacob.

He looked from the fair-haired boy to Molly. "What's happened?"

"Roger's being mean to her," Denise told him.

Molly was in awe of how brave she was.

"How?" Jacob looked furious.

"He called her 'matchstick leg.'"

Molly didn't see, but heard the thwack.

*

Jacob didn't know where his strength came from. All he knew was the rage boiling inside made him want to thump smirking Roger for calling his sister names. He couldn't remember moving, just the pair of them on the ground, Jacob on top pummeling the bigger lad's chest.

"Someone help. Get him off me!"

A whistle blew and Jacob, hauled by the collar, was pulled off Roger. Miss Crow towered over Jacob as he lay panting on the ground.

"I knew you were trouble the instant I set eyes on you."

Molly moved forward, "Please, miss, it wasn't his—"

"Quiet, girl! No one asked you." Her lips a stern line, Miss Crow looked down at Jacob. "Go at once to Miss Templeton's office and tell her you've picked a fight. Serves you right when you get the cane."

Jacob rapped on the office door with a knuckle, and a voice from within called, "Enter."

Miss Templeton sat behind her desk, spectacles at the end of her nose, reading a sheet of paper. She'd taken off her navy jacket and wore a button-down white blouse.

She looked up. "Yes...Jacob."

His anger now dispelled, Jacob felt weak and wobbly. "Miss Crow sent me because I started a fight with another boy."

The headmistress stood. "Why?"

He hung his head.

"Jacob, I asked a question and I want a truthful answer."

Jacob's hands were clammy suddenly and he wiped them on his trouser leg. "I can't say, miss."

Big boys don't cry and neither do they tell tales.

"Jacob, you've to learn that we will not tolerate fighting here at Leadburn School. It's bad enough we're battling the enemy without fighting between ourselves. I've no other alternative than to teach you a lesson."

There was silence when all that could be heard was the tick of the round wooden clock that hung on the wall behind the headmistress.

She drew herself up. "You'll do fifty lines tonight: *I must not fight or I may get expelled.*" She sat back in her chair. "Tomorrow morning at assembly you will apologize to this boy you attacked."

Jacob balked. "Could it just be the class, miss?"

"I make the rules here, Jacob."

"Yes, miss. I will say sorry." Because, he thought, he'd have his hands behind his back and cross his fingers, so whatever he said wouldn't count.

As he made to turn for the door, Miss Templeton told him, "Whatever the reason you fought, even if it seems a good one, like defending someone"—her gray eyes probed his—"you must learn to control your temper. Nothing is gained by fighting."

Jacob wanted to disagree, because weren't the soldiers fighting to save their country? But, he decided, he was in enough trouble already.

Back in the classroom, everyone turned as he came into the room and, feeling conspicuous, Jacob put on his "I don't care" face.

Miss Crow, standing in front of the blackboard, asked him, "How many lashes did you get?"

"None, miss. I got lines."

Miss Crow pursed her lips in disapproval.

CHAPTER ELEVEN

It was Saturday, and with no school Molly was at a loss what to do. Aunty Brigit surprised her by bringing out a jigsaw puzzle from a kitchen cupboard and putting it on the table. Molly was keen to start as there was a picture of different colored kittens on the lid of the box.

"Try using your left hand to pick up the jigsaw pieces," Aunty Brigit encouraged, "it will help with fine finger motions."

She didn't know what Aunty meant by "fine finger motions" but anything that helped unstiffen her fingers was worth a try. Mam made Molly do finger exercises at home that the nurse at the hospital had shown them, accompanied by little rhymes. "Round and Round the Garden" was a favorite rhyme when Molly used her forefinger to go around her palm when she was younger.

Over these past few days at her new school, Molly kept her handicapped hand hidden beneath the desk to avoid drawing attention to her starfish-like fingers. She didn't do anything that involved using both hands as the last thing she wanted was to be teased and for Jacob to get into more trouble because of her and get expelled.

Jacob had asked Aunty Brigit what the word meant that night after he'd done his lines in secret in the bedroom.

Aunty had given him a dictionary. "Look it up for yourself," she'd told him, then raised an eyebrow, "but it won't apply to such a good boy as you, will it, Smoky?"

"Expelled means dismissed from school," Jacob told his sister later when they were in bed, his face dismayed.

Molly made up her mind that if Jacob wasn't allowed in school, then she wouldn't go either, even though she desperately wanted to make friends with Denise.

Molly had thanked Denise for sticking up for her when the horrible Roger had taunted her.

"No need to thank me, I know what's it like to be called names. See these?" Denise pointed to some brown marks on her nose and cheeks. "I used to get called 'freckle face' and sometimes 'ginger, you're barmy.' But I don't any more."

"Why not?"

Denise made a fist and looked fierce and Molly was a little scared of her. "Because I threaten them with this." She grinned and became her friendly self again. "They think I'm a bully."

Molly understood, because everyone at school was afraid of bullies and they never told on them because they'd surely become the next victim.

Denise giggled. "I've never hit anybody or called them names, but don't tell." Her face clouded. "So, if Roger thinks you're my friend, he won't bother you any more."

Friend. The word loomed large like capital letters in Molly's mind. She would have to tell Mam she'd made a friend when Jacob next sent a letter. Mam had written and said she was glad they were settled in with such a nice lady as Mrs. Merryfield sounded, and that they were to be good and to write and tell her all the news. Molly had slept with the letter under her pillow every night since.

Taking a break from doing the jigsaw, Molly looked outside the sash window to where Jacob sat on a branch far up a tree in the garden playing a game. Molly didn't feel sad that she wasn't able to do the same because if one of the twins had to have a weak part of their body, she was glad it was her. She loved her brother and it would have been sadder by far if he'd been the one unable to do such things as climb a tree.

The weather had forgotten it was winter and, as Aunty Brigit came in through the stable back door into the kitchen, the air gusting in felt unusually warm.

She held up the greenery in her hand. "I'm short of rosemary for your rub." Aunty put the fragrant herb from the garden onto the draining board.

Ever since that first night, Aunty Brigit did exercises with Molly, then, with the special mixture she'd made up, she stretched Molly's ankle and massaged her leg twice a day. The heady smell (or aroma as Aunty called it) from the oils she used and the warmth of the cozy room made Molly sleepy.

Aunty told her, "That's the beauty of using essential oils; they relax the mind as well as doing the body good."

"Are they new? Why didn't Mam know about them?"

"Not everyone does, Molly, even though they've been around for thousands of years since the ancient Egyptians used them."

"What do the oils do?"

"Hopefully, help strengthen your weak leg muscles. And this one"—Aunty held up another small glass bottle she'd made up—"is for muscles held in a permanent position like yours that makes you walk up on your toe."

"What oils are in the bottle?"

Molly didn't really want to know because she didn't fully understand all the talk about oils and massages, but she was being polite because she knew this was one of Aunty's favorite subjects.

Aunty held up the bottle and read the label. "Let's see. Ah, yes! Ginger, lemon and cypress."

Molly had one question she wanted the answer to: "Will the oils make me better?"

"I can't promise, dear, but it might make an improvement." Aunty Brigit cocked her head to one side as if she was thinking. "It's kind of like magic, Molly, you have to believe in it, or it won't work."

Molly decided to believe with all her might. But each night when she took the caliper off and her heel didn't reach down to the ground, it didn't seem possible that she'd ever walk properly.

*

Jacob was sitting on a branch of the big spreading tree down the garden when Aunty Brigit called him in for his dinner.

He'd overheard one of the bigger boys in the school yard at playtime talk about snipers who lived up trees and kept an eye out for the enemy. Jacob played the game of snipers and if he saw the slightest movement on the ground, he was ready to aim and fire with his pretend wooden gun. He didn't tell Aunty about his game as he instinctively knew she wouldn't approve of guns.

He felt sad for Molly because she couldn't play out with him and climb trees. If he could swap places and be the twin who had a weakness down one side he would, because he loved his sister even though they quarreled sometimes.

These days, though, he preferred being on his own because after he was made to say sorry in assembly, when Roger had that smirk on his face, there was an anger within Jacob at the unfairness of it all. One day, though, he'd get his own back on Roger.

He went indoors and washed his hands without being told, then took his place by Molly at the table, noticing a jigsaw with some pieces joined together on the far side.

"Tuck in," Aunty told him.

Dinner was a steaming bowl of thick vegetable soup, with crusty bread smothered with butter from the local farm.

After they'd eaten and Aunty began collecting the soup bowls, she told Jacob as she picked up his, "We're out of eggs.

Be a good boy and go along to the farm and see if they've any to spare. Don't bother them at the farmhouse, though, because Mrs. Nichol isn't very well. Go in the byre and ask the Land Girl. She'll help you."

The twins looked at one another. Last night in bed they'd spoken about what the lady at the post office said about them pulling their weight and they'd tried to think of ways to help Aunty Brigit. Partly because she was old and kind for taking them in, but mostly because, if having them live with Aunty got too much, the twins might be sent to nasty Nora's place.

"Yes, Aunty," Jacob said. "But before I go, I'll help with the dinner dishes and Molly can put them away."

It was November now and Jacob had got used to living with Aunty Brigit and Smoky in the cottage. If the twins got homesick, somehow Aunty Brigit knew and she'd make them a special treat. The last time was a scrumptious cake with ration chocolate on the top. She once took them to the pictures on the bus to the nearby town of Hexham. The picture was called *Bambi* and Aunty said it was so popular it had been re-released. It was about a fawn whose mother, who he was very attached to, died and Bambi was left sad and alone. Molly cried at the sad bits and couldn't stop all the way home on the bus. Jacob told her to stop being a sissy, but he knew he'd only said this because he was upset too and wasn't allowed to cry.

The twins were in regular contact with Mam, but she still hadn't visited as she'd promised.

"Your mam's doing vital war work," Aunty explained, "and probably she can't get away."

The fact was proven in Mam's next letter. Aunty had read the letter out loud as the three of them sat around the kitchen fire after school.

I miss you both terribly but I'm afraid all leave at the fac-
tory has been canceled till further notice as we have to keep
up production to help the war effort so we can win the
war. When that happens, you'll be coming home for good
and we'll never be parted again.

The three of them had smiled broadly at one another, though
Aunty's watery eyes had looked a little sad.

"I've got used to you two rascals being around and when the
time comes, we'll miss you, won't we, Smoky?" The cat, sitting in
the sun on the window ledge like an ornament, meowed mournfully.
"But we'll be happy for you when you're back where you belong."

Although Jacob liked his hometown, especially the seaside,
he wished his family could live in the village with its friendly
people, and the countryside where he was allowed to roam in all
kinds of weather.

Aunty had told him, "As long as you wrap up and tell me your
whereabouts, you won't come to any harm."

At home it was busier and he was told to never to speak to
strangers; Granny had always insisted she knew where he was at
all times.

Though, sometimes Jacob wished he could make friends with
the boys who kicked a ball about on the village green after school.
He was happy to be with Molly but drew the line at playing girls'
games. Aunty had been surprised but pleased when he joined the
Cub Scout pack at the local church hall. But though she tried,
she couldn't get Molly to enroll in the Brownies.

"You're too shy for your own good." Aunty had shaken her
head, the skin beneath her chin wobbling. "You realize you
might be denying another little girl who is looking for a friend
just like you."

"I have a friend," Molly had said in that refreshingly direct way
of hers. "I've got Denise and I'm allowed to play at her house."

Jacob had tried to convince his sister. "I was scared too when I started Cub Scouts but the meetings are fun. Everyone's friendly and we've to help people as much as we can. In the summertime Akela says we'll go camping and learn all about the outdoors."

At Molly's look of despondency, Jacob realized he'd said the wrong thing. All the activities he spoke about were difficult for her. Molly vehemently shook her head and Jacob knew once his sister had made up her mind, nothing he said would change it.

One thing Aunty was adamant about was that the twins attended Sunday school. She told the twins, "It's my moral obligation to your mam." And so, every Sunday, the twins were packed off to church.

*

Molly, following Jacob into the bright and sunny church the first time they went, was startled by the dazzle of red, the carpet running down the aisle, the hassocks, the seat covers, and at the front, in the intricately carved pulpit, the preacher.

Aunty whispered, "That's Mr. Carlton, the curate."

Molly and Jacob sat in the pew at the back with Aunty, away from staring eyes, but the curate looked directly at them and his kindly brown eyes met theirs and he smiled. The sun shone through the arched stained-glass window at the front, which had a picture of Jesus, the halo above his head angled as though the curate wore it. Molly, terrified that a nervous giggle might slip out, clapped a hand over her mouth.

The service began, hymns were sung, prayers were said. Molly, feeling conspicuous, stayed seated in the pew because it was difficult to kneel down wearing a caliper.

Then the curate announced, looking out over the congregation, "Children, time for Sunday school. Follow Miss Hudson and make your way through to the church hall."

Children stood up from their seats and, in the uncanny

silence, trooped down the center aisle, passing the pulpit, and made their way up a flight of six stairs. Molly, trailing behind her brother, felt self-conscious as people sitting in the pews stared at her as she limped past.

The children followed the leader along a long corridor and through a doorway, and Molly tried to keep up. The twins found themselves in a large musty room where the children sat on chairs that were arranged in a semicircle. Molly recognized most of them as they attended Leadburn School. Now out of sight of the confines of the church and their parents, the children, of various ages, began to chatter noisily among themselves.

"Quiet please," the young lady at the front called and the chattering stopped. "Hello, you're new." When she smiled her wide apart eyes lit up. "I'm your Sunday school teacher Miss Hudson, but everyone calls me Sandra. Are you the evacuees billeted at Mrs. Merryfield's?"

"Yes," Jacob answered.

"We're pleased to meet you, aren't we, everyone?"

"Yes, Sandra."

"I'm new too. But I'm only standing in for Mrs. Baines, who is the real Sunday school teacher, for a couple of weeks until she gets better. Everyone is most kind and made me welcome as they will you too." She smiled at the class, then turned to the twins. "Take a seat. Will you be all right? The chairs are quite low," she asked Molly.

The little girl, flushing up from her neck, nodded.

"Would you like to tell everyone your names and where you're from?"

Molly felt too shy in front of so many strangers, even though she tried to be brave, so she left it to Jacob, who could handle such an occasion.

"I'm Jacob," he said as he looked around the class, "this is my twin sister, Molly, and we're from South Shields."

"What a coincidence," Sandra exclaimed, "I am too. Which part?"

Jacob told her where Granny's flat was. He added, "But it's not there any more as we were bombed out."

Molly heard the tremble in her brother's voice.

Thankfully, Sandra didn't question any further but told Jacob, "I heard the orphanage I was brought up in was bombed too, but fortunately the orphans had been evacuated to the country by then."

When the twins were seated, Sandra looked around the class. "Last week we talked about Jesus healing a leper and what we thought it meant. Do you remember?"

A girl with a blue ribbon in a bow in her hair at the front put her hand up. "It means Jesus taught us to show people kindness."

"And to be helpful," the boy beside her said.

"Well done," Sandra told them.

She began to hand out sheets of paper and pencils around the class.

"This week I want to you to draw an example of what you think that means, how you can think of helping someone. You can color the picture in with crayons on the table."

Everyone went quiet while they drew, until Sandra called, "Time to finish now. Who wants to be first to show their picture?"

"Me, miss." The girl with the blue ribbon came to stand at the front of the class. She held up her picture. Molly burned with shame as she looked at it; it was of a girl with pigtails who wore a brace on her leg.

She looked directly at Molly. "We should be kind and help people who have got something wrong with them."

Molly felt humiliated, as if the girl was comparing her to a leper and someone untouchable.

Everyone gaped at Molly and she shriveled. Once again, she was being singled out because she was different.

*

As Christmas approached, the days became biting cold. One morning when Jacob awoke and looked out of the window, his heart leaped in his chest as he saw a white wonderland below.

The branches on the trees were bowed low with snow and the garden, a white carpet, had a trail of paw-like footprints in the pristine snow.

As he wolfed his porridge, Aunty told him, "You go on ahead to school, there's too much snow for Molly to turn out."

"I'm not staying at home and being different," Molly said, surprising Jacob as rarely did he see her defiant.

"Molly, dear, the ground is slippery and even I'm not going to venture out and risk falling."

Molly's brow puckered as she pondered the matter.

"The snow might be quick to thaw." Aunty looked doubtful. "Meanwhile I have another jigsaw for you to do. Different kinds of birds this time. Also, we could do some ankle stretches and exercises. I'm sure all the work is improving your walking."

When Jacob left the cottage for school, in the white world around him, sounds and shouts were muffled and there was no clip clop of Mr. Nichol's horse on the road as he drove past in the milk cart, only heavy thuds. Halfway to school, a feeling of happiness that he hadn't experienced in a long time overcame Jacob. A sensation of being cocooned in the magical white world around him when he felt safe and secure.

Thwack! The force of something like a brick hit him on the ear below his cap, giving Jacob such a fright.

"Ow!" His ear stung.

An icy snowball lay on the ground. Jacob cradled his ear with a hand and saw, as he stared down, that in the middle of the disintegrated snowball was a sizable stone. *Who would do such a thing?*

Looking around, he saw Roger running up the school steps, grinning at him.

"Just wait, I'll get you for that," Jacob shouted.

"You have to catch me first." The boy disappeared into the safety of the school.

*

On Christmas Eve, Molly woke up to Jack Frost's icy pictures, an amazing sparkly tree of spiraling, swirling branches that covered the inside of their bedroom windowpane. Aunty Brigit had knitted colorful lengths of wool to place over the center wood of the sash window to stop the freezing drafts.

Jacob was already up and dressed, and he told her, "Aunty Brigit says we can have our bedroom fire on as a treat tonight but only if we promise we won't touch the fireguard."

Molly stared at the small, black cast iron fireplace with the pretty floral tile surround, set in the wall at the foot of their bed and imagined its cozy warmth.

She let out a groan of sadness. "Remember, Jacob, how Granny used to let us have the fire on whenever we were poorly and had to stay off school in bed?"

The atmosphere was charged with sorrow as Molly realized that this would be their first Christmas without Granny or Mam, and she knew Jacob was thinking the same thing.

Jacob's eyes were dull now, and he told her, "Cheer up, Molly. Next Christmas we'll be at home with Mam."

But a tightness came into her chest as she realized that they didn't have a home in South Shields any more. The thought frightening, she changed the subject. "I hope Mam gets our parcel in time."

Aunty gave the twins pocket money each week for helping with chores around the cottage—Jacob brought in the coal and ran errands, while Molly set tables and, though it took an age, swept the floors with the long-handled sweeping brush. They'd

saved their pocket money and bought Mam a box of three handkerchiefs with a flower embroidered in each corner from the
WVS bring-and-buy sale.

"It should," Jacob told her as he tied his shoelaces. "We posted
Mam's present four days before Christmas like Mrs. Leadbeater
told us. But remember, the trains are carrying munitions so
there's not much room left to carry the mail."

"Jacob, should we buy Aunty Brigit a present? Only I've
hardly got any money left after buying Mam's."

"I haven't got much pocket money left either. But I think we
should. How about some barley sugar?"

"Can you crunch them with false teeth?"

Neither twin had any idea.

They asked Mrs. Curtis when they visited the village shop
later that morning.

With a twinkle in her eye, Mrs. Curtis, standing behind the
counter, asked, "I presume they're for Brigit Merryfield?"

They nodded.

"I would say so. But if she can't and has to suck them, they'll
last so much longer." The twins didn't understand why Mrs.
Curtis smothered a laugh with her hand.

"How much are they?" Jacob asked.

"How much have you got?"

He held the pennies out in the palm of his hand.

"That's just the right amount." She beamed.

As the twins were leaving, Mrs. Curtis called, "Molly Moffatt, it's time you started the Brownies."

Molly was surprised; it seemed that everybody in the village
really did know everyone else's business.

*

The next day, Jacob felt something heavy at the bottom of the
bed as he awoke.

"Wake up, Molly, Santa's been and left us a stocking!"

He didn't really believe in Santa but pretended to just in case he got cinders for a present like Granny always warned he would if he didn't behave. Proof that Jacob's doubts were well-founded was that the bulging stockings were his. Surely elves would make their own rather than have Santa rifle through Jacob's chest of drawers?

Molly rubbed her eyes, then, sitting up in bed, reached for the stocking on her side.

"Look." She pulled something out of her stocking. "I've got a bar of soap and a puzzle book, ribbons. Oooh, an apple... What's this... modeling clay." She spread the gifts on the bed, grinning. "What did you get?"

Jacob brought out his gifts one by one. "Toy soldiers, licorice, an apple, crayons, and a tin whistle."

As they came downstairs and entered the kitchen, Molly still in her nightdress and wearing a dressing gown, the twins sang "We Wish You a Merry Christmas" to Aunty, who stood at the sink peeling potatoes.

A mouthwatering meaty aroma suffused the kitchen from the range oven. Molly went over and handed Aunty the sweeties wrapped in Christmas paper. "Merry Christmas."

Drying her hands on her apron, Aunty flushed with pleasure. Opening the gift, Aunty declared, "Barley sugars, my favorite sweets." Her eyes glistened with tears. "But the best present is having you two here." She sniffed. "Now, let's see what's under the tree."

The small artificial tree that stood on an occasional table had candles in holders, flickering on the end of the branches.

Jacob could tell Molly couldn't believe her eyes, for there beneath the tree, dressed in pink knitted clothes, was a china-faced doll.

"And these are for you, Jacob." Aunty handed Jacob a pair of binoculars. "It's time you recognized the different kinds of birds."

Jacob wanted to hug Aunty, but he held back because hugs were reserved for Mam.

"Thank you, Aunty," the twins chimed.

"There's another surprise." Aunty picked a parcel wrapped in brown paper, tied with string from beneath the table, and handed it to Jacob.

He looked at the handwriting. "It's from Mam!"

He tore open the parcel. "It's books, and a card." He gave Molly hers. "Mine's *Biggles Goes to War*." Hardly able to contain his excitement, Jacob held the book up to show the others. It had an airplane on the cover with an explosion beneath.

"Mams know these things." Aunty Brigit had a contented smile on her face.

"She must have searched all over." He stroked the book's cover, lovingly. "Because it's secondhand. What's yours?" He turned to his sister.

"It's called *Little Women* and looks very old."

"You'll love it, dear," Aunty Brigit told Molly. "I laughed and cried when I read it."

Molly, looking as if she couldn't wait to start, opened the first page.

"Breakfast next," Aunty told her, "then off we go to church."

Later, as Jacob sat on the couch that evening, the Biggles book on his knee, he reflected on the day; going to church, where Molly sang "Happy Birthday" to baby Jesus in his crib, then a plateful of chicken dinner. Jacob had eaten so much he thought his tummy would burst.

Of all the presents he'd been given, Mam's card, with the jovial rosy-cheeked Father Christmas on the front, was the best. He imagined Mam, with a concentrated little frown, writing their names and drawing kisses and hugs on the inside of the card. A warm glow enveloped Jacob as he felt contented and loved—though he'd never confess to being so mushy.

In the afternoon they'd listened to *Alice in Wonderland* on the wireless. Then Molly revealed her big surprise she'd kept for the occasion—showing how she could pick up a piece of jigsaw puzzle with her left hand. Jacob was so happy he nearly cried.

"Time for bed," Aunty called from where she sat at the table taking the meat off the chicken bones. "But first come and make a wish."

She handed Molly, sitting opposite, the chicken wishbone. They both pulled the bone and Jacob wanted to let Molly win, but his competitive spirit wouldn't allow him.

He closed his eyes and wished that he could go on living in the country and that one day soon Mam would join him.

But wishes didn't always come true, as he found out later.

CHAPTER TWELVE
January 1944

It was New Year's Day, and the three of them sat in the front room—a rare treat, Aunty told them—but Molly didn't find it so. She preferred the coziness of the kitchen.

With its musty smell and heavy furniture, long blackout curtains that reached to the floor, the room had a stark, unused atmosphere even though flames licked up the chimney.

"*There is confident hope of victory in the New Year,*" Aunty read, as she sat in a saggy wingback chair, warming her toes in front of the fire. Then she laid the newspaper on her lap and addressed the twins, who were reading their books.

"The talk in Curtis's store yesterday was that the invasion in Europe by the allies will be sooner rather than later." She shook her head. "Folk like me think it'll be spring, when the weather's better."

Aunty kept the twins informed about what was going on in the world and sometimes Molly thought it was because she'd no one else to tell. The little girl's heart ached whenever she thought of the time when they would leave and go back home. Aunty would be on her own again. Though she'd have Smoky still and she was good company.

"What will it be like after the war? Will we be able to eat anything we like and not queue?" Molly couldn't remember before the war as she was only little when it started.

Aunty heaved a sigh. "That's the thing, Molly, dear. In these parts, apart from the rationing and blackouts, I doubt much will change for many of us. Though some will have lost loved ones and their lives can never be the same. Think of all those poor souls who are getting bombed—how wonderful it will be for them to go to bed at night without fear."

Molly shivered as Granny came to mind. She liked to believe she was in heaven with Grandad; that way she didn't feel so sad.

Aunty looked stricken. "I'm sorry, dearie—me and my big mouth."

Jacob, sitting beside his sister on the lumpy floral couch, looked up from the Biggles book he was reading.

"Akela at Cub Scouts said we had to pray for Mr. Churchill because he's poorly. Is that right, Aunty?"

"It is, Jacob, the prime minister is recuperating. That's another reason why I think the invasion won't happen yet." She spoke as if to herself. "Nothing will start without Churchill at the helm. We need him to help get the second front going."

The twins looked at one another. If Aunty believed in the prime minster, then so would they.

One Saturday, Aunty told the twins as they sat eating their porridge, "Dears, Mr. Churchill's returned from Marrakech, so we can all breathe again."

Her jubilant mood was infectious and the twins beamed at one another.

"Where is Marra—"

"Kech," Aunty finished, "in a place called Morocco, wherever that is." She took a bite of dripping and bread. "To celebrate I'm going to see if them oranges they talked about yesterday in the store have arrived yet."

"Oranges!"

"Yes, all the way from Spain. Gracious me, I hope they don't have a bomb in them."

"A bomb!" The whites of Molly's eyes doubled.

"Yes. Only the other day there was talk that bombs were found in a ship carrying oranges from Spain. Whatever next." Aunty pursed her lips in disgust.

Jacob decided it was worth the risk as he was desperate to know what an orange tasted like; he couldn't remember ever eating one. "Won't there be queues?"

"For miles, probably," Aunty joked.

"I'll go if you like." Jacob wanted to be helpful. "I've to go out anyway to post Mam's letter."

Mam had been in touch to say that she'd been moved to another section at the factory.

I'm like a mole in a hole as I work underground. But I'm both happy and sad to have changed shifts. Happy because if I volunteer to do this job the supervisor said I'd be put on the top of the list for leave when the work slackens. So, it's worth working in these conditions, knowing that it'll help me see you sooner. I'm looking forward to meeting your nice Aunty Brigit and thank her for looking after you so well. I do worry about Molly's caliper and if it needs adjusting as it's been so long since she's been to the hospital.

The sad bit of working here is that I had to leave my friend Vera, who I told you about, because she isn't moving to this section. But as you know we share a bedroom and so we can talk in bed like you two do when you're supposed to be asleep and the lights are out.

Jacob had felt homesick for Mam when he read that bit as it reminded him of her nestling between the twins at bedtime.

She'd read to them from a book until, sometimes, he found himself waking up and it was next morning.

"What a good boy you are, Jacob," Aunty said now. "Then I can start baking. Oh, and while you're out can you pop along to the Nichols' farm and ask if they've got butter or eggs to spare?"

Aunty baked every Saturday morning for the week using precious rations of margarine, butter and dried eggs if she had no fresh ones left.

"I'll make some of your favorite oatmeal biscuits and sticky gingerbread," she told him. Aunty turned to Molly, who sat reading a book with Smoky curled asleep on her lap.

"Molly dearie, it's best if you stay indoors today as I'm worried the rain during the night might have turned into ice on the path and you might slip."

"I don't mind, Aunty. Denise is coming to play to escape her brothers and we've decided to play dolls hospitals." Molly's friend had four brothers, who she claimed were always teasing her because she played what they called "soppy girly games."

"Wrap up, Jacob, and here, take this before you go." Aunty reached for the jar of malt extract on the shelf. The twins were given all kinds of medicines from colored bottles and Aunty had told him that the brown sticky substance offered on a spoon was "extra vitamins to keep you healthy."

Venturing out on the icy pathways, Jacob was glad of the excuse to be outside. He wanted to check if any of the village boys were out playing. Recently, he'd taken to hanging around the village green at weekends, watching the lads playing footer. One afternoon, as he stood beside the heap of coats that were used as goalposts, the football came sailing through the air, over Jacob's head and landed behind him. Picking the ball up, he threw it to the burly lad, who ran, red faced and panting, toward him.

Jacob recognized him as Ronnie Curtis, Denise's brother, the same age as him and who attended the village school.

The lad sniffed back some snot. "Are yi' any good?"

"What?"

"At footer. Dougie hasn't turned up and my team's a man short. D'you wanna play?"

Heart pumping, Jacob tried not to look keen. "I suppose."

The lad ran off. Then stopping, he turned and, with a jerk of the head, gestured for Jacob to follow.

Ever since then if he turned up at weekends and a game of footer or cricket was taking place, Jacob found himself automatically included.

Today, though, as he expected in such slippery weather, there was no sign of his friends on the village green.

The queue, when Jacob reached the village store, went on for ages and he felt hemmed in as he was smaller than everyone.

When, finally, it was his turn, Mrs. Curtis told him, "You can only have one orange, son. Half of them were rotten when they arrived and the other half were snapped up first thing."

Jacob, sorely disappointed, resigned himself to the fact he'd have to share the orange.

But trudging on to the post office, he was cheered at the thought of the homemade oatmeal biscuit and cup of tea he'd enjoy later.

Pushing the post office door open, the bell tinkling, Jacob was met with another queue—only this time it wasn't quite as long.

"Terrible isn't it, the poor woman."

His ears pricked as he listened in to what the woman in front was saying to her neighbor, who wore a thick scarf wound around her neck so you could hardly see her face. The lady speaking wore a green wool coat with a white stripe that looked like a blanket and steel curlers that poked from the front of her headscarf.

Jacob knew that Mam would call her common as she always said a lady should look neat and tidy when she was out and about.

"They say Edie Nichol never got over the loss of her son," the lady wearing curlers said.

The two women, their eyes oddly round, had their heads together and Jacob had to strain to listen.

The lady wearing the scarf unwound it and Jacob saw she had a thin face that had hollow cheeks as if she'd sucked them in. "How many months ago did she get the telegram?"

"Last August, as far as I can remember." The lady with the curlers gave a sorrowful shake of the head. "From all accounts she was doing well."

The thin lady had an intent look on her face that Jacob associated with gossipy neighbors. "When did it happen?"

"Last night I heard. I know she had a weak heart." She shrugged. "Maybe it just gave out. I've heard that can happen with grief."

"Poor soul. It's a mother's worst nightmare." The thin lady's chin trembled and Jacob wondered if she had a son she worried about.

"Next please." Mrs. Leadbeater stared through a glass screen on the counter at the front.

"Doris Leadbeater should know." The curlers lady picked up a folded newspaper from a pile on the shop counter at her side. "She's often up at the farm to see how Edie Nichol is—was doing."

As the queue inched forward, the two women continued talking. "Have you noticed how the days are lengthening? It's now eight o'clock in the morning before the blackout ends." The lady tucked the newspaper under her arm, and the smell Jacob associated with newspapers wafted up his nostrils.

Then the ladies talked about George Formby—who Jacob knew as he played the ukulele and sang silly but nice songs on the wireless.

"I like George." The thin lady appeared happier now, Jacob was pleased to see. "He seems genuine."

Jacob was greatly surprised she knew Mr. Formby that well to call him by his first name.

When it was her turn, the lady with the green coat and curlers stood at the counter in front of the screen. Eyes narrowed, she spoke in a hushed voice to the postmistress. "It's a pity about Edie Nichol. Is it true her heart gave out?"

Mrs. Leadbeater's cheeks went pink. "I'm sure it'll be in the deaths column if the family wishes people to know the facts."

"Only she was doing so well, but you never know what's going on inside, do you? How's Mr. Nichol bearing up?"

"I'm afraid I'm no wiser than you." Mrs. Leadbeater looked at the newspaper under the lady's arm. "Now, what else can I get you?"

The lady asked for a notepad and envelopes in a voice that sounded annoyed.

When it was his turn, Jacob handed over the envelope addressed to Mam and Mrs. Leadbeater stuck a stamp on it. After he'd been served and paid the pennies for the stamp, Jacob hovered in front of the counter.

Mrs. Leadbeater raised questioning eyebrows at him.

He wanted to ask the postmistress's opinion on whether she thought it all right if he went to the farm for butter and eggs, but people in the queue were listening in. Squirming with indecision, Jacob thought the last thing he wanted was people to think him a baby who couldn't make up his mind.

"Thank you," he told Mrs. Leadbeater, and made for the door. The thing that made him decide what to do was the notion that, when Granny died, the last thing Mam would have wanted was to be bothered about eggs. He knew it was right not to go.

Even so, disappointment seared through Jacob at the thought

that this week he might go without oatmeal biscuits and gingerbread.

*

"Jacob, will you do me a favor when you come home from school tonight?" Aunty Brigit asked one freezing cold morning in February over the breakfast table.

"Yes, Aunty," Jacob answered, his mouth full of crusty bread, butter and homemade plum jam.

In his head he heard Mam say, "Don't speak with your mouth full, Jacob."

"The coal man hasn't made a delivery yet and we've only a few lumps in the coal house." Aunty shook her head. "I'll go and ask that nice Mrs. Saunders from the village if we can buy or borrow a bucketful. She's plenty to spare because her old man works down the mine." She gave a conspiratorial wink. "I'll tempt her with a jar of homemade apple chutney; it did the trick before. The thing is, Jacob…" She watched fascinated as he wolfed another bite of his bread down. "Would you call in at the Saunders' after school and carry the bucket home, because my back won't stand the strain."

Jacob waited till he'd swallowed the bread and his mouth was empty before replying. "Yes, Aunty."

"And Molly." Aunty turned to look at his sister. "You're to have the day off school as it's forecast snow."

Jacob saw the glum look on his sister's face. But even a hint of snow meant Molly stayed at home because the risk of her slipping and falling on her backside, as Aunty put it, was too great.

"How about you help me make potato cakes for dinner? You can cut out the rounds." Aunty Brigit always encouraged Molly to use her handicapped hand. "And you can fill in the time by crayoning one of your lovely pictures for me."

Aunty stood and started collecting the dishes.

She paused. "While I think on, don't forget, you two, that the Warden's checking everyone's gas masks and will call in later. It's only taken the man four years!" She rolled her eyes. She looked down at the cat, who arched her back and rubbed her furry body against her ankles. "Smoky, you can do as you like."

Smoky replied with a meow.

*

That afternoon, when dinner was over, and Jacob had gone back to school, a weak sun broke through banks of gray clouds and, shining through the window, lit up the far wall of the kitchen. Molly felt cheated. It hadn't snowed.

She got bored when she didn't go to school but if she was truthful, she felt tired, as keeping up was exhausting, especially battling to walk in this bitterly cold weather, when her ankle muscle seemed to stiffen up even worse. The idea of having a day off appealed more than she was ready to admit.

"Ta ta," Aunty called as she opened the back door wrapped up in a man's greatcoat and old, rather battered brimmed hat, and wellies. "It's not far to the Saunders' house, just over the bridge and past the store. I'll be back before you know it. I'll leave the door on the sneck."

She blew a kiss and was gone.

The cottage deathly quiet, Molly moved over to the standard wireless and, opening the wooden doors, switched it on. "Music While You Work" boomed from the grille and Molly thought of Mam working at the factory. A longing washed over Molly. She wished Mam could visit even for a short time.

She consoled herself by picking up Smoky and resting her cheek against her soft fur. She was reading *Little Women* yet again and was up to the part when Jo was leaving home. How Molly wished she had the heroine's feisty nature.

"I'm trying to be braver," she told the cat.

Settling on the couch, her novel in her hand and Smoky stretched on her lap, Molly began reading. Soon, her eyes drooped and she must have slept because when she awoke, seemingly with a start, the kitchen had darkened eerily and Molly didn't know where she was, but thought it must be nighttime.

Smoky, stretching her sleek body, jumped from her knees and, padding to the window and leaping up onto the ledge, sat and looked out. Molly, struggling to stand up from the couch, followed.

Looking through the windowpane, she could just make out beyond the back garden fence where the sky, a threatening uniform dark gray, appeared to meet with the landscape. It had snowed and the spread of the tree branches, with a thin layer of snow, reminded her of spiders' legs.

As she took in the scene it started to snow again, and the snowflakes, falling thick and fast, blotted out the view.

Molly turned and checked the wall clock.

Four o'clock. She'd slept for almost an hour.

Jacob was late coming home from school. And where was Aunty Brigit?

CHAPTER THIRTEEN

His turn to have a go on the slippery slide they'd made, Jacob was having fun with the other boys and the unruly streak in him wanted to stay longer. But the guilty side that knew he shouldn't, because Aunty would be waiting for the coal, won out.

Making his way over to the Saunders' house, he walked along the front garden path and down to the coal house at the back, where Aunty's bucket, filled with coal with a ledge of snow covering the top, waited for him.

The coal heavy, the paths icy, Jacob had to be careful where he trod as he'd nearly slipped twice. Making his way down the side path of their cottage, he placed the bucket of coal by the back door and, after knocking each foot against the wall to rid his wellies of snow, he pressed the backdoor sneck.

He walked into the kitchen, and though the light was on and music blared from the wireless, Jacob knew by Molly's worried face that something was wrong.

"Jacob, I'm so pleased you're home."

"Why, what's the matter? Are you hurt?"

"It's not me, it's Aunty Brigit, she hasn't come home yet from when she went to see Mrs. Saunders about the coal."

"How long ago was that?"

"Ages ago. I fell asleep. Jacob, even if Aunty stayed and chatted with Mrs. Saunders as soon as it snowed, she would've made for home."

Jacob knew this to be true.

"I got all wrapped up for the outside but as soon as I stepped out on the path I unbalanced and slipped and so I turned back."

Jacob knew by his sister's trembling chin she was frustrated and blaming herself for not being able to search for Aunty.

"It's the same for everybody," he consoled, "I nearly slipped carrying the coals."

Molly's eyes widened in anxiety. "Aunty's old and not steady on her feet sometimes."

Jacob picked up his wellies from the doormat. "I'm going out to look for her."

A knock came at the door.

The twins looked at each other.

The Warden, who Jacob had never seen before and who wore a helmet with a big white "W" on the front and an ARP badge pinned to his blue overalls, stood outside.

"If you've come about our gas masks—"

"I haven't, laddie. I've come to tell you that Brigit Merryfield has met with an accident and you've to go to Mrs. Leadbeater's house." He banged his feet against the doorstep and walked in. "You'd best pack a bag, you can't stay here on your own."

"What kind of accident?" Molly's voice was shaky. "Is Aunty Brigit all right?"

The Warden walked over to the range and warmed his backside.

"Mrs. Leadbeater happened to be looking out of the post office window and saw your aunt slip on the slope just before the bridge over the stream."

"Where is Aunty now?" Jacob wanted to know.

The Warden blew in his hands to warm them. "A right carry-on there was. The army was involved and two soldiers, hefty lads they were, carried your aunt to the post office. I was passing by and Mrs. Leadbeater asked if I'd go to the warden post and phone an ambulance. It took its time to get through, then Mrs. Merryfield was taken to the War Memorial hospital in Hexham with a suspected broken hip."

"Did she go on her own?" Molly limped over to stand next to her twin.

The Warden, watching her, scratched the back of his neck. "Mrs. Leadbeater wouldn't hear tell of it. She closed up shop and went with her."

"How bad is Aunty d'you know?" Jacob, afraid of the answer, felt his stomach slacken. "Will she be coming home?"

The Warden gave a doleful shake of the head. "Not tonight, sonny. There's no telling when she'll be back."

Molly's face drained of color. "Please, sir, will Aunty be all right? She's not going to ... die?"

The Warden bent forward and spoke to Molly at her level. "Don't you worry, pet, she's not that bad. Maybe an operation is due and plenty of rest, then hopefully your aunty will be as fit as a fiddle."

The full realization of what had happened and that they were about to be homeless dawned on Jacob, and he looked helplessly at Molly.

"What about Smoky?" Molly's brown eyes widened in alarm. "Who'll look after her?"

The Warden looked puzzled. "Who's Smoky?"

"Aunty's cat."

"I don't know anything about any cats." He sounded irritated. "All I've been told is to take the pair of you to Mrs. Leadbeater's place tonight until alternative arrangements can be made for both of you. Frieda will be there."

"I can't go without Smoky." Molly's face was resolute.

"Mr.—" Jacob said, knowing he needed to stand up for Molly. "My sister doesn't walk in snow—she can't go anywhere."

The Warden stared at Molly and, looking her up and down, rubbed his chin in thought. "Nobody said anything about a cripple." He spoke as if Molly wasn't there and Jacob felt his anger flare up.

"She isn't a cripple."

The Warden made a *she looks one to me* kind of face.

"When it's fine, Molly walks to school every day." Jacob proved his point.

"Hold on, sonny, I'm trying to think." The Warden's brow wrinkled. "I can't carry her that's for sure, not on a night like this. We'll both end up with broken hips."

Jacob saw Molly shrink into herself at the idea of being carried by a stranger.

"Hang on, I've got an idea." The Warden made for the door. "I won't be long."

After he'd left, Molly's expression was concerned. "D'you think Aunty Brigit's in a lot of pain?"

"I don't know. But I would think a broken hip hurts like crazy."

"What d'you think's going to happen to us, Jacob?"

Jacob decided it was useless him trying to make things better. "I suppose they'll find us somewhere else to live."

"We could stay here by ourselves and look after Smoky till Aunty Brigit gets better." Jacob knew Molly was trying to sound brave, but she didn't look as if she really believed what she said.

"Kids of our age aren't allowed to live by themselves."

"Jacob, I'm frightened. I don't want us to be parted." Molly's eyes were pools of brown misery.

She picked up Smoky and cuddled her into her chest. "Everybody we love isn't here. Mam, Granny, now Aunty Brigit." She stroked the cat's head and she purred. "And I'm not going to live anywhere without Smoky."

Jacob had never seen his sister look so determined.

*

Hearing thuds on the wall outside, Molly presumed it was the Warden arriving back and kicking snow from his boots.

When he entered the kitchen, the Warden had a young girl with him and the pair of them were covered in snow.

"This is Frieda from the post office," said the Warden. "Mrs. Leadbeater telephoned earlier to say that with the recent downfall of snow, she doesn't know when or if she'll be back tonight. I've explained the situation to Frieda and she agrees she should spend the night here with you at the cottage." He made for the door. "Things will get sorted in the morning. Is there anything you need?"

Molly didn't know if they needed anything or not but shook her head.

"Then I'll be off. I'm on duty tonight."

The back door slammed and with the Warden gone, the twins were left with the uneasy sense of not knowing what was going to happen next.

The girl stared at them with a serious face.

"I'm Jacob." Molly's brother took the lead and as always, she was glad. He held out his hand like a grown-up.

The girl shook it. "I know, Aunty Doris told me all about the pair of you."

She had an accent that Molly didn't recognize.

"And you must be Molly. How d'you do?"

Molly decided against shaking hands. She wished she had Floppy rabbit here to hug for security as meeting new people made her shy and tongue-tied.

"How d'you do," she copied.

"Who's your Aunty Doris?" Jacob wanted to know, and Molly thought him brave to ask such a personal question when they'd only just met.

"She's the postmistress who you've met, I believe." The girl took off her wet mackintosh and hung it on the hook on the back door. Shaking off her wellies, she padded over to the range.

"The fire's nearly out. Is there any coal?"

She had black hair and was quite skinny, Molly thought, gazing at the sticky-out bones on Frieda's neck and shoulders. But her big expressive eyes were friendly.

Jacob made for the back door. "I've fetched a bucketful and left it at the back door."

Later, after Frieda had built up the fire and yellow flames licked up the chimney, she turned to the twins and gave a hesitant smile. Molly wondered if she too suffered from shyness.

"I do know a bit what you're going through. I'm an evacuee too." Frieda's eyes filled with sorrow. "I'm German. My parents sent me here at the beginning of the war when it was too dangerous for me to live at home."

The twins looked at one another. Molly didn't know what to say. They'd no experience of Germans except for what they heard about soldiers and raiders. They were the enemy. Molly had never thought of ordinary children like her that lived and went to school in Germany.

The girl seemed to sense their unease. "I've lived with Aunty Doris since I was eleven and although I love it here in Leadburn, one day I hope to return home to my family."

Molly understood, as she felt the same way. She wanted to know more about Frieda's mam and dad and why they weren't here too, and was surprised Jacob hadn't asked, but her brother was unusually quiet.

Just as she summoned the courage to ask, Frieda spoke. "Have you had anything to eat?"

"We've had nothing since dinner time," Molly volunteered when Jacob didn't answer.

"I'm not hungry," Jacob announced and, with what Mam called a mulish expression, he told his sister, "I'm going upstairs to the bedroom."

He left the room and stomped up the stairs. Molly thought him quite rude.

She felt stiff and awkward left with Frieda, and couldn't shake the need to apologize for her brother's impolite behavior.

Frieda didn't look offended, only unhappy. "What would you usually have to eat?"

"There might be some potato cakes left from dinner." Molly, trying to be helpful, wanted to make it up to the girl for her brother's bad behavior.

"I can smell something cooking in the range. How about we take a look?"

Molly knew that Aunty had put meat bones in the stock pot with vegetables and was making soup for tomorrow's dinner but, she reckoned with a tight pull in her chest, there would be no need because none of them would be here.

She nodded.

Smoky meowed, as if reminding her to give her some.

While they ate at the table, Molly felt self-conscious eating on her own with Frieda. The food was delicious, but she was surprised to see that Frieda only picked at her supper.

When Molly removed her caliper and readied for bed, she said her prayers, which were always the same. *Please God bless Granny in heaven and Mam at the factory and make the war stop soon.* Only tonight she added, *Help Aunty Brigit get better.*

Climbing into bed, she told Jacob, "Why did you go off like that? If Mam was here, she'd go mad with you for being so bad mannered toward Frieda."

"She's German." Jacob's expression was serious.

Molly was disappointed at her brother's attitude. "She's friendly and nice."

"She's still a German. And it was them that killed our granny."

Jacob's lips bunched as if that was all that needed to be said on the matter.

Molly felt confused. She liked Frieda but what Jacob said was true.

Unsure how to answer, she changed the subject. "Why would her mam and dad send her away like that?" Molly wondered aloud.

"Who cares."

There was no talking to Jacob when he was in this mood and wouldn't listen.

A creak from a floorboard on the landing told Molly that someone was outside the door. Then the footsteps receded and descended the stairs.

"D'you think that was Frieda come to say good night?" Molly was stricken with conscience. "She might have heard."

"I don't care if she did." Jacob turned over and, as he faced her, she smelled toothpaste on his breath. "What did you have for supper?"

"Vegetable soup with bread and butter."

"I'm starved," Jacob wailed.

Though she was mad at her brother for the way he behaved, Molly also knew he couldn't help himself any more than she could being shy. And though she knew being hungry served him right, her gentle heart forgave him.

"You can have a bowlful for breakfast in the morning."

The unspoken words *before we leave the cottage* hung in the air.

Breakfast to begin with was an uncomfortable affair.

Jacob slurped his soup and didn't have any manners, forgetting to say please and thank you when Frieda handed him anything, and he avoided looking at her. Molly felt as though he was taking it out on her, for what happened to Aunty Brigit. As if she was the cause of all the bad things that were happening to the twins.

Frieda must have felt it too because, looking decidedly uncomfortable, she spoke. "I hope your aunty is feeling better this morning. At least she's in the right place." She continued eating the porridge she'd made. Then she looked up. "Are you enjoying school?"

Molly, eating her porridge, replied noncommittally, "Kind of."

Frieda didn't look at Jacob and told Molly, "It's difficult at first, isn't it, when you start at a new school? Especially when you're classed as different in some way. I hope the children aren't nasty toward you. You must tell a grown-up if they are."

Jacob stopped eating as if he was listening.

Molly wanted to know, "Did that happen to you?"

"Yes, because I'm German and I have an accent."

"What did you do?"

"Nothing. That's why I'm telling you."

Molly plucked up the courage to ask, "Why did your parents...?" She faltered.

"Send me to England?"

Molly hung her head and nodded.

"Because we're Jews. And hated by those in power in my country. One terrible night before the war started, Nazi soldiers came and broke the windows and set fire to property in our neighborhood and we fled for our lives. It was then Mama and Papa agreed my brother Kurt and I should be sent to England out of harm's way. They, with Grandma, would follow at a later date. Before they could escape, Papa was arrested and taken away to a camp."

"You have a brother?" Jacob wanted to know.

"Yes, Kurt. He jumped ship before it left for England to go back to look after Mama and Grandma." She looked at them with troubled eyes. "I know Kurt is alive because I got a letter from him last month, forwarded by the Red Cross, to say that Mama and Grandma have been taken to the camps too." She gasped in a breath as though steadying herself. "Kurt is in hiding and I believe he's at Papa's friend's house, probably in his cellar, out of the Jewish quarters. But I'm still terrified for his safety."

"What happened when you came to England by yourself?" Molly couldn't imagine anything worse than being without her brother in a strange place.

Frieda visibly relaxed and she gave a fond smile. "Aunty Doris heard on the wireless of the plight of the children who came from Germany and she offered to help and she took me in."

Upset by the terrible tale, Molly couldn't help but ask, her voice trembling, "What happened to your mama and grandma in the camps?"

"I don't know, I haven't heard from them since I came to live here."

A heavy silence filled the room as they all thought of the fate of Frieda's relatives.

After a while, Jacob picked up his spoon. "Could you pass me the salt, please, Frieda."

Frieda told them after breakfast was finished and the dishes were washed and put away, "It's time for me to go. I help milk the cows at the Nichols' farm and I'm late, but the foreman will understand when I tell him the reason. I also help deliver milk around the doors in the village."

"And the school?" Jacob asked.

"Yes. I'll wave if I see you."

She moved to the door and, taking her mackintosh from the peg, Frieda looked out of the window. "The snow has melted and the sun is shining. Can you make it to school?" she asked Molly, who was putting the plates away in the cupboard next to the sink.

Molly was relieved Frieda asked because she was unsure who was in charge and the feeling was unsettling. Before she could answer a rap came at the back door.

Frieda opened it and a rather flustered Mrs. Leadbeater stood there, dressed in a winter overcoat with the collar up and headscarf. She bundled into the kitchen. "What a time I've had. I didn't get home till early this morning. An ambulance was called out and, as he was coming this way, he gave me a lift." She looked at each of the three of them. "How are things here? Thank you, Frieda, for looking after the twins."

"We've been fine. Who's looking after the post office?"

"I stuck a notice on the door saying it was closed till further notice, then Peggy Teasdale who delivers the post turned up and said she'd look after things. She'd heard from the Warden about Brigit's accident." She rolled her eyes heavenward. "I swear you can't do anything without someone from the village finding out."

"How is Aunty Brigit?" Molly asked in a trembly voice. Aunty was old and Molly was afraid of the answer.

Mrs. Leadbeater gave her a kind smile. "She's had a shock but she's made of stern stuff and bearing up. They're taking an X-ray today but I reckon she's broken her hip."

"How will she manage to get around?" Frieda asked.

"That's the big question." Mrs. Leadbeater regarded the twins. "The thing is, it'll be a struggle for Brigit to look after herself let alone you two." She heaved a big sigh. "I'll have to make further arrangements. Though, where to billet you I don't know; what with soldiers and evacuees, everywhere is full—the homes that aren't are those people that balk at housing evacuees. As the billeting officer I could pull my weight and compel them to do so but I'd rather not as it usually ends badly and the evacuees tend to be removed to other premises in the end."

The twins looked at one another. Jacob's troubled eyes reflected what Molly was thinking too. They were a nuisance and no one wanted them. In Molly's case, she was extra work.

Jacob bunched his lips. "Molly and I are sticking together."

"I'll do my utmost to see that happens, Jacob."

Frieda looked at the twins in concern. "Aunty Doris, couldn't we house them?"

Molly thought Frieda kind to suggest such a thing.

"There's nothing I'd like better and I've thought about it"— Mrs. Leadbeater gave an unhappy shake of the head—"but even if we had the room, what with all my commitments and running the post office it wouldn't be fair on any evacuee."

Frieda glumly nodded as if she knew this to be true. Then she looked at her watch. "Aunty Doris, I'm sorry, I have to go."

"Yes, get yourself away." Her face relaxed into a smile, she told the twins, "Don't you worry. I'll come up with a solution. I usually do."

As Frieda put on her mackintosh, Mrs. Leadbeater called, "How's Bob Nichol doing? I haven't called in on him these past few days."

"I don't know. These days he keeps to himself. The new foreman at the farm deals with everything and Sandra and I are doing the milk round, such as it is."

Molly wondered who this Bob was, but she kept the questions she wanted to ask to herself.

"Bob's alone too much of the time for his own good," Mrs. Leadbeater told Frieda as she opened the back door. "It's still early days since Edie died but hiding away isn't going to solve anything." She bit her lip and stared into space as if lost in an upsetting thought. Then, as her eyes focused, she gave a wistful sigh, "If only Bob hadn't lost . . . but then again, 'if onlys' don't solve anything."

After Frieda left, she told the twins, "Now you two, what are we going to do about you? More to the point, who is going to take the two of you in? You're my top priority." Her expression changed and became thoughtful. Then a smile lit up her face.

She exclaimed, "D'you know, I think I've solved the problem. Off you go to school. I've some arranging to do."

CHAPTER FOURTEEN

When Bob Nichol saw Doris Leadbeater walk purposefully up the earthen track and onto the farmhouse front path, he knew trouble was brewing.

Infernal woman. Why doesn't she just leave me be? Then he was angry with himself, for he knew Doris was only doing her best to see him through his time of trouble—but Bob didn't want her help. He was perfectly content with his own company. He was done with being civil just for the sake of it and trying to find things to say to people about concerns he had no interest in. Damn it! Why didn't folk just leave him alone in his misery.

"Yoo hoo, Bob, are you in?"

Bob cursed that he'd left the front door off the latch after he'd let Tyne, his sheep dog, out first thing to do his business.

He opened the kitchen door and called along the passageway, "In here, Doris."

As she opened the hallway door, a blast of cold air tunneled along the passageway.

He led the way into the kitchen and without any formality, he asked, "Who's looking after the post office?"

"Peggy Teasdale."

Bob thought as much; the two women were as thick as thieves and had been ever since they went to the village school together. Bob, two years older and in a higher class, knew to keep out of Peggy's way as, in those days, she had a soft spot for him and didn't mind who knew it. All Bob was interested in back then was the day he'd leave school and start full time at his dad's farm. Farming was his life... Bob's eyes misted as he thought those words and pictures of his son Wilf and Edie flashed in his mind. Had he put the farm first? He didn't know; he didn't know anything any more.

"Bob, there's something I want to discuss with you." Doris's soft voice broke into his scattered thoughts. Her cheeks pink from the cold, Doris stood in front of him and her staring eyes were ponds of sorrow.

"What?"

She took off her gloves and headscarf and smoothed her curly blonde hair with her hands. The fire crackling in the background, businesslike, she told him, "I'm here in an official capacity as billeting officer."

"And?" Bob shifted uneasily. He didn't like the sound of this.

Doris chewed her lip as if deciding how to go on. "I have twins that need to be housed and you've got plenty of space here and—"

"No chance." Bob made to turn because, as far as he was concerned, the conversation was finished.

"Hear me out, Bob."

Bob didn't want to listen because Doris, with those big imploring eyes of hers, could be mighty persuasive when she wanted. "I'm not having no kids running around the place."

No way, he thought to himself, *those days are over.*

She touched his arm. "They're only eight, Bob, and they've been living with Brigit Merryfield. But she's gone and broken her hip, we think."

"That's not my problem." Bob ignored how uncaring he sounded.

Shaking her head, Doris let go of his arm. "The only other person is Nora Bates but she's only in it for the money." She heaved a troubled sigh. "Besides, Nora will only take the boy as the other twin has a problem."

"That sounds like Nora Bates. Selfish to the core."

In Bob's mind that was the end of the discussion. His gaze absently wandered the familiar kitchen: the redundant range where no delicious smells, which had always made Bob's stomach rumble, came from the oven any more; Tyne, his loyal dog, curled by the fire; the dresser with a photo of Edie and him on their wedding day. And one of Wilf, his boy, proud as punch in his uniform.

"What's wrong with this laddie?" His voice sounded gruff even to him.

"It's a girl, Molly. She has an infirmity I've never heard of before, but it means she's weak down one side and wears a caliper on her leg."

"I know nothing about girls."

"The twins don't want to be separated, Bob. Maybe if you could take them for a short spell, just till I can find someone else…"

Rage flared within Bob, a rage he found hard to control. He realized that these days his emotions were all over the place. He wanted to tell the interfering Doris that she knew better than anyone what grief was like. He couldn't look after himself, never mind two kids and one with a disability at that. He was a bloke, for goodness' sake, what did he know about childminding?

He had once known about it, Bob's traitorous mind told him, but he didn't want to go down that route to those far-off days when Wilf was the cutest little boy. Unable to express feelings, Bob bottled them up like he'd always done.

He made excuses. "No, Doris. I've heard about some of these kids. Rough as they come. Scruffy, I've heard, and some of them run wild."

Doris laughed outright. "Just like you, Bob, when you were young."

He had the grace to smile. "Doris, I can't. I…" He never

could find the right words. Edie had done the talking for them both.

"I *do* know, Bob. But you've got to get back on the horse and now's as good a time as any to start." She cocked her head. "You do know as the billeting officer I can pull my weight and force you to take the responsibility of housing these—"

"You wouldn't."

"Yes, I would. The twins need somewhere to rest their head tonight. Bob Nichol, you should be ashamed of yourself. What if they were your—"

"Don't say it, damn you!"

Doris went white. "I'm sorry, Bob. That was uncalled for. But I'm desperate. If only you saw them, you'd know why I feel the way I do. They're nice kiddies. She's shy but won't let her disability stop her doing things. He's protective and headstrong but I suspect beneath it all he's just a frightened little boy."

A reflective silence filled the room that Bob found intimidating. He was being worn down, he knew, and Doris had her "I won't give up" face on, that he knew so well from the old days. He'd had a crush on her when they were at school together, but she'd eyes only for Jack, the man she eventually married.

He never told Edie that she was second best. They'd made a life together and Bob, over the years, grew to love his wife. He knew fate had played a hand and got it right for Doris and him with their respective partners.

When Jack died in a crash on his motorbike, Doris became reclusive and withdrew into a world of her own, and Bob was the only person she allowed in. Not because of their long friendship but purely because he was the only person who spoke the truth, made her see how she was isolating herself. He'd told her bluntly that her late husband would be appalled if he saw how his forthright and outgoing wife had turned her back on the world.

"If Jack were here now, he'd tell you the last thing he'd want is for you to spend a lifetime mourning him." It had pained him to say it but he had told her anyway. "Jack lived his life to the full and you've let him down by not doing the same."

That had made her snap out of the sorrow she had been drowning in. She tore him off a strip and it was good to see the spirited Doris he knew back again. She went on to build a life of her own and Bob was proud. Though a man of few and select words, he could never bring himself to voice sentiment.

He knew Doris's game; she was returning the favor and trying to put him on the right track.

He looked at the photo of his son again, and Doris said, "You had a kiddie, you lucky thing. Some of us don't even have memories of children."

Doris could be a hard woman when she wanted.

It was true, though; he'd lost Wilf, but he still had the memories, even though they were too painful just now to conjure up in his mind.

"Okay, Doris, you win. I'll take these twins on—but only on two conditions. That you help as and when you can. As I said, I know nothing about caring for kiddies. And that you find them somewhere else to live as soon as you can."

"It's a deal," Doris told him.

*

As Doris walked along the path back to the post office, she hoped she'd done the right thing by involving Bob. He could be an obstinate bugger when he liked, which was most of the time, and would bend for no man, let alone two defenseless children. But there was no harm in him, and he was frank and he endured better than any man she knew, which was a handy trait to have, having been married to a nag like Edie Nichol.

A needle of guilt stabbed Doris and she thought of the saying, "never speak ill of the dead," though she knew it was tosh, because the truth couldn't be changed by death.

Doris gave a heartfelt sigh. *Only time would tell*, she told herself, *if I've done the right thing*. There was no denying Bob was a man's man and she doubted he'd ever cooked a meal or even washed a sock in his entire life.

The niggle of doubt grew like a worm inside her to the size of a snake.

What had she done?

*

Before the twins left for school, Mrs. Leadbeater had given them fourpence each so they could stay for their dinners, and the long day at school dragged for Jacob.

The postmistress's parting words had been, "While you're away I'm going to see about a billet. And I promise to be here when you return tonight. So, don't fret."

That was easier said than done, thought Jacob, as he sat at his desk trying to concentrate on practicing his handwriting. He was worried about where he and Molly would sleep that night. He missed Aunty Brigit and was concerned about her recovery. Aunty was like Mam and Granny; when you had a problem, you could go to her and she'd help sort it out.

Jacob didn't like being told what to do by people like Miss Crow, but family was different because they cared about you. And though Jacob liked Mrs. Leadbeater, he didn't know her well enough to believe she'd keep her promise to keep the twins together.

As he stared into space a thought struck. Before Granny was called to heaven, when the twins lived with her, she used to tell them, "You mustn't worry Mammy when she comes home for a visit. It will only upset her if she can't do anything to help. Tell me and I'll help sort the problem out."

But Granny wasn't here and there was nobody else—except Mam. Was this one of those times when Jacob should disobey Granny and let Mam know what was happening?

Thwack! Someone cuffed his ear. A figure towered over him and, looking up, he stared into the two differently colored eyes of Miss Crow.

"Stop daydreaming, boy, and get on with your work. And don't give me that insolent look."

"I'm not, miss."

"And don't answer back."

There was no pleasing her. She was always watching him and Jacob knew she was looking for any excuse to give him lines or at least a good telling off. She'd disliked him ever since the fight with Roger.

Roger wasn't a problem any more and kept his distance now; he didn't want another bashing, especially from someone smaller than him—he'd lose face with the others. Jacob always made sure Molly knew she shouldn't be alone with Roger or he might take it out on her.

"No, miss."

"No, you will or won't answer back?"

Jacob tried to figure out what she meant while the rest of the class sniggered.

"Quiet!" Miss Crow appeared to quiver as she turned to glower at the class. "Or else you'll all be spending tonight doing lines."

Thankfully, Miss Crow's wrath now turned on the other children and she forgot about Jacob.

When the bell rang for home time, Jacob, lifting the lid of his wooden desk, put his reading book and slate away. Mam called this tight feeling he had in his tummy a knot and Jacob imagined a thick rope inside with knots all the way from his belly button to his throat.

Walking home at a slow pace with Molly, the sky darkened and sleet pelted from the sky, and Jacob was glad of the gloves and scarf Aunty had knitted for him. The twins didn't speak but they knew each other's thoughts: What was going to happen when they arrived home at Aunty's?

It was a relief when they arrived at the cottage to see the back door ajar—someone inside was waiting for them.

"There you are," Mrs. Leadbeater called from where she stood at the kitchen table where she was putting butter, cheese, eggs, and a wedge of Spam from the pantry into Aunty's messages bag.

"Best you take these with you. You can eat them for tea." She gave the twins what Jacob thought was an uneasy look. Moving to the sink, she dried the stockpot and put it away on a shelf.

Jacob's gaze traveled to the range, noticing the fire had gone out and that black ashes lay in the grate, then he was startled to see the twins' suitcases standing beside the front room door.

His stomach clenched; they were off somewhere.

Mrs. Leadbeater, drying her hands on the tea towel, gave that wide, not quite real, smile grown-ups did when they wanted to convince you of something.

She looked around. "That's everything done. We can be off."

"Where to, Mrs.?" Jacob felt like a little boy again when something new and frightening was about to happen and he had no way of knowing what to expect.

"Bob Nichol who lives at the farm has agreed that you can live with him for a while." In the stunned silence, she went on. "There are sheep, cows and hens…"

"Is that the farm where the lady died?"

She gave Jacob a long, thoughtful look. "Yes, Jacob, you're right, it is. I'm going to be honest with you both. Bob is sad because his wife has died and he needs company. At a push I could find some-where else for you to stay but not together. D'you understand?"

The twins looked at one another. Molly nodded first.

"I...I want to be with Jacob. I'll stay with Mr. Nichol." Though his sister's face looked troubled, her voice was firm.

"Me too."

"Good, then that's settled. Your mother will be informed by letter what's happening."

Mention of a letter reminded Jacob of the one hidden in his drawer in the bedroom. He made a mental note to retrieve it before he left.

He dithered. Was this real trouble like Mam said? Instinct told him that it wasn't. Besides, he was supposed to give the letter to someone only when he had nowhere to turn, but Jacob could write to Mam and, if needs be, she'd sort things out.

Happier now, he concentrated on what Mrs. Leadbeater was saying.

"Mr. Nichol is a decent man." The Mrs. bustled about tidying up as she spoke. "But not very good with words. And then there's Tyne, his dog, who's getting on—"

"What about Smoky?" Molly looked startled, her eyes wide, as if she'd just remembered. "Where will she go?"

"D'you know, I hadn't thought about the cat."

"Please, let me take her." Molly looked around for Smoky. "I'll be the one to look after her."

Smoky padded in.

"I don't know..." Mrs. Leadbeater's brow furrowed as she studied the cat. "I don't see why not. I can't think of anything else to—"

"She won't be a nuisance, I promise."

Smoky meowed as if promising too she wouldn't be a nuisance.

Mrs. Leadbeater shrugged. "What's another animal on a farm."

Smoky's tail lashed as if she objected to be spoken of as "just another animal."

"Oh, and another thing. I've phoned the hospital. Brigit is going to have an operation on her hip."

Molly picked up the cat and cuddled her. "Who will look after her?"

"After her operation, she'll be transferred to Yorkshire to her daughter's until she's recovered."

Jacob's heart sank. It sounded like Aunty would be gone for a long time.

"Come on, you two, let's be off and get you settled in at the farm."

Jacob remembered Mam's letter. "I'll just check to see if everything's packed."

Before Mrs. could protest, he hurried toward the stairs.

*

"Yoo hoo, Bob, we're here," Mrs. Leadbeater called from the front doorway.

A dog came barking from behind the door.

"Down, Tyne." A man's voice spoke, and the barking stopped.

Molly had the urge to hide behind Mrs. Leadbeater. When the door opened, she had to crane her neck back to look up at the tall, burly man standing there. A black and white dog, its tongue lolling out, stood at his side.

The ruddy-faced man had dark whiskers growing from his chin and, even at this time of year, his muscled arms, protruding from his red-and-black checked shirt, looked very tanned. He didn't speak but stood aside to let Mrs. Leadbeater and the twins into the farmhouse kitchen.

Molly looked around and saw a long wooden table with dirty dishes on it and the salt and pepper still out. A dresser stood in an alcove with lots of paperwork covering the top and in front of the range fire was a chair with a cushion that had a dent in it where Mr. Nichol had been sitting.

"Bob, this is Jacob and Molly Moffatt I told you about."

The man eyed them, but his gaze didn't linger on Molly's leg brace—instead he was looking at the cat who stood at her side.

Smoky had followed them from Aunty Brigit's house as if she knew there was going to be no one left at home.

"Nobody said anything about cats." The man's stern expression worried Molly.

"It belongs to Brigit. We couldn't leave her, Bob."

"Mr. Bob"—Molly found her tongue for Smoky's sake—"you won't know the cat's here, honest, 'cos I'll feed her and let her in and out of the house."

"Hrrmph." The man reminded Molly of the giant in Jack and the Beanstalk, and she shrank back.

"Would you rather I show them around or will you do the honors?" Mrs. Leadbeater put Molly's case down on the floor.

"I can manage. Best you get back."

"If you're sure."

As she made for the door, Mrs. Leadbeater, biting her lip, didn't look at all sure.

Her hand on the doorknob, she turned. "Bob, tell Frieda if you need anything when she's here in the byre in the morning and she'll fetch me. There's makings for tea in the bag and if you need shopping send—"

"I'll manage, Doris." Mr. Bob picked up Molly's suitcase.

As Mrs. Leadbeater opened the door, Molly asked, "Will you let us know how Aunty Brigit is?"

Mrs. Leadbeater gave her a friendly smile. "Of course, love. I'm off to the church hall tonight for a salvage drive for rags. But I'll visit Brigit tomorrow night, if the weather permits for travel. I'll call in and see you afterward to tell you about her operation."

Molly wished she had the nerve to ask if she could visit Aunty too but that would be forward, as Granny would say.

After Mrs. Leadbeater left there was nothing for it but to follow Mr. Bob up the narrow staircase.

"This is your bedroom, lad." Mr. Bob opened the door to a small bedroom that had a view over the front of the house where you could see miniature workers in the faraway fields, then the main road and grasslands on the other side of the valley.

As the twins entered, they saw pictures all over a wall of the same boy at different ages: a class photograph, and one in a football team holding up a trophy and him standing by a Christmas tree with a big grin on his face as he held a toy tractor. Then in a picture frame on the far wall, a man in uniform who resembled the boy.

"That's Wilf." Mr. Bob nodded at the wall of photographs.

"Won't Wilf mind me having his room?" Jacob asked.

Mr. Bob took in a big breath and then let it out slowly before saying, "No. Wilf was killed in the war."

Molly felt sad for Mr. Bob, but didn't know how to respond. She looked at her brother, who seemed unsure what to say too.

Then Molly said, because she thought it might be of help, "Our granny died. We miss her, don't we, Jacob. But she's gone to heaven."

Jacob nodded his agreement.

Mr. Bob swallowed as if some big piece of food had got stuck in his throat. Instead of answering, he moved out of the room and along the landing, then opened the door to a bedroom at the back of the house.

The twins, following, found themselves in a bedroom overlooking fields beyond the farmhouse, where sheep and cows grazed.

This room was bigger, and with just a bed covered with a homemade counterpane and dark wood wardrobe—the same as the one in Jacob's room—it had no pictures decorating the walls.

"Your room," Mr. Bob told Molly, dumping her suitcase on the bed.

It felt cold and lonesome already, Molly thought as she looked around. She felt both sad and nervous as she'd never spent a night apart from Jacob. It wasn't because she was frightened, more that Jacob wouldn't be there to share secrets in the dark. And they often said the same things at the same time which made them giggle. Often there was no need to talk as they could sense what each other was thinking. The best part of sharing a bedroom with Jacob was listening to him breathing as he slept, and, comforted, Molly too would fall into a deep and dreamless sleep.

CHAPTER FIFTEEN

When they came down the stairs from their bedrooms, the twins didn't know what to expect. They made their way into the kitchen as it was rude to poke around someone's house—as much as Molly would've liked to.

Mr. Bob wasn't anywhere to be seen, but rustlings came from the pantry off the kitchen.

Jacob nodded to the table where there were thick slices of crusty bread piled on a chipped plate and yellow butter on a saucer. He rubbed his tummy and licked his tongue over his lips. Molly giggled; she knew he was trying to make light of things to make her laugh.

Mr. Bob appeared, his large frame filling the doorway, with a chunk of cheese and jar of jam in his hands. He moved over and set them down on the table. The dirty dishes, Molly noticed, had been deposited in the sink.

"Does Brigit fix your bread and butter and cheese and suchlike?" he asked gruffly.

"We're big enough to do that ourselves." Though Jacob had his stubborn face on, as Mam called it when his chin jutted, Molly knew her brother was just as confused and scared as she was.

To prove a point, Jacob sat at the table and, picking up a knife, he attempted to spread butter on a slice of bread. The butter was hard and the bread soft, so big holes appeared in the bread. Jacob ate it with relish as though that's just how he intended it to be.

Seeing Jacob struggling, Mr. Bob sat down, scraped butter on his knife, spread it thinly on the bread and, looking purposefully at Molly as if to say *this is how you do it*, he cut thin slices of cheese and made a sandwich.

"Mother's tomato chutney goes a treat with cheese." He spooned some brown chutney over the bread.

"Where is your mam?" Molly picked up a slice of bread.

Mr. Bob looked uncomfortable. "That's what I used to call Edie, my missus, when she was alive."

The room went quiet apart from the sound of them eating. Molly wondered if she should say "I'm sorry for your loss," as that was what Mam always said to people when a relative died.

She had the impression it wasn't easy for Mr. Bob to say or hear anything about Edie or Wilf. Her heart ached for him as he didn't appear to have any family left. Molly wouldn't know what she'd do if she didn't have Mam and Jacob to keep her happy.

The long, uneasy silence didn't seem to bother Mr. Bob, who was content to sit and stare into space while eating his cheese sandwich.

Then a series of loud barks made them all sit up. Tyne, who'd been curled up in front of the range fire, now stood barking at Smoky, their faces inches away from each other. Her back arched and tail lashing, she hissed at Tyne, then swiped at him with a paw.

"Oi! We'll have none of that." Mr. Bob moved over to Smoky and, picking her up, carried her to the door, legs dangling, and opening it, slung her out.

"It was Tyne as well!" In her distress, Molly forgot to be her timid self.

"The cat's got to learn. She stays only if she behaves."

The twins were in Molly's room, sitting cross-legged on the bed. There was only one easy chair in the kitchen and the only other place to sit apart from at the table was on the floor. Besides, the twins felt awkward with Mr. Bob and like they were in his way.

Jacob had carried the lamp Mr. Bob had given him by the handle to the bedroom. Molly could tell her brother was proud to be entrusted with the lamp on his own—something he'd never be allowed at home. Mr. Bob had told Jacob to always be sure to blow out the lamp once he and Molly were in bed.

"It's very quiet living here. Mr. Bob doesn't have the wireless on and he never listens to the news. I thought all grown-ups did." Jacob's brow creased in puzzlement. "He's not like Aunty Brigit, who talks all the time."

"He might have forgotten how 'cos he lives on his own."

"I don't know why you're sticking up for him, Molly, he threw Smoky out in the cold."

"I feel sorry for him…but not enough to want to live with him. I'd rather be at Aunty Brigit's."

"Well, we're stuck here for now."

"She'll come back, won't she?"

"Who, Smoky?"

In the yellow light of the lamp's flame, Molly nodded.

Jacob remembered his promise to Mam to look after his sister. "Course she will when she's hungry."

Molly appeared pacified.

After a while Jacob said, "I don't like the thought of going down the garden to go to this midden lavatory the Mrs. told us about, or having oil lamps to see by because they make scary shadows on the walls."

Molly looked around with frightened eyes as if some monster, like in a story, would jump out and grab her.

"D'you think," she asked, "we should stay up here for Mr. Bob to come upstairs and say good night, or should we go down and see him?"

"I think the rules are different here," Jacob replied.

He was proven right when, a few moments later, a rap came at the bedroom door.

"It's Mr. Bob," Jacob whispered.

Surprised he didn't just walk in, Molly felt like royalty (as Granny would say when someone treated her like a lady); grown-ups usually just barged in.

"Come in."

Mr. Bob poked his head around the door. "What are you two up to?"

"Nothing," Jacob was quick to say.

"Then, can you do nothing downstairs and save burning a lamp?"

"Sorry." Molly began to move off the bed. "Please, Mr. Bob, when is bedtime?"

"When you're tired."

"What if we can't get to sleep and want to read?"

"Then, come downstairs."

Molly looked at Jacob in dismay. What kind of grown-up was looking after them when he didn't have rules for bedtime?

After Mr. Bob had left, Jacob whispered, "Imagine if we can do whatever we like?"

Molly didn't like the eagerness in her brother's voice. Knowing Jacob, he'd get into all kinds of trouble.

"Mam won't be pleased."

"But she isn't here."

Molly only hoped it wouldn't be too long before Mam got in touch to tell them she'd visit them.

Little did Molly know her wish was soon to be granted.

Molly was surprised she slept at all that first night as she expected to miss her brother and to lie awake in the dark, but the eventful day had drained her and she fell asleep practically as soon as her head touched the pillow.

The next morning, when she and Jacob went down to breakfast ready for school, everything was different and strange. Mr. Bob was up and dressed and sitting in his high-backed chair in front of the range. A pencil in his hand, he barely looked up as they came in, concentrating wholly on the *People* crossword. Molly wondered if he'd been to bed at all.

Crosswords were something Granny used to do and a moment of longing for how things used to be at home overwhelmed Molly. She wondered if the pining inside whenever she thought of her granny would ever stop. Grown-ups said time was a healer but it didn't seem to be working; she felt as sad now as she had when her granny had just died.

The place had an unkempt feel. Last night's tea dishes were still in the sink, crumbs were on the carpet and all the surfaces had a layer of dust. Molly felt the need to tidy up. It was clear that her brother, however, had no such intentions—all he was interested in was his tummy.

"What's for breakfast?" Jacob's abrupt tone made Molly cringe and worry about Mr. Bob's reaction.

He didn't seem to mind—in fact, he didn't even turn around to look at them as he answered. "Help yourself, there's bread and jam in the pantry. Weetabix, if you like."

He went back to studying the crossword.

The twins had a silent breakfast. Even the sound of their metal spoons against the china dishes seemed awkward, and Molly sensed her brother's impatience brewing. She was glad when they'd got themselves bundled up for school and ready to leave the farmhouse.

It was then that Mr. Bob laid his paper on the floor and, after a mighty stretch, stood up.

He looked at the two of them squarely. "Is that you two off to do some learning?"

"Yes, Mr. Bob." Molly remembered the manners Granny had instilled in them.

"What d'you usually do about dinner?"

"Aunty Brigit makes it."

"Best you stay at school."

Molly thought that, as Mr. Bob had glanced at her handicapped leg, he was just being considerate of her walking too far.

However, Jacob, as the twins made their way to school, had a different opinion.

"Mr. Bob just can't be bothered to make dinner." He kicked a stone into the road.

The air was warmer. It had rained during the night and everything appeared to be dripping. As she limped through puddles, Molly thought it best not to reply to her brother. He needed time to get used to Mr. Bob.

When the twins returned from school neither Mr. Bob nor Tyne were at home but the farmhouse door was on the latch. Molly noted that the dishes in the sink had been washed, and then felt bad because they should've helped.

Jacob's eyes scanned the table. "He hasn't left a note." He sounded accusing.

Granny had always left a note when she disappeared, explaining where she'd gone and what time she'd return.

Jacob eyed the open pantry door. "I'm famished. I'm going to find something to eat then explore the farm. I can't wait to see a tractor close up."

A tractor didn't appeal to Molly, but she was happy to see her brother's eyes light up—for the first time in an age.

"I'm going to try and find where Smoky's hiding."

*

Molly found herself in a cobbled yard beside a big sprawling shed with a tin roof. The dungy smell in the air made her wrinkle her nose. At that moment a young lady came out of the shed doorway. She wore blue dungarees and her mousy brown hair poked out of the front of her turban headscarf. She carried an empty bucket in her hand, and as she moved toward the outside tap, she noticed Molly.

"Can I help?"

Molly was surprised to see the lady was Sandra, the Sunday school teacher. Her friendly smile of recognition put Molly at ease.

Worried about Smoky, Molly overcame being tongue-tied. "I'm looking for a cat."

"Any particular cat?"

"Smoky. She belongs to Aunty Brigit and she's run away."

Sandra's expression was sympathetic. "Frieda and I work together milking cows. She told me that your aunty had a bad fall and was taken away to the hospital."

Once again, Molly was amazed how quickly news traveled here in Leadburn.

"I like your name by the way. All the best girls are called Molly. I should know—I worked with one when I was a scullery maid and she was lovely."

Molly's chest swelled.

"Have you ever seen a cow up close?" Sandra called over the noise of the tap filling the bucket.

Molly wanted to answer because she desperately wanted to ask if she could see a cow, but shyness overcame her and she just shook her head.

"I hadn't either when I first came here. Because when you live in South Shields it's not the kind of thing you see, is it?"

Molly shook her head.

"Tell you what…" Sandra's tone was soft. "Why don't you and your brother come on Saturday morning to the byre." She pointed to the shed. "If you come early the cows will be getting milked."

A quiver of excitement raced through Molly. Wait till she told Jacob.

Sandra picked up her bucket and made to leave the yard. "See you then. Oh, and don't worry about the cat. I've seen her around. She won't starve as she was chasing a mouse."

As Molly made to find Jacob, it occurred to her that Sandra hadn't once stared at her disabled leg.

*

Later, after the twins had looked around the farm and Jacob had enthused about the machinery in the shed, they were heading back to the farmhouse, when, in the dim light of the late afternoon, they saw someone cycling up the earthen path. Jacob recognized Mrs. Leadbeater riding a cumbersome black bicycle with a basket on the front.

"Yoo hoo," she called. "A letter arrived—I thought I'd bring it up in person and see how you're doing." She dismounted the bike and leaned it against the garden fence.

Jacob opened the back gate and the three of them walked along the back-garden path and into the gloomy cottage.

Mrs. Leadbeater took off her headscarf and opened her coat. She lit the lamp and, taking a letter from a pocket, she looked around. "Where's Bob?"

"He wasn't here when we came home from school." Jacob felt his voice sounded more tale-telling than he intended.

As Mrs. Leadbeater passed him the letter, she looked vexed.

"It's from Mam." Jacob beamed at Molly.

Jacob wasn't too sure if he wanted Mrs. Leadbeater to know what Mam had to say as they didn't know the lady well enough.

She appeared to understand his difficulty and told him, "Why don't you read the letter out to your sister while I set the table for tea."

"Molly can read too," Jacob said quickly, as he knew Mam

liked people to know that Molly could do most things just as well as him.

"I'm sure she can. It's up to you."

Jacob nodded and the twins sat at the table. By the lamplight, and without removing their coats, he tore open the envelope while Molly looked at him expectantly.

A small piece of cardboard fell out of the envelope with two sixpenny pieces slotted in it. Jacob pushed one out and gave it to Molly.

My dearest two,

I'm writing this with a big happy smile on my face. I've got a lovely surprise. I haven't been well recently, nothing to worry about, just a cold I can't shift. The factory's doctor reckons I should be granted leave of absence for a couple of days and so, my darlings, I've got this weekend off and I'm coming to visit you on Saturday.

A tightness pulled in Jacob's throat and as his eyes welled with unshed tears, the writing blurred and he couldn't read another word.

He wiped his nose on the sleeve of his coat. "Mam's coming to visit."

Molly's eyes shone in the lamplight. "Read on and see what else she has to say."

Jacob continued, though his voice sounded like he had a frog in his throat—a silly saying of Granny's.

I'm wondering if your nice Aunty Brigit could spare me a bed for the weekend or the couch would do. If that's a nuisance, ask her to please find me lodgings for the night. I'll arrive sometime in the afternoon and you can show me

*all around the village. I can't wait to see you both and am
counting the hours.*

Love you, Molly Moo and Jacob, heaps of love too.

*Hugs and kisses to both,
Mam*

The twins stared at one another in disbelief.

Mam would be here in four days' time.

"She doesn't know about Aunty's accident." Molly looked anxious.

"Children, I couldn't help but overhear," Mrs. Leadbeater called over from where she was putting china cups and saucers on the table. "I've passed on the information to the evacuation scheme that you've been moved and your mother will no doubt be informed. As far as lodging is concerned, what with soldiers and evacuees, I doubt there's any vacant rooms. Rather than have your mother look further afield to find accommodation, she can share your bed here, Molly. I'm sure Mr. Nichol won't mind."

But by the concerned frown on her face, it looked like Mrs. Leadbeater didn't quite believe what she'd said.

"Will you ask him?" Jacob wasn't scared to ask exactly, but it would be better coming from a grown-up.

Mrs. Leadbeater, putting on her headscarf and fastening the ends under her chin, told him, "I'm off to visit Brigit but Mr. Nichol will be home soon, I'm sure." She gave a weak smile. "I'll call in when I get back and before I go to the church salvage meeting. I'll ask him then."

Molly piped up, "And you can tell us how Aunty Brigit's doing?"

"Of course, love."

The twins watched the dark silhouette of the postmistress going down the path from the doorway, the light from her bicycle shining a tunnel of dim light on the ground.

Jacob sensed his twin was worried about Smoky.

He cupped his hands around his mouth, and called, "Here, Smoky...Where are you?"

There was no familiar meow.

*

Later, Jacob heard a motor vehicle drive up the path before stopping outside the farmhouse. Looking out of the kitchen window, he saw the shape of a van and the outline of a figure headed toward the back door.

Tyne bundled into the kitchen, followed by Mr. Bob. He looked at the twins, sitting at the kitchen table, as if in surprise. "I see you're having tea." He took off his heavy-looking coat and hung it on the hook and, hauling off his boots, left them behind the door.

"We were waiting for you," Jacob said. He was positive Mr. Bob had forgotten about them.

Mr. Bob came over toward them. "Bit early for me." His breath smelt sour and Jacob felt the need to wrinkle his nose but stopped himself. "I'm off for a lie-down."

Mr. Bob clomped upstairs, leaving the twins staring at one another wondering what to do.

Much later, when it was pitch dark outside and Molly had drawn the blackout curtains and Jacob had lit the lamp with matches from the drawer, the twins sat at the table doing homework—a rare occurrence without being told.

A movement upstairs caused Molly to look up at the ceiling.

"Mr. Bob's up." Her voice sounded a little scared, Jacob thought.

Footsteps stomped down the stairs, and Mr. Bob's large frame appeared in the doorway. He stood in an open-neck shirt and braces that held up his cord trousers.

Stretching, he moved toward the table. "Have you not had tea?"

"We didn't know what we could eat," Jacob accused.

Mr. Bob studied Jacob. "Laddie, if you were that starved, you'd find something quick."

Molly explained, "We were waiting for you, Mr. Bob. We're not allowed to pour boiling water from the kettle."

"Hrrmph!" Mr. Bob moved to the pantry and, bringing out the same food as the night before, he placed it on the table. He told the twins, "I can make boiled eggs, if you'd like."

After they'd eaten and the twins had helped do the dishes, Mrs. Leadbeater called, a blast of cold air coming in with her as she opened the back door.

"You weren't in when I called before, Bob, and the kiddies were on their own." She sounded like Mam when she was cross about something, Jacob thought.

Mr. Bob, sitting in front of the fire, legs crossed at the ankles, looked up from the newspaper he was reading.

"I went to the mart as usual then bought some feed and oil for the lamps."

Mrs. Leadbeater put her hands on her hips. "Then off to the pub, no doubt."

"It's what I always do on mart day. Anyway"—Mr. Bob uncrossed his legs and stood up—"what's it got to do with you?"

Mrs. Leadbeater's mouth pinched and she looked up at him. "You didn't have children to look after before."

Mr. Bob hesitated and looked a little uncertain. "They're big enough to look after themselves."

"They're not, Bob."

Jacob eyed Molly as they stood by the sink listening in. Should they leave the two grown-ups to argue by themselves? But he was intrigued and he wanted to hear more.

"Our Wilf was brought up to do things for himself, to have a mind of his own."

"You and Edie did a marvelous job with your son, Bob. No one could do better. But this isn't the same. These kiddies aren't yours to mold. You shouldn't be leaving them to fend for themselves their first day here."

By the lamplight, Jacob saw Mr. Bob go tomato red in the face. "You're a busybody, Doris Leadbeater. And that sharp tongue of yours will cut you one of these days."

"Bob, I'm sorry if me talking about Wilf has upset you but these two are now your responsibility. Their parents are depending on you to look after them. They're not used to the ways of the countryside."

"Please, Mrs."—Jacob felt the need to remind the lady of the truth—"we have no dad. He died when we were little, but you don't have to worry, I can look after Molly."

Mr. Bob looked from Jacob to Molly, who stood at the sink pulling the skin at her throat.

"If I'd known there'd be this much fuss, I wouldn't have agreed to have them." He sighed, "Now they're here, I suppose I'll have to put up with them."

"And no sneaking off to the pub."

Mr. Bob glared at the Mrs. "I've never snuck anywhere in my life."

He stomped over to his coat and, donning it, dashed out of the room. Tyne stood up, ran and sniffed the bottom of the back-door, whining.

Mrs. Leadbeater, shaking her head, turned to the twins. "At least the man's talking, even if we don't like what he has to say." She gave a feeble grin. "Don't you two worry about Mr. Nichol, his heart's in the right place. Only, he's set in his ways and he gets easily upset these days." She pulled a knowing face. "I think it's best we leave telling him about your mother's visit until tomorrow."

Jacob decided he liked Mrs. Leadbeater. She spoke straight and he knew where he stood with her.

Molly came over from the sink, her face pale, as if she'd been the one arguing. "Mrs., did you see Aunty Brigit?"

"I did, love, and she's had her operation and she's being transferred to a hospital close to her daughter as soon as Brigit's up to it." Her expression was rueful. "She's still a bit woozy, but the hospital is pleased with her recovery so far. Her main concern is you, Molly. Brigit says she wants you to continue with the leg exercises and medicine she's been giving you. She asked me to help and when she feels better, she's going to send a letter telling me what oils and herbs to use."

So, it was definite now, Jacob thought, they wouldn't be going back to Aunty Brigit's. The war might be over before she got well. He made up his mind to ask Mam when she visited if the twins could go home.

CHAPTER SIXTEEN

"I couldn't get to sleep last night I was so excited," Jacob told Molly. "I did that thing Aunty taught us. I went from my tiptoes to my head and told each part of my body to relax, but that didn't work either."

It was a breezy Saturday morning and the dark gray sky threatened rain. The twins, up and breakfasted early, were making their way to the byre where they hoped to watch the cows being milked.

"It's just like Christmas waiting for Santa coming," Molly agreed. Mam was visiting this afternoon and Molly couldn't wait.

They walked in silence for a while, relishing what the day had in store for them.

"Jacob..." Molly needed to ask her brother something but until now hadn't felt able to broach the subject.

"Yes?"

"Why don't you get along with Mr. Bob? After all, he's agreed to let Mam stay in my bedroom for the weekend."

"He only let us stay with him because the Mrs. made him take us in. He doesn't want us here."

Molly didn't agree; Mr. Bob was lonely and missing his family and didn't want to be bothered with other people. She didn't even hold it against him that Smoky had run away.

Jacob, frowning, went on, "He hardly ever speaks and all he does is sit in his chair, slurping tea and reading the newspaper."

Molly decided against arguing with Jacob when his mind was made up like this. She wanted this to be a happy day.

"Listen, Molly." Jacob stood still and gazed toward the low spreading shed. "Can you hear the cows mooing from inside?"

Molly stopped and listened. "I can."

"Do we just go in?"

"I suppose so. Sandra didn't say. You go first."

The byre was lit by hurricane lamps and the first thing Molly saw was a row of deep red cows tethered in stalls either side of a passageway. The nearest cow had a watchful look about it, as though the animal was ready to flee. Molly felt a certain sympathy for the cow as that was how she felt when confronted by a stranger.

"Phew, what a stink!" Jacob held his nose.

The stalls were raised and the stench came from a channel running in front, filled with cows' muck and urine.

Sandra emerged from a stall and Molly gave her a wave.

"Hello, you two." Dressed in dungarees, her hair covered by a headscarf, Sandra said, "We're nearly done but you can watch for a while—only don't get in the way."

"We won't," Molly promised.

"Stand way back at the end of the stalls as these beasts can give a nasty swipe of the tail or worse, a kick with a hoof."

Molly didn't need a second telling.

Sandra went back to the stall and, sitting on a three-legged stool, she picked up a galvanized bucket and, clasping it between her knees, she grasped the cow's udder. Molly watched in amazement as she saw milk squirt into a pail.

As the twins made their way to the end of the passageway, they passed a stall where an old man, an unlit clay pipe dangling from his mouth, sat on a stool milking a cow.

Then a girl's head emerged over the top of another stall. She waved.

"It's Frieda!" Jacob waved back. "I'm going to ask if we can have a go at milking."

"Please don't," Molly begged, as she didn't want them to seem forward.

To her relief, Jacob did as she asked.

*

Later, when the milking was done, the twins watched as the older man, with the unlit pipe still in his mouth, led the cows, head to tail, out of the shed.

Watching him go, Sandra told them, "Mr. Jeffries is from the village and helps out, when his arthritis allows, that is."

Then, along with Frieda, she scrubbed and swilled the shed floor, took the cows' muck to the midden, then sterilized the milking equipment.

All the while, the twins watched from where they stood at the end of the stalls. It occurred to Molly that her leg must be getting sturdier for her to stand that long.

After a time, she began to worry that they might be in the way. "Jacob, maybe we'd better go."

"No, I want to see what happens next."

"That's it." Sandra came over and Molly thought she must have heard them talking. "What happens now is the milk is poured over a cooling contraption and then put into big galvanized churns that wait at the end of the track to be collected by a lorry that transports it to the dairy."

"Some get delivered to the village and our school by horse and cart," Jacob reminded her.

"That's our favorite job," Frieda told him as she joined them.

"If it was my farm, I'd want to drive the horse and cart myself," Jacob said.

Molly saw Frieda and Sandra exchange a glance.

A sad expression crossed Frieda's face. "Mr. Nichol used to, but since his wife died, he's lost interest and leaves the running of the farm to a foreman—"

"Who we hardly ever see," Sandra cut in.

"Can we go and see the horses?" Jacob asked.

"How about you come back later and you can watch the Clydesdales getting groomed? Meanwhile, you can help feed the hens." She smiled at him.

Frieda seemed at ease talking to Jacob and Molly remembered that the German girl had a brother too.

"And the pigs." Sandra led the way out of the wide shed doorway where the sky had started to clear and between gray clouds was a blue sky. She turned to Molly. "Will you manage? The ground's rather uneven."

Molly nodded. She didn't have a clue whether she would or not, but she didn't want to be left out.

At that moment, an airplane's drone sounded in the distance. As the plane came closer, Jacob cocked his head and listened. "It's one of ours but it's running on only three engines." Jacob knew all the different planes as he had always listened to them when they flew over when he'd lived in South Shields. "It's a Halifax bomber."

As the plane thundered overhead, Sandra, face upturned, waved a hand and shouted, "Go on, you can do it."

The plane disappeared into the distance, leaving a wispy white trail way up in the sky.

She sniffed. "When I see a plane, it makes me think of Alf, wondering if it could be him."

"Who's Alf?" Jacob asked.

"Me brother."

"Did he live in the orphanage with you?"

"Yes, but we hardly saw each other. The orphanage was run by a strict mistress who should never have been in charge of bairns."

Molly felt sad at that; she couldn't imagine being separated from Jacob.

"Your brother flies bombers?" Jacob looked impressed.

Frieda told him, "Alf's plane went down on the Swiss border and he was taken prisoner, but he escaped."

"Where is he now?" Molly asked Sandra.

"He came back to England after Christmas."

"Have you seen him since?" Molly knew that if it was Jacob, she'd be desperate to see him.

Sandra appeared a little upset and Molly wished she hadn't asked.

"He was due a rest but with leave suspended, he's back on operations." She grimaced at Frieda. "We're the same, worrying about our brothers. Kurt in hiding in Germany. Alf in peril in the sky."

"They've come this far against the odds." Frieda nodded at her friend. "They're meant to survive."

The two girls smiled at one another.

Molly liked being with them; they were comfortable with each other and seemed more like family than friends.

Sandra linked arms with Frieda. "We're getting too serious. Time to feed the hens and collect eggs. Come on, you two."

A bitterly cold wind had sprung up but Jacob, searching for eggs in the straw in the little hen houses, was in his element and didn't seem to mind.

Molly, standing in the field, her long glossy hair whipping around her face, felt the cold seeping into her bones. Though she was happy to watch, she hoped they would soon be making their way back to the farmhouse. But she couldn't help but laugh as the hens, strutting in their funny, jerky way, appeared out of the houses.

Then, something caught her attention. She looked past the hen houses to the top of the field where someone was hurrying toward them.

It was Mrs. Leadbeater.

*

Mrs. Leadbeater had insisted the twins return to the farmhouse with her and no amount of pleading would entice her to reveal why. Molly hadn't liked the grim look on the postmistress's face, as it reminded her of strangers when they saw her leg in a caliper. In those instances, it was a tell-tale sign of pity and feeling uncomfortable they avoided eye contact with Molly. Anxiety rippling in her tummy, she wondered what Mrs. Leadbeater felt uncomfortable about.

Now, the three of them sat around the farmhouse table, while Mr. Bob was in his fireside chair with Tyne sitting at attention at his feet. Molly felt wary of the tense atmosphere.

Mrs. Leadbeater took a big breath before she spoke. "I didn't want to tell you until we reached the farmhouse but I've had a telephone call from the factory concerning your Mam."

"She's still coming to see us this afternoon?" Jacob looked hopeful.

"I'm afraid not." Mrs. Leadbeater swallowed hard. "Jacob, Molly, I'm going to tell you something that's going to shock you."

Mrs. Leadbeater gave another big swallow. Molly looked at Jacob and he shot her a worried look back.

"You know how your mam worked in the factory and it's dangerous?"

"Yes," Jacob said. Molly couldn't speak.

"Well, there was an accident underground and she—"

"Was she hurt?" Jacob had gone white and the sprinkling of freckles on his cheeks stood out.

"Yes, Jacob. I'm so very sorry to tell you that your mam died. But it was so quick she wouldn't have known the accident had happened. It would be just like falling asleep."

Silence gripped the room and the only sound was Tyne noisily licking his fur.

Molly found she couldn't move even to lift an arm. "Our mam is dead?" The shaky voice didn't sound like hers.

"Yes, Molly and—"

"I don't believe she is," Jacob cut in. "How did she die?"

"There was an explosion in the section where she worked—"

"How do they know Mam was there at all?"

"Jacob, the factory knows who's in work at any moment of the day." Mrs. Leadbeater glanced over at Mr. Bob.

"Mam might have gone to the lav." Tears brimmed in Jacob's eyes.

Mr. Bob's chair creaked and he stood and walked over to the table. "Laddie, there's no mistake. Your mam has died in a dreadful accident."

"And they're sure it's Mam?"

Mr. Bob laid a hand on his shoulder. "Positive, laddie."

Jacob's shoulders heaved. "She had a cold, she promised to visit." His voice was squeaky. Molly wanted to comfort him, but it was as if she couldn't move a muscle, couldn't speak.

"She would be here if she could, have no doubt about that." This time it was Mrs. Leadbeater who spoke.

"When did it happen?" Jacob said.

"On the night shift. They didn't know where you both were but your mam's friend at the factory knew you were evacuees here in Leadburn. Because I'm the billeting officer they contacted me."

Jacob shrugged off Mr. Bob's hand and, scraping back his chair, he raced over to the door and out of the kitchen.

Mrs. Leadbeater stood up from her chair and made to follow, but Mr. Bob caught her by the arm and murmured, "Leave him be for now."

Molly felt bad she didn't follow him, and she was surprised she wasn't crying, but hearing about Mam didn't seem real. Mam, in her mind, was still coming to visit this afternoon. She couldn't be dead.

She stood up on wobbly legs and all she could think to say before she went up to her bedroom was, "Mam's friend Vera will be sad."

*

Later, after Molly had gone upstairs to her bedroom and Doris went up to check on her, Bob moved a dining chair next to his by the fire.

He heard footsteps on the stairs, then Doris appeared in the kitchen doorway. Her shoulders hunched; she was trembling, as if in distress.

"Come—sit here by the fire." He patted the chair beside his.

"I'm not cold, Bob." She walked over and sat next to him. "It's just hit me the poor woman's dead and it's another case of here one minute and gone the next."

"You've kept strong for those kiddies," was all he could think to say. Bob wished he was better with words. "How's the girl?"

"I really don't know, she hasn't spoken." Doris looked pained, and at a loss.

Bob heaved a heavy sigh. "It won't sink in for them for a while. I should know."

"Me too," she reminded him. "But they're only children and don't understand the concept of death."

Bob raised a quizzical eyebrow. "Like we do?" A silence followed, broken only by yipping from Tyne, who, curled at Bob's feet, presumably dreamt in his sleep. "You say they've got no one."

"The granny who looked after them died in a raid in South Shields. She was down as next of kin. It was the friend who put the factory straight."

"Did the factory know what happened?"

Turning toward him, Doris grimaced in horror. "It was in the cordite section and there was an explosion underground. That's all they said. Apparently, all news of the incident is censored and no official announcement is to be made."

"Surely the folk around would hear the explosion?"

She shrugged. "All I know is it'll just be announced in the local paper that workers were killed in an accident."

Bob shook his head. "I don't know what the world's coming to when no one speaks the plain truth any more."

In need of physical contact, Bob bent down and fondled Tyne's ear. The dog, waking up, licked his hand.

"The factory's shrouded in secrecy, Bob. And rightly so. Just think of the bombings if Jerry got a notion where the factory's situated."

"So, what will happen to the twins?"

Doris groaned, "An orphanage, I suppose."

Bob, staring into the yellow flames, refused to let his mind wander down that route. "When will that be?"

"Contrary to what you think, Bob, I'm not a know-it-all."

Stung, he sat bolt upright and said, "I was only asking."

Doris's cheeks flushed. "Sorry. I shouldn't argue at a time like this. This business has upset me and I'm taking it out on you."

"It's a bugger, all right. Sorry, language."

"Apology accepted." Doris stood. "I'm going to make something nice for the twins' tea. I need to keep busy." She moved over to the dresser in the alcove and, opening the doors, began to take out blue and white crockery.

Bob went silent as he worked something out. His mind made up, he told Doris, "The twins can stay here till things get sorted."

"Thank you, Bob." Doris gave a faint smile. She looked as though she wanted to say more and then thought better of it. She busied herself getting the table set, and then with a concerned frown she looked up and asked, "How long d'you think we should leave looking for Jacob?"

Bob didn't know. In his experience, he thought the laddie would want to be alone, but he was often wrong about such things.

He gave as good an answer as he was able. "The laddie will come back when he's ready." He stood up and made for the door. Tyne followed, tail wagging. "How long are you staying?"

"I've put a note on the post office door to say its's closed for the afternoon. Why?"

He took his coat off the hook and opened the back door. "I'm off to look for that damned cat."

*

Later, when Molly shuffled down the stairs, Mrs. Leadbeater was still there, setting the table.

Molly tried to remember which meal it was for. She'd lain on top of the bed staring at the ceiling listening to her own sharp shallow breaths for she didn't know how long. What the Mrs. had told her about Mam didn't seem real. She started to worry that she'd made it up in her mind. When she could stand the quiet in the room no longer, Molly stood up. She felt dizzy, like she was going to faint but breathing deeply seemed difficult somehow.

"We've all missed dinner"—Mrs. Leadbeater, moving over to the sink, gave Molly an intent look—"and so I thought I'd make an early tea. How about I make a meat pie and you can have potatoes with it."

"I'm not hungry, thank you," Molly said in a small voice.

"Molly, love, sit down, you're not yourself. Would you like a drink of water?"

"Yes, please."

"To be truthful, Molly, I don't know what to say about your mother's accident." As she handed the glass of water over, Molly saw how Mrs. Leadbeater's hand shook. "If you want to talk, I'll be happy to listen and answer any questions you have. Or, if you just want to sit quietly on your own that's all right as well."

"I like you being here." Molly sipped some water and then found she could take longer breaths.

"That's a start."

"Would Mam hurt?"

"No, love, she wouldn't know anything."

"She was excited to come and see us." Her voice wobbled.

"Wasn't it lovely that your mam was looking forward to something?"

"I wish I'd sent her more letters." Molly's vision blurred.

"She'd have been thrilled with the ones she got."

"I've looked everywhere." Tears spilled from Molly's eyes, and she went on with great gasps, "But I can't find Floppy rabbit..."

"There, there, love." Mrs. Leadbeater bent over and, taking Molly in her arms, squeezed her tight.

It felt good to rest her head against Mrs. Leadbeater's chest and feel warm skin through her clothes.

"Molly, just let it all go."

With a shudder, Molly did. Huge sobs racked her body, making her shoulders heave up and down and her tummy hurt. When she thought she'd no tears left, a fresh lot fell.

Then, just as quickly as the tears started, they stopped, and Molly's eyes felt sore and swollen.

Mrs. Leadbeater let go of Molly and, searching up the sleeve of her white blouse, she brought out a handkerchief.

"Here. There's a good girl. Wipe your eyes and blow your nose and we'll go find that Floppy rabbit of yours. Then, you can help me make tea."

*

Bob Nichol couldn't find the cat anywhere, but he came across Jacob sitting slumped on the wooden bench by the stream.

Bob stood over him. "Lad, you'll freeze sitting there with no coat on. Go and have a run around the stream to warm up and use up energy."

"I've run way up the road and back." The lad spoke in monotone.

Bob could see Jacob's face was red with exertion. He sat down beside the lad.

"When I lost the Mrs., I didn't want sympathy or to listen to anyone talking just for the sake of it, I just wanted to be left alone. Still do."

Jacob stared at the ground as if he'd found an insect he'd never seen before.

"The thing I'm trying to say, lad, is there's no proper way to behave when you have something like this to deal with."

Bob was startled as Jacob covered his ears with his hands and started to yell, "No, no, no! Mam isn't dead!"

What a to-do. Bob thought hard and decided the only thing to do was something he was good at: a bit of plain talking.

He reached out and gently but firmly took the lad's hands away from his ears. "It's no use denying it, laddie. Your mam's gone and there's nothing you can do about that except make her proud the way you carry on."

Jacob turned and stared at him as if he'd never seen him before.

"It won't be easy, I'll grant you that."

The lad was tight-lipped and Bob didn't want to think about the pain he was experiencing. God only knew the hurt Bob had gone through when he lost his only son.

At that moment, in the distance he saw airplanes flying low in the sky. As they screamed nearer, Bob looked up and saw five of them flying in formation.

Jacob came out of his stupor and looked up too.

"One engine," they said in unison.

"Fighters," Bob confirmed.

"Why are they flying so low?"

Looking at the lad's expression, which had changed to one of mild interest, Bob inwardly smiled. The pair of them had found common ground at last. Bob kept talking, trying to draw Jacob out. "Looks to me like fighter pilots from the local airfield training on low flying techniques."

As the planes screamed into the distance, Jacob looked up at him and it broke Bob's heart to see the expectancy in his eyes. Just like Wilf's at the same age.

"D'you know much about airplanes? I read Biggles adventures and the last one was where he was given command of a fighter squadron and..."

Bob let him talk, grateful that the lad could forget his troubles for a while.

When Jacob fell silent and the mask of anger returned, Bob stood up on arthritic knees that pained him and announced, "Time for home before we both freeze to death."

"Did you come out to look for me?"

Bob knew by the resentful tone in Jacob's voice that he was mad at life—and who could blame him.

"No, for the cat."

"Smoky."

"That's the one. Have you got any ideas where she might be?"

"Maybe at Aunty Brigit's house."

There was no need to go looking as who should come padding along, tail sailing in the air and heading straight for the lad as if she knew she was being talked about, but Smoky. She brushed Jacob's leg.

"Can she come to the house?" The lad picked up the cat and nuzzled his face into the soft fur.

Bob didn't say a word but led the way home.

"What a day."

Doris looked tired and drawn, Bob thought.

It was much later—after a grand tea of homemade meat pie followed by a solid rice pudding with a crisp brown topping, and once the twins were in bed—that the two of them lingered at the table, cups of tea in front of them.

"Worse for them," he commented.

"Poor kiddies, how can I help them get through this?" Doris looked pained.

"How did you cope when you lost Jack?" Bob sat and sipped his tea.

"I don't know, it's all a blur."

"Same here with when I lost Edie. I swore I'd never put myself through that again. I still can't get used to it."

"You never will. You just learn to live with it." Both hands on her cup, Doris sipped her tea and stared ahead with somber eyes. She looked as though she was reliving painful memories. "When Jack died, all I could think was, if only he'd been a minute sooner or, for that matter, later, taking that bend in the twisty road, he wouldn't have met with the lorry that crashed into him." She turned to him, her face desperate. "Would you believe some daft bugger explained in great detail in my company how they found my Jack on his motorbike. That was nine years ago and to this day I can't get the scene out my head."

Bob nodded. "Some folk relish the gruesome details. And there's plenty of that with this war on."

"Well, I certainly am not one of them. I'm happy to stay away when it's not my tragedy, unless of course I'm needed, like now."

The conversation felt too close for comfort for Bob.

Doris drained her cup and stood up, saying, "The thing about the twins is we'll have to keep them busy—occupy their minds so they won't have time to think."

As Bob opened his mouth to answer, a thud came from upstairs and footsteps could be heard traveling across the landing.

The pair of them looked at each other.

"That's the lad going into his sister's bedroom," Bob said.

"Poor mites, they want to be together and who can blame

them." Doris moved to the door and took her coat off the peg. "What happened to Smoky?"

"Last time I saw her she was curled up on the bottom of the lassie's bed."

Doris's face softened as she smiled. "You're a good man at heart, Bob Nichol. Pity you don't show it more often."

She opened the door and was gone.

Deep in thought, Bob took the two cups over to the sink and, rinsing them in cold water, put them on the wooden drainer. He moved over to the chair and eased into it.

What was he doing getting involved? With kiddies at that, when he wasn't even related. He'd agreed to give the twins a home temporarily, for their safekeeping and no more than that.

Doris saying "we" loomed large in his mind. The "we" that meant he'd have to take responsibility for helping the twins get over the grief of losing their mam. Bob's heart hardened. He wanted no part of it. He didn't want to feel anything for the twins because that led to hurt and disappointment, and he'd had enough of both to last a lifetime.

He'd stand by his word and give them a home until an alternative place could be found and that would be the end of it.

Bob moved to the pantry and, taking a glass off the shelf, poured himself an unusually large whisky.

CHAPTER SEVENTEEN

Life for Molly, now that Jacob was angry most of the time, was difficult. She couldn't talk to him about anything any more, especially about Mam, and the sense of isolation was overpowering. All kinds of thoughts about Mam kept running through her mind and Molly still couldn't quite believe she was dead. She kept expecting a letter from Mam to arrive or that the farmhouse door might open one day and Mam would magically appear.

The only source of comfort was having Floppy rabbit, Molly's companion since she was little, and part of the old life she felt homesick for. Molly couldn't go anywhere without Floppy rabbit for fear those short, shallow breaths would start up again when she thought she might die for the want of air. At these moments Molly talked to him—sometimes in her head—and explaining to Floppy how she felt, somehow, helped all the panicky thoughts, whirling in her mind, to disappear and she could breathe easily again.

Nor did she want to go to Denise's house to play when her friend asked. Denise had told her one day at school, her eyes shining, "Dad's a joiner at the mine and guess what he's made for me for my birthday?"

Whatever it was, Molly didn't want to know.

"A doll's house. Come and play this afternoon after school?"

Molly didn't want to go to anyone's house with a mammy and daddy, not because she was jealous, but because it would remind her of what she could never have now that Mam had died and she was an orphan. Molly hadn't known what an orphan was until she met Sandra. Being an orphan frightened her because of what Sandra said had happened to her; she'd ended up in an orphanage where she hardly ever saw her brother.

Mr. Bob had changed too as he'd gone back to not speaking. Mealtimes were silent affairs when no one looked at each other. Mrs. Leadbeater was the only one who stayed the same, but Molly found her difficult to be with because she insisted the twins kept busy. Molly didn't want to join Brownies or make new friends or even join in at Sunday school now. She felt tired and weepy and all she wanted was to be left on her own to read a book. Instinctively, she knew Jacob felt the same way, only it was different for him as he could mooch outdoors with no one around.

Sometimes, if Molly closed her eyes, she could not only sense Mam's presence but smell her perfume. But when Molly tried to imagine Mam's darling face, or softly spoken voice, she couldn't, and she was distressed to the point of blurry tears.

At first, after Mam died, Jacob crept into Molly's bed each night and, because neither of them could sleep and they wanted to take their minds off feeling sad, they'd play the game of taking turns rapping out popular songs with their knuckles on the wooden headboard while the other twin had to guess the tune. "Ten Green Bottles" was always the easiest one. Molly missed her brother the nights he stopped stealing into her room, but she didn't question why because the vexed expression he wore these days made the words dissolve on her lips.

Tonight, though, as Molly got ready for bed, she made up her mind to talk to Jacob about what was bothering him, even if it did make him cross.

Wearing pajamas and barefoot, she limped into his bedroom, noticing along the way that her left foot was not so much on tiptoe as it used to be.

The door creaked as she opened it. The room was in darkness.

"Who's there?"

"Molly."

Hands in front of her, she inched forward in the direction of the bed. "Jacob..."

"What?"

The undertone of irritation in his voice alarmed Molly and she wanted to retreat from the room. But, determined, her eyes wide and staring into the blackness, she carried on.

"Can I talk to you?"

"What about?"

Molly heard a spark of interest in his tone. Encouraged, she groped her way over to his bed and sat on the edge. "I want to ask you something."

"What about?" The bed moved as he struggled to sit up.

Bracing herself, she asked, "Don't you like being my twin any more?"

"That's a silly question."

If only she could see his face, Molly could judge what he was thinking.

She persisted. "Is it true, though?" It felt eerie speaking like this, as though Molly was talking to a ghost.

"Course not."

His voice, coming through the darkness, sounded like the twin brother she knew.

"It's just you're not the same." *There.* She'd plucked up the courage to tell him.

"Yes I am. Only..." Molly could hear the shakiness as he spoke.

"What?"

"It doesn't matter."

Determined to tell him what was worrying her, she faced where his voice came from.

"Jacob..."

"Yes."

Molly felt those quick shallow breaths starting again as she prepared to tell him what she was afraid of. "Remember the book Mam gave me at Christmas?"

"Yes."

"I've read it three times and there's a girl called Beth in it who isn't strong and she dies. Jacob, sometimes I feel that might happen to me."

She heard the bedcovers being flung back. "Don't say that!"

"I don't want to. Honest."

"You'd leave me just like Mam did."

Shocked, Molly protested, "Mam couldn't help it."

"Then why did she go back to work when she knew she might get blown up?"

Molly didn't know what to say and felt teary. She was glad of the darkness so she couldn't see her brother's angry face.

With a huge sniff, he said, "I miss her, Molly."

"So do I."

"I can't believe we won't see her again."

She heard sobs; Molly had never known her brother to break down and cry like this. She reached across in the darkness and found his shaking shoulders. She hugged him tight and, when he'd stopped crying, she climbed into the bed properly and, snuggled up together, they both fell sound asleep.

A week later, on Tuesday, which usually was Women's Institute night, Mrs. Leadbeater arrived. These days she never knocked but barged straight in, and tonight was no exception.

The twins, sitting at the table finishing tea, which never varied— bread, butter and homemade jam and, on rare occasions, cheese— looked up expectantly.

Mrs. Leadbeater told Mr. Bob, who was sitting in his chair,

"I've had a letter from Brigit. She's fine and recuperating well. She said her daughter's spoiling her. She said her main worry is the twins and she wanted me to tell you she's delighted you've given them a home, Bob, and Smoky too. Apparently, Tabitha is allergic to cats and Brigit wonders if Smoky could stay until she returns."

Mr. Bob shrugged. "I suppose so, as long as the cat behaves itself."

Molly relaxed. She hadn't had one of those scary breathing attacks when she thought she might die since the night she had found the courage to go into Jacob's room.

"When does Aunty think she'll be coming home?" Jacob said.

"Nobody knows, Jacob. It takes longer for older people to get over such things as broken hips."

She turned to Mr. Bob. "Brigit has sent a list of instructions for Molly's exercises and stretches with oils. She insists we continue as she was seeing an improvement in Molly. I suggest I call in every night, but mornings are difficult. Bob, can you do some stretches before Molly puts her caliper on in the morning and do them Sunday, as it's my day off?"

This was unexpected. Molly didn't know what she thought about this.

Mr. Bob, his brow wrinkled, thought for a while. Then, he stood and the newspaper he was reading slid off his lap and landed on Smoky, giving the cat a fright. He moved to the passageway and grumbled, "First cats and now exercises, whatever next?"

"Oh, we'll think of something, won't we, twins?" Mrs. Leadbeater grinned.

Like a heavy blanket being removed, the atmosphere lifted. Laughing, Molly looked toward her brother. The darkness, momentarily, left his eyes, and he laughed too.

*

Next morning, as the twins made their way to school together, Jacob looked out over the field beyond the farmhouse where cows and sheep grazed and lambs suckled from their mothers. He thought of Mam and was surprised but pleased when he didn't push the painful memories away.

They headed on their way to school, Molly limping at his side, book bag slung over a drooped shoulder, Floppy rabbit peeping from a coat pocket.

Jacob knew the knitted rabbit was important to Molly and at times like this, he pretended he didn't notice and he never teased. Walking along the footpath, the air was soft and warmth radiated from a weak sun. It smelled like spring was here. An inkling of enthusiasm to explore the outdoors broke through the dullness within him.

Deep in thought, he didn't notice the lace of his right shoe had come undone and, tripping over it, he nearly fell. The shoes were secondhand and didn't fit properly—as none of his clothes did these days. They came all the way from kind people in America and the children in Leadburn School were allowed to choose one item. Jacob had chosen woolen knee socks but Mrs. Leadbeater said they weren't the best choice as he needed short trousers.

"You go on," he told Molly as he kneeled on the cold ground and fastened the lace.

When he stood and saw the children, Molly among them, file up the school steps and go into the darkness of the school, a rebellion he hadn't felt in an age fired in him and he sat on the nearby wall in the sun.

His face upturned and seeing the yellow light shining through his closed lids, Jacob gave a big sigh. He felt carefree for a moment in time. But as the thought popped in his head that Miss Crow would delight in punishing him for playing truant from school, Jacob knew he wouldn't give her the satisfaction. He rose from the wall and, shoulders slumped, he walked the few yards and climbed the steps.

Gloom descended on him. One day he'd be like Biggles and be free to soar in the skies. But as he entered the school, a rumpus in the cloakroom interrupted his thoughts.

The entrance to the cloakroom was filled with a few children intent on watching something. He stood on tiptoe but couldn't see over the heads.

A voice cried out, "Give him back. I know you took him out of my pocket."

Jacob's chest tightened. It was Molly's voice.

"What would I want with a stupid rabbit? They're for babies."

"I know it was you who took him."

"Go on, then where is he? Oh look, I found him. Pity you can't reach him."

Jacob pushed his way through the children.

Roger was teasing Molly, holding Floppy rabbit over her head. With a desperate look on her face, she tried to reach the rabbit, then, trying to jump, she overbalanced and nearly fell.

"Don't be mean, Roger, give her it back," a girl shouted.

Roger hesitated, then flung Floppy rabbit over to the far side of the wall of pegs.

"Baby!" he jeered at her. "I'm surprised they let you out of the infants' school."

Roger turned, smirking, and looked straight at Jacob.

With all the grief and anger boiling inside, a need to take vengeance on the hateful Roger exploded within Jacob.

"I'll show you for tormenting my sister."

Roger's eyes widened in fear. "I found the rabbit on the floor, honest."

"Liar."

As everyone watched, Roger grew red-faced. "Well, she's such a baby. People laugh at her at school."

That did it.

"Nobody laughs at my sister." Jacob lunged forward.

Roger toppled backward to the ground and Jacob, pouncing on him, pummeled the bigger boy with his fists.

"Please, somebody, help!" Roger screamed.

Nobody did. Jacob heard the other boys yelling and encouraging the fight and, in the commotion, he didn't hear a stern voice shout, "Enough!"

All he knew was Miss Crow was now at the front and cuffing the back of his head.

"Get off Roger, this minute."

The others were quiet now, in respect, Jacob knew, and fear of the strict teacher. Miss Crow was quick to take her wrath out on anyone handy.

She yanked him by the shirt collar and, his temper gone as quickly as it flared, he stood up from the floor on shaky legs.

"Jacob Moffatt, this is the second time I've caught you fighting. I won't tolerate bullies in my class."

Jacob knew he was in for it but pretending he didn't care, he pulled a defiant face.

The teacher seethed, "Go and stand by my desk. The rest of you, into the classroom at once, and no talking."

Roger, his face gleeful, told Jacob in an undertone as he walked past, "You're for it now."

Rather than show fear, rebellion took hold of Jacob. Repeating what he'd heard the bigger girls in the school yard call their teacher, he lashed out before he'd thought the words through. "Miss Crow's a stupid cow."

Immediately the words of anger and frustration were out, he knew he'd let Mam down.

"I heard that, Jacob Moffatt, and you'll be sorry." Miss Crow's face was stern, her lips a thin line. Jacob quaked inside but didn't allow his expression to change from brazen.

"Please, Miss Crow"—Molly, wringing her hands approached the irate teacher—"it wasn't Jacob's fault, Roger was—"

"Don't tell tales, girl."

"I'm not, miss…"

Jacob was proud of how brave Molly was for trying to defend him but wished she wouldn't as she would only get herself in trouble.

"…it was Roger who started it."

"Silence. Your brother was told what would happen if he was caught fighting again."

Everyone sat at their desks; Jacob stood at the front of the class with his arm outstretched. A cold shiver traveled from his buttocks to his spine, but he wouldn't allow his fear to show.

Miss Crow, a long reedy cane in her hand, drew back her forearm and brought the cane down. The thwack on Jacob's palm could be heard at the back of the class.

"Other hand."

There was a gasp from the class as no one had been known to be caned twice.

"This stroke is for your cheek."

Jacob held out his hand again. Miss Crow brought the cane down again and caught Jacob's fingers this time; the blow stung and made his eyes water.

He couldn't imagine Biggles flinching and so neither did he. His hand stinging unbearably, not a sound escaped his lips.

Jacob looked over to where Molly was sitting. Her desk lid was raised, and she was hiding behind it; he knew she couldn't bear to see him suffer.

"You may now go to your desk." Miss Crow's eyes gleamed with satisfaction.

The urge to call her a stupid cow again overcame Jacob, but the pain of his hands won.

Moving to his desk, all eyes in the class watching him, Jacob sat at his side of the seat. His hands on fire, he grasped the cold metal of the desk's cast iron legs to try to relieve the searing pain.

*

As they trudged home after school, Molly told him, "Your hands look very sore. Put them in cold water when we get home. That's what Granny did when she burned her hand lifting the kettle by the hot handle."

"Molly, I don't want anyone at the farm to know what happened at school today," Jacob said, frowning.

"Why not?"

Jacob shrugged.

Molly didn't understand, but she could see her brother was upset and didn't want to talk about what had happened.

Smoky met the twins as they went through the cottage gate and escorted them up to the back door. As soon as they entered the farmhouse, Jacob escaped up to his bedroom.

Mr. Bob was in the pantry. He appeared in the doorway carrying a bucket of potatoes.

When he saw Molly, he raised his eyebrows. "Is it that time of day already? Where's Jacob?"

Worried she might blurt out what had happened today, Molly tried to think of something to say. "He doesn't feel very well, Mr. Bob." It wasn't a lie.

"I wanted him to take these spuds up the field, they're to boil for the pigs. I've to fix one of the fences." He gave a frustrated shake of the head. "I suppose if I want the job doing, I'll have to do it myself."

Molly was surprised as Mr. Bob usually left the running of the farm to the foreman. But recently, probably because Mrs. Leadbeater was always on at him to take an interest, he had begun to keep more of an eye on things.

Molly set the table, including a cup for Mrs. Leadbeater, who would be calling in after she'd closed the post office to do Molly's exercises and massage.

Molly placed the homemade Woolton pie—which Mrs. Leadbeater had told her was named after the minister for food—in the range oven to heat. Mrs. Leadbeater had made it yesterday as it was Sunday and her day off from the post office.

"Seeing how I was making a pie for Frieda and me," she'd told Mr. Bob, "I thought I'd make one for all of you."

The pie made of potatoes, oats, vegetables and covered with golden pastry had smelled delicious as it cooked in the oven.

"Can I have some now?" Jacob had wanted to know.

"Indeed no," Mrs. Leadbeater told him. "You've had a big dinner. It'll keep till tomorrow."

Mr. Bob eyed her suspiciously. "You don't usually come on a Sunday, Doris. Are you checking up on me?"

"Bob Nichol, I've got better things to do than to wonder what you're up to." There had been a silence, then she had said, "But you could take more interest in the kiddies."

Molly had squirmed, knowing a quarrel was brewing.

"I've told you before, Doris Leadbeater, to keep your nose out of my affairs."

Molly hadn't stayed to listen any more, because hearing the two of them argue made her tummy ache. She had asked to be excused and gone upstairs to read in her bedroom.

At times like this, she missed Mam, and longed for the reassuring hug she knew she would give her.

Now, as Molly put tea leaves in the china teapot in readiness for the meal, she wondered if she should open the oven door and check the pie or leave it until Mr. Bob returned.

Then the door opened and Mr. Bob came in, a panting Tyne behind him. Going over to the sink, Mr. Bob washed his hands at the cold water tap and filled Tyne's bowl up to the brim.

He nodded to Molly and then said the usual, "I'll make us a pot of tea."

Pouring the boiling water from the black kettle over the tea leaves, he stood the teapot on the range to let it stew.

"Where's the lad?" Mr. Bob said.

"Upstairs."

"Still? Is he still ailing?"

"I think so..."

*

Bob, looking at Molly's troubled expression, knew something was wrong. He didn't want to probe because that would mean getting involved, and he knew that once that happened, with her soulful, brown eyes, Molly Moffatt would get under his skin and Bob would be done for.

He couldn't bear to love and lose someone again; the hurt was too painful.

"Was the lad ailing at school?"

Molly wouldn't meet his eyes but held her knitted rabbit and looked scared, as if worried she might say something she shouldn't.

Something was up. If the lad was in trouble of some kind, Bob needed to know. They were his responsibility, after all, until Doris found them a new home.

Marching along the passageway, he called from the bottom of the stairs. "Jacob, get yourself down here and be quick about it. That's an order."

Bob went back into the kitchen and took the pie out of the oven. Sitting at the table, he cut the hot, seductive-smelling pie into three large portions.

When Jacob entered the room, as he put the slices of pie on plates, Bob didn't look up.

The lad sat down and Bob handed him a plate. He searched

Jacob's face for signs of sickness or guilt. All he saw was a lad who looked as if he carried the world on his shoulders.

"I'm not hungry," the boy mumbled. Head down, he kept his hands on his knees beneath the table.

Now Bob knew something was up. A growing lad didn't refuse a mouthwatering piece of pie.

Against his better judgment, Bob asked, "What's wrong?"

The lad stayed mute and shook his head. "Can I leave the table?"

"I asked you a question."

The boy shrugged. "Nothing."

"Eat a bit of pie, then you can leave the table. It's a long time till breakfast."

Bob offered the plate to the lad again.

The boy looked cornered. He gazed at his sister and it was as though a secret message passed between them. The twins often did this, Bob noticed—they appeared to know what each other was thinking.

The lassie took the plate from Bob and put it in front of her brother.

Bob decided to let the moment pass and began eating; as always, he was ravenous. It was on his second mouthful, as he was chewing, that he looked up to see Jacob cutting the pie with his fork, while keeping his other hand beneath the table.

"It's manners to use your knife." Bob spoke more sharply than he meant.

The boy brought up his other hand and picked up his knife but not before Bob saw something that sent shudders down his spine: a welt across the palm of the boy's hand.

"Show me your hand," he boomed.

The boy looked uncertain, then held out his arm.

Seeing the extent of the lashing, the black and blue bruising, Bob erupted in anger. He knew the extent of the boy's pain because he had suffered at the hands of his da, who never thought twice about giving him a thrashing.

"Who did this?" he said, trying to control his fury.

Jacob stayed tight-lipped.

At that moment Doris bundled in the kitchen doorway.

She prattled as she closed the door, "Heaven help me! Folk have gossiped all day in the post office about the invasion. Some crackpot reckoned it'll take place on March the eighteenth." She turned, her face indignant. "I ask you, how can anyone possibly know tha—" Seeing Bob's irate face, she stopped short, then asked, "What's up?"

"Look at that." He pointed to Jacob's upturned hand.

She moved closer. She folded her arms over her bosom. Her face went cherry red. "Who gave you the cane? Never Roberta Templeton."

"I doubt it," Mr. Bob chipped in. "Roberta never did resort to the cane. It must be that scrawny teacher. What's her name?" He directed the question at the girl, knowing she would cave long before her brother.

"Miss Crow," Molly whispered.

Bob turned to look at Jacob. "Was it her?"

"Yes."

"Why?"

The girl looked at her brother tentatively. "It's all my fault. If I hadn't been a baby and taken Floppy rabbit to school, none of this would've happened. I'm sorry, Jacob."

"You aren't a baby," her brother cried. "And I'll punch anyone who says you are."

Molly looked up at Bob. "Roger was teasing me and wouldn't give me Floppy back and..." Again she looked uncertainly at the lad. "Jacob got mad."

"What happened to the other boy?" Doris wanted to know.

Molly shrugged. "Nothing."

That settled it. Bob jumped from his seat, nearly knocking the table over, tea and all, and dived for the door.

"Bob. Stop! Where d'you think you're going?" Doris said.

He shrugged into his coat. "I'm going to have it out with Roberta Templeton about that woman. Look at the lad's hand. It's a damned disgrace. Whatever he did, he didn't deserve that."

"Bob, you'll do no such thing. I agree Miss Crow needs reporting but not tonight and not when you're all fired up. You'll regret what you say. Wait till the morning when Roberta will be at work. You don't want to be disturbing the woman's home life."

Bob, despite the urgency to go now, thought over what Doris said. He took off his coat.

Damn the woman. Doris was right.

*

Once the twins were upstairs, Doris sat in front of the fire next to Bob, the dregs of their tea in their cups.

She told Bob, who still looked troubled, "I'm glad you came to your senses."

Bob shook his head. "Aye, well, I'm not so sure. 'Strike while the iron's hot' is my motto."

Doris, staring at the red coals, couldn't think of an appropriate answer.

"Thing is," Bob told her, "being caned like that—and in front of the whole class—could break the lad's spirit. God knows, he's been through enough lately. Where's the woman's heart?"

Doris decided to dig deeper. "You sound like you speak from experience, Bob."

"Aye well, that's another story. Let's just say I had a bastard of a da who liked to use his fists when the drink was inside him. Pardon the language."

Doris turned to gaze at him, not wanting to press him further. So that was the story behind Bob.

Bob in turn looked like a dog caught in the act of pinching the Sunday joint. "You're the first person I've confided in about me da."

Doris, feeling privileged, flushed.

"What's with you staying on tonight?" Bob, looking thrown, as if he'd said too much, changed the subject. "You're usually rushing away to fix Frieda's tea."

"Her and Sandra are away to see *Northern Pursuit* at the pictures. I've seen it and the supporting B film—what a load of codswallop, that one was. Though I didn't say as much to the lass. Frieda could do with a night out. That nice Eddy Gibson she was seeing got called up and she's taken it badly."

"She would do, with her history, poor lass."

They lapsed into silence.

"Is it true that Sandra and the curate, Mr. Carlton, are...you know...sweet on each other?"

Doris was surprised Bob knew. "Who told you that, Bob?"

He pulled an affronted face. "I'm not daft, Doris. I've got eyes. The curate was up at the farm for eggs and I happened upon the pair of them in the yard." His cheekbones raised conspicuously as he grinned. "The way they jumped apart you'd think they were conspiring to rob a bank."

He stood and, taking her cup, he went over to the sink where he deposited both their teacups on the wooden drainer.

Back in his seat, he told her, "I know two love birds when I see them."

"This is in the strictest confidence mind, Bob." Doris tapped the side of her nose.

His eyebrows shot up. "Doris, with my social life, who am I going to tell?"

She smiled. "Only Frieda and I know. And yes, the couple are officially courting." Doris clenched her hands together and beamed with excitement. "Mr. Carlton went to see the bishop and he gave his permission. Apparently, propriety is important and so they've to court in secret until an official engagement is announced."

Bob clicked his tongue. "What a daft carry-on. Even if he is a man of the cloth, good news should be shared. Especially now, when all we hear is war news."

"I agree. But who are we to question the ways of the church?"

They lapsed into comfortable silence.

Bob startled her then by saying, "Edie liked to go to the pictures and complained when I wouldn't go with her. That made-up stuff is not for me, but I wish I'd been more sociable for Edie's sake."

"For a man of not many words you've excelled yourself tonight, Bob."

"Aye, well, believe it or not I'm finding it easy to talk to you." Looking abashed, he rubbed the back of his neck and appeared restless. Doris wondered if he regretted saying what he'd just said.

"Thank you, Bob. I take that as a grand compliment." Inwardly, Doris thought, *poor soul's lonely and has no one else to talk to.* She knew that feeling from when she lost her Jack. "You want to get out more. I don't mean socially. I just mean be more involved around the farm."

"After Edie died, I lost all interest. And what with Wilf gone, there didn't seem any point. To be honest, there still doesn't, though I am trying to get involved again."

Doris didn't answer as she didn't want to stop his flow.

"Edie blamed me for Wilf joining up when he could have been exempt and stayed on the farm. She said with all the stories I told him about the Great War, I glamorized it. He couldn't wait to do his bit in this one." Bob let out a heartfelt moan. "I was proud of the lad but now I wish I'd kept me mouth shut. He'd still be here by my side, ready to take over the farm."

"Most of us have 'if onlys,' Bob, including me. Take that day in the post office, when Mrs. Hall said her husband suffered

from gout and it was that painful he couldn't help with lambing." Doris, sorrowfully, shook her head. "If I hadn't opened my
big mouth and said Jack would turn out, he'd still be here."

Bob gave her a sympathetic look and told her, "You've no need
to blame yourself."

"Tell me that when I'm lying in bed in the middle of the night
and can't sleep."

Bob's eyes met hers and for a moment Doris could swear his
gaze became both intimate and tender.

They both looked away and Doris felt oddly discomfited.

Bob cleared his throat and coughed as though embarrassed.
He obviously felt the same way.

A door banged upstairs and footsteps could be heard on the
landing.

"That'll be the lad going back to his room again. They play
this game where they have to knock on the headboard for some
reason. They did it for a while after their mam died. Drives me
mad. But I came to realize the twins need to be together when
they're down." Bob frowned. "That bloody teacher. I could wring
her neck."

"Bob!"

"Sorry. But she makes me furious. She'd no right to do what
she did, especially when that laddie's grieving for his mam." His
eyebrows drew together in concern. "I mean, you never know
how youngsters are going to react in times of trouble. Look at
Frieda and that bother with her eating."

"The thing is, Bob, the twins need security, and being here
with you for the time being has given them that."

Bob sat transfixed as he thought on the words.

He stood up and, disappearing into the front room, he
returned seconds later carrying one of the saggy-cushioned chairs
from the floral cottage suite. Carrying it over to the range, he

placed it alongside his. Returning to the front room, he brought out the second identical chair and placed it on the other side.

Standing back, he gave a satisfied nod of the head.

It occurred to Doris, and not for the first time, that beneath Bob's tough and sometimes unapproachable exterior lay a kind and thoughtful man.

CHAPTER EIGHTEEN

March 1944

"Murdering swine! I'm going to kill you if it's the last thing I do on earth." Jacob took hold of the joystick and spoke in a voice like the newsreaders on the Pathé news at the pictures. "Biggles takes possession of the aircraft and proceeds with his dangerous mission and—"

"Please, can I fly the plane now?" Molly, sitting behind him in the cockpit, begged. "It's been your turn forever."

It was early on a sunny Saturday morning in March and the twins were playing in the back field behind the byre. The air was soft and Molly could see miles of fields, separated by drystone walls, in the valley and beyond.

The "airplane" she and Jacob were flying was made up of old rickety chairs, and some musty-smelling sheets they'd found in one of the barns.

The twins changed places, Molly shuffling forward and Jacob clambering out of the plane and moving to the back of the cockpit. Molly put on pretend goggles and made the appropriate noises as the plane took off and soared into the sky. Up in the clouds, she felt equal to anyone. It didn't matter if she couldn't walk properly; all that mattered was she concentrated and kept one hand on the joystick. Tiny figures in the street below looked up in wonder and waved.

In this pretend world, Molly could imagine that somewhere

down below, Mam worked in a factory and in her time off she'd write the twins a letter and soon she'd be coming to see them...

"Time to go down, we're out of fuel," the co-pilot behind told her and with a jolt Molly came back to reality.

Mam had died. In that moment the enormity of what that meant—that she'd never see her beloved mother again—was made bearable only by the image of Mam and Granny together up in heaven looking down on her.

"My turn again when we've refueled," Jacob told her when they were on the ground and the plane came to a shuddering halt on the runway.

As she cumbersomely climbed out of the cockpit, Molly, once again, became a little girl with a disability that people either were afraid of or ridiculed or pitied.

"Here you both are," Sandra called as she walked from around the byre. "I saw you were about while I was milking. I've been looking everywhere for you."

Her face flushed and eyes shining, there was an air of excitement about her. She eyed the plane. "What on earth is this contraption?"

Looking at the airplane through the big girl's eyes, the illusion vanished. Molly saw the construction as it really was, three chairs behind each other, and a torn sheet draped over them.

"Just a game," Jacob mumbled, blushing.

"We're flying an airplane." Molly spoke up because she'd had fun and a happy time, and she felt defensive about the airplane.

Sandra nodded in understanding. "That's what Alf used to do when we were young." She smiled fondly at the memory. "Now, here he is flying real airplanes."

Sandra had a strong Geordie accent and it reminded Molly of her hometown. An ache of longing overcame the little girl.

"That's what I'm going to do when I'm older," Jacob told Sandra.

"You'll be great at it. I've had exciting news from Alf." Sandra radiated happiness. "He's sent a letter to say he's on leave next weekend and so he'll hitch a ride north for a visit." Her eyes misted. "I haven't set eyes on him since he was interned at the Swiss camp."

"How did he escape?" Jacob asked, sounding intrigued.

Molly just knew her brother was thinking of Biggles. He was always going on about his hero's dangerous missions.

Sandra's eyes squinted as if she was recalling what she'd heard about that time. "He hiked over the Pyrenees to Spain. From there he was sent by the British Embassy to Gibraltar where he was repatriated to England by sea."

Jacob's eyes grew wide. "Did he get to kill many of the enemy when he escaped?"

"He didn't say, Jacob." Sandra looked rather amused. "I suspect he was concentrating more on staying in hiding."

Jacob seemed impressed. "I wish I could meet him."

"D'you know what?" Her eyes gleaming, Sandra gave them a wide grin. "You can, we're planning a picnic in the afternoon when Alf's here. I'd love it if the two of you came too. That's if the weather behaves and it's a perfect day like this." She turned up her head and scoured the expanse of blue sky. Then looking back at the twins, she told them, "Mr. Jeffries has agreed to do afternoon milking with Frieda."

"Ooh, thanks." Jacob's face lit up with excitement. "Then I can ask Alf all about airplanes."

Sandra laughed. "How about you, Molly? Will you come along?"

"Yes please." A sudden thought struck Molly. *Sandra goes everywhere on a bicycle.* "Will you be going on bikes?"

"No, Mr. Carlton's driving the vicar's old Morris. It hasn't been out of the garage in an age, so there's no worry about petrol."

Molly knew petrol was rationed and was only supposed to be used for special needs and war work. She was surprised the curate was coming along too and wondered why Sandra flushed pink at the mention of his name.

Sandra said, "Come on, we'll have to get a move on if you're to help delivering the milk. Mr. Nichol will be waiting with the horse and cart."

Mr. Bob had become friendlier recently and he didn't forget to do Molly's stretches in the morning any more. Most days, after tea the three of them sat together—the twins on the comfortable chairs that had mysteriously appeared in front of the range fire the morning after Jacob got the cane.

Mr. Bob always inquired about school, and then finished by asking, "Is that new teacher behaving himself?"

That was another mystery. After Mr. Bob had gone to see the headmistress, Miss Crow was never seen again. A new teacher called Mr. Reeves appeared one morning to take class. A kindly man, Mr. Reeves had graying hair. Molly liked him because he didn't make her be a reading monitor to classmates who couldn't read, but did the job himself.

Everyone, apart from Roger, who kept to himself these days, agreed they much preferred the new teacher.

With Mr. Bob taking more interest in the farm, the twins were allowed to go on the milk round at weekends, with Molly sitting beside him on the cart, while Jacob and Sandra delivered bottles of milk to villagers' doors and collected the empties.

At dinnertime the twins joined Frieda and Sandra for sandwiches in the barn, or, if the weather was sunny out, in the field behind the byre.

And life became tolerable—as long as Molly didn't let herself think about where they would live in the future.

*

The following Saturday Molly drew back the blackout curtains, and she was relieved to see a bright sun shining from the blue sky. The picnic was on.

Mrs. Leadbeater called in at the farmhouse before opening

the post office, a wicker basket in her hands. She placed it down on the table, her round face beaming, and removed the tea towel laid over the top: "Ta da!"

Molly and Jacob gaped at the laden basket of mouthwatering food. A plate pie with a golden crust, Spam sandwiches cut into triangles, a quiche made with beetroot, onion and cheese, and a carrot cake.

"All homemade for a special occasion," Mrs. Leadbeater told the twins, then looked guilty, as if she'd said something she shouldn't.

Later, as the twins made their way down the track to wait for the motor car, Jacob asked Molly, "What d'you think the Mrs. meant by a special occasion?"

"Maybe it's special because Sandra's brother is here and she's happy that Alf is safe?" Molly guessed.

Alf had arrived safely in Leadburn last night. He couldn't stay at the Land Girls' hostel, where Sandra lived, and so the curate had arranged for him to sleep at the vicarage for the weekend.

"I feel sick with excitement," Molly confessed, as she kept an eye on the road. "I hope I feel better by the time we eat the picnic."

"Me too," Jacob said, to Molly's surprise. Unlike her, he could cope with unusual situations.

Molly tried to think of what Mam would tell them: *It'll pass once we get going.*

As if on cue, the motor car, driven by Mr. Carlton and with a stranger in the passenger seat, came into view along the stretch of road.

The ancient-looking Morris stopped and the rear door opened and Sandra's head poked out.

"Hop in, you two!" She took the wicker basket from Jacob.

The twins did as they were told and sat either side of Sandra. She told them, "You know Mr. Carlton, the curate."

The curate turned in the driver's seat and his brown, caring eyes met Molly's. "We've never formally met. Pleased to meet you."

Molly, feeling self-conscious, gave him a bashful smile.

Jacob said, "We're pleased to meet you too."

"And this is my kid brother, Alf." Sandra's face was aglow with happiness.

Alf was wearing an RAF blue-gray uniform and he had the same sand-colored hair as the twins, and green twinkling eyes. "How d'you do, both. Sandra's told me all about you." He gave a boyish grin. "There's nothing like the folks of Shields, right?"

Jacob beamed.

"The people from Leadburn are nice too," Molly quickly put in, in case the others felt left out.

The grown-ups laughed and she didn't mind; everyone appeared in a good mood.

Mr. Carlton drove the car along the narrow and twisting roads, passing a landscape of fields, some with workers, others with an abundance of sheep and dear little gamboling lambs. Alf and Sandra talked nonstop, mostly about his escape from the Swiss internment camp.

Molly noticed Jacob was leaning forward and listening intently to their conversation. She was happy looking out over the countryside, thrilled at the sight of the leggy lambs in a field that looked like a green carpet.

"I can't believe you're here," Sandra told her brother now, her eyes sparkling with happiness. "After the war's over, I won't allow anything to separate us ever again."

"You don't want me crowding your life," Alf told her.

"Oh, but I do, you're family. You belong."

Mr. Carlton took his eyes off the road, momentarily, to look at Alf by his side. "I would agree with that."

As she listened to the grown-ups talking, a thought struck

Molly and she felt sad. The twins didn't have a family and they didn't belong to anybody any more.

*

"Whereabouts is this pool, Sandra?" Mr. Carlton wanted to know. "It's difficult without any road signs to go by."

Jacob knew that signposts had been removed to confuse the enemy if ever they invaded.

As the motor car rattled along through the countryside, houses lining the road and a pub with a fox on the sign outside came into sight.

Sandra was looking at a road map in her hands. "This must be Wardhaugh village; it's the only place around here on the map."

No sooner had they entered the tiny village than they were motoring out the other side, heading for open countryside without another house in sight.

Jacob piped up, "What kind of pool? Will there be fish in it?"

"I doubt it," Sandra told him distractedly. She leaned forward, and told Mr. Carlton, "I recognize where we are. You follow the road for some time and there's a stone ruin of a building you can see off the road."

As they passed the ruin, Jacob asked, "Can we stop and take a look?"

The ruin, with pitched roof and windows that had no panes in them, looked as though it had once been a house. He imagined all kinds of secrets that might be hidden inside that no one had investigated.

"Another time," Mr. Carlton told him, turning back to give him a smile.

Sandra went on, "As I recall, you turn somewhere at the top of that hill, see… where the church with the white painted windows is. The track should be on the right just before you reach the summit."

Mr. Carlton turned right at the track and, following it

beneath an overhang of trees, the track opened to reveal a glade where a stream torrented over high rocks into the swirling waters of a pool below.

The car slowed then stopped and, as they all got out of the car and stood on the lush grass surrounding the pool, the only sound that punctured the air was the waterfall as it pounded the waters below.

"The first time I came here, it seemed like I'd discovered a fairy glen," Sandra told the twins.

"How on earth did you find it?" Alf wanted to know, looking spellbound as he watched the crystal-clear waters gush over the rocks.

"I didn't. Someone brought me here."

"Who? Do I know them?"

"No, Alf. He was an American who flew planes like you." She gave a sad sigh. "He was one of the unlucky ones who didn't make it."

Jacob saw a look pass between Mr. Carlton and Sandra, as if they shared a secret.

The curate looked deep into Sandra's eyes and smiled. "We'll always remember him."

"With fondness," she told him. Then she turned to the twins. "Come on, you two, give us a hand to get the food and rug from the boot of the car. I don't know about anyone else, but I'm famished. And by the looks of things"—she held up the wicker basket—"we've got mountains of food."

Mr. Carlton, who was wearing a sports jacket and flannel trousers and dog collar, shook the tartan rug out onto the grass. Sandra handed out plates and, sitting on the rug, they all tucked into the delicious-tasting food.

It must be the fresh air that made him hungry, Jacob decided, because he ate every morsel on his plate and he could have eaten more. His appetite had returned and it was the first time since—but there his mind slammed shut like a book. He felt disloyal to Mam when he felt happy.

Afterward, while Sandra cleared away, Jacob went over to where the waterfall cascaded from the rocks above and sat on the grass. Mr. Carlton strolled over and sat down beside him and chewed a blade of grass.

"Times like this, I wish my mum was here to share the moment," he told Jacob.

Jacob stiffened. He wondered how the curate knew that was how he felt. He felt teary because Mam was missing out.

"I miss Mum, dreadfully." Mr. Carlton gazed into the distance as if he was avoiding looking at Jacob.

"Is she in heaven?"

"No, but I don't get to see her very often as she lives a long train ride away. I know she wouldn't want me to be sad as mums like their boys to be happy."

They sat quietly together for a while, then Mr. Carlton spoke. "The good thing is when I am missing her all I have to do is close my eyes and think of some happy time we spent together." He turned to Jacob. "Memories are the most precious things—and no one can take them away."

"I could sleep for a week." Alf's booming voice broke into the conversation.

Jacob turned and saw him lie back on the rug and put his hands behind his head.

Mr. Carlton stood up from where he sat by Jacob. An eager expression on his face, he told Alf, "Not now, you can't." He made his way over to the Morris and, opening the boot, produced bottles of wine and lemonade from the boot of the car.

"Let the celebrations begin."

Alf sat up. "What celebrations?"

Sandra's features softened as she looked at the curate. "Mr. Carlton—Matthew—has asked me to marry him."

A stunned silence followed. Jacob felt like an intruder. He didn't know quite what to say or, indeed, if he should say anything. He could tell by the soppy look on Molly's face she was gripped by what was happening.

"What!" Alf looked stunned. "It's a bit sudden, isn't it?"

Mr. Carlton put the two bottles on the rug and took hold of Sandra's hand. "I've loved your sister since the first time I saw her when she came to Leadburn."

This was getting far too mushy for Jacob's liking.

Sandra told them, "The bishop insists we're to court in secret. But I wanted us to get engaged while you're here, Alf. We won't announce it for a while yet but it's important that you're the first to know and that I tell you in person." She turned to the twins. "We're happy to share our good news with you both."

Alf's face split into a beaming smile. "Congratulations," he told the couple. He shook hands with Mr. Carlton and kissed his sister on the cheek. "I'm in shock, but in a good way!"

Jacob decided, after what Mr. Carlton told him, it would be all right to be happy.

He asked, "Did Mrs. Leadbeater know? Is that why she baked a cake?"

Sandra nodded, laughing. "Frieda knows too. In fact, this outing was her idea when she heard Alf was coming home. She and Mrs. Leadbeater planned it all."

"No spilling the beans, mind." The curate ruffled Jacob's hair.

"I can keep a secret, I'm a Cub Scout." Jacob's voice came out more huffily than he intended.

"I won't say anything, either," Molly said, but she looked, Jacob thought, as if something troubled her.

As the lemonade and wine were opened, they all chinked cups and the grown-ups toasted, "Peace and happiness for the future," and Jacob forgot that he was worried about his sister for the time being.

*

Later, alighting from the Morris and waving goodbye to everyone as the car drove away, Jacob let out a contented sigh.

What a smashing day, he thought to himself.

He waited for Molly to catch up and, as they trudged up the
earthen path toward the farmhouse, he turned to his sister, who
seemed unduly subdued. "One of the best parts was when I spot-
ted the minnows in the pool—only it would've been better if I'd
had a net and could've caught one."

Molly didn't answer but trailed beside him.

"What's the matter, Molly?"

She stopped and, as she turned toward him, he was startled at
her pale and anxious expression.

"Jacob, where are we going to live when the war's finished,
now that Mam's..." She swallowed hard, and looked at him with
sad eyes.

Jacob stiffened. "I can't think of that right now."

"Sandra said she and Alf had no family and they were sent to
an orphanage. That might happen to us."

Jacob felt helpless. He didn't know what to say.

Until now he hadn't thought beyond his misery. Mr. Bob had
been kind billeting the twins, but he didn't really want them
there and Jacob felt in the way. After the war finished, Mr. Bob
would likely want to go back to living on his own.

Jacob's thoughts turned to Mam and how he'd promised to
protect his sister.

"Maybe when Aunty Brigit gets better and she returns home
we can live with her. She's old but we could manage if I helped
with the jobs and shopping."

He saw Molly cheer a little at the prospect. "Now I've worked
out how to hold things better, I'll help too."

"Whatever happens, Molly, we'll be together, and I'll look

after you." He reached out to hold her hand and tried to give her a reassuring smile.

Though he sounded brave, inside, as he thought of the future, Jacob was quaking.

*

One night, the table set, Molly and Jacob were sitting waiting for Mr. Bob to join them for tea when Mrs. Leadbeater appeared in the kitchen doorway, a letter in her hand.

"Where's Mr. Nichol?" she asked, looking around.

"He's out in the field with Tyne to see if any more lambs have been borned," Molly told her.

"Born," Mrs. Leadbeater corrected automatically, as she moved over to the table and sat opposite the twins.

"I've received a letter from Brigit Merryfield," she told them, and Molly detected concern in her eyes. "I'm afraid Brigit's taken a turn for the worse—the poor dear's had a heart attack."

Molly was speechless. She glanced at Jacob, who looked as shocked as she was.

"Brigit was taken to the hospital but has been discharged and she's back at her daughter's and doing well, by all accounts," Mrs. Leadbeater was quick to reassure them. "There's a letter inside the envelope for you two." A troubled expression crossed her face. "Before you read what Brigit has to say, you should know she doesn't know about your mam's accident." She shook her head, unhappily. "Would you like me to read her letter for you?"

"Yes please." Jacob's voice sounded trembly.

Dear Jacob and Molly,

Just when I was doing fine this had to happen. But that's what life's like when you're getting on. I don't want you to worry about me, though, as I'm on the mend now. Due, might I add, to all the homemade remedies I'm taking. My Tabitha and her husband have a large herb garden and I'm in my element.

The thing is, now my youngest granddaughter has left home, there's a large bedroom going spare and Tabitha and her husband have invited me to move in permanently. Tabitha says it makes sense as it will stop her worrying and save a lot of her time traveling back and forth. I've come to the conclusion that living here with my family is something I'd like, as I'll see more of my grandchildren who live close by. But you both are family too and I wanted to look after you until the end of the war when you could go back home and live with your mother. Of course, I worry about Smoky because she obviously can't come and live here with Tabitha's allergy.

But as Tabitha says, you're in good hands and I can always visit when I feel up to it. As far as Smoky is concerned, nobody owns a cat—Smoky taught me that, she chose to adopt me. Treat her well and she'll stay with you as she's a clever cat and knows where she's best off.

So, my dears, forgive me my promise to give you a home until the war is over and let's pray that won't be too long, then you can go home to your mother where you belong.

Yours, affectionately,
Aunty Brigit. XX

PS Keep up the exercises, Molly, and please write and let me know how you get on.

There was an uncomfortable silence. Molly covered her face with her hands in distress.

The words played back in her in her mind. *Then you can be back home with your mother where you belong.*

Mrs. Leadbeater spoke. "I wondered if we should tell Brigit about your mam but after a lot of thought, I suggest we take the route of 'ignorance is bliss.' That means when a person doesn't know something, it's kinder not to tell them the truth because it will only upset and worry them when there's no need. If we tell Brigit about your mam's accident, she'll only fret and she's too poorly to do anything about it. I suggest we wait till she's stronger. What d'you think?"

Jacob looked at Molly, and Molly knew they were both thinking the same; their hopes of a home with Aunty Brigit had died.

They nodded.

"We're getting along fine as we are, aren't we?"

Molly didn't need to look at her brother. They were fine for now but what would happen in the future?

Molly was afraid of the answer.

"Yes, Mrs. Leadbeater," they both replied dutifully.

CHAPTER NINETEEN
April 1944

Molly thought that Easter time was pretty in the countryside. Yellow gorse bloomed in the hedgerows, pretty purple flowers hung in village window boxes and the trees were the greenest Molly had ever seen.

One Sunday, Molly sat with Sandra and Frieda in the field behind the byre in the warm sunshine eating dinner.

"Is that Mr. Humpty you're eating?" Sandra grinned as she opened a lemonade bottle filled with cold tea she'd brought from the hostel.

At the church service that morning Molly had won a prize for the best decorated Easter egg—Humpty Dumpty sitting on a wall. The idea was Molly's but the wall was too difficult to make with her stiff fingers, so Mrs. Leadbeater had helped out. The prize, a scrapbook with a page of pictures of film stars, was presented by Mr. Carlton. When her name was called out as the winner, Molly could've died with embarrassment at the very idea of walking down to the front in view of the whole congregation, but then the thought of owning the scrapbook spurred her on.

Molly nodded. "Yes. I felt bad cracking Mr. Humpty's head, though."

"It's only an egg." Frieda laughed.

Frieda had become a good friend to the twins, especially as

she understood what it was like to be an evacuee and have a home elsewhere that she might never see again.

In the early days of their friendship, Sandra had warned the twins, when Frieda was out of earshot, "It's best to avoid asking questions about her family as it may upset her. As you know she's had no word since she left Germany at the beginning of the war and she gets sad sometimes, though she doesn't show it."

The twins understood because if anyone inquired where they were evacuated from and then added, "You'll be pleased when the war's over and you can get home to be with your family," the words hurt like a stabbing pain.

A little frown riddled Frieda's brow. "Did Jacob decorate an egg? I didn't see one."

"His cracked when it got boiled in the pan and Mr. Bob said he couldn't spare another one."

"Where is Jacob today?"

"Playing cricket on the village green with his friends."

"It is good to be outdoors in the sunshine." A faraway look came into Frieda's eyes. "I wonder if Kurt ever dares go out from his hiding place in the cellar to feel the sunshine? I hope not, but knowing him, he will."

In the silence, a look of surprise crossed her face as if she hadn't intended to speak out loud.

Even though the sun was warm on her back, a shiver ran down Molly's spine.

"How old is Kurt?" she blurted, without thinking.

"He was nine when I last saw him." Silent for a moment, Frieda's eyes grew wide as if she calculated his age and was surprised. "He's fourteen now."

It struck Molly, as she looked beyond the farm and over the road to where gangs of Land Girls worked in the fields, that soon she would be nine, the same age as Kurt when he jumped ship. She couldn't imagine doing anything so brave.

She knew Granny's cautions—*be careful you don't slip and break a leg; it's too dangerous to go on a swing when you can't hold on and you might fall and crack your head*—were because she feared Molly would get hurt. But the warnings had only helped make her afraid and prevented her from trying new things.

She was tired of being scared. Besides, being anxious didn't keep you safe—bad things still happened even when you took care. Look what had happened to Granny and to Mam.

Mam always said Molly could do anything if she put her mind to it, and from now on, she resolved, she'd take Mam's advice. She couldn't rely on Jacob to fight her battles forever—it was time she changed her ways.

Molly snapped out of her reverie, noticing that Sandra was making big eyes at her, and she realized she mustn't ask Frieda any more questions about her family.

"Molly," Sandra said in an over-bright voice, "why don't you help bring the cows into the byre? Mr. Jeffries is off work this afternoon. It's not too far."

It was well-known that Molly wasn't too keen on cows, especially walking among them, as their hindquarters were enormous and she was afraid of their hooves.

Granny's voice of warning came into her head: *Careful, you might get trodden on.* Molly hesitated, but only for a moment.

"Yes, I'd like that. As long as I can bring a stick."

*

It was a Monday when Jacob, standing in the queue at the village store, heard the rumors about the invasion.

There were four people in front of him, and it would take an age before he got served. All he'd been sent for was the weekly ration of eight ounces of sugar as they'd run out at the farmhouse.

Mr. Curtis, his arms folded, stood behind the counter and seemed in no hurry. "I reckon the invasion's this Saturday because the moon along with the tide is exactly right," he told old Mr. Jeffries, in the front of the queue sucking his unlit pipe.

A rather fat lady in a tweed costume and green velvet brimmed hat, who stood behind Mr. Jeffries, piped up. "My hubby is in the National Fire Service and he says there's hardly anyone left as they've all been deployed down south. Apparently, the roads are clogged at times with convoys."

Mr. Curtis tapped the side of his nose and said under his breath, "Watch it, Mrs. Rochester, loose lips and all that."

The lady's face went beetroot red. "Silly man, as if spies would be here in the village store queue."

"You never know, Mrs.," Mr. Jeffries said through clenched teeth as he held onto his pipe, "what them Jerries are up to. Any one of them would give their right arm to know the exact location of the invasion."

Mrs. Rochester bristled. "I'd be grateful if you'd take that filthy pipe out of your mouth when you're addressing me." She pulled back her shoulders and turned to Mr. Curtis. "And I'd be obliged if you'd do your job and serve customers instead of gossiping. Some of us have important council meetings to attend."

Mr. Curtis pulled a "she thinks she's somebody" kind of face at Mr. Jeffries.

"What was it you wanted, Joe?"

Mr. Jeffries, taking the pipe out of his mouth, looked purposefully at the woman behind. "I'll have me week's ration of cheese and tea, please."

As Mr. Curtis weighed two ounces of cheese on the scale and gave the old man a two-ounce packet of loose tea, Jacob found himself wondering what would induce anyone to part with their right arm.

"Anyway, Joe, why do you suck that disgusting pipe all day?" Mr. Curtis asked as he handed over the rations.

"It helps me to give up as baccy is a rare commodity these

days and I can't get any." He gave Mr. Curtis a piercing look. "Even with the village shopkeeper, my mate."

Then, with a sour look at the lady behind, Mr. Jeffries left the shop.

Later, the packet of sugar in his hands, Jacob headed back to the farm, worrying about what he'd heard. If the invasion was imminent then the war would soon be over. What would the twins do then? A pain came in his jaw, and Jacob realized he'd had it clenched ever since he'd left the store.

CHAPTER TWENTY

May 1944

"Molly, are you limping?" Sandra asked late one Saturday afternoon.

They had finished milking, the work for the day was done, and they were readying to go home—or in Sandra's case to the hostel—for tea.

"She always limps," Jacob said, stating the obvious.

"I've noticed too," Frieda put in. "Molly's walking differently. It's more of a hobble, as if her leg hurts."

It did, but Molly wasn't saying. She had painful blisters from her caliper but she didn't want to make a fuss. She was afraid that if she was taken to the hospital to rectify the problem she wouldn't be allowed to return.

She'd overheard Granny once telling a neighbor, as the two of them stood gossiping on the front step and Molly, unbeknown to them, played in the under-the-stairs cupboard along the narrow passageway, "When we first took the bairn to the city hospital to see the specialist, guess what he said?"

"I haven't a clue."

"He only advised that she should be put in a home for cripples. Can you imagine? Just dumping your bairn without a care. That certainly isn't the Moffatt way. I don't know what the man was thinking."

Molly didn't want to imagine. If she went to a home for crip-ples, Jacob wouldn't be allowed to be with her. The fear of hospi-tals and being taken away had never left Molly.

At teatime, Mrs. Leadbeater arrived unexpectedly, and Molly knew the reason why; Frieda had mentioned her leg.

Mrs. Leadbeater had a nasty cold that lasted over a week, so while she stayed off work, Mrs. Teasdale took over the post office. This meant Mrs. Leadbeater didn't get to see Molly to do exercises. And Mr. Bob was too busy helping with lambing these days to help Molly with stretches on a morning. So, it was easy to hide the blisters and Molly had hoped they'd get better by themselves before anyone noticed.

"Let's have a look at that leg of yours. Sit down while I take the caliper off."

Mrs. Leadbeater looked thinner, Molly thought, and peaky, as Granny would say.

With the caliper leaning against the chair, Mrs. Leadbeater, when she saw Molly's bare leg, exclaimed, "Oh, love, how long have you had these blisters for?"

She scowled at the bubbles of skin, filled with clear fluid, which Molly knew from experience would hurt like blazes once they burst.

"A few days," she admitted.

"The blisters have been caused by pressure sores from where the strap on your caliper has rubbed. Have you had them before?"

Molly admitted, "Granny used to take me sometimes to the hospital to have adjustments made."

"Why didn't you say?"

Molly had no intention of explaining. She felt downhearted she was being a bother.

The Mrs. must have noticed because she quickly put in, "It's not your fault. Your limb has probably grown and you need a new caliper fitted."

Molly was delighted the leg had grown, because her other fear was that her disabled leg wouldn't grow like her other one.

"I still don't know why you didn't say you were in pain, though?"

Molly didn't like to say she dreaded a visit to the hospital, so she kept quiet.

"No matter. We'll see what can be done." Mrs. Leadbeater smiled a patient smile that always helped put things right. "By the way, it's time you and Jacob called me something different."

"How d'you mean?"

"'Mrs. Leadbeater' makes me sound like I'm a stranger."

"What should we call you, then?"

"How about you call me Aunty Doris, like Frieda does—but only if the pair of you would like to."

"Oh, yes, please." Molly gave a big smile. Just wait till she told Jacob. Calling the Mrs. "Aunty" sounded like the twins had family, after all.

"That's settled. Now, where did you get the last caliper fitted?"

Remembering the day Granny took her to Edgemoor hospital, Molly's throat tightened and she couldn't speak.

"You're a brave lass and deserve a treat," Granny had told Molly as they had walked out of the hospital entrance, not long before Granny died. "How about a bag of chips from the chippie down by the beach? But we can't go on the sands as there are still rolls of barbed wire in case of a Jerry invasion."

They'd taken the trolleybus down to Ocean Road and bought chips at a white-painted kiosk, then they walked to the park with swans swimming on a lake and they sat on a bench where they could see the bandstand on the rise of a grassy hill. Molly remembered the feeling of security that felt like a hug that she had had sitting beside Granny eating hot, greasy chips from a cone of newspaper.

That had been her last outing with Granny.

"Sorry, love," Aunty Doris's soft voice said, "to press you, but it's important you tell me which hospital it was. Was it the local one in South Shields?"

Molly nodded. "The specialist sent me to see a nice man called Mr. Russell and he fitted me with a caliper."

"That's a tremendous help. I'll have a word with Doctor Shepherd."

At the end of May, sitting on the train as it roared, billowing steam, into South Shields railway station, Molly could feel her heart racing, causing a pain in her chest.

She looked out of the window and imagined Mam that last day, running to keep up with the train, her hair flying, blowing a kiss and waving.

Don't forget to write, she'd mouthed.

Molly blinked hard.

When the train stopped, Mrs. Leadbeater, leading the way, stepped off the train onto the platform, and helped Molly, in her trancelike state, follow.

Aunty peered at the throng of people milling around, mostly men in uniform, some saying goodbye to tearful families.

"When in doubt," said Aunty Doris, "ask a policeman, but typically there are none about when you need one."

She made for the entrance with Molly trailing behind.

"D'you know"—Aunty stood stock still and breathed in deeply—"I can smell the sea air."

Molly smelled it too, the fresh, salty air, the sea gulls swooping overhead making a peculiar *keow keow* cry. She loved the seaside and South Shields smelled like home.

"Could you tell me, please," Aunty asked a stranger, an elderly gentleman who wore spectacles and who, minding his own business, looked startled, "how to get to Edgemoor hospital?"

Following the man's directions, the pair of them walked down the hill to busy Fowler Street, where they caught a trolleybus. The journey around the town that followed took Molly down memory lane. It was when the trolley passed the Regent Cinema, still showing signs of damage from the bombing in May last year when the twins were buried in the rubble, that Molly began to tremble uncontrollably.

Aunty Doris, putting an arm around her shoulders, gave Molly a reassuring hug.

"That's where I used to live." Molly pointed through the window to the bottom end of Perth Street. She glimpsed telling gaps between a row of terraced houses that belched grimy smoke from tall chimney pots, and there wasn't a brick left where the Moffatts' house once stood. Molly couldn't believe that the family had lived out their lives on such a tiny space of land.

The trolleybus made its way up Stanhope Road, past some shops with awnings at the front.

Leaning toward the window and looking out, Aunty announced, "This is our stop." She tinged the bell.

Following the passengers along the aisle, Aunty helped Molly alight from the platform.

As they passed through the gateway, fear of the hospital loomed large in the little girl's mind. Looking up the path to the imposing red brick building ahead, Molly longed for the space and greenery, and the security of Leadburn.

Later, after they'd seen the specialist and Molly had been measured for a new caliper, trailing along the smelly, lengthy hospital corridor to the exit, Aunty Doris declared, apparently to herself, "Typical, all was fine when he asked the questions but he balked when I asked mine. I'm none the wiser than when I went in. And why is it we have to wait so long for a new caliper to be sent?"

All Molly knew was she was relieved the hospital visit was over and she was free to return to the farmhouse. The measurement for the new caliper took an age and the adjustments to her existing caliper, as she lay on the table, hurt her leg.

A harassed-looking Aunty Doris told her, "The man barely spoke but when he did at least he redeemed himself by advising we rub Benzoin on your skin to toughen it up."

"Not if the skin breaks," Molly reminded her.

"Heavens, no. The last thing we want is for you to suffer any more pain."

Aunty, pursing her lips, became thoughtful and Molly hoped that the rant, as Mr. Bob called her outbursts, was over.

It wasn't until they were outside the hospital gateway and in the fresh air that Aunty became herself again.

"I'm sorry, Molly, if I went on in there, but I wanted to find out more about your disability than I already knew." She shrugged. "Maybe the man didn't have the answers and he was too high and mighty to say." She smiled down at Molly. "You've been a very brave girl and deserve a treat."

At the same words Granny had spoken, Molly felt teary, but she blinked hard to stop the tears from falling.

Aunty Doris checked her watch. "I haven't a clue where to go to eat."

She looked into the distance as if she'd spot a café.

Molly said, tentatively, "Granny once took me to the seaside where we ate chips in the park."

"That'll do me fine. I've not been to the sands for years so we'll make the time. There's no hurry to get back." Aunty started walking. "I suggest we go back to the place where we started from. Do you know the way to the beach from there?"

"I think so."

"If not, we'll just follow our noses to the sea. We can't go far wrong."

Molly felt a twinge of misgiving, but Aunty Doris had a twinkle of excitement in her eyes that prevented Molly from saying, *Please could we just go back to the farm and see Jacob, Mr. Bob and Smoky.*

Instead, she followed Aunty toward the bus stop.

Back in Fowler Street once more, Molly pointed along Ocean Road.

"The beach is that way."

Crossing the road, they passed the cinema where Aunty had to stop and read the billboard outside to see what was on.

As they continued walking, Molly began to feel tired. She'd forgotten how far they had to walk to reach the beach and the blister under the strap on her ankle was hurting even though her caliper had been adjusted at the hospital.

There were lots of shops and restaurants on one side of the road but the spacious pavement where they walked was lined with tall and impressive guesthouses. Though they walked slowly, Molly felt the need to stop for a moment to rest. She moved over to one of the guesthouses out of the way of passersby.

Aunty, who'd walked on a little way, read aloud the name of the guesthouse that was displayed on a pane of glass above the front door.

"The Sands. What an apt name."

The building, Molly noticed as she stood at the bottom end of a side street, had a blue and white striped awning which gave a holiday feel and a small front garden that surrounded it all the way round to the side of the house and—

"Ow!"

Someone hurrying down the side street bumped into her and, unbalanced, she nearly toppled over, but with an effort just managed to stay upright.

"Watch where you're going," a man's brusque voice said.

Shocked, Molly looked up into the icy blue eyes of a very tall man.

"Excuse me." Aunty Doris hurried over. She looked up at the gentleman. "It was you who didn't look where you were going and nearly knocked the bairn over." Her lips a thin line, she added, "I think an apology is due."

As the man looked Molly up and down, she noticed his smart gray and white pinstriped suit, then looking down to avoid his eyes she saw his brown leather laced-up shoes that were shiny new.

"Madam, I've no time for this. There's no harm done. Good day to you." With long strides he moved quickly away and, looking both ways, crossed the main road to the other side of the street, then went out of sight amongst a throng of people.

"What a cheek!" Aunty Doris called after him, "Thanks for the apology. I'm glad you care."

A bit embarrassed as passing people stared, Molly told Aunty, "He can't hear."

"I know, love, but it makes me feel a lot better. Now then, are you all right?"

"Yes, thank you. I just got a fright." Molly gave a tight smile, trying to look as if she was fine.

"Look, there's a café. How about we go and get a plate of something to eat. Then, I don't know about you, but I'm ready for home."

CHAPTER TWENTY-ONE

As Edward Fenwick senior strode along Ocean Road, he heard the infernal woman with the crippled child screeching after him, but he didn't hear what she had to say. Not that he cared anyway.

He walked along King Street and over the marketplace, heading for Laygate and home. Edward abhorred using public transport and avoided doing so whenever possible. And motoring in the Humber with this war on was out of the question, even though he did own two garages.

If he'd had sense, he reflected not for the first time, he'd have got rid of the garages as soon as it was evident war was looming. But in those days, when motor cars were for the rich and adventurous, who would have guessed what was ahead. Petrol was the first commodity to be rationed, and worse was to come when, in 1942, the availability of petrol for private use was completely withdrawn. Cars became a rare sight on the roads much to the children's delight, as local streets became their playground. Then, when Edward's son was called up, the haulage side of the business went by the wayside.

He walked for a while lost in thought, then, making his way along Frederick Street and turning into Barton Road, Edward, seeing the shuttered-up building, registered that the garage looked derelict. He made for the side door of the empty showroom and, putting the key in the lock, entered the building and made his way up the stairs. He opened the door to his flat—which had been intended only to be a stepping stone for him and his wife when they first got married all those many years ago but now here he was all alone with only a bottle of whisky to keep him company at night.

Placing the black money bag he was carrying onto the table, Edward removed his coat and hung it over the back of a chair. Moving over to the mahogany cabinet beneath the window, he opened the doors and turned the knob on the wireless. Glen Miller's band playing *A String of Pearls* blared through the mesh grille. Turning down the sound, Edward made his way over to the sideboard and poured himself a whisky before sinking down into the cushions on the couch.

The saving grace that had allowed him to keep up the lifestyle he'd grown accustomed to was the foresight he'd had back when the garages were thriving; he'd bought two run-down properties in Salmon Street off Ocean Road and converted the houses into two up and down flats. Now he managed to live off the rents.

There had been many women over the years ready to take on the role of Mrs. Fenwick. Edward wasn't interested for two reasons: the first was that no one could replace his beloved wife and the second was that he was happy with his way of life, where no demands were put upon him. His fear was, once a woman got her foot in his door, that would be the end of the simple life.

Placing the glass on an occasional table, he undid the laces of his shoes and, easing them off, sank back with his feet up on the couch.

This is the life.

Edward closed his eyes and found himself reliving, in his mind's eye, the altercation this afternoon with a tenant in one of his flats. Though being a landlord had monetary advantages the drawback was the tenants, especially Mr. Reed, who rented a downstairs flat and hadn't paid his rent for three weeks, and neither did he intend to.

The man didn't work, Edward knew, but, as a soldier in the Great War, he'd been injured and he would have a pension.

"I'll not pay a penny until you fix the damp in the scullery. And the floorboards in the kitchen are rotten. I daren't walk on them for fear I go through."

"You pay a pitiful rent," Edward had retorted. "If I start doing major repairs, I'll have no alternative than to increase the rents or else I'll go bankrupt."

You almost are, he told himself.

"Man, what a joke. You charge the highest rent in the area. I'd be gone from this dump if it wasn't for the fact that with the bombings there's no decent property to be had."

"Then stop your whingeing and pay me my rent."

The man, who was wearing only a vest and trousers with braces, had flexed his arm muscles.

As Edward had withdrawn, the man guffawed and slammed the door.

Edward, mortified, had hurried down the street and, trying to regain his composure, he hadn't been paying attention to where he was going. He didn't see the girl but the next thing he knew, he'd bumped into her. The child looked like a waif and he'd realized she was a cripple.

Opening his eyes now, Edward sat up and picked up his glass, gulping some whisky.

If the vulgar women hadn't screeched, Edward might have apologized but, he'd decided, it wasn't worth bothering with that class of person.

At that moment the newsreader's voice on the wireless caught his attention. "Allies at Anzio link up with—"

Edward didn't listen any further. What interested him was news about the invasion, when it would happen and herald the end of this bloody war, so he could start making plans for the business again.

He drained his glass and, stretching, he yawned. Eyelids heavy, and with the voice droning from the wireless in the background, Edward afforded himself the luxury of letting his eyes droop.

Bang.

Bang.

Bang.

The noise woke Edward and with a start he leapt from the couch. Not a bloody raid, not at this stage of the war. The banging didn't stop and Edward's befuddled mind realized someone was banging on the knocker of his front door downstairs.

Padding down the dim stairs, he looked through the peephole and saw Patricia, his daughter-in-law, staring back at him.

My God, her face was a picture of excitement—something Edward had never witnessed before, apart from at the wedding. Patricia's look was usually one of cool resignation in his company, as if she knew he only suffered her presence.

What his son saw in this plain girl Edward couldn't fathom. Tall and willowy thin, with no curves, she wore round glasses which, irritatingly, she kept pushing up her nose, and had mousy brown hair that framed her face to her chin.

"Patricia's intelligent, Dad, and knows her own mind, and we talk nonstop for hours." Edward junior's face had been animated when first he spoke of his girlfriend.

Talk! Edward was flabbergasted. His memory of when he and his wife were courting was one of carnal lust as they couldn't get enough of each other and be damned with the dangers.

"A good conversation, my boy, can be had on the train with a stranger."

"Not the kind of conversations that I have with Patricia." His son's tone was aloof.

Edward wasn't sure if he approved of this new Edward junior who answered back and wasn't afraid to cross his father any more—though part of him was a little impressed.

Edward junior had met Patricia at the tennis club and when he brought her home to meet his father, nothing had prepared Edward for the meeting with his future daughter-in-law. He expected someone upper class, with polished manners and an attire that spoke of money, and who worried about the impression she'd make on her future father-in-law, not this shabby-looking girl who took his breath away with the boldness of her stare.

His son had fussed, chatting about Patricia's so-called attributes; she'd been to university and had now become a teacher. As he prattled on, Edward had looked at his father in that hangdog, wanting-to-please kind of way.

"Edward, it's not an interview, I'm sure your father will make his own mind up about me without your trying to convince him I'm worthy."

"Isn't she wonderful, Dad," his son had said, gazing adoringly at Patricia. "She's never afraid to speak her mind."

Edward declined to answer. He didn't like this young lady's audacity.

Later, when they were alone, Edward had told his son, "Women are out for one thing, security. Patricia is only interested in you because you come from a family of means."

He overlooked the irony of the fact that all those years ago, his own future father-in-law had said the same of him.

Edward junior was furious and surprised his father by standing his ground. "That's outrageous. Patricia is independent and has means of her own."

Edward was gratified his son appeared to have spine, after all.

"That's the cleverness of a certain type of manipulative woman, my boy. They can wrap a gullible soul around their little finger. What happens when she gets pregnant and must leave work? Better by far to meet someone of your own class who—"

"Dad, if I'm lucky enough for Patricia to agree to marry me, I can assure you neither of us will want a penny of your money.

We'll make it on our own. I plan to go back to college and become an accountant."

Edward bit his tongue. He'd hoped his son would see sense and tire of the girl.

Then the war had started and Edward junior had joined up. And he had felt a certain pride when he saw his son in uniform.

But the couple hadn't parted and when they'd finally married in forty-two, he had insisted he pay—wanting to keep in with Patricia because she was to be the mother of his grandchildren— for what was luckily a small wedding.

Now, at the bottom of the stairs, he pulled back the bolt and, opening the door, pasted a smile on his face.

Patricia wore a guarded expression, reinforcing his suspicion that the woman was no fool and could see through him. But whether he liked her or not, Patricia would one day be the bearer of his grandchildren and more than anything he wanted the name of Fenwick to carry on. For what would be the point of building a business, as was the plan, if his son didn't produce an heir.

"Patricia, my dear what a lovely surprise," he said—which her being here was, because he could count on one hand how many times she'd visited over the two years the couple had been married. "Come in, come in."

"No, no. I'm afraid I can't stay, I'm in a hurry to prepare a meal for tonight. That's the reason I'm here—to tell you I've received word from your son. He's got a pass and intends hitching a lift home for the night." Her brow creased into a concerned frown. "Reading between the lines, I suspect like so many of the forces he's to be sent down south."

Edward's stomach lurched. His son was in the Northumberland Fusiliers and his battalion was under the command of Home Forces—where Edward would prefer him to stay.

"Can I see him tonight?" Edward felt his hackles rise at the indignity of having to ask when he could see his own son.

She looked startled. "If you don't mind, I'm planning a special night for just the two of us. Tomorrow, though, early morning would be fine, when I go back to work and before Edward leaves to go back to his battalion."

Of course Edward minded not getting his own way. Then a thought occurred. This might be the only chance in an age when the pair could make a baby together.

Edward beamed. "Of course, dear, I wouldn't dream of interfering. Tomorrow, first thing, will do me fine."

They said their goodbyes and, closing the door and padding up the stairs to prepare a lonely meal of corned beef and fried potatoes, Edward's mind working overtime, he was surprised to find that he felt envious of the young couple.

CHAPTER TWENTY-TWO

June 1944

"Bye, Aunty Doris," Frieda called as she left the upstairs flat to go to work.

"Ta-ra," Doris called back. "Tell Molly I've had no word from the hospital yet about her caliper."

"I will."

The downstairs door slammed and Doris started putting the breakfast dishes away. Frieda only ever had porridge but at least she polished the lot off in the bowl now. She'd maintained her weight for some time and thank God the problem of her refusing to eat at all was a thing of the past. Doris still lived on a knife edge worrying in case the same thing happened again. Doris was convinced the carry-on was something to do with Frieda's nerves. But who wouldn't be living in hell, with all the rumors circulating about what was happening to Jews in those labor camps in Germany. The certain knowledge her loved ones were detained there must terrify her. And the lass agonized over her brother because there'd been no word since that one letter. The worry over family had taken its toll and Doris knew Frieda was suffering, though she'd never admit it.

The wireless on in the background, Doris folded the blue and white checked tablecloth and, placing it in a drawer, looked up at the wall clock.

Time to open the post office.

Downstairs, as she unlocked the door, Doris peered out of the pane of glass at the blue skies of a new day, and for no reason at all, the hairs on her neck stood up.

Later that morning, when Doris was about to serve the next customer, Peggy Teasdale burst though the doorway and interrupted, an intense look on her face.

She said, "It's begun. It's been on the news."

"What has?"

"The invasion. The allies have landed on the Normandy beaches."

A collective gasp went up from the queue and Doris clutched her chest.

A feeling of hope for the future tinged with anxiety overwhelmed her, with the thought, *what are our lads going through over there?*

"Where is Normandy?" one of the customers wanted to know.

Doris delved into a drawer and brought out a map she kept for this kind of thing. Spreading the map on the counter, she pored over it. She pointed with a forefinger. "There's Normandy on the northern coast of France."

"Pin the map on the door so everyone can see," Peggy told her.

"Have you got anyone over there?" was the general question followed by sighs of commiseration for those that had. Doris couldn't bear to think of the boys who'd end up as casualties.

All she craved, as she served behind the counter, was to rush upstairs and listen to the news for herself.

At one o'clock sharp, she shut up shop and, hurrying upstairs, switched on the wireless in the kitchen.

"This is the BBC Home Service. Here is a special bulletin read by John Snagge. D-Day has come."

As she listened, a surge of happiness mingled with relief

rushed through Doris and, tears rolling down her cheeks, she was glad no one was here to witness her weakness.

Then, a desire to share this massive news with someone overwhelmed her and the one person who came to mind was, surprisingly, Bob Nichol.

*

Mr. Bob wasn't in when Molly and Jacob arrived home early from school. This wasn't a surprise; these days he was always doing jobs around the farm and organizing the gangs of Land Girls in the fields, because he'd given the foreman the sack.

Molly remembered that it was Aunty Doris who had brought things to a head one night after she'd massaged and stretched her ankle.

Aunty had moved over to where Mr. Bob sat, minding his own business, in his chair, reading the newspaper, and had declared, folding her arms, "You want your hammers, Bob Nichol, letting that lazy good-for-nothing foreman of yours get away with murder."

Mr. Bob, looking startled, dropped the newspaper on his lap. "How d'you make that out?"

"According to Frieda he never shows up early enough for milking and he's no help with the churns. Some folks are canceling their milk order and taking their business elsewhere." Aunty's vexed face looked scary. "Furthermore, Sandra says Jessie, the forewoman at the hostel, is never informed how many Land Girls to send to the farm and the gangs are never organized."

Mr. Bob, open-mouthed, looked perplexed. "I didn't realize I—"

"Then it's time you did if you don't want to lose this farm, as it's fast going to wrack and ruin."

Molly, stroking Smoky on her knee, wished they'd stop arguing as her tummy was hurting.

"It's time you stopped wallowing in your troubles and got on with your life."

Mr. Bob, his face purple, leapt from the chair. The two adults glared at one another.

Mr. Bob made a dive for the door, and without changing into his wellies or taking Tyne with him, he banged the door as he left the farmhouse.

Aunty Doris stared after him, looking upset. She shook her head, "Sometimes," she murmured as if to herself, "you have to be cruel to be kind."

Nothing, as far as Molly knew, had been said since, but every morning after that Mr. Bob, Tyne at his heels, left the farmhouse early to run the farm.

Now, as the twins stood in the farmhouse kitchen Molly told her brother, "I didn't want to leave school early, did you?"

"No, the news was too exciting. Especially when Mr. Reeves showed us the map and put little pin flags where the invasion was taking place." Jacob's eyes were shining. "And I wanted to hear more about the landing craft, and about the RAF planes that had been in the first attack."

Molly thought of Alf and wondered if he'd be taking part in the invasion in his airplane. She hoped not.

"I wish I knew what was going on. I feel left out," Jacob said.

Molly felt the same way too. "We could put the wireless on."

So that's what they did, but Jacob soon got bored as there was only a Music and Movement program for schools on the BBC. He went outside to fly his cardboard model airplane instead. It was a warm day, and he left the door open. Molly could hear him making exploding noises as the plane, zooming in the air, dropped pretend bombs that landed in the garden.

When Mr. Bob came home at teatime, he and the twins shared their news as they sat around the table eating sausages made from the farm's pig.

"A treat for the occasion," Mr. Bob told them.

The door opened and Aunty Doris appeared, a big smile on her face, waving a Union Jack flag on a stick.

"Everyone in the village has chalked V's on their front doors." Aunty's eyes sparkled.

"What does that mean?" Molly wanted to know.

"Victory," Jacob told her. "Even a dunce knows that."

Molly was too happy to do what she normally did when her brother got cocky—kick him under the table with her good leg.

Later, the windows open to let fresh air in, Aunty Doris told them what folk were saying in the post office.

"According to Mr. Jeffries the landings will have taken the Germans by surprise because they'd been fooled into thinking the invasion would take place at Calais, wherever that is. Peggy Teasdale said thousands of allied troops landed on the beaches in Normandy at the outset…"

As Aunty continued to talk, Mr. Bob went quiet.

"What's wrong, Bob?"

"I'm thinking of all those brave boys." He let out a heavy sigh. "Many of them won't be coming back."

Aunty nodded toward the twins. "Don't take the shine off the day for them."

"I disagree, it's right and proper they should understand the sacrifice."

Aunty nodded.

Molly knew Mr. Bob was thinking of Wilf, and she understood something of what he was going though, because she too had lost someone she loved in the war. As she thought of Mam and Granny, overwhelming sadness tugged at Molly's heart.

That evening, they gathered around the wireless to hear the King's speech.

"Four years ago, our Nation and Empire stood alone against an overwhelming enemy, with our backs to the wall."

As the voice came through the grille, Molly was awestruck that she was actually listening to His Majesty the King. But she didn't understand most of the speech and when the King said, "I hope that throughout the present crisis of the liberation of Europe there may be offered up earnest, continuous and widespread prayer," she asked Aunty what that meant.

"That we all pray, love, to get us through this difficult time."

Molly nodded. She'd do as the King asked when she prayed at bedtime.

"Such a stirring speech," Aunty Doris said, a hand over her heart, when the broadcast finished.

"Does the invasion mean that the war will be over tomorrow?"

Molly hoped so because it was the twins' birthday at the weekend—but she tussled with her feelings about that. Though it was the twins' special day (as Mam called it) and she was excited to be a year older, Molly didn't know if she could bear celebrating without Mam. It was the same last year, just after Granny died; the twins were too shocked and sad even to think about their birthday. They were living with Bessie and she surprised them by saving up her coupons to make them a birthday cake. Mam gave them some silver coins and told them they could spend it on anything they wanted. And when the twins blew out the homemade candles, made from gas tapers, with the end sharpened to make a wick, Mam's eyes had shone with love and pride.

Bittersweet memories of birthdays past crowded Molly's mind as she remembered when the family were all together.

Then, as she tuned in to the present, it occurred to her that the grown-ups mightn't even know it was nearly the twins' birthday and it would be rude and embarrassing to tell them.

"No, love." Aunty shook her head. "I'm afraid we're quite a way off from that happening but it is the beginning of the end."

Mr. Bob turned off the wireless. "Mark my words, Hitler won't take this lying down. We're for it now."

"I'm sick and tired of war," Mrs. Curtis from the store announced one Saturday morning as she stood behind Molly in the post office queue. "The thought of going through another winter with blackouts is too unbearable."

Molly had been up at the farm helping to collect eggs when Frieda had collared her. "Aunty Doris says to tell you your new caliper has arrived in the post from the hospital."

Though the Benzoin the doctor had recommend to toughen her skin had worked, Molly still had some discomfort with the leather straps. So, leaving the egg hunting to Frieda, she'd limped her way slowly all the way to the post office.

Aunty told Mrs. Curtis, "Shame on you, Jenny, when you've got the luxury of knowing that Hitler's new weapon isn't going to blow you to kingdom come."

Mrs. Curtis looked shamefaced. "You're right, poor souls in London. What have I got to complain about? I wouldn't wish them doodlebugs on me worst enemy."

Aunty smiled at Molly. "Your caliper's in a box and it's a big parcel. I'll bring it up to the farmhouse in my dinner hour and we'll have a try at putting it on then."

Molly eyed the large parcel wrapped in brown paper on the counter, and nodded.

"Pity it didn't arrive the day of your birthday for an extra present." Aunty winked and smiled.

Despite Molly's doubts the grown-ups had known about the twins' birthday.

Aunty had explained at the time, "I have a form that has your birthdate on it."

The tea table had been set with crockery when they came

home from school; Molly, who'd felt lonely and missed Mam throughout the day, had felt her spirits lift.

When Mr. Bob came home, he told the twins, "We're to wait for Doris to arrive after work before we have tea."

Further surprises happened when Aunty came in followed by Denise and her brother Ronnie, bearing gifts of a homemade card and sixpence for each of the twins.

From the pantry Mr. Bob brought out egg sandwiches, tarts filled with plum jam, a blancmange, a wobbly jelly and four bottles of lemonade and a birthday cake, with candles made from gas tapers cut into four.

Remembering the candles on last year's cake, a twinge of both homesickness and sorrow had washed over Molly. Looking at Jacob's solemn face, she knew he was experiencing the same feelings.

"You can't be missing out on a party on your birthday." Aunty Doris beamed. "It was Bob's idea to invite your friends."

"But you saw to all the food," Mr. Bob said as he marveled at the food on the table. "There must be a week's rations here." He turned to the twins. "Doris and Frieda brought it up to the farm when you left for school this morning."

Watching Mr. Bob as he carried two fireside chairs to the table, Aunty chipped in, "Oh, and by the way. Frieda and Sandra send happy birthday wishes. They're working late or they would have called in."

Overwhelmed by such thoughtfulness, happiness had radiated through Molly and, her throat tightening, she struggled not to cry.

"Oh, thank you," she simply said.

"Thank you from me too." Jacob's eyes drawn to the table, Molly knew he was impatient to start on the food.

Afterward, the children played pin the tail on the donkey and musical chairs accompanied by music played on the wireless.

When it was time for Denise and Ronnie to leave, clutching birthday cake wrapped in a homemade serviette in their hands,

Molly's eyes went glassy with tears. And as the twins watched their friends go, Molly slipped her hand into Jacob's. They exchanged a look that said they'd had a good time and felt part of a family again.

"My Denise said she had a grand time at the party." Mrs. Curtis's voice broke into Molly's thoughts. "Apparently, Ronnie scoffed his fair share of the food. I swear that lad would eat till he burst if he got the chance." At the thought of her grandson, she gave a fond smile.

Remembering the earlier conversation, Molly asked, "What's a doodlebug?"

Aunty told her, "I had a traveler in the other day trying to flog his goods and he said the doodlebug's like a plane but it has no pilot." She looked furtively around the post office. "Rumor has it that London is the main target by the enemy for the new weapon. The man reckoned between twenty and a hundred are launched every day on London."

Mrs. Curtis butted in. "People talk about it more now but the newspapers and wireless only refer to recent attacks." She rolled her eyes. "Tell that to Londoners who've put up with the deaths and devastation from the infernal weapons for the past few weeks."

"Poor souls." Aunty shook her head. "Their nerves must be shattered. All these years of war and they're still getting it in the neck."

Molly couldn't believe what she was hearing. Despite what Aunty had said, she had thought the invasion had ended the war.

She moved from the counter and Mrs. Curtis took her place. "I hear tell that folk are leaving London in their droves."

"Who can blame them, but you know what that means?"

Mrs. Curtis pulled a questioning face.

"More evacuees to contend with."

CHAPTER TWENTY-THREE

July 1944

"The reaper and binder is amazing," Jacob told his sister the first night he returned home after watching the harvesting of corn in the fields. "If you could see how it worked, the gadgets, levers, wheels and cogs, you'd want to watch it working all day."

Even if she did have the stamina to follow this reaper and binder around the field, Molly knew she wouldn't want to as it wasn't her idea of fun. She'd rather play dolls with Denise.

Molly loved gazing at the waist-high fields of golden corn, swaying in the breeze. Then when the workers came—prisoners of war, voluntary labor clubs, Land Army gangs—to help harvest the corn, it was sad because the corn was reduced to stubble.

"It helps to feed the nation," Mr. Bob, ruffling her hair, told her.

These days, Mr. Bob was hardly ever at home. Aunty Doris too, as billeting officer, was kept busy with the arrival of evacuees from down south. Jacob was in his element following the horse-drawn reaper and binder around the fields all day. And so Molly was left by herself for a lot of the time.

"It cuts the corn and binds it into sheaves…" Jacob was telling her.

Molly didn't have a clue what her brother was talking about but tried to look interested. Then, looking down at the state of his legs, she was dismayed. They were red and scratched and looked very sore.

"What's caused that?" she said, concerned.

"The stubble from the corn after it's been cut."

"Is it painful?"

"No, just itchy," he said, looking down at the scratches.

"You won't be going back."

"Yes, I will. I've got an important job." His chest expanded. "When the Land Girls' water bottles are empty, I've to run to the tap in the yard and fill them."

"My job's important too," Molly told him huffily. Molly helped the women from the village feed the workers, and though she couldn't carry trays or heavy teapots, she could spread margarine on bread and make dozens of sandwiches, and she felt she was doing her bit.

Molly liked the routine of her days, though she was lonely at times. After the workers' afternoon break, when all the doorstep tomato (which were plentiful at this time of year) sandwiches and scones were eaten, dishes washed, the kitchen spick and span, Molly would hang up her apron, and, rather than be on her own, she liked to go and watch the workers in the field and help with menial tasks wherever she could.

With all the fresh air and good food, she'd put on weight, her hair had become glossy, and her cheeks had grown pink from the sun. The new caliper was more comfortable, and Molly found she could walk better than ever.

Life for Molly had become settled, and she lived in the moment, trying to forget her concerns about the future.

One night, when they were all home and listening to the nine o'clock news, Aunty Doris arrived, looking harassed and tired.

"What are you doing out so late?" Mr. Bob asked.

"Frieda's out with Sandra and I felt like a bit of fresh air."

Mr. Bob fetched her a dining chair and set it in front of the range beside his.

"What a life. I had another lot of evacuees arrive yesterday and there's been the usual outcry of no room at the inn." She shook her head. "Of course, there's room for them now that the army's left. Only some folk just don't want to let on they've got the space." She heaved a weary sigh. "I know you can get rough kiddies, but they're children, after all, and to be cared for in times of war. Poor things, they'd had a long train ride and were exhausted when they arrived, some tearful."

"Where did they sleep?" Molly wanted to know.

"Thank goodness the WVS ladies turned up to lend a hand. We fed them and gave them blankets and they slept on the village hall floor, but d'you know what? The queer thing was because of the flying bombs, they were so used to going into the shelter they didn't undress for the night." She turned to Mr. Bob. "Can you imagine what those kiddies must have gone through at home?"

"So, did you get them fixed up?" he asked.

"I certainly did. Though I was reluctant, I used my powers of coercion. It did the trick."

Molly didn't know what the word "coercion" meant but assumed Mr. Bob did as he nodded.

"If it happens again the twins could double up and we'd have room here for another evacuee."

Molly felt herself squirm. She wouldn't mind sharing with Jacob again, but she thought of this as her home and had quite forgotten she was just an evacuee like the rest.

"Bob, you're doing enough by keeping the nation fed and by billeting the twins."

There it was again, the reminder that this wasn't Molly's home.

Aunty went on, "The other side of the coin is the evacuees can be wary of their billeted family and consider them either too posh or snobby and they can't settle in." She shrugged. "Sometimes, you just can't win."

"The main thing is, you try." Mr. Bob put his hand over hers and smiled. "How about I make you a cuppa?"

Later that night when Molly was lying in bed in the dark, Smoky, beside her on top of the sheet, stood up and stretched. Molly felt the cat pawing the sheet as she usually did when she wanted something. At times like this when Molly was sleepy, she wished the cat could talk to say what she wanted instead of having a guessing game.

Molly giggled at the thought of what Smoky might say.

Jumping from the bed, Smoky could be heard meowing at the bedroom door.

"You should have decided you wanted out before you followed me upstairs to bed."

Molly sat up and felt on the locker top for the torch Mr. Bob had given her. By the beam of light, she limped over the floorboards and, opening the door, followed Smoky, tail sailing upright in the air, to the top of the staircase. Molly held onto the banister rail and made it down the stairs, intending to let the cat out by the back door.

Moving along the passageway, Molly heard voices from the kitchen. Mr. Bob and Aunty Doris were still in the kitchen talking. Molly didn't mean to eavesdrop, but hearing the serious tone of Aunty's voice and the word "evacuees," she couldn't help herself.

"...Yes, Bob, I agree but let's hope the evacuees have a home to go back to." Aunty's voice was hushed and Molly had to strain to hear.

"It makes you wonder what kind of world we'll be living in then." Mr. Bob's voice.

"A chaotic one I have no doubt, what with house shortages, austerity and goodness knows what else. What is certain is it won't go back to the world of 1939 when this all started, like some folk expect. And think of all those who have lost loved ones."

There was a long silence.

"What about the twins?"

Molly stiffened.

"What about them?"

"Did you ever inquire about an orphanage?" Mr. Bob asked.

A cold shock wave surged through Molly.

"I did inquire about the one in their hometown but it was bombed earlier in the war. I hasten to add all the orphans had been evacuated to the country beforehand," Aunty Doris replied.

"What about orphanages around these parts, Stockbridge and Carlisle?"

"Carlisle's full to capacity. I don't know about Stockbridge."

"Doris, I'm not blaming the poor mother, but wouldn't you think, especially with the war on, she would've made some kind of arrangement for the twins if anything happened to her?"

Aunty Doris replied but Molly didn't catch what she said.

"Surely the twins have some relatives that could take them in. What about the father's side? Do you know anything about him, Doris?"

"Only that he died."

Molly put her hand over her mouth to make sure her gasps of dismay wouldn't give her away.

"The mam must have had friends who she confided in. Maybe if we seek out neighbors where the family lived, someone might know something that could help."

"For a man who says he doesn't want to get involved, you certainly try and help a lot, Bob." Aunty yawned. "I suggest we leave things as they are. There's time enough when the war's over and by all accounts that shouldn't be long. Do you agree?"

"Aye. Fine by me. Besides, there's no other option. Those two need a home and by gum, I'll find them one."

Molly didn't wait to hear any more. Laboriously, she climbed back up the flight of stairs, the meowing Smoky following.

"I can't let you out as they'll hear," she hissed at the cat as she made her way to her brother's bedroom.

*

"Jacob, are you awake?" Molly's voice came from the doorway.

"Yes."

The beam of light from her torch spotlighted him.

Molly came closer, then sat on the edge of his bed.

"Is something wrong, Molly?"

He was startled when she burst into tears. "Mr. Bob doesn't want us living with him any more."

"What d'you mean he doesn't want us?" Jacob felt angry that Molly had been upset like this.

"It's true, he asked Aunty Doris about orphanages because he wants us to live in one."

Between sobs, Molly told him about what she'd heard in the passageway. She finished by saying, "He's waiting till the war's finished, then we'll be sent to an orphanage."

Jacob, feeling himself go weak, didn't know how to answer.

Now that Miss Crow had left and Mr. Reeves was his teacher, life had changed and Jacob liked going to school. He didn't feel as if everyone was against him. He'd made friends with the village boys and played cricket with them on the village green. He was used to living here where he knew everyone, and the farm with all the machinery and living in the countryside was where Jacob wanted to be—now that he couldn't go home.

"Why doesn't Mr. Bob want us?"

"I don't know, Jacob. Maybe he just put up with us because there was nowhere else for us to live like those other evacuees."

Jacob felt so upset about Mr. Bob. He'd thought he genuinely cared for them, after all they'd been through together. Then, a flash of anger took hold. So what if Mr. Bob didn't want them. He didn't care. It would be up to him to find somewhere for Molly and him to live.

Molly sniffed hard. "Jacob, on our birthday Aunty and Mr. Bob made us feel special and I felt we belonged here."

"I know, I felt the same. Like we were family."

"Now"—Molly's voice squeaked—"Mr. Bob wants to put us away in an orphanage. Why, Jacob? We must've done something wrong."

Jacob thought hard but couldn't see how. He reminded himself he was a Cub Scout and the motto was to "Be Prepared." An idea formed in his mind.

"We could run away, Molly, and hide in that old stone ruin we saw the day we went to the pool."

His mind warming to the idea, he imagined the life the twins could lead. Him fetching wood for a fire and catching rabbits to eat, and—

"Where would we wash?" Molly's voice broke into his thoughts.

"In the stream."

"It would be dark at night?"

"We've got torches."

"Jacob, I don't think I like your idea. Me and Smoky don't want to live without taps and where there's no people or shops."

Jacob's shoulders sagged as he realized Molly would find living in a ruin on uneven ground difficult. He needed to find a more practical solution.

Molly's face was ghostly white in the torch light as she told him, "But if you think we should live in that tumbly-down building, I'll be brave and come too. It'll be better than an orphanage. I'll live anywhere as long as it's with you."

As he wracked his brains, Jacob was only half-listening, but he perked up when Molly said, "Mr. Bob said Mam should've made some kind of arrangement in case anything happened to her."

As Jacob thought of the scene at the railway station with Mam, he remembered the letter hidden in his bedroom.

Find a grown-up, Jacob, that you trust and give the letter to them.

"Molly, I've thought of something."

Her face looked up at him, pitifully hopeful.

You're a sensible boy, Jacob, you'll know when real trouble happens.

CHAPTER TWENTY-FOUR

August 1944

Molly stood in the queue at the village store, and, as usual, the topic of conversation was when the war would finish.

"I reckon the ceasefire will be sometime next week," Mr. Curtis told the waiting queue as he poured sugar into a blue bag.

"Nonsense," a lady at the front, whose shining brown hair was fashioned in a victory roll hairstyle, remarked, "it's sure to be sometime at the end of October."

There were a lot of *Hear, hear*'s from others in the queue.

"But the allies have captured and liberated Paris." Mr. Curtis weighed the bag of sugar on the scales, then handed it to the lady. "You can't tell me it's not going to be long now."

"All I know is," Mrs. Curtis, wearing a white overall and standing next to her husband behind the counter, remarked, "it's a good sign that most of the fireguard duties have ended and we can now have dimmed lights."

"Aye, but it's not the same for the poor buggers on the coast," the lady told them as she put the sugar into the wicker basket she was carrying. "They aren't allowed a dim out."

There were tuts of disgust at such bad language.

Molly tuned the chatter out, and scoured the shelves to see if she could see any tins of sardines or Palmolive soap she'd been sent for.

Two ladies behind were talking in loud voices. "Did you see

the announcement in the local paper about the curate and that Land Girl who works up at Bob Nichol's farm?"

Molly leaned forward and looked along the queue to see the two ladies who spoke. One of them, a skinny lady with a pointed nose and chin, reminded her of the Wicked Witch of the West.

The other lady, wearing a long coat and felt hat, even though it was a warm summer's day, replied, "You mean the lass who helps deliver the milk? Mind you, not that I get mine from Mr. Nichol any more."

"That's the one."

"What about them?"

The queue went quiet as everyone listened in.

"Hurry up and say," a man's voice shouted, "don't keep us all in suspenders."

Everyone laughed, Molly too, as she knew the man was making a joke.

The witch lady pursed her lips then continued in a quieter voice and Molly had to strain to hear, "They've only gone and got engaged."

"They never have. There's been no sign of anything going on."

"It said in the announcements by his parents they were proud to announce the engagement of Mr. Matthew Carlton and Miss Sandra Hudson and so forth."

At that moment the till rattled and Mr. Curtis's voice asked, "What can I help you with, bonny lass?"

"A tin of sardines and Palmolive soap, please."

Molly couldn't wait for tomorrow to see if Sandra wore an engagement ring.

"It's a diamond, tiny but adorable." Sandra held out her left hand.

"It's beautiful." Molly couldn't take her eyes off the ring.

Sunday school was over, and she and Jacob had stayed behind.

Sandra went on, "We thought now was the right time with

the end of the war in sight." She gave a sad smile. "Only I wish Alf was here to see the ring."

"He was here when you properly got engaged, though, when there was just us."

"You're right, Molly, and that's what counts." Sandra gave her a warm smile.

Jacob, head bent mutinously, kicked the wooden floor with the toe of his shoe. He hated mush, Molly knew, while she could gaze at the sparkly ring forever.

"Why didn't Mr. Carlton give you the ring before?" he asked.

"Because when we found out Alf was coming to visit, we didn't have time to go shopping."

Jacob took a yo-yo out of his pocket and wound the string around it. "I'm going to play outside."

Molly knew her brother was bored with the goings on.

"Are you coming?" he asked her.

Sandra turned toward him and gave him an apologetic smile. "I'd like a word with Molly, if that's all right with you?"

Jacob nodded and left the church hall.

Sandra tucked her hair behind her ears. "Molly, I've something very important to ask."

Molly was worried. She didn't like it when grown-ups used this serious tone.

Sandra took her by surprise by giving a girlish giggle. "How would you like to be my bridesmaid when I get married?"

A warm feeling radiated in Molly's chest. She beamed. "Oh, yes please! Will I get to wear a pretty dress?"

"You certainly will. Yellow is the color I'd like for you. I've asked Frieda and she's agreed to be my bridesmaid too."

"But what about—" Molly gazed down at her caliper.

"If it worries you, we'll get a long dress."

Bubbles of happiness bounced in Molly's tummy. Then a thought struck, and the bubbles burst.

"Will you be getting married now or after the war?"

Sandra looked puzzled, as if it was a strange thing to ask.

"I expect after the war as it'll be finishing soon. I'd rather like a Christmas wedding, but Mr. Carlton will be too busy and..."

As Sandra continued to talk, Molly's spirits deflated and she struggled to stop the tears threatening to spill.

If the wedding was after the war, Molly and her brother mightn't be here by then.

*

Jacob was practicing walk the dog to fill in the time while he waited outside for Molly.

He flung the yo-yo from his hand down to the ground and the taut string, like a lead, pulled the yo-yo along the ground. He should've been elated because this was the first time he'd mastered the trick, but instead Jacob felt nervy and jumpy.

Jacob thought about the letter Mam had given him. Why hadn't he opened it and seen for himself what it said? He immediately felt guilty. He couldn't let Mam down. She'd been strict in saying he shouldn't read it himself, but give it to someone he trusted.

But who? Though he liked them, it didn't feel right to ask Sandra or Frieda. Mr. Bob wasn't to be trusted; he'd have the twins live in an orphanage.

He wished Mam was here, but that was silly because then he wouldn't need anyone to read the letter. As the idea to open the letter himself got stronger, Jacob was firm. He wanted to please Mam.

Jacob remembered the curate telling him by the pool that memories of a loved one were precious and no one could take them away. Jacob smiled as he remembered Mam.

As he put the yo-yo away into his pocket he looked up at the heavens. The day had an end of summer feel and the gray clouds, hovering low in the sky, threatened rain.

Jacob closed his eyes.

If I'm supposed to give the letter to someone, how do I know who, Mam?

He opened his eyes and it was as if Mam had given him the answer.

Someone I feel close to.

Jacob smiled. There was only one person it could be.

*

Molly came out of the church hall to find a mist had settled over the village and fine rain was in the air. Jacob stood stock still in front of a gravestone looking as if he was intently reading it.

Though Molly was excited about being a bridesmaid, the thought of her not living here by the time the wedding happened made her have that frightening feeling, like she couldn't breathe properly, again.

"Guess what Sandra wanted—" she began, but Jacob, jumping back, startled her.

"What a fright you gave me. You shouldn't creep up like that."

"I wasn't creeping. Anyway, what were you doing?"

"Thinking hard."

She was just about to tell him her news, when Jacob surprised her by saying, "I've got a secret to tell you."

"What secret?" Molly couldn't help feeling cross; she didn't think Jacob kept secrets from her. "What kind of secret?"

"Something Mam gave me to keep."

This made things worse as Mam knew the secret too.

"I didn't tell you, Molly, because you know how you sometime blab when you don't mean to..."

"So, what is it?" She couldn't disguise the huffiness in her voice.

"A letter."

As the fine rain soaked the twins through, Jacob told his sister what had happened the day they left Mam at South Shields railway station, and the instructions she'd given him.

"Why didn't Mam tell me about the letter?" Molly felt hurt and left out.

"I guess she thought it best only one of us knew. She always kept us equal even when she made chips. Remember how we all used to count them on the plate?"

Molly did and, as she laughed at the memory, her lenient heart forgave Mam. Deep inside she knew whatever Mam did was for a good reason; she always looked out for Molly and loved both twins equally.

"Molly Moo, we love you," Jacob chanted.

Rain dripping down her face like teardrops, Molly laughed, but then she frowned and asked her brother, "But who can we give the letter to? Who do you trust?"

*

They sat in their pajamas on Molly's bed with Smoky between them, their wet clothes slung over a chair and a towel over each of their shoulders.

Jacob slid from the bed and went into his bedroom and, opening the wardrobe door, he felt on the top shelf for the letter. Mr. Bob never came into his bedroom so there had been no need to hide it.

He took the envelope to Molly, who sat waiting.

"And you've never peeked to see what's inside?" She looked astonished.

Normally, if Jacob was told "you can't," it brought the bad out in him—Mam's words—and made him more determined to do whatever it was.

"It's in your nature, son." Mam had looked pityingly at him. "Like father like son. You're just like your dad. He had a defiant streak too."

At the time, Jacob had stared blankly at Mam because sometimes once they started to complain, grown-ups forgot to stop.

Climbing on the bed beside Molly, the letter in his hand, he told her, "You know when Mam looked concerned because she wanted us to do something?"

Molly looked at him with brown pondering eyes. "You mean like the time I refused to wear my caliper because it hurt my ankle too much and Mam said it was for my own good, so I could walk properly one day."

"Yes. That was the kind of look Mam had that day when she told me never to open the letter. She trusted me, Molly, and when she died I could never..." His voice wobbled.

Jacob didn't trust himself to talk for a bit. Molly too looked weepy. Brushing his achy eyes, he showed Molly the letter in his hand and they both looked at Mam's handwriting.

To whoever it may concern.

"Jacob. Who are you going to give the letter to?"

"Aunty Doris."

Molly nodded solemnly. "I'd choose the same. Or, if Aunty Brigit was here and hadn't gone to live with her daughter, I'd be killed for choice."

They both looked at each other as Molly used Mam's phrase.

"Let's ask her tonight." Molly, Jacob could see, was excited at the prospect.

"No. I don't want Mr. Bob to be there."

"I agree." Molly looked sad. "I liked Mr. Bob. Maybe he just wants to live on his own now that his family have all died."

"Molly, you always try to make excuses for people. Mr. Bob has let us down." Jacob copied the phrase Mr. Reeves always used at school when a pupil did something wrong.

"When shall we ask Aunty Doris, then?" Molly asked.

"Tomorrow. We could go to the post office in her dinner hour."

*

Doris was sliding the bolt into place in the post office door when the twins appeared and looked through the pane of glass.

Jacob held up an envelope.

"I'm closed," Doris mouthed. "Come back after dinner."

They'd had all morning to post their letter, she reasoned. Then a stab of guilt poked her for not letting the kiddies in.

Pleeease, Molly mouthed, and who could deny those pleading brown eyes.

Doris pulled back the bolt.

"Couldn't a stamp wait till after dinner?" she grumbled as they bundled in. She opened the lid to the counter and walked in.

"We don't want a stamp . . . we want you to read a letter."

Doris looked at Molly's intent expression in bewilderment. "Why me? You can both read."

Jacob piped up, "It's a letter from Mam. She left it the last time we saw her. She told me I had to give it to someone I trust."

Doris's blood ran cold. "What nonsense is this?"

If they were adults, she'd swear they were either crackers or drunk.

"It's true." Molly, surprisingly, gave a decisive nod. "Mam gave Jacob a letter at the train station when we left. He's to give it to someone when we're in trouble."

"What kind of trouble?"

"Mam said I was sensible and would know when the time came."

Doris was alarmed. "So, what kind of trouble are you in?"

The twins shared a look and pressed their lips together. It was obvious they weren't going to say.

Doris had never heard the like. Then it dawned on her. Of course! Contrary to what she and Bob had thought, Mrs. Moffatt had probably made a will and left instructions for the twins in case of her demise.

"Give it here." She held out her hand.

She slit the envelope open with a miniature ornamental sword she kept behind the counter. Conscious of the twins watching her, she pulled out the single sheet of paper.

As was her wont these days, Doris held the letter at arm's length to read it to herself.

To whoever reads this,

Firstly, thank you, I'm so very grateful the twins have found a friend they can trust. Whatever kind of trouble they are in please contact me at the address below. (It's the accommodation for staff members at the munitions factory where I work.)

If this isn't possible, I can only assume one thing—that I didn't survive.

If that is the case, there's so much I'd like to say but for reasons I can't explain here I'll make this letter short and to the point.

A lump lodged in her throat and Doris paused. This was a woman after her own heart, she thought; she was a no-nonsense, plain speaker.

I've no worldly goods as we lost them when the bomb demolished our home. And no finances apart from the weekly wage that I earn. The point of this letter is the question of who will raise the twins and, on that matter, I will have to reveal the truth of the past.

I am an unmarried mother and their father is not who they think—he isn't dead as the twins believe. This was a fabrication to make them happy. Wrong, I know; I was planning on telling them the truth when they were older and more able to understand. Their father is Edward Fenwick and he can be contacted at the address over the page.

Please seek him out and inform him about the twins.
My prayer is that he will behave honorably as their father
and reunite with them, or at least have the decency to pro-
vide for them in some way.

    Lastly, please do your best for my beloved twins and tell
them the facts with kindness in your heart.

Yours sincerely,
Martha Moffatt

Doris didn't dare look up as she was aware the twins were looking expectantly at her and she didn't want them to see she was welling up.

Dear God, it must have been heartbreaking for the woman to write such a letter knowing she might never see her precious children again. Doris sniffed hard. She was determined to break the news to the twins in simple terms and as gently as possible. She cleared her throat, and looked at their hopeful faces.

"Why d'you think we keep secrets?" she began.

The twins looked at each other in bafflement.

"So we don't get into trouble," Jacob told her.

Dear Lord, instead of helping, Doris was making things worse.

She improvised, "If I keep a secret, it's either because I'm not ready for people to know or, if I tell it might hurt someone."

"Like when you're not invited to a birthday party and everyone else is and someone tells you," Molly chipped in.

Doris's heart went out to the little girl.

"Yes, Molly. That's one good reason. It's unkind to tell that person, isn't it, as it will only make them unhappy?"

She nodded.

Jacob was fidgeting and Doris knew he was getting impatient.

"So, this is what this letter's about. A secret your mother kept." Doris felt the atmosphere tense. "She couldn't tell you because she thought you were too young and she was protecting you from being hurt. It was important to her you knew this secret and so this is why she left this letter."

"What secret?" Doris detected a look of caution in Jacob's eyes.

"It's best I read the part of the letter that tells you."

Doris held the letter at arm's length again, and peering at it, she found the right place.

She read out loud, *"Their father is not who they think—he isn't dead as the twins believe. This was a fabrication to make them happy. Wrong, I know; I was planning on telling them the truth when they were older and more able to understand. Their father is Edward Fenwick and he can be contacted at the address over the page."*

She looked up at the two perplexed faces.

"You see, it says here that you have a daddy and he didn't die after all, and we've to contact him."

The twins stared at her.

"Why couldn't she say before?" Jacob asked.

Doris decided they would have to know one day. "Normally, ladies who have babies are married and people can be unkind to both the lady and her children if they aren't. Your mother kept the secret to protect you."

"Why didn't this other dad marry Mam?" Molly asked, a bewildered expression on her face.

"You only have one dad, Molly, and he is Edward Fenwick." Doris knew her words hadn't sunk in and that she'd have to be patient. She decided to be as truthful as she could. "And he left before you were born."

"I don't like this Edward." Molly's eyes looked darker than usual, then Doris realized her pupils were dilated. Poor love, the bairn was probably in shock.

"Why did he leave?"

"I don't know, Jacob. Your mam didn't give a reason."

Doris was careful not to elaborate as she didn't want to color their impression of Edward Fenwick or give them false hope.

"Listen carefully, both of you. Your mam was very brave and must have loved you so very much to bring you up on her own."

"And Granny," Molly prompted.

Doris smiled. "Of course."

Jacob's face contorted in puzzlement as he thought of something.

"Why does Mam want us to find this Edward now?"

This was the bit Doris found tricky. Had she done the right thing, telling the twins about their real dad? Or, should she have waited until she'd contacted him to see his reaction? The twins need never have known if he'd rejected them again. But it was Mrs. Moffatt's express wish that the twins should know about their real father.

"Maybe we could live with him," Molly told her brother. "We wouldn't be put in an orphanage then and—"

A swift shake of her brother's head made the little girl put her hand over her mouth as if she'd said something she shouldn't.

This was moving too fast for Doris's liking. "Let's just wait and see what happens," she told them.

"He might have other children." Jacob looked as if he hoped this wasn't true.

"Why would he when he left us? Did he know he had twins?" Molly's face was a picture of confusion.

Because the man was a cad and probably married and ditched the poor woman, was Doris's thought, but she wouldn't burden them with her imaginings.

"We don't know anything about him. All we know is your mam wanted us to try and find him."

Doris thought her heart would break when she saw their little faces look pathetically pleased at the mention that this was their mam's idea.

"How will we know where our—this Edward lives." Jacob wore a guarded look.

"Your mam provided his address on the back of the letter."

"Where does he live?"

"South Shields."

Molly drew a sharp intake of breath. "He lived beside us all this time and we never knew."

Doris didn't want to be drawn into that particular conversation. "I'll write to him and see if he still lives at the same address."

"Will he write back straight away d'you think?" Molly asked.

"Let's just wait and see, shall we."

Part of Doris hoped she wouldn't succeed in finding the scoundrel as she couldn't bear the twins to have any more sorrow in their lives. But you never knew, maybe this sorry affair could have a happy ending.

It wasn't until Doris braved the rain later that night and made her way up to the farmhouse that a thought struck her. Molly had spoken about being put in an orphanage. Doris was convinced neither she nor Bob had mentioned an orphanage in the twins' hearing, but you never knew when they might be in earshot. Doris used to sit beneath the table when she was little and hear her parents have all kinds of conversations that were too grown-up for her innocent ears.

Maybe that's what had happened with the twins. It was just the other night that she and Bob had discussed orphanages. Had the twins overheard? Was this what had made Jacob decide to share the letter with her?

When Doris reached the farmhouse, the twins were in bed as Doris had planned. Sitting in front of the range, she told Bob, "I'm not sure I should be telling you this, but I can't do this on my own and I need someone I trust to talk it over with."

"Why, what's happened?" Bob looked concerned.

Doris explained about the letter.

A slow smile spread over Bob's face. "That's champion news. Let's hope the man is worthy of the twins and will give them the home they deserve." He sat back in his chair and thought for a moment. "But what made the lad think he was in trouble enough to give you the letter?"

"That was my very thought, Bob. I've an idea that one, or both of them overheard us talking about orphanages and they're afraid they'll be sent to one."

"It's too late to worry about that now. It's what happens next that counts."

"Poor loves, they're terrified of being separated."

"We'll make sure that doesn't happen." Bob's voice was gruff with emotion.

He stood and went over to the dresser and, opening a drawer, brought out paper and a fountain pen. He put them on the table and pulled out a dining chair and gestured with his head for Doris to sit.

"You'll be better than me putting the words on the page," he said.

Doris walked over to the table. "What am I going to say?" As she sat, Bob pushed the chair in. He was such a gentleman, she thought.

"We'll think of something. The man has to face up to his responsibilities."

Their eyes met and lingered, and Doris saw something deep in Bob's eyes. She felt herself blush and dropped her gaze.

As she picked up the pen, Doris hoped, for all their sakes, that this Edward Fenwick would turn out a decent sort—but she had grave misgivings.

CHAPTER TWENTY-FIVE

October 1944

Mr. Bob was removing his yellow waterproof as Jacob turned up at the side door. They both hurried indoors.

Aunty Doris stood at the range, stirring a pan of something that smelled deliciously like vegetable soup. Jacob's tummy rumbled. He looked with a hopeful expression at Molly, who sat doing her weaving at the kitchen table.

She looked up and shook her head to tell him that no post had arrived.

Aunty Doris had sent the letter to the Mr.—Jacob didn't know what to call this new dad and decided to call him the Mr.—and the twins had expected him to reply immediately. That was wishful thinking Jacob realized now, as days, then weeks passed. There were lots of reasons why he mightn't have been in touch, including that he was a spy and away on an important mission and he'd be thrilled when he returned home to discover he had a son who would definitely follow in his footsteps one day. Deep down, Jacob knew he was fabricating the truth because he was sorely disappointed and trying to make himself feel better. In reality, he was worried that the Mr. couldn't care less that he had a son.

Aunty was here at the farmhouse temporarily cooking for the volunteer workers in the fields who helped with potato picking. Mrs. Teasdale was running the post office because she was at a loose end.

Jacob overheard Aunty tell Mr. Bob, "Peggy's son, Bobby, is never in the house these days. She offered her services so I can help out here. I would swear the woman has her eye on the post office—given the chance."

"Where is Bobby?"

"He's in the Scouts and they're doing a marvelous job supporting official war work, apparently."

Jacob went to sit beside Molly at the table. She had a mini loom made of cardboard that she was able to hold in her stiff-fingered hand. Taking up a needle threaded with yarn, she went under and over the tape fixed to the cardboard and ended up with a colorful square that could be used as a hand protector for picking up hot pans and kettles.

Aunty Brigit had sent the kit along with a letter to Aunty Doris telling her to start Molly off weaving as it would help with fine motor skills.

"Brigit calls it a pincer grip," Aunty Doris told the twins.

The image that came into Jacob's mind was a crab with sharp pincers and he had no idea what that had to do with Molly's hands. She'd fumbled with the loom at first and wanted to give up, but he gave her credit for sticking with it; now her hands worked fast and she was proud of the squares when they were finished.

Mr. Bob went to stand in front of the range fire. His hair, sopping wet, fell over his brow.

"I could do without this rain. I've never known such a low yield of taties. Some of the volunteer workers have done a bunk." He let out a burdened sigh. "What with rain-sodden skies, ankle-deep mud and back ache added into the bargain, who can blame them?" Lines etching his face, Mr. Bob's eyes looked droopy with tiredness. He rubbed his eyes with his hands. "Have you heard about them V2 rockets?"

Aunty looked up at him. "I've heard mention of them in the post office."

"One of the farmhands was on about them. He says it's reported the bombs are that fast you don't hear them coming. Then, with a loud *whumph* the rocket crashes and explodes without warning and anyone it lands on is a goner."

Jacob wanted to know more but he saw Aunty Doris stiffen. She pointed with a wooden spoon at Mr. Bob and nodded toward the twins. "For Pete's sake, we don't need to hear about weapons of terror."

"You can't hide from the facts, Doris."

Aunty shook her head as if she disagreed and continued stirring the soup. "Sit down, Bob, and have a yourself a hot cup of tea."

"I can't, I've just come in to collect the telephone number for the ministry offices in Hexham. I need more hands to help pick these taties. I've asked for more Land Girls but I doubt there's any to spare."

Jacob thought of the Cub Scout Law, to always do your best, think of others before yourself, and do a good turn every day.

"Can I lend a hand to pick potatoes?" he asked.

Though he'd lost faith in Mr. Bob, Jacob reckoned he wouldn't be helping him but for the war effort.

Besides, he wanted to fill in time as the rainy weather meant he couldn't play out. All he thought about when he was bored stuck in the house was when the letter would arrive from the Mr.

Mr. Bob looked at Aunty Doris. "It won't do any harm."

Aunty pointed the spoon at him. "Neither of you is leaving this house until you've had a hot bowl of soup."

*

The next morning, when Molly drew the bedroom blackout curtains back, she was pleased to see the rain had stopped. She didn't want to spend another Sunday in the house thinking about why the Mr. hadn't been in touch yet.

She decided to go up to the farm and give Sandra a woven square for the cook at the hostel because she'd be handling hot pan handles and would need a hand protector.

It was a blustery day and the tops of trees rocked back and forth. Molly, head bent against the wind, made her way up to the byre.

"Hello, Molly, what brings you out on such a windy day?" Frieda greeted her.

The stalls were empty, Molly noticed and Frieda, wearing blue dungarees, was shoveling muck and urine from the channel running in front of the stalls and piling it into a wheelbarrow.

Molly tried in vain to ignore the stench and it took a big effort not to hold her nose.

"I've been making these." She brought one of the squares from her mackintosh pocket. "I brought one for Sandra to give to the cook at the hostel. It'll help stop her hand getting burnt. It's a—"

"I know what it is."

Molly was surprised how sharply Frieda had spoken and, as she leaned on her shovel, it seemed she couldn't take her eyes off the woven square.

"Where's Sandra?" Molly asked for something to say.

"Helping with the potato harvest." Frieda, still gazing at the square, looked miles away in thought. "Papa had one of those in the bakery. Mama made it for him." Frieda looked up and, her eyes focusing, she told Molly, "Papa ran a bakery business at home in Berlin."

It seemed to Molly for a moment that the world stood still as they stared at one another, both of them surprised Frieda had spoken about her family.

"I can't remember if the square was woven or not." It seemed very important to Frieda that she did remember and she looked upset. All of a sudden, tears leaked from her eyes.

Molly didn't know what to say or do. She sympathized with

Frieda, waiting for important news too—only she'd been waiting for a much longer time.

These days, all Molly could think about was their dad, what he looked like and if he had a Geordie accent and would he ever get in touch. She wished she could speak to Jacob about him but somehow talking to her brother these days was difficult as he seemed edgy all the time.

Although Sandra had warned Molly that she shouldn't mention Frieda's family, she wondered if that was the right thing to do. All she knew was if nobody ever asked about Mam or Granny, she'd be upset.

She took the plunge. "Did your papa own the bakery business?"

Frieda looked at her with sad eyes. Molly felt bad and wished she'd kept quiet.

Then Frieda wiped her eyes with the back of both hands and began to speak. She told of the baker's shop below the apartment where they lived and how her papa went around the neighborhood with a horse and cart delivering his goods. She spoke of her mama, how she made clothes and ran the house, and her grandma, who lived in with them and liked to think she was boss but everyone knew it was Mama who ruled the house. Then Kurt, who was stubborn, and his mama despaired because he was always getting into trouble.

"He sounds just like Jacob," Molly butted in.

Frieda shook her head and smiled. "Brothers, eh!"

"If Jacob and me got parted I wouldn't be as brave as you are." It was easy to talk to Frieda now.

"At first I was very scared but Aunty Doris helped."

Molly thought about telling Frieda about Aunty Doris helping the twins and how they were waiting for a letter from their dad, but then decided now was not the right time.

Instead she said, "I hope you get another letter soon from your brother."

Frieda shook her head. "Molly, I've never told this to anyone, but I believe my family may not have survived the camps. That is why it is good to talk with you about them. In my mind I like to think of them in the apartment above the bakery shop in Berlin, Mamma, Papa, Grandma and Kurt. And though I miss them every day I'm fortunate to have a home here with Aunty Doris."

Molly felt sorry for Frieda but understood what she meant; she felt the same way about Mam, imagining her working at the factory. But though Molly had a home for now, it wouldn't be for long. If their father didn't come forward and claim them soon, it would be too late, and Molly couldn't bear the thought of what might happen then.

CHAPTER TWENTY-SIX

Edward Fenwick senior, a glass of whisky in his hand, relaxed in his chair after a Saturday morning at the golf club. The torrential rain had stopped these past couple of days and conditions had been dry enough to play golf. He'd phoned Teddy Finchley from the garage showroom downstairs and organized a game.

Edward grunted in displeasure at the memory of his ball going into the crater, the result of bombers being dispatched to Berlin last December. Poor beggars, it was said that twenty-nine planes were shot down over Jerry territory and foggy weather on their return caused twenty-one of the others to crash in Britain. One poor blighter lost his life when his bomber ran out of fuel and, though the crew bailed out, the pilot in the Lancaster nosedived and crashed into the ninth hole of Edward's golf club—hence the bloody big hole that cost Edward the match.

Even though, as the club rules permitted, he was allowed to pick the ball out of the crater without penalty, the interruption cost him his concentration and put him off his stroke. He kept damn well missing the hole.

He leaned back his head on the plush cushioned chair and, jaw clenched, saw in his mind's eye the smirk on Finchley's face when his ball ran smoothly over the green, down the hole and he'd won the match. Blast him.

Edward sat up and took another swig out of the crystal glass. He was lucky he could play golf at all, he reminded himself. Part of the course had been closed at the beginning of the war to save on labor and other costs, but the War Agricultural Committee hadn't served notice to plow up the remaining nine holes for food production and furthermore the clubhouse hadn't been requisitioned for military training as it was near the coast.

His frustration at losing to Finchley still rankled and made Edward edgy. Good thing Penelope, his latest girlfriend, wasn't here or else he'd pick an argument; then, as usual, she'd frustrate him by imagining it was something she'd done and she'd be sugary nice to him. He gave a lascivious grin; making up afterward would be worth it.

Times like this, he sorely missed his wife. She had fire in her belly and could match in him in any quarrel. He gave a long drawn-out groan. He'd never find a love like that, nor would he want to; he was too set in his ways, though he did get lonely at times.

He drained his glass.

The thought that gnawed at the back of his mind came to plague him again and he knew that this was the source of his frustration, why he couldn't settle.

That damn letter that came all those weeks ago that he'd tried to push to the back of his mind but didn't succeed as the words kept coming back to plague him.

Mrs. D. Leadbeater,
The Post Office,
Leadburn,
Northumberland

Dear Mr. Fenwick, you don't know me and I suspect this will come as a great surprise (if not a shock!) but there is no other way to tell you than be forthright with the truth.

I am led to believe that you knew a certain Martha Moffatt. I'm sorry to inform you that Martha unfortunately died in an accident at a munitions factory where she worked.

Edward had paused. This did come as a shock. Memories of Martha came flooding back, from the time before the war when the garage was booming and life looked promising.

He read on.

Martha got pregnant and went on to have twins, a girl and boy called Molly and Jacob. After the bombing last year, the twins were evacuated to Leadburn in Northumberland where they live at present. Martha gave Jacob a letter. An insurance, I suspect, for their future in case anything happened to her. Jacob has recently given me the letter.

This letter explains that Edward Fenwick is the father of the twins. I quote, "Their father is Edward Fenwick and he can be contacted at the address over the page. Please seek him out and inform him about the twins. My prayer is that he will behave honorably as their father and reunite with them, or at least have the decency to provide for them in some way. Lastly, please do your best for my beloved twins and tell them the facts with kindness in your heart."

This Leadbeater woman went on to say, Mr. Fenwick, I leave you to decide what is to be done, but the thing is, the twins, with no other family that I know of, are without a home after the war is done. I would urge that you take responsibility for them.

Your faithful servant,
Doris Leadbeater

Ever since he had opened the letter, Edward had been in a quandary. He wanted someone to carry on the Fenwick name, but the responsibility lay with his son and his wife to have a child within the family and not some waif born out of wedlock. But it nagged at Edward that this boy, Jacob, had Fenwick blood running through his veins.

Though he'd deliberated long and hard, Edward still couldn't decide what was to be done. One thing he knew: soft-hearted Edward junior must never know about the letter. The bottom line was to tell this interfering woman that it was a case of mistaken identity, but Edward had to be certain that this was the best course of action. The alternative was for him to send money to the busybody, then dismiss the problem from his mind. No one, especially his son, need know. The problem with this decision was that Edward had no money to spare.

Deciding against another drink, as it would make him sleepy for the rest of the afternoon, Edward realized he was hungry. He hadn't stayed for a tot of whisky at the clubhouse with Finchley as it would entail listening to the man bragging about his four grandchildren. The man liked nothing better than to get in a dig, reminding Edward how unfortunate it was he wasn't a grandfather. It was hardly worth drinking at the club these days as the stewardess stuck strictly to the rules and provided only one stingy glass per week for members.

Edward had hoped that when his son had had a night pass months ago before he was sent down south, the young Fenwicks would have spent it wisely (his estimation of wise) and that an announcement of a grandchild would have followed. As the weeks passed and he heard nothing from Patricia, that hope faded. He was beginning to feel concerned now that she couldn't provide a much-wanted grandchild.

Moving to the store cupboard, he opened the door and stared at the sparsely filled shelf. Beans—no, they gave him wind. Sardines; he couldn't face those aga—

The phone began to ring.

Edward left what he was doing and hurried down the staircase and, going into the office, he picked up the black receiver from its cradle.

"Hello."

"Edward, Patricia here."

A sliver of irritation ran through Edward. For God's sake, why did she insist on calling him by his first name? It was disrespectful in one so young. He was her father-in-law—why didn't she just call him Dad?

"Patricia, my dear, how lovely to hear from you."

"I've just rung to see if you're in. I need to come over and see you."

"It'll be a pleasure to—"

"I'll be there shortly."

Click.

Edward didn't know what to think. Her rudeness appalled him. Patricia was never one to chit-chat with him, but she might at least give a semblance of being polite. He wished he'd had the foresight to tell her not to bother coming but curiosity got the better of him.

An inkling of an idea surfaced in his brain and Edward felt a tingle of excitement run through him.

Could it be that she was pregnant? Maybe that's why he hadn't seen her. But the time had come when she couldn't avoid telling him because she must be . . . Edward calculated; it was five months since his son was home. Patricia, thin as a rake, possibly wouldn't have shown at first, but now, with only four short months to go, it would be obvious she was expecting and she'd feel duty bound to tell Edward, who, after all, was the grandfather. By golly, that's it! Wait till he told Finchley he was going to have a grandchild.

Climbing the stairs, the broadest grin split Edward's face and made his cheeks ache. He'd boil a kettle and make a pot of tea and bring out the block of Cadbury's chocolate he kept for a special occasion. Patricia was his favorite person at the moment and it would pay him to be civil.

The kettle whistling on a low gas, a quarter of the block of chocolate snapped into small pieces on a plate waiting on the occasional table, Edward sat on the couch, drumming his fingertips together as he waited impatiently for Patricia arrive.

Bang.

Bang.

The sound of the doorknocker echoed up the staircase.

Edward bounded down the stairs and opened the door.

"Patricia, poppet, what a lovely surprise I got when you call—" He took in her puffy eyes, ashen face. "Come in, whatever's the matter?"

Surreptitiously, he let his gaze drop to her abdomen and though she wore a camel coat, he could tell there was no sign of a baby bump.

She'd lost the baby. Disappointment flooded Edward and he felt himself slump.

Ushering her up the stairs, thoughts whizzed through Edward's mind. All his hopes and dreams of the past half hour were not to be; he couldn't bear it. And no gloating to Finchley. But there was hope for the future. Edward clung on to the thought. Patricia could get pregnant after all. That ray of hope was enough to help Edward cope with the situation.

He led the way into the living room. "Here, let me take your coat. I'll make us a—"

"Edward it's best if you sit down. I've had news about your son. Please, Edward, prepare yourself for a shock."

He couldn't take her words in at first.

He met her reddening eyes, and a shiver of fear crawling down his spine told Edward that life for him would never be the same again.

"Is he..." He couldn't say the words.

Patricia opened the catch of the black handbag she was carrying and, rifling in it, she brought out a telegram.

Edward sank down onto the couch. He felt sick.

She took the sheet of paper out of the envelope and handed it to him. "Read for yourself." Her voice hoarse with emotion, he saw compassion in her eyes. In that moment Edward understood more what his son saw in Patricia.

His hands shaking, he began to read.

We regret to inform you that your husband Corporal Edward Fenwick was killed in action...

A sob escaped Edward and he couldn't read any more for tears blurred his vision.

How long he sat in a stunned state of misery and pain he couldn't tell but when his mind focused and he took in the surroundings, he realized the kettle had stopped whistling.

Patricia appeared with a cup in her hand. "I've sweetened the tea and I suggest you drink it."

Still wearing her coat, she handed the cup to him.

"Aren't you having one?"

She shook her head. "I'm awash with tea."

It seemed strange, but the mundane was what they needed to cope with the situation as anything more serious might tip them into a display of anguish—which neither of them wanted.

Edward knew that the person they needed right now wasn't each other.

"When did you receive—?" He handed her the telegram.

"Early this morning. I came as soon as I was able to." Patricia swallowed hard as she put the telegram back in her handbag and struggled to hold herself together. "I wanted to tell you in person."

"I'm grateful."

Edward couldn't stand this polite conversation; all he wanted to do was scream blasphemy at the gods for allowing this to happen. His only son dying in some foreign land.

"You don't have to stay."

A flicker of relief crossed her chalky white, distressed face. "If you're sure?"

He asked, "Is there someone…"

"My parents are staying with me. And you?"

He nodded, not trusting himself to speak.

She gave a lingering look at Edward junior's picture on the sideboard as she passed.

The volume of unspoken words like a brick wall between them, the parting was awkward.

Again, she swallowed hard and blinked rapidly as if trying to stop a waterfall of tears threatening to fall.

"Stay where you are, I'll see myself out." She moved toward the door, then, her hand on the doorknob, she turned. "There'll never be anyone like him," she said in a wobbly voice, then she was gone.

Left alone, the silence hemming him in, Edward couldn't believe that just a short while ago he had been brim-full of hope and happiness for the future. Now he had nothing. How could life be so cruel.

The enormity of his son being killed hit him in the chest like a golf ball; Edward felt he couldn't breathe and felt panicky. He'd told Patricia there was someone he could share his grief with but the truth was there was no one. Patricia might come around for a time, more out of guilt than any real desire to see Edward, then a new life would beckon and their paths would never cross again.

A rage inside made him pace the room like a tiger wanting out of its cage. Edward didn't know what to do. He moved to the kitchen, where he threw the sweet, lukewarm tea down the sink. Moving to the sideboard, he poured himself a stiff drink from the decanter. He drank it in three gulps, then poured another.

He looked over to the mantelpiece, to the photo of his late wife, young and devastatingly pretty, with their son as a toddler on her knee.

The tears came then unbidden, rolling down his cheeks and dripping from his chin. He cried for his son who he'd never see again but mostly Edward wept for himself because of the loneliness to come.

A thought struck and, sniffing hugely, he wiped his nose with the back of his hand.

Glass in his hand, Edward went over to the sideboard where he took the letter from the letter-rack. Picking up his pen, he moved to the table and, sitting in a leather-seated dining chair, he put his glass on the gleaming tabletop.

He thought for but a minute, then began to write.

Dear Mrs. Leadbeater,

Thank you for your correspondence.

I am indebted to you for telling me about Martha Moffatt and deeply saddened to hear of her untimely death. Martha was an employee at the garage I owned; I did know she was pregnant and that it was my child she carried. She left my employment and has never contacted me since and I never knew about the baby's birth. I have worried about the child over the years but thought it wise not to interfere in Martha's life. That she gave birth to twins is delightful news as is the fact that I can change their fate. As the twins' father it is my moral duty to see that they're provided for. We will discuss this matter further when we meet…

Edward leaned back in the chair and cast his mind back to those long-ago days. He'd known from the first Martha was different when he'd interviewed her for a job as typist at the firm. She wasn't cowed or afraid to voice an opinion when Edward made demands upon his staff she didn't agree with. She was bold and had spirit and reminded him of his late wife. Yet, there was an innocence to her, that only youth and ignorance from living a deprived life could bring. There was no doubt in his mind that, given a different station in life with all the advantages that would bring, and with her stunning looks, Martha would have gone places.

Despite the age difference, Edward couldn't help being attracted to her. But the rules of being her boss and the fact she was only half his age told him Martha Moffatt was strictly off limits.

Then one evening, when they had worked late, he had offered to drive her home because of the torrential rain outside. Eyes sparkling, she'd flashed him an eager smile. Edward had known by the time they had arrived at the top of her lane that she was infatuated with him and that he should've opened the door, said "good night" and left it there. But they began talking and got to know one another better.

Martha's energy and exuberance for life affected him and he felt young and vibrant once more, just like the days when he and his wife were courting. So, when Martha told him the age difference between them didn't matter because she loved him, Edward, flattered, had ignored the voice of caution in his head and kissed her. He hadn't meant for the affair to go any further.

On her birthday, Edward had introduced Martha to champagne. They were sitting on the couch in his flat when he presented her with a square, black velvet box. His son was safely out of the way playing poker with friends; they always played cards long into the night and he knew that Edward junior would stay over.

Martha, opening the velvet box, had gasped.

Lips glistening in the soft light of the standard lamp, she told him, "I've never had such a beautiful gift. It looks very expensive. Are you sure?"

That's what he found refreshing about her. Martha was honest to a fault about how she felt, no matter the cost, but maybe that was because of her youth. Life teaches you to be wiser.

In answer he placed the string of pearls around her neck and, closing the fastening, he couldn't resist the curve of her neck and kissed her milky white skin.

Had it been his intention that night to seduce her, Edward wondered now. He remembered her being giggly and adorable as he led the way through to the bedroom. They lay on the bed and, as she unbuttoned his shirt, he saw the wanton look deep in her eyes and the ache of desire overwhelmed him. He took her in his arms and gave her a lingering kiss. There was no doubt she was eager and consenting, and there was no denying Edward's excitement knowing that he would be the first.

The only time he was a cad was when he told the girl he loved her. In truth he did, in a way, but it had never been on the cards that he'd make a go of it with her. Edward admitted he'd felt bad about how he treated Martha but, at the time, it was unthinkable to be linked with scandal. Not only was it bad for business but it was socially unacceptable that he'd a had an affair with a young employee. Edward had his reputation to think of. Besides, his son was infatuated with the girl, Edward knew, and it would have wrecked the fragile relationship between them. Maybe he should have done things differently, Edward considered.

He shifted uneasily. He would make amends now by putting the record straight and abiding by Martha Moffatt's wishes to provide for her offspring. What more could he do?

Feeling better now that he was doing the right thing, Edward poured himself another drink and, heart heavy, relived the pain of losing his son. Tears welled in his eyes. Mother and son would be united, while he had a lifetime of loneliness to contend with.

What if... The solution popped into his mind. It could work. Edward got back to writing the letter.

CHAPTER TWENTY-SEVEN

Early November 1944

"A letter has arrived and I think it's from Edward Fenwick," Aunty told Molly as she came into the farmhouse after school and put her book bag on the fireside chair.

Molly felt her heart rate quicken. She looked toward the dresser where a white envelope was propped up against a black-and-white picture of Mr. Bob's son in uniform.

"Best we leave opening it till Jacob arrives home." Aunty Doris, her expression tentative, hauled the pulley with wet washing on it up to the ceiling with the cord. It was drizzling and too wet to hang the clothes outside.

Molly knew what Aunty said was the correct thing to do but impatience made her cross with her brother for not being home from school too.

"Where is the lad, anyway?" Aunty said. "He's never about when he's needed."

She sounded irritated. Molly decided this wasn't the time to spring her surprise; she'd leave it till later.

"Gone to a friend's house to swap foreign stamps for his collection," Molly said. This was Jacob's new hobby and, though pleased he'd finally made a friend, Molly was ashamed by the stab of envy she experienced. "He won't be long because it gets dark quick."

Later, when Jacob and Mr. Bob arrived home, the four of them assembled around the table.

Mr. Bob eyed the letter in Aunty's hand suspiciously. "Who's going to open it?"

"You can, Bob, if you like."

Molly looked over to where Jacob was sitting and, seeing his vexed expression, she felt nervous and hoped her brother wouldn't cause trouble. He was upset Aunty had told Mr. Bob about their news as he felt it was their secret and he didn't trust Mr. Bob; he hadn't forgiven him for wanting to put the twins in an orphanage.

"Not me. It's not my business," said Mr. Bob.

"I will then." Aunty Doris opened the letter and began to read in her head.

Molly felt her tummy knot.

"Woman! Tell us what it says." Mr. Bob's voice was unusually sharp and Molly understood then that both he and Aunty were anxious, just like her.

"He starts off by thanking me for being in touch and for telling him where you were because he was worried about you." Aunty looked up and smiled. "He was surprised there were two of you because your mam never told him when you were born. And he'll explain everything when we meet up."

When she went back to reading, a little frown furrowed her brow.

She read from the letter, *"As the twins' father it is my moral duty to see that they're provided for."*

"What does that mean?" Mr. Bob interrupted.

"Have patience, Bob, and we'll find out." She scanned the letter. "He goes on to say we'll discuss the matter when we meet." She looked up. "Listen to this bit."

> *"I plan to come to visit Leadburn to meet with the twins and tell you my thoughts on how they are to be brought up…"*

Mr. Bob frowned. "I don't like the sound of the man's tone—"

"Bob, hush." Aunty made big eyes at him and nodded at the twins.

"We don't know anything about the man," Mr. Bob said.

"We know he's their father."

"I want to look him over. When did he say he's coming?"

Aunty scanned the letter. "This Saturday. He says he'll find his way to the post office and meet me there."

At this piece of news, excitement mingled with dread surged through Molly, making her body trembly. She was going to meet her real dad—but what would his reaction be when he met her?

*

Later, when the twins were in bed, Doris sat before the fire, Bob at her side, the newspaper on his lap. Tyne, stretched out with his head on his front paws, watched Smoky, who sat on her haunches beside him, ears pricked as if listening in to what was being said.

Doris told Bob as they both gazed into the fire, "There's been talk in the village over the weekend about the PM's statement in parliament."

"Why?" Bob gave a querulous frown. "What's Churchill said?"

Doris raised her eyebrows. "For someone who daily reads the papers, you're badly informed."

"I've a lot on my mind at the minute." His tone was defensive.

Doris stretched down and absently stroked Smoky's silky fur. "He talked about the V2 rockets which means that now at last the papers can report what's been going on in London."

"I doubt it. It'll be like them V1s, the precise details won't be given." Bob paused as if he was thinking things through. Then he cocked his head. "What else is being said in the village?"

Doris watched as Smoky, disturbed by the stroking, stood up and, stretching, padded off. "Mrs. Teasdale says the war isn't going to be over by Christmas and that they're predicting another six months."

At this piece of news, Bob blew out his cheeks and let out a sigh of disgruntlement.

Doris knew the feeling. Another Christmas of rationing and making do. She continued. "Then, at the WI meeting this week, folk grumbled because the British Legion have asked us to do the poppy-selling this year."

The pair of them lapsed into an unsettling silence, avoiding the main topic of conversation that took precedence in their minds.

When she could abide the quiet no longer, Doris approached the subject. "What's your interpretation of the letter, Bob?"

"Beats me." Bob scowled. "This Edward Fenwick is not a plain talker."

"I agree," she said. "Does he mean providing for the twins in the sense he's going to fork out money or that he's going to give them a home?"

"Who knows?" Bob folded his arms across his chest. "The man doesn't mention if he's married or got a family. In fact, we know nothing about him." His eyes narrowed. "It's my guess he was married and he deserted Martha Moffatt."

Bob was getting worked up, Doris could tell, but she needed to talk this through. "What gets me is, he knew she was pregnant and says he worried about the baby. So, why did the couple part? You could be right about him being married."

Bob tutted in disgust. "Even if the man did think he was interfering, you'd think he'd try and find Martha and his baby... check if they were all right. He could've done it discreetly."

Doris shook her head worriedly. "We'll just have to wait till Saturday and see what he says."

"It doesn't seem right the man just turns up and decides the twins' future." He gave an impatient snort.

"Calm down, Bob. He's the only family we know of, and I for one am grateful he answered, even if I am skeptical. If he does have a wife and other children, this will be difficult for him. He could have just ignored the letter and got on with his life."

"I suppose you're right." Unfolding his arms, he met her eyes. "But I'll hold judgment till I hear what the fella has to say."

There was a drawn-out silence.

The thought that had been bothering Doris came foremost in her mind. "Bob..."

Staring into space, he blinked and focused. "Yes."

"Is it me or have the twins changed toward you?"

"They have." Grimacing, he scratched his jaw. "It's since that business about them overhearing us talk about an orphanage."

"You should have a word with them."

"No, Doris." His tone was sharp. "We don't know what the future holds. Life's taught me that. The twins have to make their own mind up about me. I've given them a home when they needed one. Let's just leave it at that."

There was a pause, as, distractedly, he folded the newspaper and gazed ahead in thought. "Having bairns about has helped change me, though, took my mind off me troubles. But for them I'd still be the morose sod I was before they came." He turned and looked at Doris, an apologetic expression on his face. "Pardon the language."

"You've come on wonders, Bob. I admit I hoped having evacuees would bring you out of yourself." She grinned at him. "God knows, you needed something. Are you going to continue running the farm on your own?"

"I know no other way of life." He shifted in his chair. "I only hope I haven't left it too late, winning folk over and getting the milk business back on track."

"Where there's a will, there's a way, Bob."

He smiled his slow smile and deep in his eyes she saw warmth and affection.

Caught off guard, she babbled, "Now that the harvest's in, it's time I returned to the post office. The last of the workers will be gone this week and you don't need me any more. Besides, I've left Frieda to fend for herself too long. And though I managed to get some done between all the cooking, I've a mountain of village affairs to catch up on."

Doris knew she was gabbling but she felt unsure about how to handle the way Bob was looking at her.

"All I can say, Doris, is thank you, I couldn't have manged harvest time without you."

His broad smile, she noticed, made the lines, carved from his nostrils to his mouth, bunch up his sun-bronzed cheeks.

Flustered, she stood. "It'll be good to get back to the old routine of just Frieda and me."

The smile slipping from Bob's face was replaced by a resigned expression.

*

Meanwhile, upstairs, Jacob sat on Molly's bed.

"I wish we could stay here," Molly said, looking sad.

Jacob knew Molly was nervous about meeting their dad—afraid of his reaction when he first saw her.

He couldn't think of a reply that would comfort her and said simply, "Molly, we can't any more."

She plucked at the woolen blanket on the bed. "I want us to live with our father but we don't know anything about him."

Jacob grimaced in concentration as he searched his mind to make things better. He recalled Mam's letter and how she wanted them to find their father. "He must be nice because Mam liked him enough to make him our dad."

Molly didn't cheer up as Jacob had hoped and, instead, her face clouded with uncertainty.

The twins knew now the facts of how they were born. Denise had told Molly after she'd overheard the big girls talking in the school yard.

Molly had passed on the startling news to her brother. "You have to kiss and hug a lot and then the dad puts a thing inside the mam and they have a baby."

Squirming, Jacob couldn't meet his sister's eyes. "What kind of thing?"

"Denise said some kind of instrument from the doctor's."

It was the kissing and hugging bit that disgusted Jacob.

Again, he tried to convince her even though he was full of doubt himself. "We didn't know Mr. Bob before and he turned out all right...I suppose."

Jacob wished the Mr. had sent a picture because sometimes you could tell what someone was like if you saw their photo. His insides seemed to wobble whenever he thought of the Mr. but he experienced excitement too, though he would never tell his sister.

Molly, appearing a little happier, told him, "Jacob, I've got a surprise. I would've told you earlier, but I forgot because of the letter."

She wore a tantalizing smile like always when she shared a secret.

"What?!"

"This morning before I went to school and before I put my caliper on, I tried to walk and guess what?"

"Just tell me."

"The heel of my left foot nearly reaches the floor and I don't walk right up on tiptoe any more."

"That's such good news, Molly. Wearing your new caliper must be working."

"And the stretches and massage oil that Aunty Brigit sent," Molly said loyally.

"We'll have to write and tell her." He added, "Let's go down and tell Aunty Doris before she leaves."

"She hasn't seen my foot lately; she's been so busy."

As the twins walked along the passageway and entered the kitchen, they saw Mr. Bob, sitting with his shoulders hunched, staring into the fire.

Hearing the twins, he looked over to where they stood in their nightclothes in the doorway.

"Is something the matter?"

"We've got something to tell y—" Molly began but Jacob cut in. "To tell Aunty Doris."

"She's gone," Mr. Bob told them, a sad expression on his face.

The excitement of the next day overshadowed the events taking place in the twins' life.

It was afternoon playtime at school when everyone stopped what they were doing, skipping, playing hopscotch, or simply milling around, and looked up at the plane flying high in the sky, Jacob included.

A shivery cold day, he shaded his eyes from the low winter sun.

"It's one of ours," he shouted, as the plane flew in the distance. "A Halifax bomber—and it's on fire."

As everyone watched, fascinated, no one answered and Jacob was disappointed because his boyish pride liked to show off his knowledge about planes. The memory of that day when he and Mr. Bob had watched the fighter pilots from the local airfield screaming overhead, flitted through his mind. Jacob had been distraught because he'd just found out about Mam's accident. Mr. Bob had seemed kind and such a good sort at the time. But

Jacob had learned a big lesson since that day; he couldn't trust his judgment of grown-ups.

Flames were shooting from the port wing of the plane by now and a plume of smoke trailing from it; it was losing height. Then three white parachutes appeared, like large white umbrellas, and floated downward toward the ground.

"Hurrah," everyone in the yard screamed.

Far in the distance, the plane plummeted downward, then went out of sight, and seconds later a crimson hue lit up the horizon.

In a subdued mood everyone got on with the rest of the day, but there were lots of murmurings, wondering if all the crew had managed to bail out.

Play time over, Jacob traipsed with the others back into school. He wished he could talk over with someone what he'd just seen.

He had an amazing thought. What if being interested in planes was something that had been passed down from…his dad.

Jacob walked jauntily back to the classroom. He couldn't wait till Saturday.

After tea, Aunty Doris arrived unexpectedly and filled them in. "The word is the bomber was on an exercise when an engine caught fire and the pilot went down with the plane." She shook her head slowly side to side, looking sad. "He probably stayed at the controls so the bomber wouldn't crash in a built-up area."

"The brave lad," Mr. Bob commented as he washed his hands under the cold water tap at the sink.

"Life's short," Aunty told him. Their eyes met and a peculiar look passed between them that Jacob didn't understand. "You've got to grab your chance of happiness while you can."

Mr. Bob gave an almost unnoticeable nod and the two grown-ups smiled at one another.

Later that week Jacob heard that the plane had crashed somewhere in the Rookdale area and he wished he had a bicycle so he could go and investigate the wreckage at the weekend.

"But the Mr. is visiting on Saturday," Molly told him when she heard.

"I know but not till the afternoon and I'm not going to hang around till then." Rebellion flared within him. He knew that he'd been feeling that way a lot recently, ever since he'd heard the twins might end up being put in an orphanage.

"Oh, me neither. I've got butterflies already just thinking about it." Her face became grave. "Frieda is helping do the mail for the comforts fund so that Aunty can shut the post office early and be with us when we meet the Mr. I'm going to spend the morning with Sandra."

"Why?"

"Because that bomber crashing during the week set her off worrying about Alf. She hasn't heard from him in a long while."

Jacob felt mean. He was only thinking about himself, and it was just like Molly to think about everyone else.

On Friday at teatime Aunty Doris arrived carrying a Victoria sponge she'd made, in a round tin.

"What's the occasion?" Mr. Bob's eyes savored the cake as it was placed in the middle of the table.

"Molly's success at taking the first steps to walking properly." She chuckled. "One of these days you'll be able to chuck that caliper away."

The twins looked at one another. They knew perfectly well

Aunty Doris was trying to keep their spirits up as tomorrow was a big day.

The next day was cold and misty. Clouds hung over the rooftops, and a light drizzle soaked those villagers foolish enough to venture across their front doorstep.

The post office bell hardly tinkled all morning, enabling Doris and Frieda to pack the few essentials and goodies that were to be mailed by Special Services Mail to men and women serving both at home and abroad.

"That's my lot done." Doris placed a brown paper parcel on top of the rest on the floor.

She checked the time. "One o'clock. Time to shut up shop and have a bite to eat." She turned to Frieda, who sat across the table tying string around her parcel. "There's a bit of corned beef left. I thought I'd make sandwiches for dinner. I suspect Mr. Fenwick will want something to eat."

Doris didn't relish the prospect of being host to the man for dinner but needs must, as they say.

"None for me thanks, Aunty."

Frieda, as she placed her last parcel on the floor, looked up as though sensing she was being gazed upon. "Honestly, Aunty Doris, I'm fine. Remember, I ate the big piece of cake you brought from the farmhouse last night at our tea break and I'm still full."

Doris nodded and smiled. "Of course, love. Silly me, I forgot."

Later, eyeing the plate of sandwiches on the table, Doris, nervy and jittery inside, found she'd lost her appetite.

"I can't stand being idle any longer." She called through to Frieda in her bedroom, "I'm going downstairs to wait for the man."

"Okay, Aunty."

Trooping down the stairs, Doris began to tidy up shelves and drawers. It was as she put pencils in a pot on the counter that she saw, through the shop windowpane, the single decker bus trundle by.

Her heart beat a little faster.

As a rule, Doris didn't suffer from anxiety as her pragmatic mind told her it never did anyone any good. But, as she waited for the man who, at any minute, would appear in the shop doorway—Doris's nerves in a state—she felt sick to her stomach.

For the twins' sake, she hoped this Edward Fenwick was the sort of person the poor lambs deserved after all they'd been through. It didn't matter what he looked like or, indeed, what worldly goods he had; the main thing was if he had a caring spirit.

At that moment the front gate opened and someone walked up the garden path. Doris peered out of the window. The man, tall and elegant looking, wearing a trilby hat, gray, pinstriped suit, crisp shirt and red tie, beneath an open brown overcoat, seemed much too old in his bearing to be the person who Doris expected. He carried in his hand an enormous black umbrella that hid his face.

Doris, unlocking the door, opened it.

Hearing the doorbell tinkle, he looked up and as their eyes met, Doris knew because of the likeness, without a shadow of a doubt, that this was the twins' father. Then she gasped. She also knew she'd seen this man before and where. Of all people! Doris stiffened—it was the insolent man from South Shields that day.

*

Molly was surprised when Mr. Bob went through to the front room and lit the coal fire because everyone knew there was a campaign to save coal and families were only supposed to heat one room.

She sat in the kitchen filling the time by putting scraps into her scrapbook. Then Mr. Bob called, "Come through, the pair of you. He's here."

She heard the front door open and shut, and then voices coming from the front room.

The man, when Molly entered the room, was taking off his hat which dripped water on the mat. He was old like Mr. Bob. Molly was dumbfounded.

He looked around the room and then his gaze fell upon Molly. Looking her up and down, his smile froze and a look of dismay crossed his face.

Mam used to say in instances like this, "It's as if the bairn has some kind of contagious disease."

"This is Molly." Aunty Doris, with her arms crossed, her face like thunder, looked and sounded cross.

"Hello there." The Mr. pulled at the rim of his shirt collar as if it were too tight.

Molly felt herself shrink; his icy blue eyes were those of the stranger who'd bumped into her that day in South Shields. But he didn't seem to recognize her.

Jacob entered the room then. He looked a little flushed and had an eager sparkle in his eye.

"And this," Mr. Bob told the Mr., "is Jacob."

The Mr. relaxed when he saw Jacob, and he gave a broad smile. Placing the umbrella he was carrying and his hat on the arm of a wing-backed chair, he held out his hand.

"Pleased to meet you, young man."

"How about tea?" Mr. Bob raised his eyebrows at Aunty Doris.

The man spoke up. "I've been telling Mrs. Leadbeater, I brought sandwiches for the journey but only drank water. I'd appreciate a cup of tea."

Aunty Doris flounced out of the room. There was an uncomfortable silence while she was gone.

When Aunty returned and gave the Mr. his tea, she sat on the arm of Mr. Bob's chair.

Mr. Bob looked at her in a peculiar way as if he was surprised she was so quiet.

"How was the journey?" he asked.

"Fine."

"Was it raining when you left?"

"No."

There was a long, drawn-out silence. Molly, sitting next to Jacob on the couch, felt awkward and she began to fidget with nerves.

Sitting on the chair opposite Mr. Bob, the Mr. took a sip of tea.

Then he asked, "How about we get down to business?"

While the grown-ups talked, Molly tried to follow what they said but, deflated, she couldn't concentrate. She just knew the Mr. was put off by her disability because he acted like people often did, pretending Molly wasn't there.

"Wow!" Jacob, sitting between the Mr. and her on the couch, made Molly start. "You own a garage."

"Two," the Mr. told him, "and property." He looked at Mr. Bob and Aunty Doris. "After the war I intend to buy a larger property as the flat I own over the showroom has no garden."

"So, you intend to have the twins live with you?" Aunty asked outright, and Molly was all ears now.

"Why . . . of course. As soon as it can be arranged."

"Mr. Fenwick, are you married? Because quite frankly you are older than I expected. Have you any other children?"

"Doris!" Mr. Bob looked perplexed.

"I quite understand." He nodded to Aunty. "And in your position, I'd ask the same thing." The Mr. placed his cup and saucer on the floor before him. "My wife died years ago of cancer. I've lived on my own ever since. I met Martha when she worked for me as a typist and I was smitten by her straight away and she felt the same way. The years between us simply didn't matter." He paused. "You ask if I have any children. My wife and I had a boy, Edward. But"—he gulped and looked sad—"he was killed recently in action."

"Oh, I'm so sorry." Aunty indeed looked upset, and exchanged a glance with Mr. Bob. Molly was sad too because when someone you loved died and you couldn't see them again, it was too terrible.

"Finding out about the twins came as a gift sent from heaven." The Mr. looked at Jacob, who'd been taking everything in. "Soon you'll have a proper home and be back where you belong in South Shields. Would you like that?"

Jacob nodded enthusiastically.

Molly wanted the Mr. to include her too, and, when he didn't, a sick feeling of unworthiness overcame her.

The three grown-ups carried on talking about the war and other topics that didn't interest Molly, wages and what would happen when the war finished and men would come home wanting jobs. Then it was time for the Mr. to go.

As they all stood by the doorway, the Mr. told Mr. Bob, "I'll be in touch in the near future." He ruffled Jacob's hair. "So long, son. See you soon." Then, as if as an afterthought, he added, avoiding looking at Molly, "Bye, dear."

"Jacob, did you like him?" Molly padded over in the darkness and sat on the end of his bed.

Jacob shone the torch on her face. "He's smashing, isn't he? See, it's like I knew it would be, the Mr. turned out nice, after all."

The torch beamed on his face and he pulled a silly, scary expression to make her laugh. It was good to see him happy and Molly wished she felt the same way.

"He wants us to live in a house up somewhere called Cleadon and we'll have a garden and—"

"Don't you want to live in the countryside any more?"

Molly had missed the conversation when the Mr. had talked about Cleadon because she wasn't paying attention; something was troubling her.

"Yes, but maybe Cleadon will be the same as living out in the country if we have a garden. We can't stay here. Mr. Bob doesn't want us any more."

How could she tell Jacob what was bothering her: the fear that neither did the Mr.

*

"So, what did you think? For a start, I got a shock at how old the man was," Doris said, handing Bob a cup of Horlicks, and sitting beside him on the couch. The coal embers, a smoldering red mass, still gave out adequate heat in the chilly room that had a forsaken, mildewy smell.

"About what?"

She shook her head. Bob could be obtuse at times. "The visit, of course."

"Are the twins settled in bed?"

She knew him well enough to know he was still mulling things over and wouldn't make a comment until he was ready. Besides, neither wanted to be overheard by the children.

His hair tousled and a fresh, outdoor smell emanating from him, Doris was struck by how solid and dependable Bob appeared.

"The twins appear to be okay, but with Molly you never know because she's a dark horse and keeps things to herself. Something must be up though because she won't let go of Floppy rabbit. Whereas, Jacob seems quite excited. But then that's him, isn't it, jumping in the deep end without thinking. Once he gets his mind off those darned motorcars, reality might sink in."

"Aye. The lad can be a bit thick-skinned but his heart's in the right place." Bob took a sip of his drink. "Did you get the impression that the fella was acting peculiar with Molly? Distant, like?"

"Funny you should say, but yes, he seemed to favor Jacob." She bit her lip. She was going to tell Bob about the incident in South Shields but decided against it, as that might color Bob's judgment and it was bad enough her being biased. To be fair, the man had probably just been having a bad day. She closed her mind to the voice of reason telling her the man was an oaf and had acted unreasonably.

Bob took another sip of Horlicks and lapsed into preoccupied silence.

It felt relaxing, sitting together comfortably like this, discussing the day's events.

The perfect end to a day.

That's what Jack, her husband, used to say, when he gave her a cuddle as they sat together on the couch listening to the wireless. Doris was long past the stage of welling up whenever she thought of her late husband; in fact it was rare she thought of him these days. She didn't feel guilty because she knew life had to go on and that's what her Jack would've wanted, but she did feel infinitely sad: for herself, because she'd lost the love of her life, and for him, because he was too young to die.

Sitting here comfortably with Bob brought about that feeling again that something was missing in her life. What was it all for? Was she just treading the days till she was no more? Doris didn't want that. She took a sneaky look at Bob's profile. Could she love again?

A thought struck Doris and she involuntarily giggled.

Bob turned toward her. Eyes crinkling, he smiled expectantly. "Come on, then, share the joke."

Doris couldn't. How could she share Peggy Teasdale's idea of how to know if you loved someone?

"If you can wash a man's dirty socks and underpants," Peggy had told her, a knowing look on her face, "count yourself smitten."

"It's nothing, just something someone said once that tickled my funny bone."

Bob nodded and seemed to accept she wasn't going to tell him.

He looked back at the embers in the grate. "What I think is…" Bob's ruddy face looked troubled. "I don't know what to make of the man."

"Edward Fenwick," Doris clarified.

Bob gave her a look that said, who else?

"On the surface he seems plausible enough and I do feel sorry for him, the bloke's had it tough. God knows, losing your wife then a son in this ruddy war is something I wouldn't wish on anyone—"

"But…" Doris hurried him along because she could tell he was getting emotional.

"Gut instinct tells me there's something fishy going on. Did you notice he never said why him and Martha Moffatt separated? Something isn't right."

Doris sat up upright. "I did, Bob. I mean why on earth, if the woman was expecting, would she leave the man she loved. And he professed to have feelings for her. It doesn't make sense. I agree with you. There's something fishy about his story. What are we going to do?"

"There's nothing we can do, love. He's their father."

"Then I hope, for the sake of the twins, we're proved wrong."

CHAPTER TWENTY-EIGHT

December 1944

One Saturday morning as Molly had nothing to do, she wrapped up in a coat, knitted mittens and hat, and made for the byre to watch the milking. She had something on her mind she wanted to ask Sandra.

With Mr. Jeffries sitting in the stall next to the Land Girl, Molly decided to leave asking her question till later.

Sandra, as she sat on a three-legged stool in one of the stalls, told Molly about a rehearsal for a pantomime in the church hall that afternoon.

"What's a pantomime?" Molly asked. She made sure to stand well back from the cherry colored cow's rear end and swishing tail.

"You've never seen one?"

Molly shook her head.

"Golly, it's too difficult to explain. I know, why don't you come and watch?"

Molly gasped, "Can I, really?"

"I'm sure Mrs. Curtis won't mind. Beware, though, she'll probably rope you in to act as one of the village children."

"What does Mrs. Curtis do?"

"Every year the village puts on a pantomime and Mrs. Curtis writes the script." Sandra grasped the cow's udder and squirted milk into a pail. "The proceeds go to the comfort fund and the like."

"Are you in this pantomime?"

"For my sins, yes."

Molly wanted to be brave and this would be the perfect opportunity. Then, thinking it through, she decided that standing on a stage in front of people might be a bit too daring.

Later, as Molly stood in the church hall, the rehearsal over, she clapped enthusiastically. Sandra walked down the stage steps and joined her.

"So, what d'you think of the pantomime?"

Molly told her, "It was a bit silly but very funny and I couldn't stop laughing. The huge giant's feet sticking out of the side stage at the end was very clever."

"Yes, that was an ingenious idea of Mrs. Curtis'. Younger kiddies will think the giant really was there and did fall from the top of the tree."

Sandra, playing Jack in the pantomime, wore knee-length jodhpurs, thick woolen socks, a white blouse, green sleeveless jacket and a peaked hat with a feather. She reminded Molly of Robin Hood in the film *The Adventures of Robin Hood* that Aunty had taken the twins to see at the pictures in Hexham.

With the hall buzzing with villagers all talking at once about the rehearsal, Molly decided that this wasn't the time to ask her question. It was later when everyone had gone home and Sandra, key in hand, was ready to lock up, that Molly approached the subject.

"Sandra."

"Yes."

"Can I ask you something?"

Sandra laughed. "Depends what it is."

"It's about your wedding. Have you decided yet when it is? What if I'm living in South Shields by then?"

The Mr. had written to Aunty Doris telling her that the arrangements for housing the twins was taking much longer than expected but he'd be back in touch as soon as he could tell her more.

That night, when the twins had been making their way up the stairs to bed, they heard Mr. Bob, sitting in the kitchen with Aunty, explode, "What does the fella mean 'housing the twins'? It's not fair keeping us in limbo, not knowing if the twins will be here over Christmas or not."

"Shush, Bob, you'll upset the bairns if they hear," Aunty told him. "The man told us he was looking for a bigger place to live. And houses these days are at a premium with all the bombing."

Molly didn't care if the man never got in touch because she had a bad feeling about the whole thing. She felt excluded and decided it might be her disability that put him off. Molly felt sad as she wanted a daddy to love her as she was, just like Mam and Granny had done.

As Sandra put the key in the church hall lock, her brow knitted, she told Molly, "I must admit, I had thought you'd probably have left before the wedding takes place."

Aunty Doris had told Frieda and Sandra about the Mr.; there were no secrets between the three of them as they were close, like family.

"Matthew and I have decided to get married after the war's finished, most likely sometime in the summer. Don't worry, Molly, we'll figure something out. You will be a bridesmaid and get to wear that pretty yellow dress. I promise."

A rosy, warm glow wrapped like a scarf around Molly and lasted till she got back to the farmhouse.

"A letter has arrived from Mr. Fenwick," Jacob told Molly as she came into the kitchen from outside.

Aunty, Mr. Bob and Jacob were all seated around the table, waiting for her.

Hanging her coat on a peg, and wanting to put off the moment of truth as she was afraid what the letter might say, she moved to the fire, and warming her hands, her fingers tingled as they thawed.

"Molly, hurry up." Jacob's face was a picture of impatience. "I can't wait to hear what the letter says."

With a feeling of impending doom, reluctantly, she moved over to the table.

"According to Bert Curtis," Mr. Bob was telling Aunty, "the Home Guard had a final parade following the 'stand-down' order. By gum, that's something I'd like to have seen."

Mr. Bob sat in his place at the end of the table with Tyne, ears cocked and alert, at his side as usual. Molly found the familiarity of the scene reassuring.

"Crikey, that makes it real...the war really is ending." Aunty rifled in her handbag as she spoke and brought out the letter.

The three of them looked at her in suspense.

"I'll make it quick," she told them, "I have to chair the Welcome Home Fund meeting in half an hour."

She opened the letter then took a deep, calming breath.

"Read it out loud," Jacob begged.

Dear Mrs. Leadbeater,

As I advised you in my previous communication, I'd be in touch when I'd made suitable arrangements for the twins. I am pleased to inform you that this is now in place, as I've found suitable accommodation to rent—a house in Cleadon Hills. It has vacant possession and a big garden for Jacob to play in. Everything has fallen into place as these things do when something is meant to happen. A former employee, Mr. Alan Pearson, whose family has been bombed out of their home, has agreed to rent the flat

*above the garage showroom, that I'm presently living in
until it gets sold. And so, my plan is to move to the house
in Cleadon at the beginning of January, as it would be
inconvenient over Christmas.*

"Inconvenient for who?" Mr. Bob snorted.

"*Bob*." Aunty glared at him, then continued.

*With this in mind, I'd be grateful if you'd bring the twins
to my new premises on Saturday the thirteenth of January,
by which time I will have the place prepared. The directions are enclosed and I will reimburse you.*

Now for . . .

Aunty went quiet but continued to read the letter to herself.
Her neck turning pink, she placed her free hand over her heart.

"Damn the man!"

"What is it, Doris?"

Molly looked at Jacob and saw alarm on his face, and she felt
the same way.

Aunty Doris gave a sort of helpless look at Mr. Bob, then
handed him the letter. "Here, read for yourself."

Mr. Bob scanned the letter and his face went purply red like it
did when he got really mad. "Of all the blood—"

"Bob, this is their father, remember. We have no say in the
matter." Aunty Doris jumped in, her expression desperate.

"Tell us what the letter says!" Jacob pleaded, while Molly sat
still and quiet because she just knew this was about her.

Aunty Doris turned toward her. "Love, it seems you're not
going to live with your father and Jacob, after all." Her face
showed deep concern.

Molly's tummy lurched. She couldn't believe what she was
hearing. She wanted to cover her ears and escape from the room.

"Why not?" Jacob asked from his side of the table, his expression disbelieving. "Where else could Molly live?"

"A place called Trevally's."

"Whereabouts is it?"

"Gosforth way?"

"But why there? Why can't Molly live with me any more?"

Molly's heart thudded in her chest and a shudder ran through her body; she was sick with fear.

"Listen, Jacob, I'll read this part of the letter."

It's in the child's best interests that she lives in Trevally's where she will receive the best care and all her needs will be catered for.

Jacob leapt up from his chair and it overbalanced with a crash. "Molly doesn't need to be cared for; she can manage on her own. Mam always said so. If she was here..." Jacob's chin wobbled as he spoke. "Besides, I promised Mam I'd look after Molly." His chest expanded, and he wore that obstinate look that Mam told him would get him into trouble one day. "If Molly's not coming to live in South Shields, then neither am I. Nobody can make me."

Molly's fear changed to sadness, as she knew differently.

Later, when the twins were supposed to be in their own rooms, they lay in Molly's bed huddled beneath the blanket.

"Molly, it's up to us to think of something," Jacob whispered. "We could run away like I said before. Remember, to that tumbledown place? Anything's better than being separated."

Molly knew trying to solve the problem was useless, though she was desperate to think of something. But Jacob's plan wouldn't work. "We couldn't stay all winter, Jacob. Even if we

had something to burn on the fire and torches, they'd run out.
And it would be dark."

Usually, it was Jacob who worked things out, but tonight he
didn't seem to be able to think things through properly.

"We'll take lots of money for torch batteries."

"Where will we get the money from?"

"I don't know. We'll figure that out too."

"But we only get pocket money."

"You're not helping, Molly. Don't you want to stay with me?"

Molly was stunned he could ask.

"I'm sorry, Molly Moo. I know you feel the same as me. Why
don't I just tell the Mr. I won't live with him without you. He'd
have to change his mind then, wouldn't he?"

Molly didn't think anything would change the Mr.'s mind.
She'd seen the distaste in his cold stare. She wished she didn't
have her disability because then the twins wouldn't be parted.

"Jacob, you heard what Aunty says, we don't have any say
in—" she began, then stopped when Jacob put a forefinger to his
lips.

He slipped from beneath the covers and by the light of his
torch, moved toward the bedroom door.

"It's Aunty Doris back from her meeting," he whispered. "Mr.
Bob and she are talking downstairs. I'm going to listen to what
they say. It might be about us."

Molly knew she shouldn't as it was sneaky, but the temptation
was too great. "Wait for me."

The twins crept out and sat halfway down the stairs in the
dark, heads against the spindles, listening to the voices that came
from the kitchen.

"He thinks it's in the child's best interest." Mr. Bob's vexed
voice drifted through the open doorway and up the staircase.
"Tommy rot! The bloke means his own interest."

Silence.

At that moment, Smoky jumped on Molly's knee, giving her such a fright, she jumped and nearly gave them away. The cat's silky fur brushed Molly's neck, as though the cat was comforting her.

"If you ask me," Mr. Bob fumed, "the reason the bloke wants to live elsewhere is he doesn't want folk to know he's fathered the twins. All this rubbish about 'worrying over the years.' He never tried to find his own bairns. I feel sorry for the man that he's lost his son but his behavior in this is downright despicable. The bottom line is he doesn't want a physically handicapped child on his hands."

"But a home for cripples, Bob. An institution. The man has no heart. What did he call her? A defective. If he were here now, I'd slap the man's... bloody ignorant face."

As she listened, a cold feeling, like ice sliding down her back, made Molly shiver.

"I hate the Mr.!" Jacob forgot to whisper.

"Shh! They'll hear."

"I don't care if they do."

She took his hand. "Come on, Jacob. Let's go back upstairs."

Molly knew her brother had heard enough—as had she.

Back in the bedroom, she fell limply on the bed.

"Jacob, what's a fective?"

"I don't know, but whatever it is you're not one. I'd punch the man if he says it again."

"I don't think I'm one either." Molly's nerve faltered. "Jacob, I'm scared."

Although she loved Jacob, she didn't want to talk with him any more—not about this. She thought how happy her twin had been at the prospect of living with... his father, and Molly was consumed with sadness and guilt. Jacob had now turned against the Mr., all because of her.

"Let's not talk about it any more tonight. Night, Jacob."

"Night night, Molly Moo." He moved toward the bedroom door. "Don't worry, we'll think of something so we can stay together." His voice sounded flat and she knew he was only trying to cheer her, as he'd no more idea than she did what to do.

Then he was gone, back to his own room.

As Molly climbed into bed, Aunty's words played in her head. *I'd slap the man's... bloody ignorant face.*

As she stared in the darkness at the ceiling, Molly gave a shuddering sigh. Everyone was getting vexed and it was because of her. If Molly wasn't here, Mr. Bob wouldn't be purple in the face mad and Aunty wouldn't swear like she had and Jacob... he'd get to have a garden to play in and see the motor cars.

If Molly wasn't here, all the people she loved would be getting on with their lives.

It occurred to her that whatever happened, the twins would be parted. If Jacob refused to live with the Mr., probably, he would get mad too and the twins would end up in an orphanage where they'd be separated anyway.

Lying in the dark, Molly knew what she had to do. The time had come for Jacob to be on his own without Molly hindering him. It wasn't his fault nobody wanted her. If Jacob lived in an orphanage with rules, he'd disobey them and always be in trouble. Then he'd get angry and end up horrible again. Molly wanted what was best for him, because she didn't want to be the cause of his misery.

If ever there was a time for her to be brave, then this was it.

Where could she go? All she knew was she wouldn't go to this Trevally place where fective people lived.

Smoky jumped up on the bed and onto Molly's tummy with the lightest of touches. She imagined Smoky's staring green eyes, inches away from her face.

Then, an idea struck. Molly started to make plans.

CHAPTER TWENTY-NINE

The room had that cold, echoey feel that places do when a life-time's possessions are packed away ready for a move. Edward had left a few pieces in place so that it held a semblance of home and so that he could at least spend the remaining days in the flat in relative comfort. The decanter, crystal whisky glasses and photographs of his beloved wife and their son still took pride of place on the sideboard. The irony of those three things representing his life didn't pass Edward by. Christmas was coming and he had no one to share it with.

But not for long.

It was late evening and he hadn't eaten but, after meeting up with Teddy Finchley at the golf club's Annual General Meeting, Edward needed a whisky. He moved over to the sideboard and, recollecting Teddy's insufferable gloating over being elected Club Captain, Edward poured a healthy measure of whisky and drank it down in one gulp.

He poured another.

The clubhouse, that afternoon, had been lit by candlelight as the electricity had failed, but thankfully the heating was working for the occasion.

The congratulations over, his face grinning with triumph, Teddy, sitting next to Edward, had addressed him in a loud voice.

"I thought you'd run for Club Captain, old man." His gaze swept the rest of the committee sitting around the table. "I guess, with me being front runner you knew you didn't stand a chance."

Teddy guffawed and Edward, had he not been a gentleman, would have punched the man's arrogant face.

Teddy stood and, raising his glass, announced, "Here's to a successful year and the end of the war when youngsters will return from the forces." He puffed out his chest. "Thanks to our perseverance in these troubled times, they'll have a golf club to come home to."

Feet stamped on the floor, as glasses were raised. Edward hadn't joined in. As he'd sipped his one tot of whisky, an overwhelming desire to tell the infernal man standing beside him about his son and his future plans engulfed Edward.

He was glad he hadn't, Edward considered now, as, glass in hand, he moved to the couch and sank into its cushions. For awkward questions would surely have followed. Why was he bothered? he asked himself, taking another swig of whisky that burned as it hit the back of his throat. He was done with Finchley, finished with the lot of them.

The move was a new start—the beginning of a new life.

His mind drifted to the house of his dreams he intended to rent. The double entry gates and sweeping drive to the arched front door, a spacious kitchen that overlooked the large garden to farmland and the hills beyond. What had really attracted Edward was the agent's description of the property—occupying *a highly desirable location on a prestigious avenue.* This was the kind of estate he'd worked for and aspired toward all of his life. The kind of property he'd promised his wife all those years ago, when they'd moved into the flat above the showroom.

Swigging another drink, instead of the expected high, thoughts of the two people he'd loved dearly and lost overtook his mind. *Life is cruel—and short.* Edward polished off the rest of the liquid in his glass.

As though a reminder, the roar of a lone airplane overhead made him sit up, alert. *Damn the war, you can never relax.* Edward rose and, moving to the sideboard, poured himself another stiff drink. Returning to the couch, he noted that the plane was droning in the distance, and breathed a sigh of relief. He'd never been able to differentiate the different engine noises which meant he never knew if it was a raider or not. Not that it made any difference if a bomb had your name on it. He reclined back on the couch, his mind conjuring up a bomb with *Mr. Edward Fenwick* written on it. The sound of his own laughter startled him. Looking at the glass in his hand and seeing he'd already scoffed most of its contents, Edward told himself to steady on.

But the news of those ruddy doodlebugs of late had made him, along with most town folk, nervy and tense. For Jerry, looking farther afield than London to terrorize, had posed a new threat. Heinkels, flying over the sea, carrying the flying bombs beneath their wings, launching them to reach industrial and coastal towns. Edward knew that with its docklands and armaments factory, it was only a matter of time before this area was a target. Even if it wasn't, sometimes the range was miscalculated and flying bombs devastated populated areas; the poor sods didn't stand a chance.

Edward drained his glass. Just about to stand up and pour himself another, he hesitated. If he intended to make plans for the future, he needed a clear head and so he'd better abstain. Trouble was, Edward was alone too much and had no one to distract him from the dark moods he suffered of late.

Again, he told himself, *not for long.*

Penelope came to mind, then. Edward couldn't decide if he should make a go of it with her or not. On the plus side, she'd help with the practical side of running a large home. Women's work, cooking, ironing, that kind of thing. Now that Edward was to be a responsible parent, giving in to temptation where women were concerned was out of the question, and Penelope would be a perfect partner. He was fond of her and if he did make a commitment, he'd be faithful.

He sat for a moment, his head befuddled with thoughts, then he stood, albeit nearly falling over. Just a wee drop more and that would be him done drinking for the evening. Unsteadily, he made his way over to the sideboard. *Just a small one*, he reminded himself. Picking up the decanter, a thought struck him, and he chuckled. In his mind's eye he saw Penelope, wearing a frilly apron, a duster in her hand. Then the thought struck him; who was he kidding? Penelope wouldn't know which end of a feather duster to hold, not that she would ever attempt such a thing, even for him. And, as far as Edward was concerned, he didn't want commitment or to be faithful. There'd only ever been one exception—and that was his darling wife.

Edward welled up at the thought of her.

He poured his drink and, placing the decanter back in its place, his mind conjured up Martha Moffatt. Now there was a smasher, if ever there was one. He wondered if she'd ever had a lover after him. He was a lucky beggar whoever he was. He imagined her pretty face, wide apart eyes and engaging smile. It wasn't just her youthful looks that had attracted him but the genuineness of the girl and her downright stubbornness. Which, hopefully, their boy might have inherited. Edward raised his glass.

"To my son."

Surveying the glittering crystal against the light, he vowed he'd learned his lesson with Edward junior, God rest his soul. He wouldn't push Jacob to be a miniature him but let his son develop to be his own person.

Edward saw the future in his mind's eye. Him standing with the dads at football matches, Jacob's face when he received his first new bicycle—for judging by the insinuations made by Mrs. Leadbeater, Martha had struggled to make ends meet. A stab of shame poked Edward, but he quickly discarded the thought to the back of his mind.

Swaying into the kitchen area, he placed his glass on the bench beside the cooker. He bent down and, almost toppling over, brought out a small frying pan from the under the sink cupboard. Lighting the gas ring with a match on the third try, he put the pan on top with a knob of lard.

His thoughts rumbled on. Martha Moffatt's naming of their son was admirable, but Edward had always known that, given the chance, the girl had the makings of having class. He didn't regret his actions of the past; he knew that if he went back in time, he'd do the same thing again, as he'd had a certain standard to maintain.

Not any more, he told himself as he sipped his drink. Because from now on he was free of everyone to do whatever he liked.

The lard sizzling, he put his glass down and put the large lamb chop the butcher had given him from under the counter for an exorbitant price, into the pan. Edward mentally shrugged. That was the penalty of living with this war on when you weren't prepared to go without.

As the fat sizzled and spat, Edward resumed thinking where he'd left off. He wondered if Martha were here now and he saw her would the older version still appeal. That would depend on how life had treated her, his picky self decided.

He stabbed the chop with a fork and turned it over.

At the thought of starting over again with his son, a heady excitement grew in Edward. He brushed aside thoughts of Jacob's twin. What he planned was best for everyone concerned. He shook his head. It distressed him to see the poor disabled child and Edward doubted she'd even notice where she was because it was obvious, from the brief time he saw her, when she hadn't uttered a word, that the girl was ignorant about what was going on.

He raised his glass. *To the girl, may her new life be...* he searched his muddled mind; what word would befit the occasion... *sufficient*—a splendid word to fit the bill.

The room smelling of cooked lamb chop, Edward, placing his glass down on the bench, stretched forward and opened the window beside the cooker.

He nodded. No one could say he hadn't been admirable to his dear son's wife. He'd written to Patricia telling her his intentions to move as Edward felt a loyalty to his son to do so. He gave a dramatic sigh. No doubt, Patricia's life would move on and she'd find someone new and Edward would be an embarrassment as a previous father-in-law.

What to do about the business. Buying and selling cars could be an option but he'd need bigger premises for a showroom and he didn't plan on selling up—

A noise from outside made him pause. He took the spitting pan off the gas and opened the curtains a crack, and, swaying from side to side, he peered out. In the distance and in the brilliant moonlit sky he saw, keeping well apart, three small aircraft. As they approached nearer, they made a peculiar buzzing noise.

Pan in hand, Edward froze in fear.

Doodlebugs. There was a distant explosion, then a red hue came into the night sky.

Another doodlebug zoomed overhead, then the third, and as the engine cut, the sound ceased.

Edward didn't have time to wonder if the buzz bombs were after the docks, or, indeed, the new life that he'd be missing out on. His last thought, just before the explosion, was that he'd be reunited with his beloved wife.

CHAPTER THIRTY

Molly chose Sunday as she didn't have to go to school and so Jacob wouldn't miss her.

She sat at the breakfast table and ate her egg and crusty bread—the hens hadn't laid many eggs recently and so the breakfast was a Sunday treat. Molly tried to look as if nothing unusual was happening today but any loud noise made her jump and she was afraid she'd give herself away. But everyone ate breakfast as normal.

Afterward, when Sunday school started, Molly got upset when she realized this was the last time she'd see Sandra and that she wouldn't be a bridesmaid at her wedding. But she mustn't dwell on these thoughts or else she might lose her nerve.

When Sandra told the class the parable about the Good Samaritan, she finished by asking, "So, what d'you think the meaning of the parable is?"

A boy answered, "Someone doing a good deed by helping a stranger."

Molly reckoned, though her brother wasn't a stranger, she was about to do a good deed for him. She hoped she'd do enough good deeds so that when it was her turn to die, she'd get to go to heaven because then she'd be with Granny and Mam. For some reason the thought made her teary.

"Molly, pet, are you all right?" Sandra came and put an arm around her shoulders.

She nodded. Sandra being kind made Molly feel worse. Usually, she could talk over whatever was bothering her with Jacob, but he was the last person she could tell. She reminded herself that from now on she had only herself to rely on, and whatever the future held, Molly resolved, for Jacob's sake, she must stay brave.

At dinnertime, even though she had no appetite to eat the mince and mashed potatoes put before her, Molly cleared her plate as she didn't know when her next meal might be. Then, as Mr. Bob prepared to leave to take the scraps to the pigs, Molly smiled at him.

"Goodbye, Mr. Bob." She felt teary again as she realized she'd got used to his ways and had grown quite fond of him.

He gave her a queer look. "I'm only going up the field, lassie, not to the Hebrides." Shaking his head, he laughed, then, taking hold of the bucket, he left.

Molly turned to Jacob, busy at the table with his stamp collection. "I'm off to watch the last dress rehearsal of the pantomime."

"Ta-ra." Engrossed with the latest stamp he'd swapped, her brother didn't look up.

Molly knew if she met his eyes, Jacob would suspect something was up. Besides, she'd probably cry and so it was for the best. She climbed the stairs and, entering the bedroom, cumbersomely, she knelt on the floor and brought her suitcase from under the bed. She'd packed the night before and Molly hoped it held everything she needed, though she'd never been to an orphanage before and so she was unsure.

In her mind she went through the list yet again. Torch, clothes, her favorite book, weaving, Floppy rabbit and bread and dripping from last night's tea in a paper bag in case she got hungry.

Putting on her outdoor clothes that lay on the bed, Molly felt in her coat pocket for the pennies she'd been saving for Christmas. They jingled in the lining.

Despite being very afraid, some force drove her on and, as she looked at Smoky curled asleep on the bed, Molly knew Jacob would be amazed the way she'd thought everything through.

Only he wouldn't be by her side as normal.

Then it was Smoky's turn. "Bye, Smoky. Don't worry, Mr. Bob's kind at heart and he'll let you live here."

The cat looked up. "Meow."

Molly put the note she'd written earlier on her pillow and left the room.

Slowly, she descended the stairs, then moved into the front room—and it felt unreal, as if Molly was playing a part in a film. She opened the front door and, stepping outside, got her first fright.

Molly hadn't taken into account that these days it was only half-light by mid-afternoon. She didn't know how long it would take to get to Stockbridge or even where it was, but she knew to travel anywhere you started from Hexham bus station.

She made her way to the bus stop in the village. As she waited, Molly was glad it was Sunday so that everything in the village was closed and Aunty Doris couldn't be looking out of the post office window.

It seemed an age before the single-decker bus trundled up the road and, as she climbed aboard the platform, Molly shivered. The bus was empty except for a couple of Land Girls sitting together at the front, and she found a window seat at the back.

"Where are you off to on your own?" Mrs. Turnbull, in her conductress uniform, frowned in puzzlement as she stared down at Molly.

This was something Molly had never thought of, and she felt suddenly worried that Mrs. Turnbull would surely tell Aunty Doris.

"Hexham." As the conductress opened her mouth to speak, Molly quickly put in, "How much does it cost, please?"

When Mrs. Turnbull told her, Molly brought out the money from her coat pocket and counted out the pennies.

Thankfully, the conductress moved on to collect the fares from the Land Girls.

As the bus rattled along the twisted roads, Molly realized she'd only been on the bus a few times and though she knew Hexham was the last stop before it returned, she couldn't help but worry she might get lost. It was one thing to imagine the journey from the safety of the farm but quite another when she was all alone on the journey. It had never occurred to her that when she'd traveled before there'd always been a grown-up to make the decisions and all Molly had to do was follow and enjoy the trip.

At Hexham, alighting the platform and feeling Mrs. Turnbull's eyes on her, Molly limped out of the bus station, along the main street, then she hid in a shop doorway.

Jacob would be proud. His favorite game, when it was dusk and he was allowed out, was to track unsuspecting villagers (supposedly spies) by following them. He'd hide in doorways and if they did turn around, they never suspected that a British agent was tracking them.

Peeping out occasionally, Molly was rewarded when she saw the bus she'd just traveled on leave the bus station, heading once more to Leadburn.

Staring wistfully in the direction of Robb's departmental store, whose windows she knew would be decorated for Christmas, Molly resisted the temptation and made her way back to the bus station.

"Excuse me," she politely asked a lady bus driver sitting behind the wheel, "could you tell me the stand for the bus to Stockbridge?"

"Over there, see." The driver, who gave a rather tired-looking smile, pointed to a single-decker bus at a stand.

"Thank you." Molly made her way over and climbed aboard. As she walked past the rows of seats, she felt everyone's eyes upon her.

She sat beside an elderly lady with gray hair and apple-pink cheeks.

"Hello, dear, it's a bit dark for you to be out on your own." Her voice was croaky, as if she'd worn it out.

"I'm—" Molly panicked. This was something else she hadn't planned on. People noticing she was traveling on her own. She'd better think up a good excuse or else she might be told to get off the bus and go home.

She crossed the fingers of her right hand behind her back as Jacob told her it meant a lie didn't count.

"My granny is meeting me off the bus." Even though her fingers were crossed, Molly felt herself flush in shame.

She thought she might have given herself away, but the lady only smiled pleasantly.

"That's nice, dear, that you visit your granny. Your mammy would see you to the bus stand, I expect."

Rather than tell another fib, Molly nodded.

The bus started up and as it pulled out of the bus station into Hexham's main street, the conductress made her way up the center aisle taking fares.

The bus rattled out of town and the scene outside changed. Molly saw trees lining the road. Heart pounding in her chest, she stared into the blackness outside and realized she was off into the unknown.

"Wardhaugh, love," the man in front told the conductress.

"That'll be four pence."

The conductress took a green ticket out of the rack she was carrying, then she punched a hole in it with a machine. She handed the ticket to the man. "In future mind your cheek. I am not your love."

He guffawed.

The lady next to him shook her head and tutted.

"Single to Sinderhope, if you please," the lady told the conductress.

"Eight pence, please."

Molly gasped in horror when she saw the lady hand over the silver coin and pennies. She'd only three pence left, a small fortune she'd thought, but now Molly wondered if it would be enough to take her to Stockbridge.

When it was her turn to pay, Molly asked the conductress, "Is Stockbridge farther than Sinderhope?"

"Yes, it's the next stop."

Molly's tummy seemed to turn over and she felt sick with fright. She didn't have enough money.

"Is that where you're going?" The conductress's forehead puckered into a frown.

"Oh, no. I was only wondering. I'd like a half fare to..." she thought quickly, "Wardhaugh, please." She handed over the pennies.

"Her granny's meeting the bus." The elderly lady smiled reassuringly at the conductress.

"Who's for Wardhaugh?" the conductress called.

The bus had been traveling for quite a while and at each stop, the conductress had called the name of the place, saving Molly the worry of when to stand up.

The elderly lady who'd sat beside her had got off the bus at a place called Lowgate, not very far out of Hexham.

The man who sat in the seat in front stood up and walked down the aisle. Molly picked up her suitcase, and making her way unsteadily down the aisle, followed him.

When the bus stopped, the man alighted from the platform, and with long strides, made off into the blackness toward a building that had a dimmed light shining from its doorway.

The biting cold made Molly shiver and, putting her suitcase on the ground, she pulled the collar up on her coat.

The conductress called from the bus, "Can you see your granny?"

Fingers crossed behind her back, Molly answered, "No, but she won't be long, she doesn't live far away."

"Come on, we can't wait all night." The bus driver sounded impatient.

For an instant, as she stood alone, Molly had the urge to clamber back onto the security of the bus's platform.

Then Jacob appeared in her mind and, with huge effort, she resisted temptation and called, "I can see her now." She picked up the suitcase and limped off along the road toward the building with a light.

The bus drew away from the curb and took off down the road and was soon swallowed up in the dark. The rumble of the engine was a distant sound and then there was only silence. Molly was frightened. She'd didn't know where she was and even if she did want to return to the farmhouse, she hadn't any money left to pay the bus fare.

She wished Jacob was here. Even in the worst times when terrible things happened, they'd been together. At that moment the moon came from behind the misty veil of clouds and Molly could see the immediate area around her. A little bit of confidence came back. Mam had always told the twins if they were ever lost to seek out a policeman.

Molly dithered, then came to a decision. She had to stop being a baby and think what Jacob would do.

She approached the building and squinted up at a sign above the doorway. She saw a fox. Molly knew now where she was. The last time she'd seen the sign was when Mr. Carlton drove past in the motor car on their way to the picnic spot where Molly saw the waterfall.

The stone ruin.

Like a tap being turned on, a plan poured into Molly's mind—and suddenly it all seemed perfectly simple. She would sleep the night in the old ruin and tomorrow, first thing, she would set off to the roadside and hitch a ride to Stockbridge. That's what Sandra's brother Alf told her soldiers did when they had a pass and wanted to travel home. Now, Molly even knew which direction she needed to go.

Refusing to give in to the terrors of the blackness beyond, Molly moved on.

She'd been limping along for ages, the suitcase in her hand weighing her down one side, when the clouds thickened and blocked out the light from the moon. Molly knew she should stop and find her torch in the suitcase. It had started to rain and she needed to get to the stone building as quickly as possible. The good thing was she just had to follow the straight road. Then it occurred to her she wouldn't see the ruin as it was off the road.

Putting her suitcase down on the ground, she used her good hand to open the catch. Rifling in the clothes, she felt the torch halfway down. Closing the suitcase again, she heaved herself up and, switching on the torch, by its beam she could see beyond the road, but no sign of the building.

Managing the suitcase and torch was difficult as her handicapped hand couldn't hold either. She remembered what the Mr. had called her. Molly made a determined face. She'd prove him wrong; Molly wasn't a fective—whatever that was.

The solution popped into Molly's head. If she carried the torch in her coat pocket and used it every now and again to check the area, she'd see the building. That way, her good hand would be free to carry the suitcase and she could save torch batteries into the bargain.

Proud that she could work things out for herself, Molly staggered on.

The driving rain had changed to sleet, she saw by the light of the torch, and it was soaking her through. Molly began to shiver.

She thought of the fire at the farmhouse, the warm glow and the heat that warmed her.

Putting down the suitcase, the fingers in her mittens were so cold that even with her good hand, she found grasping the torch in her coat pocket difficult. Her ankle too had stiffened as it did in cold weather. Shining the torch beam off the road to the grass beyond, she saw no sign of a building.

Deflated, Molly put the torch back into her pocket and, picking up the suitcase, she struggled on, uncontrollably shivering by now.

When she started to walk uphill, something told Molly this was wrong and, turning, she decided to trace her steps back along the roadway. In her fuzzy mind she felt disorientated. Turning left, she struggled over a grassy verge aware that her shoes were soaked through. She realized then that she was lost and her befuddled mind remembered that no one knew where she was and she could die out here.

As her tongue licked the salt tears on her lips Molly admitted she wasn't brave—she wanted to be back safe with Jacob at the farm.

Defeated, her drowsy brain admitted she'd no energy left to go on. She dumped the suitcase and switched on the torch, which took a supreme effort as her hand somehow couldn't find the pocket of her coat. Pointing the beam in front, Molly saw a black shape in the distance that could only be the building she searched for.

Summoning all her strength, and breathing in slow panting breaths, she found the energy to reach the stone building and collapsed in the doorway. Lying on the ground, all she wanted was sleep. Eyes closed, it registered somewhere, through Molly's exhaustion, that she didn't feel the cold any more.

Unaware that the building had no sheltering roof and that the sleet had changed to thick flakes of snow, Molly lay oblivious on the stiff grass.

CHAPTER THIRTY-ONE

"How about we have leftover taties fried for tea?"

Mr. Bob sat in his chair in front of the range fire, legs stretched and wearing his work dungarees and stockings with holes in the heels. He'd helped with milking the cows to allow Sandra to go to the final pantomime rehearsal.

Jacob looked up. "Ooh, yes please, Mr. Bob."

Even though he'd had Sunday dinner, Jacob was starved. Earlier, after doing his stamp collection, he'd kicked a ball around in the back garden, then, when it started to rain, he came inside to play with the Meccano set Mr. Bob had recently given him which had belonged to his son.

"We bought it one Christmas for Wilf when he was about your age," Mr. Bob had told him.

Jacob was surprised but nevertheless pleased, as it was the first time Mr. Bob had spoken to him about Wilf. All kinds of questions flitted through Jacob's mind, but instinct told him, when he saw Mr. Bob's downhearted expression, this wasn't the time.

Jacob now understood that Mr. Bob got lonely for his wife and son and nobody could replace them. Mr. Bob had got furious the way their father treated the twins, especially Molly, and Jacob had to admit the farmer wasn't so bad after all. He mightn't want the twins to live with him because he was happier on his own, but Mr. Bob still wanted what was best for them.

"I'll look after it," he'd promised, taking the big box Mr. Bob handed over to him.

"Aye, it might as well be used rather than sitting in a cupboard."

Now, as he sat on the kitchen floor, Jacob attempted constructing a car, but it was a lot trickier than he'd first thought.

"It's a while till teatime, yet," Mr. Bob said, and Jacob's tummy rumbled with anticipation. "What time does the rehearsal finish, d'you know?"

Jacob shrugged; he didn't have a clue.

Mr. Bob went back to reading the newspaper.

While he worked, Jacob's mind went back to worrying about how he could avoid living with the Mr. because there was no way he was leaving Molly. Jacob would never forgive the man after the way he'd treated his sister and what he'd called her.

Jacob was aware now he'd been kidding himself all along. That night when Molly asked him if he liked the Mr., he should have been truthful. He was nothing like Jacob had imagined. He was old—more like a granddad—and he was a complete stranger. Jacob had only pretended he wanted to live with him because he so badly wanted a home and a dad to call his own. He was ashamed at letting Molly down because he'd known the man wasn't interested in her, but Jacob had convinced himself that everything would work out just fine. Deep down, Jacob had sensed the man was false and didn't really want him either. Jacob realized now; his son had died and the Mr. only wanted Jacob to replace him.

He'd tell Molly all this when he said he was sorry and that he'd never be disloyal again. He would find some way for them to be together even if it was living in an orphanage.

Satisfied with his plan and eager to tell Molly when she came home, Jacob continued making his car.

Not long afterward the door opened and Aunty Doris, looking drenched, bundled into the kitchen.

"I got halfway here when it started belting down with sleet. Me feet are soaked through from the puddles." She undid the laces of her black lace-up shoes and pulled them off. Taking off her coat and headscarf, she shook them over the linoleum floor. "I've come for eggs, Bob, if you've any to spare." Jacob saw her roll her eyes. "As if I haven't got enough to do, I volunteered to donate a cake for the Coming Home Fund raffle." She came over to stand by the fire.

"I'll have a look." Mr. Bob stood up and went over to the pantry.

"Bob, have you heard about them Jerry planes coming over? They launched an attack on industrial towns up here in the north."

"Is that right?" Mr. Bob's voice came from within the pantry.

"The report said there was over twenty-five of them Heinkels headed toward the coast. Apparently, before they reached the coast they launched the doodlebugs they carried under their wing so they had more range."

Shocked, Jacob stopped what he was doing to listen.

Aunty went on, "The bombs were aimed in the direction of Newcastle—and some folk say they were after the armaments on the Tyne. Some landed in South Shields and civilians were killed in their homes."

"Poor souls, at least they wouldn't know much about it." Mr. Bob appeared carrying brown eggs in a bowl.

"Fancy, though, the war just about to finish and you cop it now." Sorrowfully, Mr. Bob shook his head.

"I don't want all the eggs." Aunty changed the subject and Jacob was glad because he didn't like to hear about people being killed by bombing—especially in their hometown.

"Just as well because you weren't getting them all." Mr. Bob gave Aunty a cheeky smile.

Aunty rolled her eyes at him. "Two will do."

Mr. Bob put two eggs on the table and took the rest back to the pantry.

When he returned Aunty said, "I'd best be getting back. I don't want to be out if the weather gets worse."

"I'm worried about the lassie." Mr. Bob's brow creased in concern. "She's still out there and you know what she's like if it snows. It's difficult for her to walk as it is."

Jacob told Aunty, "Molly's at the pantomime rehearsal at the church hall."

Aunty Doris shook her head. "No, she isn't. The rehearsal finished ages ago. I know because Sandra locked up, then came to see Frieda, and the two of them are talking weddings in my kitchen."

Mr. Bob looked puzzled. "Where is she, then?" He looked at Jacob. "Did she say she was going anywhere else?"

"No." A pang of guilt poked Jacob. He'd been too busy with his stamp collection to take any notice when his sister left. An icy shiver ran down his spine.

Mr. Bob went over to the door and took his greatcoat, that he wore in the first war, from the peg. "She might have slipped and fallen. I'll go and search." He pulled his wellingtons on and, opening the door, disappeared into the night.

"Can you think of anywhere your sister could be?" Aunty asked.

Jacob couldn't. It wasn't like Molly to go off on her own. His twin instinct told him something was wrong and the first inkling of fear pierced him.

Jacob waited anxiously until Mr. Bob returned, coming into the kitchen, shivering with the cold and shaking off his soaked greatcoat.

"She's nowhere to be seen."

Jacob could see by the uneasy look in his eyes that Mr. Bob was worried.

Moving over to the fire, Mr. Bob told Aunty, "I've been down to the post office and Sandra says Molly didn't turn up at the rehearsal."

Jacob's tummy went rock hard.

"Then where on earth can she be? She can't have gone far." Aunty Doris looked worriedly at Jacob. "Can you think of anywhere?"

Jacob didn't have a clue; he was reeling at the fact that Molly, of all people, had told him a fib. *There must have been a good reason*, his inner voice told him.

He shook his head.

"How about we check her bedroom?" Mr. Bob suggested.

"Good idea, Bob. That might give us a clue."

Jacob didn't see how, but he followed the two grown-ups upstairs.

"I don't usually go into the twins' rooms," Mr. Bob told Aunty as he opened the door, "Wilf liked to keep his bedroom private."

"What about changing beds?"

"They do it themselves. Look, there's a note on the lassie's pillow."

Mr. Bob picked up the sheet of paper. Glancing at it, he handed the note to Jacob.

"It's for you, lad."

Feeling their eyes on him, Jacob began to read to himself.

I'm sorry, Jacob, I told you a fib but I had to make up something to leave the house. I want you to go and live with the Mr. and have a garden and motor cars. I'm leaving and I don't want you to find me because it won't do any good because we'll be put in an orphanage and parted anyway. I'm going to live in one because there's nowhere else. I don't like the Mr. and I'm glad I'm not living with him. If I tell them at the orphanage I've no one, they'll have to take me in.

As he read the note, Jacob felt his chest go tight and his breaths became shallow and fast.

> *I've got a plan and I'm proud because I thought it all up by myself without your help. But I'm upset I won't see you for a while. When Mam and Granny died and I knew I'd never see them again that made me really sad. This way, when we're old enough, Jacob, we can live together and I'll see you again every day. I know I can stay brave till then.*
> *Ask the Mr. if Smoky can live with you and look after her.*

> *Love and hugs, Molly Moo who loves you. xxxooo*

Jacob looked up at Aunty and Mr. Bob. A big lump lodged in his throat; he couldn't speak even if he wanted to. Molly had planned this all along and she was only thinking of him, while he…he was selfish and had thought only of himself. But he would never have believed she would run away like this. Guilt consumed him; Molly had done this all because of him.

"What does the letter say?" Aunty's voice said.

Too distressed to speak, Jacob handed her the letter.

Reeling with so many questions, and no answers, Jacob didn't know how long he stood frozen to the spot as the grown-ups read the note in silence.

"Oh, Bob we've got to find her." Aunty's voice registered in his mind. "This is serious, Molly could be anywhere. It's dark now and wet out there."

Terror gripped Jacob's throat. Anything could happen to his sister in the dark. He looked up at Mr. Bob. His face was grave, like somebody had died. The thought made it harder for Jacob to breathe.

"I'm going to knock on Colin Metcalf's door. The police need to be involved in this."

Mr. Metcalf, Jacob knew, was a special constable and helped the police when needed as the nearest policeman was stationed at Hexham.

"I'll wait here with Jacob. Hurry, Bob, we have to act fast."

*

While they waited, Aunty quizzed Jacob about where he thought the orphanage was where Molly would go. Jacob didn't have the faintest clue; he didn't know of any.

When Mr. Bob returned, he didn't look relieved like Jacob had hoped.

He approached the table with a worried frown and without taking his coat off, he told Aunty, "Colin's Mrs. answered the door. I told her it wasn't a social call and wanted to speak to Colin."

"Was he in?" Aunty's anxious tone scared Jacob.

"Aye. And when I told him what was up, Colin used his head."

"What did he say?"

"That we should check to see if Molly had left the village before organizing a search."

Jacob, unable to sit another moment, rushed up to Mr. Bob. "We should search the village now. What if Molly's hurt and—"

"Woah, laddie. We took that into account." He turned to Aunty. "It was nigh on the hour and the bus was due, so we hopped it to the bus stop. When the bus arrived, Elsie Turnbull was the conductress."

"But Molly's never been on a bus on her own," Jacob put in, confused.

"She has now, lad. According to what Mrs. Turnbull said."

Jacob was dumbfounded. He saw in his mind Molly hauling herself up onto the platform and lumbering down the aisle. He wracked his brains. Where would she be making for?

Aunty stood up. "Was Elsie the conductress all afternoon, Bob?"

"She was and furthermore"—he directed his gaze at Jacob—

"your sister boarded the bus late in the afternoon and got off at Hexham."

Jacob was amazed at Molly's daring. He knew she would have the money because she saved her pocket money, whereas he couldn't spend his quickly enough on a comic or sweeties.

"Did Elsie say what the bairn did at Hexham?"

Mr. Bob scratched his head. "After she got off the bus, she headed for town. That's all Elsie knew. She feels bad as she had wondered if she should say something, but she'd decided Molly always seemed such a sensible lass."

Aunty Doris held her chin in her hands. "So, what do we do now?"

"Wait," Mr. Bob said.

Jacob couldn't bear to wait. All possibilities flashed through his head, including her being found by a spy who...he slammed his mind shut. That was only make-believe and he'd had enough of that. Molly was in real danger and it was time for him to be sensible and think hard because only he could work out where she might be. The quicker she was found, the better it would be for his sister's safety. His mind shied away from what Granny would be saying if she were here, all the harm that could befall Molly.

Mr. Bob's voice penetrated his thoughts. "Colin's phoned Hexham police station to report the matter and he says he'll be in touch as soon as he hears anything."

Aunty folded her arms and looked appalled. "So, we're just supposed to twiddle our fingers and wait?" Jacob knew that Aunty was on his side.

Mr. Bob, looking desperate, said, "What else can we do? I'd be out there now if I had any idea where to start looking."

"I know, Bob, sorry. It breaks my heart to think she's out there feeling unloved and all alone. If only she'd said something."

"Oh, Doris," Mr. Bob groaned, "we've been over this before. Our hands are tied—there's nothing we can do."

Aunty pursed her lips as if she didn't agree. "She's only a child and we were supposed to be looking out for her and here she was thinking we were going to dump her in an orphanage."

Mr. Bob's face seem to sag. "Not we, Doris, me. It's my fault that she's that upset she's run away, and I feel terrible."

Jacob felt worse. Mam had asked him to look after Molly and now she was gone, and it was all his fault. If he hadn't gone on about motor cars and living in South Shields, Molly wouldn't have got this idea that she was stopping him from doing what he wanted. He shouldn't have dithered. Why hadn't he got in touch with the Mr. straight away? Told him if Molly couldn't live with him, then neither would he. At least in an orphanage they'd both be in the same place. Because, Jacob realized with a shock, he was scared to be without her. Ever since they'd left home when everything was different, pretending he was Biggles was the only way Jacob could deal with all the new things that were happening. Deep down he was frightened but was afraid to let it show, and so he got angry and started fights. Molly was just herself and never tried to be anything else and there was something about her that calmed him and made him strong. If anything happened to Molly, he would be…he would be…

"There, there, Jacob, don't cry." Aunty's arms came around his shoulders and she hugged him tight. "We'll find Molly, you'll see." But her shaky voice told him she didn't believe it and was only trying to reassure him.

Big boys don't cry. Jacob didn't feel like a big boy, or like Biggles. He was only himself—Jacob Moffatt—and he wanted his sister back by his side so badly that it hurt.

Later, when the hands on the round clock on the wall pointed to seven o'clock, a knock came at the kitchen door.

Jacob, after a good cry which hurt his tummy and made his

shoulders go up and down, didn't feel either silly or ashamed that he'd cried like a baby because he now felt better somehow, even though he was still frantic about his sister. He sat up and watched eagerly as Mr. Bob answered the door.

"Hello, Colin, any news? Sorry, come in."

Mr. Metcalf walked through the doorway and Jacob saw he wasn't wearing his uniform but an outdoor coat that reached down to his wellingtons. He searched his face to see if he could find any hint to what news he was bringing.

Mr. Metcalf nodded at Aunty Doris. "Hexham station has been in touch. They've been searching around Hexham but with no luck. An officer made enquiries at the bus station and was just about to give up when the Stockbridge bus came in. On further inquiry the conductress revealed that a young girl had got on her bus earlier on the outward-bound journey and said she was being met by her granny."

"It can't be Molly," Jacob cried, "she hasn't got a granny."

"Which stop did this girl get off at?" Aunty Doris wanted to know.

"Wardhaugh. They can only spare one copper and he's doing a house to house search in the village."

"But Molly doesn't know anybody. Why would she go there?" Mr. Bob sounded perplexed.

"She must have her reasons, Bob. Maybe it's somebody she's met that we don't know about."

Jacob knew that couldn't be true. Molly wouldn't have kept a secret like that from him.

"That's not like Molly," Mr. Bob agreed, "I reckon it isn't her. It would be a wild goose chase searching Wardhaugh. Meanwhile, she's somewhere out there in the cold."

Jacob had been wondering why the name of the place sounded familiar and suddenly he knew. Relief flooded through him. "It is Molly!" he cried. "And I know where she's going."

All their eyes were upon him.

"Sandra and Mr. Carlton took us in his car to a pool with a waterfall. We passed through that village called Wardhaugh and saw an old ruin. Molly's hiding there."

"How do you know?" the special constable asked.

Jacob said, "Because, when we heard we'd be put in an orphanage, I wanted us to run away and we talked about living in the old ruin."

Mr. Bob let out a tormented sigh.

"What stopped you, then?" Mr. Metcalf's face had that disbelieving expression grown-ups have when kids say something far-fetched.

"Because...we decided it wouldn't work."

"Well I'm not sure, it might be a waste of time and we need to find her fast. I'm not interfering with what headquarters are doing and getting them to send a copper on a wild goose chase."

"Please, please, can we go? I know she's there." Jacob was desperate.

"Colin"—Mr. Bob's voice was firm—"have you any better ideas? How about we go take a look—it's better than just hanging around here."

"But why would she go there?"

"If she is there, Colin, you can be the one to ask her."

Jacob decided whatever happened, he liked Mr. Bob from now on.

The four of them sat in the old car that rattled as it swung around corners and made them swerve in their seats. Mr. Bob sat in the passenger seat with Mr. Metcalf driving, while Jacob was in the back with Sandra. As Sandra knew the way, Aunty had insisted that she come with them while Aunty stayed at the farmhouse in case there was any news.

"I don't want kids in the way, you stay here," Mr. Metcalf had at first told Jacob.

Even though the man was a special constable, Jacob was ready to argue. He'd said again that he was going, his fists clenched as he spoke.

But it was Mr. Bob that changed Mr. Metcalf's mind. "Colin, the lad comes too. I'll see to him." His voice had suggested there was no arguing.

Jacob had looked at Mr. Bob with gratitude and Mr. Bob had nodded his head and given him a small smile of reassurance in return.

The sleet had turned into rapid snow and by the light of the sidelights—that were their proper size now, as the regulations hadn't to be followed—Jacob saw, as he looked through the front window, it was coating the ground.

He knew Molly's poorly leg wouldn't cope with slippery ground or with the perishing cold. He'd heard one of the laborers at the farm say that out on the moors when it snowed it could be "freezing to death weather."

The thought made Jacob go as white as the snow.

They passed through the village and saw the pub on the right with a dim light in its doorway.

"Sandra, can you see if we're anywhere near, yet?" Jacob heard the tension in Mr. Bob's voice.

"If only the moon would come out fully," Sandra told them, "so I could see properly. The ruin should be somewhere around here on the right."

The moon was veiled behind the clouds; the light wasn't bright, but you could see out of the car.

"I'll slow down so you can take a good look," Mr. Metcalf said.

As they crawled along the narrow road, Jacob strained to see from the back seat.

He jumped when Mr. Metcalf shouted, "Look in front. I can see a building off the road. Is that it?"

"It'll be the ruin, it's the only place around," Sandra said, trying to see too.

When the car stopped, Jacob was the first to climb from the car, heart thumping in his chest. All three adults had torches and, as they switched them on, the round beams of light helped them to see.

It had stopped snowing but the air was biting cold this far out in the countryside. Jacob felt the icy air hit the back of his throat as he took each breath. A shudder of horror swept through his body. How could Molly survive out here?

"Spread out." The special constable's voice was the voice of authority. "That way if she is here, we won't miss her."

Mr. Bob took Jacob's small hand in his big one. "Stay with me, laddie, we don't want you getting lost."

They trod over the stiff snowy grass and Jacob got the sense of the vast space all around, where no sound but the crunch of their feet on hardened snow broke the silence, and not a light shone in the night sky.

"Hang on." Sandra's voice came through from just ahead. "I've found something." Jacob froze. Silence. "It's a suitcase." Mr. Bob gripping his hand tighter, they made their way over to where her voice came from.

As Jacob approached Sandra, he could see she was bending over something on the ground.

"The catches are frozen and it won't open." She stood up and shone her torch on the suitcase.

Seeing his sister's suitcase, a sob escaped Jacob. "That's Molly's suitcase, but where is she?"

"Spread out," Mr. Bob told them. "She's here somewhere. We've got to find her, the lassie could freeze to death out here."

It didn't take long to reach the ruin. Jacob, wrestling his hand loose from Mr. Bob's, ran the last few yards.

And then, by the light of a shadowy pale moon, he saw Molly lying on the ground just inside the doorway and ran to her, throwing himself down on the snow beside her.

The feeling of not being able to breathe gripped Jacob but he knew he needed to overcome it to shout out to the others, for Molly's sake. "She's here," he shrieked at the top of his lungs. "She's here!"

The others caught up.

Sandra knelt beside Jacob on the ground. She shone her torch on Molly's face.

Her face white, Molly's eyes were tight shut and her skin was cold.

"Is she going to be all right?" Jacob's tummy slackened and the words rushed out in a squeak.

Her clothes were soaked through and her hand, where she'd lost a mitten, was icy cold.

Sandra put her fingers on Molly's neck. "Her pulse is weak and slow. She might have hypothermia. In Red Cross classes we were told to remove wet clothes and the casualty should be warmed gradually. But move them gently."

Mr. Bob put the torch on the ground. Shrugging out of his greatcoat, Mr. Bob, with a gentleness Jacob had never seen before, helped Sandra take off Molly's sodden clothes down to her navy knickers and then he wrapped her in his coat, holding her tight in his arms to warm her.

Jacob had never been so scared. "What's wrong with her? Why won't she wake up?"

"She's unconscious, we've to take her straight to the hospital," Mr. Bob said gently.

Sandra, by the beam of her torch, led the way, Mr. Bob

following, Jacob tagging along at his side and Mr. Metcalf bringing up the rear. As they made for the car, Jacob heard someone sobbing, and in surprise he realized it was him.

Sniffing hard, he climbed into the car; Mr. Bob sat in the front with Molly, still lifeless in his arms.

The car set off and Sandra turned to him, saying softly, "Molly is very ill, Jacob. We must pray that she pulls through."

Molly's words played in his head from the time she'd told him about the book she was reading. *There's a girl called Beth in it who isn't strong and she dies. Jacob, sometimes, I feel that might happen to me.*

Jacob didn't want Molly to die—and it wasn't because he was thinking of himself, that he'd be alone, or having realized now that it was his sister who was the stronger of the two—but because it wouldn't be fair on Molly. She was sturdier and starting to walk properly. She deserved some time without wearing a caliper, playing out like other children. She'd put up with so much in her life so far, and it wasn't fair.

He let out a quivering breath. He loved his sister and didn't want to be parted from her.

Tears streamed down his face and his chest hurt. If she did die, then she would be with Mam and Granny in heaven. But the thought didn't make Jacob feel any better.

CHAPTER THIRTY-TWO

"When will Aunty Doris phone the hospital?"

Jacob sat at the breakfast table feeling hollow inside, but not the kind of emptiness that made him want to eat. He hadn't slept a wink last night; he'd lain in bed willing it to be morning when he could find out how Molly was doing in the hospital.

A concerned look on Mr. Bob's face, he eased into a chair opposite Jacob. "Early, I should think. She'll let us know the news as soon as she can."

The urge to race down to the post office and find out what was happening overcame Jacob.

Last night, Mr. Metcalf had driven his motor car to Hexham hospital where Mr. Bob, followed by Jacob and Sandra, had carried Molly into casualty. A nurse had led Mr. Bob into a cubicle where he'd laid Molly on a high bed and then a screen was pulled around her.

When Mr. Bob came to sit and wait with the others, he told them he'd been asked a lot of questions and that they were looking after Molly now. After a while, a doctor, who looked lots younger than Mr. Bob and wore a white coat and had a stethoscope hanging around his neck, approached the group. At his grave expression, Jacob's tummy gave a peculiar cold quiver.

"Molly's had quite an ordeal. She has hypothermia and is under strict observation until there's an improvement. She's being sent to a side ward."

"Can one of us stay with her?" Sandra asked.

As a porter came by with a trolley and disappeared behind Molly's screen, the doctor shook his head. "I suggest you go home and telephone the ward in the morning."

Mr. Bob turned to Jacob. "Your Aunty Doris can ring from the post office."

Jacob didn't want to leave Molly alone when she was ill, but he'd had no choice.

This was all his fault, he knew, and now he wished again that he'd got in touch with the Mr. earlier, then Molly wouldn't have run away.

He would send a letter to the man now.

"Mr. Bob..."

Mr. Bob, gazing into the space before him, focused on Jacob. "Yes?"

"Have you got a notepad and an envelope I can use, please?"

Mr. Bob looked about the room and got up. "They're around here someplace. I'm not a letter writer myself, if I can help it."

Before Mr. Bob had a chance to look, the kitchen door opened and Aunty Doris, bundled up in her outdoor clothes, hurried in.

She came over to the table, her cheeks apple-red from the cold. "I'm in a rush. I haven't got long before opening time."

"Have you phoned the hospital?" Jacob asked.

"I have. It took forever to get through." She unraveled the scarf from around her neck.

"What did they say?"

"That she's much the same."

"When can I go and see her?" Jacob knew his twin would want him by her side.

Aunty put a hand on his shoulder. "Visiting is an hour in the afternoon and night but..." She eyed Mr. Bob as though for support. "I'm sorry, Jacob, children aren't allowed on the ward."

Stunned, Jacob looked from one adult to the other. "I need to be with Molly."

Mr. Bob shook his head. "It's the rules, laddie."

Jacob's shoulders slumped and he felt defeated.

Then he remembered the letter. "Aunty, have you still got the letter from . . . Mr. Fenwick?"

"I have. It's still in my handbag. Why?"

"I just wanted to look at it."

Jacob needed it for the man's address.

Later, Jacob sat at the table, pencil in hand, struggling over what to say.

Mr. Bob had gone out to mend a fence, and had told him before he left, "Have the morning off, but it's best that you go to school this afternoon. It's no use sitting around moping."

But going to school wouldn't stop Jacob thinking about Molly. Anger that he wasn't allowed to see his own sister erupted in him, then he remembered what Mam had always insisted: *Never accept the word "can't."*

Jacob thought hard about how to find a way to see Molly. He knew instinctively that, even if she was asleep, she'd know he was at her side.

Jacob began to write as concentrating, hopefully, would take his mind off his fears about his twin.

He put his name and the address of the post office at the top of the letter.

> *Dear Mr. Fenwick,* (He knew that was the proper way to start a letter—even though the man wasn't a dear person to Jacob.)

> *It was nice of you to ask me to live with you but now that you don't want Molly, I don't want to live with you any more. Even if you have got a big garden and cars in a*

garage. Molly and me have never been parted and I want to be with her. If you let her live with you too, I would change my mind. It's up to you.

Jacob, hesitating, bit a fingernail.

But only if you say sorry for calling her names and never do it again.

Again, he paused, but decided that was everything he wanted to say. Signing the letter, he put it in an envelope and, licking the flap, he sealed and addressed it. He would use his comic money to buy a stamp.

He would post it before he went to school. Putting on his coat and thick socks and wellies because it was cold and foggy outside, Jacob thought that, although he didn't like the man and would rather not have him as a dad, it was better than the twins living in an orphanage. Jacob would live anywhere if it meant he and Molly could stay together.

That afternoon at school was torture as all Jacob could think about was Molly poorly in the hospital. His hands shaky, he got ink smudges all over his exercise book. But Mr. Reeves didn't scold him for carelessness like he normally would.

At playtime in the school yard, Denise came over to ask how Molly was doing.

"How d'you know she's in the hospital?"

"Miss Templeton told us all in assembly this morning. We said a prayer for Molly."

"Who told Miss Templeton?"

Denise shrugged.

News traveled fast in the village, Jacob knew, but he assumed it must've been Aunty Doris.

"Me and Molly are best friends," Denise told him solemnly. "I'd like to visit her. D'you think I could?"

"Children aren't allowed," Jacob said sadly.

"Not even a brother?"

"It's the rules. I can't."

Then he thought of his mam's saying again, and Jacob made up his mind. One way or another, he was going to visit his sister, and see for himself how she was doing.

It was after Aunty had been to the hospital the next night and was reporting about Molly, that Jacob had a brainwave.

"How is she?" Mr. Bob wanted to know. "Sandra visited this afternoon and said that she's worried about the lassie."

"I didn't stay long, Bob. Sister said it was best." Aunty bit her lip. "She's developed a cough and become breathless." With a worried expression, she looked at Mr. Bob. "They suspect pneumonia."

Jacob had a dragging down sensation that made him feel weak. Granny had spoken that word when old Mr. Todd who lived next door to the family in Perth Street, and who gave the twins black bullet sweeties, had gone to the hospital and died.

Jacob remembered because Granny had called the pneumonia, "The old man's friend."

"Is Molly going to die?"

Aunty bent down and stared hard at him, which was never a good sign. "Pneumonia's a serious disease, Jacob, and we have to pray for Molly to get better."

Some inner instinct told him he had to see Molly, as him being there would help her find the will to fight. It was pointless telling this to a grown-up; they wouldn't understand, as he knew it only made sense if you were a twin.

Then he had an idea. "Aunty, has the side room got a window?"

Aunty frowned in puzzlement. "Yes."

"Can I go to the hospital tomorrow and see Molly through the window?"

Aunty paused, then said, "I don't see why not." She turned to Mr. Bob. "Jacob could take the afternoon off school and go in with you."

Mr. Bob nodded.

Next morning, as Jacob sat eating Weetabix and Mr. Bob picked up the scrap bucket to take up the field to the pigs, the door opened and Aunty walked in.

"Doris, what are you doing here at this time?"

Aunty's face looked stern. It could only be news about Molly, Jacob thought, and his stomach twisted with fear.

Aunty took off her heavy coat, scarf and gloves, and came to stand next to him.

"Jacob, I've had a lady on the telephone and she was enquiring about you."

"Me. Who was it?"

Aunty shook her head. "A Mrs. Patricia Fenwick."

Mr. Bob looked shocked. "I knew it. Fenwick was phony. He did have a—"

"Bob, wait. This was his son's wife. The son that got killed, remember?"

Mr. Bob put the bucket down. His brow crinkled. "What did she want?"

Aunty turned toward Jacob. "Apparently you wrote to your... to Mr. Fenwick—your dad."

"I did." Jacob worried he was in trouble and felt the need to explain. "But only to say I would live with him only if Molly was allowed."

Aunty's face softened. "I'm not accusing you, Jacob. It's just the lady saw your letter and was confused. She didn't know anything about the pair of you. She telephoned the post office to see what was going on."

"So why didn't Fenwick get in touch?" Mr. Bob said crossly.

"Bob, he couldn't." Aunty appeared awkward, as if she didn't know how to go on.

"Just spit it out, Doris."

"You remember me telling you about those Heinkels carrying flying bombs and some landing in South Shields killing civilians?"

"What's that got to do with anything?"

Aunty turned to Jacob. "I'm sorry to have to tell you but... one of those civilians was your dad. Patricia said a bomb landed on his home." Aunty came and put her hand on his shoulder. "She explained that his flat was destroyed but she discovered your letter in the downstairs lobby."

Jacob's spoon, full of milky Weetabix, clattered in the china bowl. "The Mr. is dead?"

"I'm sorry Jacob, yes."

Jacob sat up straight. He wasn't sorry and he didn't feel guilty because his relief surpassed any other feeling he might have. He didn't have the fear of having to go and live with him any more. He was now free to stay with Molly. And even though he was his real dad, if Jacob was honest, he couldn't feel sad; he could never have liked the man because of the way he'd treated his sister.

That afternoon, in the hospital grounds, Jacob stood on tiptoe peering through Molly's side ward window. The cold seeping through his shoes from the concrete ground, his feet were frozen.

It didn't matter, nothing mattered, except him getting a glimpse of Molly through the pane of glass.

Cows mooed from the distant mart where farmers bartered for livestock, but the sound didn't distract Jacob. His full concentration was on what was going on in the room.

He watched as the nurse, in a purple and white striped uniform and starched cap, moved away from the bed and disappeared out of the door.

Molly lay in the bed, her face as white as the sheet that covered her. Eyes closed, not a muscle moved.

Jacob willed her eyes to open.

A hand came on Jacob's shoulder then, and he jumped with fright.

Mr. Bob towered over him.

He crouched down and looked at him intensely, concern in his eyes. He said gently, his voice close to a whisper, "Molly's not doing too well, lad. She's nigh close to death. But Jacob, she'll not be in any pain. She's in God's hands now."

As Jacob stared at his adored sister, his lips moved. *Molly Moo, love you with all my heart . . . and I always will.*

EPILOGUE

June 1945

The organ in the little church of Leadburn resounded with the triumphant sound of the "Bridal Chorus."

Jacob felt very important in the hand-me-down trousers and shirt and tie he was wearing. He did as he'd been told, moving one step, then pausing, then another step, in time with the bride, who, having no family, had chosen him to walk her down the aisle.

Frieda, dressed in a pretty yellow frock and carrying a posy of flowers, walked in front.

Passing the smiling people, who stood in pews watching the procession move down the aisle, a mixture of happiness mingled with sadness engulfed Jacob. He wished Mam could be here.

As he walked past, Mr. and Mrs. Curtis nodded and Aunty Brigit, sitting alongside her daughter, Tabitha, gave a big smile and waved.

When the groom turned and saw the bride walking toward him, his eyes crinkled and a delighted smile spread his face. She looked pretty in a navy frock with white buttons and flared skirt, small hat with a flower at the side and a veil, wrist-length gloves and navy peep toe shoes. When the groom lifted the bride's veil, she winked at him.

Waiting at the bottom of the aisle, Molly, wearing an identical dress to Frieda's, took the flowers the bride handed over. Jacob beamed with pride seeing her, knowing what this meant to her.

Before the service began Jacob, as instructed, moved over and sat down in the front pew. Molly came to sit next to him and, giving that shy, unsure smile of hers, she put the flowers behind her on the pew and held out her hand.

Taking Molly's hand, Jacob held on tightly as if he'd never let go. For, although his twin had finally recovered from pneumonia, it had taken a very long time and, according to Aunty, Molly was still frail and needed to be built up.

Since Molly had come home from the hospital, nothing had been said about the twins being put away in an orphanage and Jacob assumed the reason was because Molly wasn't well enough yet.

As for him, Jacob didn't care what happened to the twins, as long as Molly was alive. A round of applause from the congregation startled him and, looking up, he saw the groom kissing the bride—the kind of mushy stuff that made Jacob flush to the roots of his recently cut, short hair.

Then, the organ started up again and, as it played rousing music that Jacob somehow felt in his chest, the bride and groom walked down the aisle and out of the church into the glorious sunshine.

*

At the reception, held in the village hall, where the guests were seated at long trestle tables with white cloths covering them, Molly felt special as she sat, Jacob next to her, with the rest of the bridal party on a raised stage.

The scene reminded her of when the war had finished weeks ago, and the village had held a street party.

Molly, still rather weak then, had been content to sit and watch the fun. Red, white and blue bunting was displayed everywhere in the village, while Union Jack flags, poking out from windows, blew in the breeze and people danced to a piano in the street. As Hitler's funeral had passed—which involved Mr. Bob leading his milk cart with a coffin on top—everyone had cheered and clapped.

Now, the reception meal over, dished up by a catering service and consisting of parsnip soup, followed by chicken, new potatoes and vegetables, then apple pie and custard, Molly sat back in her chair with the fullest tummy.

Alf, out of uniform, and wearing a smart navy suit, shirt and tie, stood up and chinked his long-stemmed glass with a spoon. He ran his fingers through his hair in a nervous fashion. Molly didn't blame him, for although she was determined to be brave these days, she'd die of fright if she had to stand up and speak to all these people.

All eyes upon him, Alf began. "Ladies and gentlemen, firstly, I'd like to say I'm honored to be chosen to be best man. I don't know what the groom was thinking of choosing me and I hope I don't mess it up for him."

There was a shout from Mr. Curtis sitting below. "Didn't you know, fella, that's what a best man's for."

When the laughter had subsided, Alf carried on. "We're all gathered here on this happiest of occasions but sadly there are those who didn't make it." He raised his glass. "And so, I'd like to make a toast to absent friends."

Chairs scraped as everyone stood, raising their wine glasses with somber faces as they repeated the toast.

Molly's eyes traveled around the table, as she took in the people who'd been her friends over the past eighteen months or so. She wondered if they'd be sad when she lived elsewhere.

It occurred to her that almost everyone who sat at the table had lost someone dear.

Sandra and Alf, who had no parents. Sandra, though glad to have her brother home for the wedding, was a little sad because Alf had re-enlisted in the RAF. Mr. Carlton, who looked happy just to be sitting at Sandra's side. Mr. Bob and Aunty, who'd both lost loved ones and had rebuilt their lives. Then, Frieda with Eddy Gibson, recently demobilized, sitting beside her listening intently to everything she said. Frieda said he was just a friend, but Molly knew differently.

Frieda had recently had a telegram from Kurt. Her hand shaky, Frieda had solemnly passed the buff-colored piece of paper to Molly when they sat together behind the byre eating dinner.

"Read it for yourself," Frieda had told her.

Papa survived Dachau! Camp liberated. Papa at Herr Unger's house with me. Mama, Grandma perished in transport to Auschwitz. Berlin in ruins. In the Russian zone. Movement difficult. We're safe. Will see you one day. Loving brother, Kurt

Molly was horrified and hadn't known what to say. Then she'd felt bad because she wasn't being a proper friend. All Frieda wanted was someone to talk to. Molly knew this because that's how she felt after Mam died.

"I'm sorry about your mama and grandma dying."

"I knew in my heart they had." Frieda gave out a quivering sigh. "I'm glad they were together and didn't suffer the camp."

"And your papa and Kurt are alive."

Frieda had given a trembly smile. "I can't believe it is true. But I worry what condition Papa is in after being in the camps for so long. And what life is like in Berlin." She paused, then her chin lifted. "No matter how difficult it is, when the time seems right, I am going to visit. They are my family." She gave a pained look. "Though I won't live in Berlin any more. My home is here in Leadburn."

Molly had been pleased at that. She liked Frieda and was glad she was staying. Though the thought reminded Molly that she didn't know if she and Jacob would still be there by then.

Alf's voice penetrated her thoughts again. "Seriously though, in such an uncertain world and when both have suffered tragedy in their lives, it's wonderful they've found love again." He grinned. "I hope all their troubles will be the plod of four-legged friends."

The guests laughed heartily.

"Please raise your glasses to the health and happiness to the bride and groom."

Everyone stood. Molly, joining them, raised her glass of lemonade.

There were cries of "Speech...speech."

The groom looked unsure, then, taking a deep breath, he stood up.

Mr. Bob looked different when he didn't wear his work dungarees. Spruced and shiny, his unruly hair flattened with Brylcreem, he wore a suit (that looked a bit tight around his waist as the material stretched), shirt and tie, and a white carnation in his buttonhole. Molly thought proudly that he looked very smart.

He fished in his pocket and brought out a slip of paper. He held it at arm's length, then scrunched it up.

"I don't need that to remind me what to say. I didn't think I wanted to go on after...you know...and thought I'd never be happy again, but life has a funny way of proving you wrong. I fell in love again, with Doris." He beamed down at his wife.

Aunty Doris blew him a kiss. There was a blast of noise as people cheered and stamped their feet.

"My wife and I—" Shrill whistles came this time. "Would like to thank you for the good wishes and for joining us on our wedding day." He paused as if he'd forgotten what to say next.

"Bridesmaids," Aunty Doris whispered.

"I know," he told Aunty, then turned to the guests, a mock disgusted look on his face. "See what I have to put up with?"

Everyone laughed.

"I'd like to make a toast to the bridesmaids—aren't they beautiful?" The guests murmured their agreement. "And not forgetting this handsome young lad who agreed to walk the Mrs. down the aisle."

Molly had never seen Mr. Bob so jovial and relaxed. Marrying Aunty seemed to be doing him good.

"To the bridesmaids and Jacob."

Again, everyone repeated the toast and took a sip from their wine glasses.

Molly didn't squirm as she'd expected but calmly smiled, pleased that Mr. Bob thought she was beautiful.

Mr. Bob sat down.

Sandra, from across the table, pointed an accusing finger at Molly with an amused expression on her face.

Molly knew she was referring to the yellow frock she was wearing, the same color as she was due to wear next month when she was bridesmaid at Sandra's wedding. Aunty had sworn her to secrecy about the color of the dress, and seeing as she had already bought the material, Molly thought it best not to say anything.

Molly gave a rueful look back and Sandra laughed and blew her a kiss.

A cozy feeling came into the hall as everyone started chatting and laughing, then, as a chinking was heard, a hush settled over the guests.

"The bride and groom have a special announcement." Alf beamed and sat down.

As Mr. Bob and Aunty Doris stood, Molly saw the expectant gaze on the faces of the guests below.

Mr. Bob looked at Aunty, who nodded and smiled. "It's customary"—he looked around the faces below—"for the bride and groom to give gifts to the bridesmaids. Frieda received hers before the ceremony."

As proof, Frieda showed off a necklace with a pearl drop that hung around her neck.

Mr. Bob went on, telling Jacob, "Of course, we couldn't leave you two out. This is for both of you." He handed Jacob an envelope.

A puzzled frown on his face, Jacob brought out a slip of paper. He began to read and his eyes grew bigger with excitement.

Molly begged him, "What does it say?"

Jacob beamed at his sister and read the note aloud. "Will Molly and Jacob Moffatt please do Mr. and Mrs. Nichol the honor of being their adopted children and living with them permanently at the farm."

A collective gasp of pleasure filled the village hall.

The twins gawped at each other, as the news sank in.

Molly finally found her voice. "Can Smoky live with us too?"

"Tyne insists she does," Mr. Bob joked.

Jacob and Molly stared at one another in wonder and amazement, and then grabbed each other in a hug they never wanted to end.

ACKNOWLEDGMENTS

I am blessed to have lovely supportive and caring people in my life and I would like to take this opportunity to say thank you to all of them.

As ever huge thanks to my husband, Wal, thanks for all you do and for putting up with me. You know I couldn't do any of this without you.

Heartfelt thanks to Sarah, Kim, Noelle, Natasha Hodgson, Becca and every one of the hard-working professionals that make up the Bookouture team. Thank you for your help and support for getting *The Lost Children* ready for publication. I am so fortunate to be with Bookouture.

Once again, I'm indebted to the insightful Vicky Blunden. Working with you has been fantastic, and as ever, your input and suggestions have vastly improved the story. Special thanks to Christina Demosthenous for your continued belief and encouragement and for always being there for me. I'm truly grateful.

To my lovely family Tracy, Andrea, Joanne, Phil, Nick, Gary, Gemma, Dale and Robbie, Laura, Tom and Will—life is enriched with all of you in it. Thank you to my friends and all those at Border Reivers, for their support and delight at my writing achievements.

Lastly, to you, my readers, who took the time to read *The Lost Children* and review it—and to the book bloggers—a heartfelt thank you.

YOUR BOOK CLUB RESOURCE

READING GROUP GUIDE FOR
THE LOST CHILDREN

A LETTER FROM THE AUTHOR

Dear Reader,

Firstly, thank you for choosing to read *The Lost Children*. I can't believe I've written four books, and it just goes to show if you follow your dream and have faith, it can come true. However long it takes!

The idea for the novel began when I was doing research for a previous book and read accounts of children being evacuated in WWII. It was when I saw photographs of bewildered looking children standing at a railway station, their name and address pinned to their clothes, that the full implication of evacuation hit me. How could any parent, I wondered, send their precious child to complete strangers faraway in the countryside, with no idea when they might see them next? I tried to imagine myself being one of those parents, the maternal struggle within, wondering if, indeed, you were doing the right thing. Would the host family treat your child right? What if your child was homesick or ill and needed you? The stark reality was that, with the ever-present threat of enemy raids, if they did stay at home, you could lose them forever.

As I wrote the scene with Martha and the twins—their departure at the railway station—I endeavored to keep all these emotions in my mind, aware that a mother's instinct would be to stay brave for their child's sake. Then the moment of departure when reality hit and the train pulled out of the station and you waved your final goodbye. The lonely walk home, the empty house, with all the distressing "what ifs" nagging in your mind.

I choked up when I wrote that scene, my own children, when they were young, in my mind's-eye.

Much has been documented about how evacuated children were unhappy living in the countryside with their host families but then I discovered accounts of people who enjoyed the experience and learned a different way of life. Some former evacuees reported it was difficult going back to towns and cities and kept in touch with their host families after the war finished and returned over the years for holidays.

So, the seeds of the twins were planted and I wanted them to experience the positive side of evacuation with Brigit Merryfield—a character I loved from the moment of her inception in my mind.

It was as if the twins had always lurked in the recesses of my mind as I recognized them from the beginning. The surprise was how their characters developed throughout the story. Jacob, the seemingly strong one, protective of his sister. Molly, with hidden strengths, who suffered from cerebral palsy—something close to my heart.

It was heartbreaking researching CP, the lack of both compassion and treatment back in those days.

Then came the characters of Doris and Bob, who I introduced in an earlier book. I wanted to explore what became of them. I so wanted a happy ending for them both and the twins, and it seemed only right and fair they ended up together as a family. I imagine them living happily ever after at the farm—not forgetting Smoky and Tyne, of course!

The setting of *The Lost Children* is in the fictional village of Leadburn in the beautiful Northumberland countryside where I live. As ever, I aspired to keep the research as accurate as possible and to give a true account of life on the Home Front during WWII.

I do hope you enjoyed reading *The Lost Children* and the happy ending left you smiling.

Warmest wishes,
Shirley

DISCUSSION QUESTIONS

1. Were you shocked by an employer saying, "We can't have customers seeing a pregnant woman on the premises?" And by Martha being sacked on the spot?
2. Do you think Martha was right to refuse Bessie's offer to help bring up the twins? Was it for the best to have them evacuated instead?
3. Were you appalled by the attitudes toward children with cerebral palsy? And by the specialist telling Martha, "Take the child to Trevally's home for crippled children?"
4. Was Martha right to keep the twins' father a secret from them?
5. Did you think it wise for Doris to hand over the twins to live with grumpy farmer Bob Nichol?
6. Which twin was inwardly stronger and why?
7. Did Edward Fenwick have any redeeming qualities?
8. Which character did you like best and why?
9. Did the twist in the epilogue surprise you?

YOUR
BOOK
CLUB
RESOURCE

VISIT
GCPClubCar.com

to sign up for the **GCP Club Car** newsletter, featuring exclusive promotions, info on other **Club Car** titles, and more.

 @grandcentralpub

 @grandcentralpub

 @grandcentralpub

Journey to the past with more unforgettable historical fiction from Shirley Dickson. Read the *USA Today* and *Wall Street Journal* bestseller everyone is talking about!

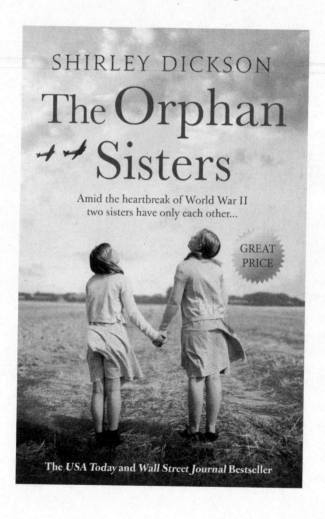

SHIRLEY DICKSON

The Orphan Sisters

Amid the heartbreak of World War II
two sisters have only each other...

GREAT
PRICE

The *USA Today* and *Wall Street Journal* Bestseller

ABOUT THE AUTHOR

Shirley Dickson lives under the big skies of Northumberland, United Kingdom, with her husband, family, and lucky black cat. She wrote her first short story at the age of ten for a children's magazine competition. She didn't win but was hooked on writing for a lifetime. For many years she wrote poetry and short stories and got many rejection slips. Shirley decided to get serious about writing novels when she retired, and she has now written two stirring World War II historical novels. Shirley says she is a prime example to "never give up on your dream."